Three hundred years ago, it was time.

The world spun as it always had, men rose and men fell, kings reigned and empires waned, and it was time. Men remembered a Savior Who came, and the world changed for a time. Then men forgot, and the world spun again as it always had.

And it was time.

There was nothing particular about it—some trees, some rocks, and a creek spilling over an unimpressive waterfall into a shallow pool.

Three hundred years ago, it was hidden. An invisible shield cast over an ordinary piece of land where a Tutelo Indian caught a fat trout in the cool stream only the day before. So hidden the Indian would be the last to have looked upon it for centuries to come.

Waiting, aging, growing—untouched, untainted, and unseen

Waiting for him

Waiting for us.

The Glen.

Back to the Glen

Carla Coon

© 2014 Johnson Press

Back to the Glen / Carla Coon

First Edition, Paperback published August 2012

Printed in the United States of America

ISBN : 978-0-9854434-3-6

10 9 8 7 6 5 4 3 2 1

Cover photos: *Cabin in the Woods* by Nomadic Lass, CCPL
Silhouette Girl by Glenda Otero CCPL
Creative Commons Public License2.0
Poem: *Lost Liberty* by Robert Fuller Murray
Song: *We Will Rock You* by Brian May

JOHNSON
PRESS

To my sister Tricia,
who has always been there for me.

1

Regrets

He was in front of the pack with the other worshippers only seconds behind. The man who'd taken the boy couldn't be very far ahead of them. His hand shot along the wet wall, steadying his way in the winding tunnel. The cave was dark. Bulbs strung every twelve feet gave off only a weak yellow glow. He caught a glimpse of the man cradling the boy like a new bride and turning a corner in the cave where the path split. There was no question where the man was headed. Too fast, he rounded the same corner and slipped on the smooth rock. He managed to catch himself and push back from the wall, righting his lanky limbs and barely slowing his pace.

It was his job to guard the chamber—his alone! But he messed up, left his post to enjoy some of the ceremonies in the Hall of the Sacrificial Stone. He figured no one could have gotten past those three fiends outside that only looked like Rottweilers. How did this guy get to the kid? It didn't matter now; he had to get him back. His tail was on the line.

Behind him, he heard a roar as more and more worshippers entered the narrow labyrinth of passageways that wove through the mountain cave. Shortly they would all know their sacrifice had been taken. This guy had no clue what he was dealing with. There were nearly two hundred coven members here tonight who would literally tear him limb from limb when they caught him.

The passageway narrowed, slowing his progress even more. Stalactites hanging like icicles from the ceiling lessened then disappeared altogether, as did the stalagmites encrusting the floor. The tunnel began to climb steeply, and cold slabs of low, overhanging rock forced him and the man carrying the sacrifice to duck. The two made their way folded at the waist like plebian slaves bowing to their master. The ceiling, he knew, would stay low like this till they were practically out. It was uncomfortable, his long legs angled like a spider's and spread out as far as the narrow channel would allow. Only one body at a time could make its way into or out of the limestone cave. Somewhere ahead, about a hundred yards off, lay the four-foot wide egress. Minutes later, he sniffed fresh air, warmer and dryer. It was just steps to the opening now. Awkwardly with his back hunched and his head tilted up, he kept his eye on the man holding the kid, who despite being more encumbered was surprisingly nimble. For the first time, he noticed a black covering on the man's head and realized with slight surprise the guy must be Jewish.

Oh, crap! They were practically out.

He watched the man straighten where the tunnel opened to the entrance. Abruptly the Jew turned and stared at him, a fixed and feral look in his eyes. Even as a lesser, he could sense great power in this strange man; in fact, he'd been sensing it the whole time he was chasing him. Now with the guy turned around and confronting him face to face, the ominous feeling grew to a menacing proportion. He stopped dead in his tracks unsure if perhaps the man was reaching for a gun, at least he told himself that was why he was stopping.

Frozen, he watched the Jew reposition the boy to his hip. He raised his free arm high above his head as if he were wielding an invisible sword. In one swift motion, he pulled the imagined instrument down through the air. An incredible force of power flashed from the man's arm. A laser beam sliced across the ceiling of the cave, splitting the rock. The ground below and the rocks above him trembled.

Too late, he realized what was happening. Instinctively he turned and ducked, spidering his way back towards the inner cave as fast as he could. He barely passed two dangling bulbs, when a bible-sized rock broke loose in front of him, landing inches from his feet. He leapt over the boxy thing, at the same time hearing a thunderous tumult. The banging din rippled forward. Rocks crashed one upon another behind him, sealing the cave entrance shut. Still bowing like a common serf anticipating a blow from his master, he ran smack into the arms of another lesser, leaving the two instantly enmeshed.

2

Looking past their tangled embrace, he saw a horde of coven members.

"Back," was all he could think to scream to warn them, but even as he opened his mouth to yell it, a large piece of rock slammed into his head. In seconds, it was raining boulders.

Black . . . everything went . . . black.

The first thing that registered was pitch black as if he'd been dropped in a well of ink. Next came the heavy weight pinning him to the ground, followed by searing pain. His arm, his head, his back were on fire with it—making it impossible to distinguish if it was truly dark, or if the blackness was actually a product of his own blinding pain. Along his left leg, he felt another body squirm. A warm, oozing wetness surrounded his limb, and he speculated if it was his blood or the person's next to him. It didn't matter. This was it for him. He could feel himself slipping away; the screaming chaos beyond the rocks faded; the pain that had been stinging his arms and legs turned to a dull, numbing cold. He wanted to enjoy the release of pain as a calm chill spread over him, kicking in like a Percocet.

Instead, a sharp sense of deep regret seized his heart, squeezing it in a vice-like grip, more painful and searing than any of his injuries. He saw it clearly, this path he had chosen, this life he had been enjoying, something was horribly wrong. He suspected it then, even while living it; only now, every cell in his mortal body knew it, lamenting each hapless, unexamined moment. His heart slowed till his lifeblood ceased to flow through the highway of veins. Only then did he see the full state of his soul. Too late . . . too late . . . . A terrifying realization spread over him, sucking him into an eternity of regret. He released his final breath and ceased to exist in this world.

2

The Day After

AUGUST 15, 2006

Clarice walked through the dark woods, following the curving ascent of the land toward their house. Mournfully silent, the forest hugged her as she passed among its towering trunks and under its thick canopy. Her trudging steps seemed to reflect the confusion of her mind, which labored to sort out the incredible events of the last twenty-four hours.

Jackson was safe. That was the most important thing. He had reached the sanctuary of the Glen. Her husband would have to accept it as she had. Their six-year-old son must stay in the safety of the Glen alone, hidden from them and the world. What choice did she and John have? The Glen like Eden of old now lay invisible somewhere within the borders of their five hundred acre property. Knowing it had to be this way and accepting their son's fate could hardly ease the pain of losing him. John and she would need each other more than ever.

Clarice plodded along the trail blazed by the ATV with some loose notion that they would have to hike back here later and retrieve the vehicle from where it lay stuck in the mud. Such a practicality seemed out of place after all that had happened, and her thoughts as bleary as the morning mist drifted instead over the distant past—the secrets she'd kept from John, the worries over what was wrong with their son, that ball of pain she'd carried everywhere—*gone, gone, and gone.* Clarice's step picked up with an almost animated relief, realizing that whatever else had gone on and whatever lay ahead, she was through denying her gifts. *Gifts?* Did she just call them gifts? Something lifted inside her, or more precisely, she acknowledged that it *had* lifted, leaving her as weightless and carefree as a school kid on the first day of summer. All at once, she couldn't wait to see John – to be in his arms. She was ready to share her life with him, all of it, everything she had hidden, held back, and denied.

Her thoughts cleared, leaving only a picture of John and the priests back at the house. When she and Jackson had reached the Glen in safety and watched the entity retreat, her relief had been so great; it had driven thoughts of the others and what they were facing far from her mind. Feeling chilled and more than wondering about them now, she hurried her steps. The air was damp with fog that would soon coat everything in morning dew. Clarice glanced down at her once-white polo and favorite jean skirt, both covered in grass stains and dirt. The shirt stuck to her in places with dried blood. It was torn from the collar across the sleeve, baring one shoulder. She refused to think how it had torn. Concentrating on the path, she watched one dusty sneaker follow the other up the hill.

Dawn was lifting the curtain of night unveiling a few of the wide trees close to home that stood among the slimmer maples. The ancient trees spared once-upon-a-clearing a century ago were always such a peculiar contrast to the young maples. Clarice recognized the mammoth oak ahead, the same one where she had found Jax that day he had wandered off. Something dark bulged from the trunk. A second later the lump materialized as a body smacked face first against the tree. Clarice rushed forward to find the mangled body of Gabriel Katz.

"Oh my God, my God!" Her hand flew over her mouth, stifling the gag reflex that threatened to throw up on the deceased. Blood was everywhere. His shirt was ripped open, revealing an enormous gash from one shoulder blade to the opposite hip where white bone protruded through his dark slacks. A mass of black curls matted with blood parted around a deep pit in his skull. It looked as if he had been thrown against the tree like a rag doll and then slid down with his arms upstretched. Etched into the rutted bark, just above his

6

fingertips—as if he had reached to touch them before dying—were two words: *Thou Win.*

At once Clarice saw her son standing by this very tree six months ago, after she'd been frantically searching for him. She pictured the stone falling from his hand when he saw her coming. He'd run to her, then. She never questioned why he held the stone. *Thou Win*—these were Jackson's words. Her little boy must have carved them that day. *What could they mean?*

But look at this man! Without thinking, Clarice placed her hands under his torso and pushed, releasing his death grip on the tree. The body turned towards her, and she gasped at the mutilated face. Rigor mortis would set in; he shouldn't stay this way. The deceased suddenly slid further to the ground, making Clarice jump back. If possible, he looked even more pathetic now, his back a cockeyed twist, one arm flopped out and dangling from its socket. There was no way she could leave him like that. He deserved better than that . . . better than *this.* She swallowed hard, gingerly picked up one bloody wrist, and laid it over his chest. Lifting the other arm, her stomach turned as the limb sagged unnaturally, apparently broken at the elbow. His kippah lay near. Clarice retrieved it, shook a leaf off, and placed it on his head. Kneeling by his side, she lightly brushed her fingertips over the eyelids. No good, they remained open. She bit her lip and made another pass, shutting out the cold stare.

Sitting back on her heels, the rising sun shed more light on his poor face . . . her son's protector. What did she know about him, except the incredible bravery she'd seen last night? Did this Gabe have family? Where was he from? How did he find them? She knew nothing, yet this man had given his life for her son. He'd been tortured by that evil entity, literally torn to shreds for her son. Dear God, how could she ever repay him?

Seized with grief and gratitude, Clarice leaned down to kiss the cold forehead. She remembered when she was ten and her mom made her kiss her grandmother in the coffin. The entire Martin family did it that way. As difficult as it was, and it wasn't much really, she always felt it was something to show that she loved her grandma and would always remember her. Sitting back up, Clarice heard the sound of crunching leaves. She bit her breath as the noise drew near, drawing her eyes to the path. With relief she recognized both of the figures coming up from the darker woods—one silhouette, the tall, powerful build of her husband next to the shorter, rounder figure of one Father Tom.

"Oh John!" Clarice gulped the words she'd intended to yell scrambling from her knees. She took off, almost falling on her face before covering the fifty yards straight into her husband's embrace. Wordless they held each other tightly then kissed, her slender five foot four reaching familiarly for John's burly height. In that kiss, they poured everything: their sorrow over leaving their six-year-old son in the Glen, their relief over his safety and theirs, and everything they'd been through in the last twenty-four hours. When he released her, their eyes met, searching through tears. What she saw there, Clarice told herself later, shouldn't have surprised her, but John's hurt slammed into her like a Mack truck. She'd cut him deeply in keeping her secrets, hiding herself from him. His eyes said it all: *I thought I knew you—thought I knew us.* Those seconds felt like eons, staring into his pain and riddled with guilt! Of course, John thought he knew her. They shared everything . . . everything but that, she reasoned even as her mind raced to excuse herself. How could she have told him about her ability to see the spiritual world and the incredible things she saw when she had spent a lifetime denying her gift? How? How would she ever have explained leaving her body and literally flying as a spirit when she couldn't understand it herself? In those intense seconds, her eyes begged his for understanding. Yet all she saw reflected in those big, brown, honest eyes was her own betrayal.

Without warning, Father Tom, who'd been standing shyly a few feet off, sprang past them towards the oak tree. "Rabbi Katz!" he cried with John and Clarice hurrying after him. "Oh no, such a good man. Look what it did to him!" The young priest dropped to his knees. The two men stood there absorbing the shocking scene while she tried to process the fact that apparently this man had been a rabbi. Clarice looked at Father Tom, his white collar hanging loose over his blood-spattered black suit, noticing his injuries for the first time. The boyish face was smashed and bloody, and his once slender nose hooked to one side and likely broken.

The priest's fleshy hand formed the sign of the cross over the body. She surveyed John's face, whose handsome features were bruised and battered with a black eye, cuts, and a swelled blue cheek. She gawked surprised she hadn't noticed it all before. Even John's giant hands were purple and puffy with every knuckle torn open. This finally triggered an inventory of her own. Aches and pains leapt to sudden life all over her back, and she remembered fighting those bodyguards with John and being slammed to the ground.

Bewildered Clarice watched the priest with a kind of numb interest as he began some kind of rite for the dead over the Jewish man's body. Father Tom shifted his foot, placing it just an inch from a small puddle of blood. Her mind flashed to a larger lake of blood, the one she'd seen last night around Roxy. She remembered floating above her best friend as if she were a patient having an out-of-body experience. *Oh God, Roxy is dead too!* She had not even had time to process what she'd seen, let alone grieve. Roxy, her Roxy, brutally murdered, her body sprawled out on the floor of the health food store like so much trash.

Clarice turned abruptly from the corpse and bloody pool, stifling a gasp and throwing cupped hands to her mouth. Pictures of Roxy burst upon her—Roxy in one of her outlandish getups, Roxy's long limbs exiting the little yellow punch bug, Roxy at the water cooler throwing her head back in one of her irresistible and uncontrollable laughing fits. "Oh God," Clarice cried, flinching at the memory. John's heavy hand went between massaging her unbelievably sore shoulder and patting her super tender back. But his show of concern was so welcome, there was no way she would say anything. A few minutes later, wiping her watery eyes with filthy hands, she turned back around, escaping John's unwitting torture and hearing the priest's words. Father Tom continued mumbling prayers taking a small, plastic vial from his pocket and sprinkling the rabbi's body. How odd that the priest thought nothing of blessing a Jewish man with all these Catholic prayers. Then again, nothing should surprise her after all they'd seen since yesterday.

Yesterday! It was only yesterday that Roxy had come for Jax and unsuspecting, delivered him to the enemy. So many deaths and sacrifices made for her son! Clarice turned to look at John grateful for

9

the healing waters of the Glen. What would she have done if this Gabriel Katz, a rabbi, had not shown up on the path and helped her get John to the water? *Ack*, she couldn't think anymore. This man in front of her had given his life to bring their son to the hidden sanctuary in the woods. It was all too fantastic, too surreal. It was also one scary big mess. Straight away, she thought of the old priest, Father Simeon, wondering if he was still at the house, if he was even . . . As if reading her thoughts, the priest finished praying over the body and stood addressing them with calm authority.

"We have a lot to discuss before we call 911." His voice and demeanor had changed from the shy, young priest they had met that first time. "Let's each go over what we know and try to figure this out." Tom turned to Clarice. "First I need to know if you feel the way your husband does that Jackson is safe."

She looked at the normally pubescent, now pulverized face with his straight brown hair in the boy scout cut and his soft shape. She couldn't get over the new confidence he was showing. Either this whole trauma had changed him, or they had never seen this no nonsense side of the happy go lucky acolyte.

"I *know* he's safe. I delivered him to the Glen myself."

"So, the Glen—the mural on his bedroom walls— it's right here in these woods somewhere?"

"Yes." She studied her sneaks, trying to find words for the Glen. "It's hard to describe. The whole area is . . . like being in Eden. It's much more fantastic than the mural. Its borders are . . . well, an invisible wall or something that keeps out evil. It saved me from these three dogs once." She peeped at John hoping to judge his reaction, but he was looking down at the body of Rabbi Katz.

"The dogs in your painting? The canvas in your studio that made Father Simeon faint?"

"Yes, he saw the evil portrayed in them. They were demonic not corporal dogs . . . fiends from hell, I guess." She searched the priest's face for any sign of disbelief then continued. "I was jogging when they came out of nowhere. I ran like mad trying to stay ahead of them, and then I felt the Glen pulling me. When I reached its borders, the dogs howled and disappeared. The same thing happened last night when

Jax and I reached the Glen. The black entity,"—she stopped, hugged her cold arms—"it just swirled up in a tornado and disappeared."

"Can we go back and get him, now that it's safe?"

"No!" both she and John spoke in unison. She shot John a look.

"You understand?" He nodded. "Oh, thank God I was afraid I wouldn't know how to tell you. But John, I *was* going to tell you," she emphasized. "No more secrets, I promise." He said nothing, didn't even look at her. Again, she couldn't read him beyond the hurt look. The three began walking back to the trail, which before long became the path John had been forging since they moved here. They were still a good three hundred yards out from the house and yard.

"So this Glen is a sanctuary? Does he just stay there, all alone?"

"Yes Father," John answered, "but I think we all know he's not alone."

Clarice's eyes studied the beaten path leading to the house, feeling a bite on the ball of her foot every other step. She tried to ignore the pebble and think of a way to explain the Glen.

"It's like *Brigadoon*, you ever seen the movie?" Neither the priest nor her husband answered. "Brigadoon is a legend, a town that mystically appears once every hundred years. These hunters, Gene Kelly, Vince—er, no Van something . . . anyway, they stumble on this Scottish village that just appears in the mist. Only the people act and dress like they're from hundreds of years ago. Then after a time, the hunters learn they have to leave Brigadoon before midnight or it will disappear again for a hundred years, and they'll be stuck in it." She watched John's purple profile nodding, and Tom, his broken nose crookedly pointing down watching his step. "The Glen, well, it's not like that, but it reminds me of the movie because no one could see or enter Brigadoon until some heavenly clock revealed it again."

"Hmm," Father Tom mused, "in Genesis, after the fall, Eden was said to be guarded by angels with flaming swords."

"Something like that. All I know is we won't see Jackson or find the Glen till the preparation for his mission is over." Clarice stopped, did a quick hop unsuccessfully fishing for the pebble in her shoe.

"But he's only six!" Father cut in, stopping with Clarice.

"Father," John said, a little sharp, "you're not making this any easier on her."

11

"Oh, I see . . . you're right of course. We better move on," the black-clad priest said and resumed walking. "Clarice, what happened to the Rabbi back there?"

"All I know is," Clarice said, grunting inwardly as the ball of her foot came down again on the tiny annoyance. "Gabe was leading Jackson to the woods, when John and I were fighting off the bodyguards in the backyard. I was slammed unconscious—"

"That fat a—" John said, biting his intended word, "ape threw you like a wet fish. I thought he broke your back. I was fit to kill after that."

Clarice touched her husband's arm. "All I could think of was that those guys were after our baby." She turned to Tom and half studied the flattened nose as she spoke. "Anyway, when I came to, John was fighting both guys, and this giant black swarm was headed towards the woods. I took off to find Jackson and Gabe Katz."

Father Tom nodded, breathing through his mouth. The nose looked painful. "Oh, that was just after the exorcism."

"Exorcism!?"

"Yes, Father Simeon performed one. There was a legion inside that old man; it was incredible evil."

Clarice recoiled at the thought of the blackness being a legion of devils but continued, "Well, I found Jax running on the path alone. I put him on my back; he held on like a monkey, and I raced like mad for the Glen with that black thing behind us. Once we reached the borders, the entity swirled up and disappeared. Later on, Jax told me his protector had ordered him to run; so that's how they got separated. Gabe—Rabbi Katz," she corrected, "he must have stayed to face the evil alone."

Tom puffed, and Clarice realized he'd been keeping up with her husband's long strides. As a runner, John's pace never bothered her, but the priest was definitely favoring his right knee. She slowed her step to match his while John outstripped them. "Do you want to stop?"

"No, I'll be fine," Tom said, trying to smile but ending more in a grimace. "The rabbi told me something in the car on our way up here," he wheezed, "how he'd known his whole life he had some important task to perform. I believe he had a power in him just to defeat that evil. Father Simeon called it Tzaddik."

They passed between the tool shed and garage. Clarice shook the still-at-large pebble to her instep and glimpsing what was left of the shed door. She gawked at the gaping hole where the ATV had smashed through and at the boards she had hacked free, which now resembled shredded wheat. All of it evoked an image of John slumped over the seat, impaled with the giant metal bar sticking out the front and back of him as if he'd been skewered for a luau. Father Tom put a hand on her forearm and leaned in to speak, thankfully drawing her away across the driveway towards the front yard. She concentrated on the crushed white stone of the drive, listening to his unexpectedly low voice. "Simeon didn't make it," he said, just as they reached the front yard. Clarice slowed her step, immediately jolted by the two dead bodies on the grass. Father Tom continued to hold her arm and escort her. They stole past the scene in slow motion with a respectful hush. The corpses lay like fallen wizards. The old bearded priest was face up by the huge oak, and the ominous stranger lay face down on the other side of the tree. Through his gray hair ran a streak of black like the reverse of a skunk's tail. Piercing the base of his skull, a gold crucifix stood in macabre irony, leaning over like a hastily stuck cross on a freshly dug grave.

"Oh my God," she choked under her breath. How much more could she take of blood and death? She inched past the long cadaver, mindful of the crucifix planted like a flag on foreign soil. As if it wasn't hard enough before to make out the nasal sound coming from the smashed face of the young Father Tom, he spoke so low now, both she and John strained to listen.

"I was the one . . . I killed him, but . . . " He paused then his words rushed together suddenly more audible. "He was choking Father Simeon, squeezing the life out of him! I was . . . had been knocked unconscious on the porch. He used some devilish magic on me. My mind was . . . he was assaulting me with images and . . . my own sins. Then my—my body it levitated. He made it slam back and forth between the pillars." Clarice looked up at one of the stone pillars seeing blood and visualizing the tour de force that had crushed his

13

face. "When I came to, I heard Father Simeon finishing the exorcism. He called the man Menger, Christian Menger. He—"

"Father Simeon knew him?" John cut in.

"No, no, I'm sure he didn't. I don't know how he knew the man's name." The priest shrugged. "I saw an enormous legion of devils escape him, pouring out from every orifice of his body. A jet-black swarm of them headed for the woods. That must be what you saw." Father Tom looked from the remains to Clarice. "After that Menger went nuts screaming about losing the power they gave him. He began choking Simeon." The purple profile of the young priest was pained with worry, his voice full of remorse. "I—I had no choice. The crucifix . . . it was all I had. I was too weak to stop him any other way." Father Tom buried his face, gripping his brown hair. Clarice patted the priest's back and thought of how horrific it had to be for such a religious man to have been forced to kill someone, and in such a way—with the symbol of his own faith!

"That's when I came out front," John added. "The two bodyguards saw the blackness swarming across the sky; we all did, and it was like after that they just wanted to be done with me. They quit fighting and just ran." Across from her, John flexed his swollen hands, and Clarice's heart lurched. She pictured bathing and dressing the open sores.

"I know," Tom said, backing away from his own ghoulish handiwork and looking toward the other corpus delicti, the body of his mentor. "I was kind of dazed holding Father Simeon, but I remember the one with the long hair. He ran up to the body and rifled the pockets. I think he got Menger's wallet before the bigger one came out front. That one spat on the body, and they both left."

"Yeah, I saw them take off in that black Caddy they came in," John added.

Tom jolted around with an out of place, almost gleeful look. "Oh my gosh, I know the license. Praise God, I memorized the plate!"

After John called 911, the three of them sat on the porch steps waiting for the police. Clarice tried to tend John's wounds using a cold, wet hand towel from the hall bathroom and a bowl of ice water. But John pulled away from her curtly telling her to see to the priest.

14

The dried blood on Tom's face was acting like its own bandage for the smashed nose, so all she dared clean were his forehead and chin before he begged her stop. Meanwhile John had fetched the mohair throw from the living room couch and thrown it over the old priest's body, his upper body that is, as the scanty breadth of it covered less than half of him. His long legs peeped from under his black cassock and ended in a pair of black oxfords; the feet flopped in opposite directions. The body of Christian Menger lay uncovered. Mercifully, from where they sat, it was mostly out of sight behind the oak.

"What about Jackson? What will we say?" Clarice asked, removing her left sneak and rummaging for the cause of her torture. She pulled it out peering at it, surprised to find the persecuting shard so tiny.

"We'll tell the truth," the priest got off the stoop to address them. Clarice flicked the stone into a bush.

"What?" John said incredulous.

"He was kidnapped last night," Tom said, obviously leading.

"Well, yeah."

"You don't know where he is, that is, you can't find him, right?" They both looked blankly at the priest. "So you don't know where he is, right?" His voice looped up on the last word.

"I guess so," Clarice said, still no idea where the priest was headed, but impressed with his apparent calm and command of the situation. She felt like Dr. Watson waiting for Sherlock Holmes to explain some rudimentary point she was missing.

"No, you *know* so!" he sounded triumphant and firm. "What good could come of the entire truth? We tell them a six-year-old boy is living in that woods there, but you can't find him cause he's in some mystical paradise, but don't worry cause he's safe. Listen to how impossible it would be. We'll be locked away in a mental ward or worse. And Jackson must be protected. Who knows how many others are out there ready to harm him."

It wasn't much of a plan, Clarice thought, slipping her foot back in the sneaker, and she had no idea how they would explain the carnage. Aside from the ruse of pretending their son was still missing, the three agreed to tell the police everything they knew, leaving out any talk of black forces or preternatural happenings.

15

* * *

Three police cars showed up within the hour. By noon, the place was crawling with Ithaca police, ambulances, crime investigators, detectives, photographers, and news crews. All three of them were taken into custody and separated for questioning. All three were made to surrender their bloodstained clothes and were fingerprinted. Clarice was in a room so like the ones she'd seen on TV it was laughable with its cafeteria, folding table, metal chairs and a wall full of what had to be a two-way mirror. A policewoman had given her blue police sweats that smelled faintly of deodorant and sweat. Sitting there trying not to be too weirded-out wearing somebody else's none-too-fresh workout clothes, Clarice concentrated on the line of questioning she knew was coming – the murder of Roxanne Cassan, her former coworker at the *Binghamton Journal.*

"Are you familiar with Macromania, Mrs. Miller?" Clarice shook her head eyeing the squinty-eyed, beer-bellied cop. "It's a health food store on Main Street in Binghamton. Workers walked into a bloody mess there this morning, Mrs. Miller. Do you know what they found?"

Course she knew. Hadn't she seen it last night when her spirit hovered above Roxy's murdered remains? Studying blue-tipped fingers, she prepared herself to look properly shocked. Grief stricken and horrified would be easy, she decided, no faking required. Sergeant Blaine scrutinized her. She felt it but kept her eyes on her hands holding the coffee cup in front of her.

"They found the body of a Roxanne Cassan, sliced up pretty good." He leaned in. "Your best friend, I understand."

"Oh my God, what? Roxy? Roxy Cassan? Who, what . . . what are you saying?"

Well, she'd hardly win an Oscar, but hopefully her performance sounded at least as shocked as she still felt over poor Roxy's demise. So many questions she needed answered. Even though she was certain that psychic Harriet had done it, she had no idea how Roxy had been fooled. The image of Roxy's body face down in that pool of blood gushed before her, legs hooked back in a splattered double-u, her throat slit, those ridiculous orange capris painted with her own blood. She thought of the colors so vivid and clashing, the cherry blood on

16

the tangerine pants, crimson on her slashed purple shirt—*Oh God, even in death, Roxy's outfit managed to be shockingly mismatched.* Her Roxy, who loved life and every day wore a crazy, eye-popping ensemble that screamed I'm alive and I'm glad to be alive. The less Roxy's getups matched the better she liked them.

"Oh God!" Clarice howled.

That did it. There was no trouble giving the officer the expected reaction. Her sobs broke loose and continued long after Blaine disappeared to join the others watching her behind the two-way mirror.

"She looks pretty dang shocked." A skinny detective said to Blaine.

From his seat at the head of the long table, Sergeant Matt Blaine looked at the rookie, who was leaning casually on the corner of the table and glancing over his shoulder at Clarice Miller. Only he wasn't being casual; he was feigning coolness – his wannabe, TV drama, cop show idea of how he thinks detectives act. The kid always pissed Blaine off.

"Doesn't mean squat, Hitchko."

"What you think, Sarge?" Hitchko sounded sarcastic. "She offed her best friend and took her own son?"

"Listen up, bucky-boy," Blaine busied himself lighting a cigarette before continuing—even though there was a ban on smoking in the whole damn building now. He always said and did things to remind junior detectives how far down the ladder they were from him. "You better start thinking she did it," he puffed, "he did it," Blaine pointed behind him with his cigarette at John Miller in the other observation room across from Mrs. Miller, "or they both did it." He rolled his cigarette between his fingers then took another drag.

"The priest could've done it." Another cop in the room spoke up, one too new for Blaine to even name. What the hell, was the academy farting these guys out?

Blaine was silent studying John Miller through the glass. Even if Blaine didn't already know about the man's construction company, he looked the brick-wall type, the kind that worked with his hands. Miller was likeable too, a man's man—the sort of guy Blaine would toss back pitchers with down at Pete's after work. But those stalwart good looks and honest eyes could fool you. He knew something wasn't right in their stories, no matter how sincere they seemed to be. He'd been on the force for twenty plus years and had more closed cases under his belt than any one of the five guys in the room. Hell, than all of 'em together.

"Let's go over what we know," Hitchko piped up again.

"Why, you writing a friggin book?"

"Take 'er easy, Sarge." Detective Schroeder, fatter, older, and greyer than Blaine, leaned out the door and yelled into the squad room, "Get Blaine some coffee before he explodes all over Hitch."

"Fine," Blaine said, flicking his ash in someone's (the kid's he hoped) coke, "tell us what we know, junior." Hitch remained unruffled, another good reason to hate the prick. He reclaimed his coke and tossed it in the garbage.

"We got four vics, three here in Ithaca, and one in Binghamton. A rabbi from Boston, a priest from Maine, a—"

"And a blond walk in a bar. Sounds like a frigging joke," Blaine snickered.

"*Shh*," Schroeder grinned.

"One old man and a redhead," Hitchko continued, nonplussed. "And one missing kid, Jackson Miller. The priest admits he killed the old guy but says Vic One was choking Vic Two, the bearded priest.

"Forensics will confirm that Hitch, don't trouble your pretty little head."

The new guy turned from looking at Mrs. Miller and spoke, "The Millers and the young priest all say they never even met the rabbi till yesterday."

Schroeder whistled. "Did you see that stiff by the tree?" Everyone in the room had. "I don't even see how that could of been done by a person."

The room fell silent, and the men looked either out one mirror at Mrs. Miller or out the other side of the room at her husband. The door popped open, and the captain leaned in. "We have a license plate from the priest for a black Deville he says Vic One drove. We need a description of the two guys the couple says they were fighting when the priest stabbed the first guy. They took off in that caddy. You need to wrap it up." His finger twirled. "There's a kid missing, and the FBI is due any second."

Blaine swore. "FBI, Cap'n?" Blaine squashed his butt in a cup lid. "I'm gonna be on that couple like sap on Clark Griswold till we figure this crap out and find the kid… or his body. Screw the Bureau."

When approached again, Clarice tried an entirely new tactic. Blaine had brought her hot coffee, a stack of photos and a load of barely disguised accusations. "Mrs. Miller," Blaine loomed over her or rather his gut did, his cheap aftershave competing with her none-too-fresh borrowed sweats, "we just have a few more questions."

Clarice had had it. "I refuse to waste another second like this." She stood, flung the full cup across the room at the wall, almost shocking herself. Hot splatters of black coffee ricocheted in all directions, hitting Blaine, herself, the mirror, the floor and door. "Do you hear me? Find my son, dammit! You should be finding my son." She heard herself shrieking, sounding as crazed and mad as a mother with a missing son should sound. Not a hard card to play, she found, letting her pent up emotions run like a faucet on full.

John must have taken a similar tack as she heard his voice booming through the precinct. Eventually husband and wife were sitting in a room with a police artist. They were asked to describe the two bodyguards who had arrived with Menger and kidnapped the boy. Unfortunately, both she and John had been so focused on saving Jackson that the faces of the two men refused to materialize. They gave a fair physical description, though. Both were muscular football types. John guessed the bigger guy with the crew cut at six three and two hundred seventy pounds. The Italian looking guy with shoulder-length, wavy black hair and deep-set eyes was maybe six one and two hundred and ten, about John's height and weight. As a fellow artist, Clarice promised the officer that when things calmed down, she would try to sketch the men herself.

After two hours with the police artist and as many as twenty hours being questioned, they were released. When they got home, the house was crawling with authority figures. Most prominent were the FBI, who set up a workstation in their great room, SOP—standard operating procedure to wait for any ransom calls or notes. Father

Tom was being held in the murder of Christian Menger. Police were searching for one Harriet Mansfield, a missing worker from the health food store, and a pair of thugs driving a black Cadillac Deville, DTS with the license plate BNF-6646.

3

Back at the Ranch

Sergio and Mark took off from the Miller property like two bats out of hell. Sergio drove the luxury sedan looking as if he were concentrating hard on the road. Instead, he was preoccupied with the logistics of his and Mark's circumstances. Both men were tall and well built, but Mark would have to be described as lumbering. A good word for someone like Mark, a square-jawed guy in a military crew cut, tattooed arms and a mind as disencumbered as they come. Mark would rip you to shreds on command with a conscience as clear as a newborn babe. Then again, his own conscience meter was about nil, too.

Sergio Valenti saw himself as a guy perpetually caught up in circumstance. From seven years to twenty-seven, Sergio had learned to more than roll with the punches. To look at him, a quintessential swarthy Italian, model shoulders over a tight waist, lush waves of long black hair, you'd never guess the numbing cold that strangled his heart, a heart that once never wanted anything more than to get along and experience love. The deep set eyes over high cheekbones looked tough, penetrating and practical, set on one thing and one thing alone —survival. After a lifetime of circumstances, Sergio knew only how to calculate for his own survival. Every hand fate dealt him seemed to force him to ensure that first. After that was secure, and only if that was secure, Sergio could be a fair, stand-up kind of guy.

At present, he and Mark both looked as if they'd gone ten rounds with Mike Tyson. That Miller guy, about Serge's own size, had a nasty ground and pound, wailing on him like a crazed animal. What could you expect; they were threatening the guy's family, after all. When

Mark flipped the puny wife like a wet rag, Miller went nuts and was able to hold both he and Mark off. Sergio felt bruises forming where he sat. He was used to ignoring pain, though. He stole a look in the rear view mirror at a bloody slice across his chin, chastising himself for getting hit in the face. Someone might have said he was vain the way he could dodge and ward off blows to the face in any fight. In reality, he was just good at it from a lifetime of scrapping to keep his place, to not get walked on, and sometimes not get killed. *Ooo*, his ribs were sore, and his wrists felt like someone was holding a blowtorch over them.

Mark, his bulk filling the passenger seat, sniffed loudly and turned to Sergio, who was leaning over the wheel in thought. Serge got a good look at Mark's war wounds: pretty impressive swelling over his left temple, a growing ball on the end of his nose, and a ripped lip. Both their knuckles were blue but untorn. Regular workouts on the bags and each other, kept their fists iron strong.

"So," Mark said, "what are we supposed to do now, Judas?

"Don't call me that, mamaluke!" Sergio refrained from the obscenity he would have added, falling back on harmless Italian slang. Better not to set Mark off, he decided. They had to stick together, at least for the time being. The master used to call Sergio Judas to remind him of his past, like he needed reminding. He'd betrayed his friend and mentor for drug money, and was a hair's breadth from being ripped to shreds by a gang of dealers, when the master swooped in to save him. It was a long downward spiral, but from that day on, he was a slave to the Master. Mark was called Cain for similar reasons since he'd murdered his own brother. But the master was dead, and Sergio never wanted to hear those pet names again.

"That piece of dirt is dead in hell," Sergio said, checking his speed, no sense being pulled over by a cop; he had other plans. "Anyway, what's the difference? We're done; we're free! It's over, Mark."

"Yeah, feels good too." Mark snorted, rubbing his stubby hair. "No more ranch, no more bodyguard crap, and kidnapping girls for him. *Ding dong, the Master's dead*," he sang.

"Not the tune, guy" Serge said, feeling irritated.

"How do you know, you some kinda *Wizard of Oz* expert? I don't care anyway. It's a good song for today." Mark dragged his hand up over her perpetually allergy-ridden nose and continued humming his own rendition of the melody. He leaned over the back seat rooting for his cigarettes. Mark wasn't the sharpest cheese on the shelf, but he got it right. With *him* dead, they were free. Probably only till they all met in Hell, but for now, they were as free as the monkeys in Oz.

They needed a plan though, Sergio realized, turning up 79, leaving Ithaca. "Who knows how many dead bodies up there and nearly two hundred more in the cave back at the Ranch. Gonna be a truckload of investigating. Friggin' pigs everywhere."

"How they gonna know 'bout the Ranch?"

"Maybe they don't know," Sergio drummed the wheel a second thinking. He stopped when it quickly irritated his tender wrist. "They might have these plates, though, right? We need a plan fast."

"What about the Ranch?" Mark lit a cigarette and cracked the window. Morning was dawning with fog covered valleys and green rolling hills. It would be another nice day. "Oh, man," Mark blew smoke back in the caddy instead of out the window, "what about all them worshippers trapped in the cave-in? They were only there for the sacrifice, not their fault. Still can't figure out how that happened, you know? I was by the barn, watching them dogs go nuts chasing something. Then I hear this huge crash, sounds like thunder, man. Guess that's when the Jew got the kid out, but I didn't see him till too late. Anyway, we should dig 'em all out."

"Stupido!" Sergio dared to cuff the thick head, same way a dad might discipline a son. "We can't do that. There's elders in there. If one of them comes into power, it could be worse for us. *He's* dead, isn't he? We're his guards, aren't we? They'll blame us. No chief, I'm free, and I'm stayin' free!"

Even Mark could see that. Mark was silent pulling on his cigarette. It was hard to judge if he was offended. The guy was a loose cannon normally, and with no direction from the master, he was capable of anything. Mark took another drag and flipped his mirror down, exploring his facial wounds. He might look to Serge for the direction he used to get from the Master if Serge played him right.

23

Sergio yanked the wheel, made another turn, a plan already forming in his mind.

"You had a good idea, Mark," Sergio said. "We need money and a different car. Then we can blow this state. We're heading up to the Ranch." Mark flicked the cigarette and looked at Sergio, a smile slowly spreading across his face. "Even if the master left a connection to the Ranch," Sergio went on, "I think we have time to get stuff. He had money, and there's like a hundred of the worshipper's cars up there right now. We can split the cash, friggin' take our pick of wheels, and take off. Nothing ties us to him, nothing that's not in that desk."

Nearly three hours later, they pulled up the long dirt drive onto the Ranch in Cobleskill, NY. They drove through the gate, which uncharacteristically hung open on the barbed wired fence. A sea of parked cars lay in a field to their left, looking like a used car lot. They passed the stone barns and bunkhouse, and continued up the hill to the old farmhouse. They parked out front next to a yellow Volkswagen Beetle.

"Oh yeah, I forgot," Sergio said, sore muscles and bruised ribs whining as he got out of the car, "that Harriet woman, the psychic drove that bug up when she delivered the boy. Member we threw her body in the ditch after he killed her." Sergio walked once around the Volkswagen stretching his arm and popping his right shoulder blade. He'd need a good rest tonight, he decided, and then he'd be fine.

"So why did the master kill her even though she brought the boy," Mark asked, uninterested in the bug and walking to the porch.

"She killed some lady in Binghamton, the one the master psyched into kidnapping the boy. She made a huge mess, that's why he offed her."

"So that's her car?" Mark sniffed forcefully, gaining the porch.

"Naw, she drove a red Corolla. She was up a few times after her initiation. I think the bug belongs to the chick he tricked into taking the boy, the one the psychic killed."

Sergio joined Mark, who stood waiting for him. He flung the front door wide open, and together they crossed the short foyer. Sergio turned right, stepping into the parlor room, that gaudy red space of chandeliers, oriental rugs, and gilded mirrors. At the head of the room stood a black polished desk, and behind it, a high back chair of red leather. Mark went directly for the chair and plunked himself on the makeshift throne.

"Ha ha—look at me, Serge!" Sergio ignored him. "Hey Judas," he shouted when Sergio wouldn't indulge him. "Eat this, I got the power!" Mark jumped from the chair and shook.

"What's wrong wichoo?" Sergio said.

"It's … the chair. It's haunted, man. Feels ice cold like he's still frickin' in it!"

"Shaddup will ya! Let's just get the shcarole and get out."

Sergio manhandled the locked drawer thinking, and at the same time trying not to think, how it would be just like the master to somehow still be in that chair. The lock wouldn't budge. Sergio flung the chair out of the way. He climbed under the desk, lay on his back and gave the drawer a violent kick. He got back up. Mark yanked it open and began pulling out a pile of loose cash. Sergio quickly reached in the back of the drawer after him for a small silver case and pocketed it while Mark wasn't looking. There was a good chance Mark didn't even know about the case, and even if he did, he might not know its significance. He also didn't seem to know Sergio had lifted the master's billfold off the dead body. It sat safely tucked in his left back pocket, and might have felt cold too if Sergio allowed himself to dwell on it.

Mark looked lost or mesmerized; Sergio wasn't sure which.

"Here," he said, scooping the pile. Sergio began dealing the cash out like Monopoly money, one for you, one for me style. He could have counted and divided it, but he was positive Mark would suspect he had cheated him.

* * *

While they trashed the desk and parlor, both men were completely unaware of a pair of bare feet creeping down the oak stairs. Scared, Jessie slid one foot down to the next step, froze, listened to the guards then slid the other foot down to join its mate. She was really too scared to understand the random words she caught from the foyer. She definitely figured out their master was dead, that evil creature, who had invaded her mind and will with just his eyes. It made sense *he* was gone. In some way, after that first eye contact, she had been able to sense his presence whenever he was down here. She'd

25

heard him screaming in the yard last night, a primal scream that went right through her. It sounded like he lost something. Before that, all night long there had been comings and goings on these stairs. After midnight, everything was dead quiet, even the damn dogs must have been locked up. She'd begun working on the door hinges in her room with the fork she'd secreted away some time before. She'd been waiting for just such an opportunity when she wouldn't be heard. Jessie knew she was the only "guest" at the house at present, according to the pig who brought her here.

Gaining another stair, she tried to think of anything she knew, so she could formulate a plan to get out of here. It was all so bizarre though, and her mind went back to the day she had been taken. Months ago, she had been walking downtown on her way to get soda—soda for Pete's sake. It wasn't the best part of town, but she'd never expected that kind of trouble. A big guy jumped out of a van, grabbed her, and pulled her in, shutting the door. As it drove off, she fought and kicked till he practically had to sit on her.

She was thrown into this dark, smelly barn with a mess of filthy, half-dressed women. It stunk like no barn she had ever been in. She figured out why as she watched one of the women go to a pile of hay in the corner and defecate right in front of her. She remembered freaking out. They were in wide stalls, and there were iron bars like cell doors across each stall. Five women were in her stall. They looked sick and crazy. Two were covered in sores. A short brunette with knotted hair told her to just sit against the wall and watch how it worked. Told her to stay clear when guards came and try not to be noticed, or she would get picked. She shivered at the thought.

When a guard did come in, a squirrelly redhead with a leering grin, he threw a pile of food on the floor—looked like garbage for pigs. The girls rushed forward, pushing and fighting, shoving food in their mouths as fast as they could, till the pile disappeared. Scared shitless, Jessie asked no questions, just sat against the wall and watched through the night.

In the morning, there was a lot of yelling and screaming when at least four men came in to herd them all outside. They ordered them to strip, and when she hesitated a fast hand slapped her face so hard, she fell into some other woman who told her, "Just do it, honey."

They were hosed off like animals as other men shoveled out the stalls and threw fresh hay down. They redressed, grabbing random items off a pile of, (she supposed), clean clothes, fighting over pieces like rabid dogs. Jessie managed to obtain a paisley shift too short for her long legs. They were lined up for the "test," which she found out later was a pregnancy test. They had to squat over a bucket, one after another and pee on a stick. But Jessie didn't need any test. She already knew that she was pregnant. Looking back, she wondered if they had known too, and if that was why they had kidnapped her. She thought she remembered seeing one of the men who kidnapped her, hanging out at the clinic just days before she was abducted.

Now, Jessie stood on these stairs frightened out of her mind, her hand cradling her swollen belly. She had to get out of here—had to find a way. She crept to the next step. Another two feet and she'd reach the double doors to the room they were in. The heavy wood doors were wide open, but she figured she could slip behind one and hopefully remain undetected till they left.

She made it and stood as still as stone, listening to their plans. They were talking about some cave-in and a bunch of trapped "worshippers." Jessie knew after months in this house that these people were in a cult, satanic she guessed. Thoughts of what they planned to do with her and her child haunted her daily. She'd been moved to the main house the day after being taken, the very day of that humiliating pregnancy test. She was placed in a bedroom, with its own bathroom and told over and over how lucky she was, how she would be taken care of, and how many privileges she had.

Her life was straightforward. She saw a doctor, once a month, there in her room. She was fed three decent meals on trays no less. She had TV and magazines, a few clothes, and best of all, she was unmolested.

The two men mentioned the girls in the barns. That meant the other barn she had seen also held kidnapped women. How could this place lie so undiscovered? It was incredible!

Sergio lit a match, threw it into the bronze waste can by the desk. The papers took, and a small flame jumped up.

"Hey, I gotta get my gear outta the bunkhouse," Mark said.

"Me too. Hey Mark, two minutes tops. Whatever you can fit in one bag; capisce?" Sergio looked at Mark making sure he got it, before he dropped the bigger bomb on him. He'd gone over and over it in his head. He saw no way out. No other way. Nada! He grabbed Mark's arm.

"Have to gas the girls in both barns. Have to, Mark."

"What? Why, they had it bad enough. Why not let 'em go?"

"Man, why you gotta be such a friggin 'stunad'. They seen us. Hell, you and I kidnapped most of 'em! You think they're not going to have sketches of us plastered on every post office and police station wall across the country?"

Mark stood there running his hand back and forth over his nose. The master had a plan in place for the girl's destruction all along if ever the ranch were discovered. They'd both been drilled in the procedure. But to actually do it . . . Sergio felt an involuntary shudder rush over his spine. It was all he could think about the whole way up here. No matter how he looked at it, nor how he turned it over in his head, they had to take care of the girls. Mark and he needed time to get away, and every one of those poor creatures could ID them. Mark shook his arm free.

"Think about it Mark," Sergio spoke low still unsure. "We gotta do it. Every one of them girls knows my face, yours too. We'll fry for what we done, for our part in what he done." He used bad English, aware he was using bad English. It was like a language between thugs, and it always seemed more effective with Mark. "The master always had a plan for that. He showed us."

"Yeah, the canisters," Mark sounded robotic. "We seal shut the windows, pop open the cans, toss 'em in and boom, they're dead."

"We're really doing them a favor," Serge said, walking over to the window and looking down towards the stone barns. "Think'a the nightmares them girls 'id have. They could never make it in the real world again."

Mark couldn't argue with that; even he understood the girls were more like animals now. This was kind of a mercy killing.

Both of them were done. Sergio shot a wad of spit onto the red chair for good measure. "I gotta hit the can, first." He left Mark, each of them holding their wad of cash, not entirely sure Mark wouldn't jump him for his. As he walked, his ears pealed for any sudden move by Mark, his mind quickly went back to the girls. *Why, they had it bad enough. Why not let 'em go?* he heard Mark's words echoing his own thoughts.

Sergio stood in front of the toilet stunned. *Oh my God,*—his mind screamed to a being he was sure did not exist—*am I that far gone?* I'm the animal, not them. He saw their faces, their mangled hair; his gut hurt just thinking of his part in stealing their lives. The coven was sick. His actions were so controlled by *him*. There was the element of his own fears, his need to survive, his need to stay out of prison that allowed the master to bend his will. Sergio's fall from grace began as a kid, continued in the streets, and was completed by the coven. He was a minion. He never admitted that to himself. He always tried to preserve just a part of himself, just a tiny speck of his free will. He practiced making his mind blank before the master; he guarded his true thoughts, keeping a part of himself free from his actions.

Since being free of the master—actually the moment the master died—something very real lifted from his soul as if a barbell that had been crushing his chest were removed. Sergio began to reclaim something of himself. An unfamiliar feeling of remorse and regret crept over a part of his cold heart he would have sworn was dead. It made no sense to him, but in this moment, he decided the girls could not be killed; he wouldn't do it. He couldn't. He'd find a way to run, to hide, and not be caught. Sergio Valenti flushed the toilet and zipped his jeans.

Jessie released her held breath. She only wanted to save herself and her unborn child and leave this compound alive. Nothing she could do would stop them. It wasn't her fault about the girls. It wasn't her fault. No way would she risk getting caught. With no small twinge of guilt, she turned her thoughts to practicalities. The only cover available was down by the two cars that were parked out front close to the house. She had watched through the cracked door as the bigger guard left heading toward the barns. Then the other who had been in the bathroom left but turned heading to a different building. Jessie emerged, stood in the doorway peeking. She watched him disappear from sight and she ran like hell. Crouched between the black Deville

29

and a yellow Volkswagen Beetle, she could see the front of the barns and beyond that to the field full of cars behind it.

All around the barn windows were propped open with pieces of two by four, and the square-headed big one with the crew cut was shutting them by knocking the wood out with a rake. Each window flopped down with an ominous bang. Jessie watched helpless. He dragged a box from the side of the barn and pulled his shirt up over his chin. He removed fat canisters from the box and began snapping off the top of each can and rolling them into the open barn door. She could hear the hiss and see a vapor shoot into the air. After more than a dozen, he slammed the door, bolted it, and shoved some piece of foam at the bottom. He dragged another box to the second barn and began more cans tossing them in the same way. Cockroaches, Jessie thought, as if they were merely setting off bug bombs. She tried not to be sick and prayed she wouldn't hear the girls' screams. She noticed keys dangling down in the yellow car. Keeping a constant eye on the man, Jessie started making moves to get inside.

In a complete fog, Sergio rummaged through his drawers and the floor of his room shoving random items in a duffle bag. He assumed Mark was below filling his own bag in the room shared by the six guys who worked the ranch. Sergio got his own room when he was moved up to top bodyguard for the master. He thought of Lou, Juice, Banger, Danny and Nate, trapped in the cave this very minute. He saw no possible way to free them without letting elders out. Not sure he would anyway; every one of them would kill him at the first sign by an elder. Sergio always suspected that they could sense an inner disloyalty in him. He wondered if they would feel different, too, with the master dead or if they were more like the lessers, who pined for all this coven BS.

He sat on the edge of his bed wondering for a moment where he would go, how he would get out of the country, and fast. He listened and realized he didn't hear anything downstairs. He took his bag and headed down, seeing Mark breathless on the landing, holding a wait a second finger up and moving towards his room.

"Mark, I want to talk to you about the girls," Sergio said a little confused at Mark going the wrong way and having no packed bag with him. Getting no answer, he followed him and stood in the doorway as Mark threw things off a closet shelf, ending with a brown backpack in his hands.

"It's done, dude. No worries."

"What? Done, when?" Sergio sounded panicked.

"Just now. I did it just like we learned." Mark's brow curled into a question.

Sergio tore from the room and bounded off the cement porch. He slowed down, listening for cries screams or even a cough as he approached the stone barn. Lifting the bolt and about to slide it back, he realized he heard nothing . . . nothing at all. The doors and windows had insulation nailed to them; the place was practically airtight. No one could have escaped the fumes, which the master had told him were ten times more lethal than the hydrogen cyanide used in Nazi Death Camps. Sergio leaned his head against the door, pounding it with his fist.

By the time Jessie opened the car door and slid into the seat, the guards were headed towards the field of parked cars. Crouched down, she continued to watch both men weaving in and out the rows, peering inside vehicles and trying door handles, obviously looking for a car to take. She would not make a move till they drove off, that was for damn sure.

The big one with short hair got in a very distinct car. Jessie knew her cars—the one passion she could share with her drunk dad. He drove off in a sweet 1993 XJ220 Jaguar coupe in British racing green. The man with the dark Italian look was out of sight, farther down the hill. Not one minute later, Jessie heard another engine turn over and drive off. She waited exactly three minutes before turning the ignition key in the beetle.

On her way down the dirt drive, Jessie stopped the car by the stone barns. Holding her hand over her womb, she listened out the open car window—not so much as a cough. They must have died quickly. She caught herself thanking God as if he even existed in this hellhole. She sped down the dirt drive, through the open gate, and out of the barbed wire compound, planning to put as much distance between herself and this place as humanly possible.

4

Sergio

Sergio Valenti pulled away from the Ranch satisfied with his choice of a silver BMW. Nerds and their hide-a-keys. He'd watched Mark drive off ahead of him, relieved to be rid of him. There was more chance that they'd be fingered together, than apart. He never wanted to see him again. What Mark had done—what they'd done— they had to do, he told himself again, realizing he might be telling himself the same thing for a long, long time. He watched the roof of the house and the barns disappear in the rear view mirror, vowing to leave it all behind, and telling himself the girls were at peace, waking in a better place, human again, whole and untortured. So why were his hands shaking and insides twisting in a knot? He squeezed his hands on the wheel, literally getting a grip. It was no use; he had to stop and fast. He was driving west on 88 toward Oneonta and had just passed a rest stop. He swung the car onto the shoulder, looked for the hazard lights for all of two seconds, gave up and threw the car door open, retching with a heaving vengeance. A couple cars whizzed past doing eighty. One nearly sheared off his open car door and his head with it. He shut the door on the waning sound of the angry horn, and crawled over the stick shift to exit the passenger side. Landing in a long-legged heap on a patch of weeds, he held his head down between his legs. He hadn't eaten since last night, so the somersaults his stomach was performing were unproductive except for some gastric acid. He sat there a long time, letting his body decide when it might be through. Finally, he determined enough was enough and stood erect. He knew the girls deserved so much better . . . . He pounded the hood of the car and took off, walking along the shoulder of the highway and telling himself again and again they were better off.

Sergio could not have said how far he walked or even how long, but the sun had kept track of time, and it seemed well past noon when he returned. It was hot as blazes by the time he got back in the car. He cranked the AC and listened to classical Jazz spill from the stereo of the BMW. Sergio Valenti pulled back onto the road, determined to compartmentalize what was left of his conscience. A talent he'd honed to perfection since he was young. He studied the hills of New York, a rolling blanket of lush green mounds on a checkerboard of farmland, spotted with small towns and houses. Sparkling sun glinted off the Susquehanna River, snaking its way alongside as if following the highway. He hadn't lived a whole lot of places, but it was hard to imagine anywhere better looking than this part of New York in the fall and summer. In the car, stifling hot August air was being replaced by the air conditioner, pumping cool air faster than any car he had ever known.

Sergio shifted on the warm leather, noting a lump in his pocket. He'd almost forgotten. He rifled in his pants for the tiny silver box. Holding it in one hand, his thumb popped the lid open. Out of it fell a gold key, bouncing off the console between the seats and landing in the cup holder. He glanced down at the key's distinctive square profile of rectangular teeth. Still holding the box, he steered using his forearms and ripped at the old velvet lining until it tore. He felt a scrap of paper and freed it, letting the silver box drop to his feet.

"Knew it!" he yelled out loud and laughed, holding the tiny scrap of yellow ledger paper. He knew he remembered correctly, the day he'd spied the master slipping a yellow paper in the box just when Sergio had entered the room unexpectedly. The Master was getting old—*had* been getting old; he was dead now. He must have been worried he'd forget the number and bank, or maybe he had worried he'd die and the contents would be forever lost. Either way—Sergio stared almost unbelieving at his good fortune—this tiny piece of paper with an address on one side and a number on the other could very well be his ticket out of this mess, maybe enough to start a new life. Un-frickin believable! His luck was really turning around; so was

34

the car. He took the next exit and swung back heading east on 88 toward Schenectady.

Sergio punched the address into the BMW's computer to search for what he was sure was the location of a bank. Sweet, these wheels had internet and everything. This car is outrageous! Had to belong to an elder. But which one? His skin bristled, and the classical Jazz suddenly annoyed him. He pressed the seek button on the steering wheel a few times searching for a tune, but ended up stopping on the news instead. He listened hard, waiting to hear anything about a murder in Ithaca. If they did find the ranch, they'd sweep every inch of it for prints. Too bad he couldn't have burned it all to the ground, but that would have brought cops like bees to a beer can. Years ago, in the early days with the master, when he was being sucked in deeper and deeper, the master had told him that his connections were wiping Sergio's record clean, supposedly even his prints were removed from the system. It might be true. He would have had every reason to see that Mark and he were invisible, what with all the risky kidnappings.

Madonn! Sergio thought, cranking the stereo, he had to stop thinking about stuff he couldn't control.

Forty-five minutes later, hearing the GPS announce, "Destination on right." Sergio pulled the beamer past the First Colonie Bank of Albany and turned into its parking lot. He sat there a tad mystified, for Sergio, barely familiar with bank accounts, had no clue how safe deposit boxes worked. After a couple of minutes, he noted the time 3:45. Don't banks close at four? Not wanting to wait until tomorrow, he finally exited the car intending to find out something today. He entered the bank and shyly approached the first available teller, a pretty, Asian number, who gave him an immediate flirting smile.

"*Ciao,*" he began falling back on his Italian looks. Girls seemed to love that. "I was thinking of renting a safe deposit box, but I'm uh, a little confused how it all works."

"Well, we're about to close . . ."

"I know, I know," Sergio shrugged and held his hands palm up pleading, "I just wanted to understand the process.

"Oh, that's no problem," she said reaching for forms, her silky black hair swinging forward. "These are the forms you need to fill out and—"

"Uh, I wondered if you could just sort of walk me through it? I mean where does my stuff go? How about my key. How big are the boxes? I don't know squat about this stuff." He leaned on her counter, gave her a lusty grin, totally aware of his effect on women.

"Um . . . maybe, I . . . " She looked to her left where two other tellers tapped away on keyboards then back at the lobby where zero people waited in line. "Sure, yeah, I guess I can walk you through the procedure. Let's see, after you obtain a box, you get a key. When you want to get in your box, you visit a teller—"

"Like you," Sergio tapped her shoulder, pulling his hand away after just the barest slide of his hand down her arm.

"Right, me," she laughed a silly nervous sound. "Well, after you sign the admission form, and we verify your signature—"

"How, I mean, electronically or what?"

"No, I'm afraid we're still in the dark ages here. The bank checks the signature against the initial one on file, this pink card here." She tugged the card out of the forms she'd taken with her. "After that, the manager or if he's tied up, a teller, me, ha-ha, brings the day gate key and the key for your box—"

"*Oop*, lost me, I thought *I* had the key for my box?"

The girl kept moving as she talked, opening the vault, and walking down a short corridor. "Every box has two keys, the bank's key and your key. The box cannot be opened unless both keys are inserted. Even the bank can't get into your box without your key." They reached a small room filled with safe deposit boxes. "The teller or guard hands you your box, and leads you this way." They stepped across the hall to a small empty room with a long cherry table and a few chairs. "This is the viewing room. The bank official will give you privacy if you desire and stand right outside this room. When you're done, you close the box and hand it back to the official. The box has an eyebolt in case you want to add another small lock of your own."

Sergio left the bank knowing one thing. He wasn't getting into that safe deposit box, unless they accepted his signature for the Master's. And that was okay. He smiled, that was just fine with him.

Using cash, he checked into a nearby motel in Colonie on Wolfe Road. It was one of those motels with outdoor stairs and a cement porch running past each of the second floor rooms. The outside door was a must. He hated the idea of being cornered in a hotel—elevators, tight hallways, busy lobbies. That and the fact this motel had a weight room where he could workout. His room was smack dab in the middle on the second floor. Sergio threw his duffle bag on the bed and turned on the TV, flipping for news. His stomach was in knots, but growling with hunger. He glanced around the cheap room, it had a fridge, but no bar or snacks. He wondered if he would throw up pizza if he had some delivered. Forget it, business first. He dumped his bag on the bed, and out fell a mess of papers and junk he'd kept in his nightstand drawer, two pair of jeans, and exactly one sock. They left in such a big hurry he hadn't packed one shirt, not even boxers. Stupido, what was he thinking? Anyway, lucky thing the papers were there.

Sergio Valenti was a man of few talents by his own measure, but one of them was about to pay off big time. Ever since he was a kid in foster homes, he'd practiced forging signatures. With a good fake, he got out of classes, used credit cards, even passed a few checks. He had a knack too, noticing angles, swoops in letters, anomalies. His habit was to study every signature he saw, especially while it was being scratched out. A hobby really, he'd lie in his bunk at night and practice Mark's, some other worker's, or usually the scrawling signature he saw being signed most often, the master's.

His hands finished shuffling papers and landed on the one he wanted. Boom there it was over and over on the page, that long loose capital C and the wavy line swooping into what looked like a capital M or N also ending in a flowing wave. The master's signature was calculated, he was sure, to hide his real name, whatever that was. Sergio pulled the sheet to his lips and smacked. "Yes!"

He reached for the master's billfold; his license would be Serge's ticket to the vault. He'd never seen him with one, but he had to have one right? The master did drive. He flipped the wallet open, pulled out the card. To the left of his picture, for the world to see was his name! As wigged out as Sergio was, looking at the face again, he began to laugh, really laugh. The master, his torturer, sooo mysterious. Yeah, right. He spit aiming a wad in the can by the cheap dresser.

"Christian Menger, Christian Menger, ha, ha, ha, unbelievable, just unbelievable!" He held the license and spun around in triumph,

"*Pomposo pavone*, you were too good to be called anything by your lessers. HA! All along, you just hated your given name. It flipped you out that your mummy and daddy named you Christian, the biggest Christian hater of all time. Ha, ha, ha." Sergio could hardly stop, the relief of a good laugh, the very sound of it a huge release.

It was Wednesday. He would bone up on the signature and look for a license doctor to fix the picture on the master's license. He'd hit that bank a sap, but for now Sergio was calling for pizza, hitting the sack, and later the weight room and a bar, in that order.

* * *

More than several days went by before Sergio even saw the weight room, let alone a bar. He ate that night, curled up like a pricked caterpillar and slept on and off for two days. By the time he got up on Saturday, the bank was closed. He spent the weekend between the weight room, a Planet Fitness, and a local bar, catching the news every chance he got. So far, he wasn't in it. Millers were all over it, though, and so were those priests, one dead and one behind bars for killing Menger. Ha, if they knew what the master was they'd pin a medal on that priest. He watched with a purposeful, detached interest, except he found it weird the kid was still missing.

It was Monday. Armed with the key, the numbers, and a plastic grocery bag shoved in his jean pocket, Sergio entered First Colonie Bank. Just as he'd hoped, his little oriental friend was not working, else he'd have to avoid her. He had found a license doctor on Saturday easier than he thought, but the job was lousy. Any nickel bouncer could peg it for fake, but his picture was on it, and if his little hired helper did his part, the manager would barely glance at his ID anyway.

Sergio got in the short line, wishing it had been busier. This bank was so basement, not much of a noon crowd. Whatever, each teller would be busy with some transaction, and eventually the manager too. Shifting his shoulders, a little bead of sweat trickled down his back. He stepped forward; he was next. The girl teller would be best, but it probably didn't make a hill of beans difference. It was just girls seemed to let him get away with more than guys. Sergio spied the kid he'd hired not an hour ago, lanky, crazy orange hair, two henna tattoos—a dragon and a snake. The kid stood coolly by the bank doors. Seemed a smart kid, played the plan back to him twice without a single mistake. It should work.

Here goes, Sergio thought, stepping up in line. Damn, he was getting the male teller. Fat guy, greasy hair, looked about thirty.

"Uh yeah, hi. I need to get in my safe deposit box?"

"What number?" the teller asked, looking bored.

"236."

The man slid his can off the stool, went to a card catalogue file, and extracted the pink card and sheet of dates and signatures. Sergio gave a quick glance out the corner of his eye to make sure orange slice wasn't dealing his hand too quickly.

"Sign here Mr. Menger, and I'll call the manager for verification. He'll need your license." His heart racing, Sergio made a slow play of getting the doctored license from his wallet. The teller pushed the piece of paper over to him and left to get the manager. Sergio looked at the paper, about a dozen of his master's wavy CS signatures, each followed by a date. The last one was six months ago. Taking a breath and exhaling slowly, Sergio dated it and scrawled an identical signature on the first blank line at the same time the manager arrived holding the pink card.

"Sir," he said nodding and then scrutinizing the new signature. "ID please."

Sergio smiled and slowly began to hand the wallet to the man.

"Uh, you'll have to remove it," he said not taking it.

Sergio pulled the license out, and on cue, the kid erupted in a shrill scream. All eyes went to the front.

"I HATE THIS BANK!" The kid flailed his tattooed limbs. "Why won't you give my dad a loan? I want to know why, why." Each word was louder than the last, accompanied by fake tears and stomping back and forth like a crazed toddler.

Sergio slid the license toward the manager, to regain his attention. For a second, the manager looked as if he would make Sergio wait, but Sergio made a quick show of checking his watch and huffing. The manager gave the license the expected cursory look and handed it back to Sergio, his eyes on the kid, who by now was surrounded by a loan officer and a guard. He was yelling something about his dad losing his job, his mom going to divorce him, and how it was all the bank's fault. The kid was doing a bang up job for a c-note.

"Uh, it's fine, Eric," the manager said with a rap on the counter. "Take Mr. Menger on back, I have to see to this."

"Meet me over there," the teller pointed a chubby finger towards the day gate, and re-filed the papers, before obtaining the two necessary keys. He passed through the gate, hearing the end of the performance with the kid yelling, "F--- you all," and conceivably storming out as planned.

Alone in the viewing room, Sergio eyed the long metal box, grateful there had been no secondary lock he would have had to pick. He hesitated, then fast turned the key, and swung open the long lid. His heart skipped a beat. On top lay an envelope with words scrawled across in the Master's hand.

> *Read this first.*

Sergio picked it up, unsure. "*Bastardo,*" he muttered, reluctant to obey one last command. He pulled the sheet of paper from the envelope and read:

> *If you have opened this safe deposit box, then I have passed from this life. What you find here, you must know, comes with a price. You will pay for all you take. Enjoy while you can. We will meet again.*

Sergio stared at the words, which in his core, he suspected were true and powerful. Meant for an elder, perhaps, but still cursing any that enter, like Tut's tomb. He could walk away, take nothing, owe nothing. Could even toss his half of the cash from the Ranch in the box, lock it up, and throw away the key. He could; he should.

Sergio stood there debating, several realities washing over him. His picture could be on the news at any time. They could tie him to the kidnappings, murders, gassing the girls, a thousand crimes. He would never see the light of day, and who knew how many of these cultists he would encounter behind bars, if he didn't get the death penalty, that is.

What choice did he have? What choice had he had for years now? For Sergio Valenti, life never seemed fair. It seemed to him a string of predetermined choices, the kind with no way out. He found his hands investigating the contents of the box—several manila envelopes, a passport, a black velvet bag, and cash. His fingers flipped through the stack of hundreds. He picked up the passport; staring back at him was the face of his master, nameless for all the years he had known him.

"*È mucchio di ossa,* ," he said, staring at the picture and calling his former master a pile of dead bones. "*Affare fatto.* See you in Hell, just like we planned."

With that, Sergio shoved all the contents of the box in the plastic bag, locked the empty box, and handed it back to the teller, who was waiting patiently in the corridor. He went straight to the car parked and found orange slice leaning against the driver's side door. Nudging him out of the way, he flashed the other fifty he owed him then shoved it in the kid's pocket and hopped in the beamer. Sergio Valenti pulled out of the First Colonie Bank parking lot, richer than he'd ever been, and oddly aware of being more in debt than he'd ever thought possible.

5

Questions & Answers

Monday afternoon, Clarice returned home from a short jaunt with Sergeant Blaine to go over sketches at the Police Station. They had run the gauntlet, and from the porch, she gazed beyond all the cameras closing in on her. Their front lawn looked like a Paparazzi circus: snapping flashes of light, news people with fat microphones where their mouths should be, trailing wires attached to enormous video cameras, news vans with equipment spilling out like campers at a state park. Her brain hurt; her legs felt like liquid stumps. Would these hounds be here every day? When would they go home? Of course, Jackson had only been "missing" for a week.

"Mrs. Miller, Mrs. Miller," they screamed, and her eyes wandered with no idea which face to look at and thereby give permission to assail her with another question. She saw four or five different mikes and noted at least one familiar face from Channel 9 news, a youngish brunette named Renee James, who looked at her with sympathy. They seemed to work it out amongst themselves and the loudest questioner, a graying middle-ager from TV 12, took front stage.

"Mrs. Miller, do you believe Jessica Fuhlible's story that she used Roxanne Cassan's car to escape this cult? Do you believe she had anything to do with the kidnapping of your son?"

Clarice wished John were here. He was at the office, but he, too, could be suffering a similar assault downtown. Neither of them could very well turn news crews away when as parents of a missing child, they should be grateful for any media coverage. She'd heard the breaking news of this girl found driving Roxy's car two states away and the fantastic story she told about being held captive on some property in Cobleskill, NY. Even now, the police were locating the property. Clarice stuttered, "I..I only know as much as you." This was terribly unsatisfying to the pest-a-razzi, and shouts of "Mrs. Miller, Mrs. Miller" erupted anew.

"Mrs. Miller," Renee James piped up, her face hidden by the giant mike with a square nine on top, "is there anything you want to say to the kidnappers if they are listening right now?"

This wasn't hard. Her words would be sincere enough, her sorrow genuine. "I…we just want our son safe and unharmed." Things got quiet and more fat mikes worked their way forward, wagging in the air looking like an ugly crop of Black-eyed Susans. Their holders held arms up and crouched out of site for their respective camera crews to have a good shot at her. Clarice took a wavering breath and stared blankly into the cameras. "Please we just want our son back. If you have him, don't hurt him. He's so special." She caught herself talking to angels, pleading with God. "Please bring him back, let him go. . .whatever it is you took him for, he's . . . he's just my baby. I want him back"—her breath caught and cascaded out the word—"back, uh…uh…back home with us. Please, Oh God, please . . . " She broke down unable to continue, and a good thing too. Any minute, her heart would have burst to a full-fledge begging God himself to let her baby go.

Finally, Sergeant Blaine of the Ithaca Police took her by the shoulders, turned her around, and pushed her into the house, closing the door, and turning back to address the news crews. Clarice leaned against the other side of the door hearing him and struggling to regain her composure. And she *had* to regain control or Blaine might break her down and get at the truth.

"That's enough folks," he shouted over them. "We're doing the best we can. Please give the Millers a little space. Commissioner Tynan will answer your questions downtown. You gotta clear out, you gotta let 'em breathe."

"Sergeant, Sergeant," the hounds turned their questions on him. "What do you know of the Fuhlible story or this cult in Cobleskill?"

"C'mon now," Blaine said. Then he shouted over the continuing racket, "No comment. No comment. Keep it up and I'll have you pushed back to the road."

Inside, the house was dark. Every blind had been drawn against the invading cameras, rumormongers, and reporters. Blaine was the only officer here now. All week, the house had been crawling with every kind of official and agent, even all night. Some of them slept on couches and some in John's office. Since she and John had only cells and a Tracfone number, the police and FBI were able to track calls without actually being at the house. By the end of the week, the police decided to vacate, leaving only Sergeant Blaine, who stayed twenty-four seven when he wasn't out badgering poor Father Tom, her work friends, or John's clients. No ransom calls had come as yet, and of course, none would.

"Would you like me to get you a cup of coffee?" Sergeant Blaine asked her.

Clarice looked at the heavy-set officer with graying hair, a Dunkin doughnut gut, and a permanently skeptical face. He probably wanted a cup himself. "Oh Sergeant, that's nice of you, but I'll make us coffee. You'd get lost in that kitchen." She wiped her wet eyes, burning from lack of sleep. "I could get lost in there myself. We've only been here six months." *Great,* she thought, *why did I remind him of that?* She felt weird in his presence, like he knew things weren't adding up. She wondered if he thought she'd killed her own son.

They had at least cleared her of any involvement in the death of Rabbi Gabriel Katz. The coroner concluded only a bear could have mauled him that way and thrown the man's body against the trees where they had found his blood. But she and John's weak answer as to why the rabbi was even there wasn't helping anything. Early on, they had decided it was easier to tell as much of the truth as possible, and the truth was they had no idea how or why Gabe Katz had come to their house. At least they didn't know what drew him. They told police they believed he was searching for them, and they had no idea if he knew Jackson had been kidnapped. No, they didn't know him or anyone in Boston, and they had no knowledge of the photo found in his rental car of one of Clarice's paintings.

45

Blaine pulled a stool from under the island and from there watched the TV in the adjacent great room while Clarice filled the coffeepot with water and scooped grinds into the filter. "They should know something more as soon as they find this place the girl is talking about. Don't worry, Mrs. Miller, we'll get to the bottom of things, alright." His assurance sounded more like a threat to her, and Clarice willed herself to smile gratefully at the man. Just then, Blaine snapped to attention and heaved his weight off the stool.

"They found it!"

Clarice followed the sergeant into the family room, snagging the remote and turning up the sound. A helicopter view showed dozens of cop cars screaming up to the so-called Ranch. It looked familiar to her, even though she'd only seen it looking translucent when flying over the land in spirit form. News coverage went on for hours. Officer Blaine was on the phone constantly trying to squeeze out information from his superiors and anyone else he knew on the scene. He seemed resentful or maybe just frustrated that he wasn't there. While the news crews had only rumors and what pictures they could steal from the air, Blaine was able to confirm via his contacts much of what they found. It was horrific.

The house on the top of the hill and the bunkhouse were empty, and twenty-six women were found dead in the two barns. Plates on a black Cadillac parked in front of the farm house matched those Father Thomas O'Donnell had given police. More and more discoveries unfolded as the night wore on. Clarice watched incredulous. Every time the cameras panned the surrounding area, she searched for cars. It made no sense. Where were all the cars she had seen when she had flown about in spirit form that night? The only conclusion, the one she did not want to believe was that the hundreds of worshippers must have escaped the cave.

* * *

John walked into the small visiting room to wait for Father Tom. He looked at the smudged two-way mirror then across the room to the camera mounted in the corner, wondering who might be observing him. The table had brown metal chairs only on one side. John sat a moment then twisted his chair, making an embarrassing squeak until his back was partly to the mirror. He arranged the chair next to him as well. Propping his elbow on the table and his head in his hand, he looked at the big round clock, watching the second hand tick its way around and trying not to dwell on the fact that his pastor and new friend had been locked up and charged with murder. He crossed his leg and quickly uncrossed it, noting his work boots still had dried mud on them. He went between staring at the clock and down at the floor. Finally, the door opened, and Father Tom, wearing a bright orange suit and handcuffs, swung past the guard. The prison uniform looked wrong with his Boy Scout face and clean cut hair. It leant none of that dignity of his black habit. To top it off, the overalls were too small and too short, making Father Tom even more of an object of pity.

"You have fifteen minutes," the guard grunted. "I'm right outside the door."

Handcuffs jingling, Father clumsily pulled his chair even closer to John, keeping his back turned to the mirror.

"John, we're alone but maybe not so alone, capisce." He put his head down so his chin was on his chest, leaned his forehead practically to John's, speaking low. "This is how we'll talk whenever we have something paranormal to relate." Tom sat back up, lifted his head looking for John's acceptance.

"Have you spoken to your lawyer yet? How can you explain it all to him?"

"Yeah, we met. He's a canonical lawyer that the diocese sent, a priest, John, so I was able to tell him everything I know."

"Church lawyer seems hardly the thing for a…a murder case. He any good, Father?"

"Well, actually Monsignor Graham used to be a trial lawyer in Los Angeles. He called just an hour ago saying they found the property owned by Christian Menger and one horrific mess there too." John nodded. "Graham guessed it won't be long till I'm out on bail or even have the charges dropped for self-defense, or actually some other term, I've forgotten, but it means I was saving someone else's life, which I was."

"That's good. I heard the same news about the barns and the girls, or at least as much as I could grab at the office. Reporters are following us everywhere. Ken, the owner of Bookworm Joe's next

47

door—you ever met Ken?" Father Tom shook his head. "He chased them off, pulled me into Bookworm's, and locked the coffee shop up. We watched the news in there. Ken told me he was actually the one who sent Rabbi Katz to you at Saint Elizabeth's that day when he was looking for Clarice."

"Do you know why he was looking for Clarice?" Tom asked. John's head shook. "The rabbi told me he'd been having these dreams of your son Jackson and of this flying woman." Father's chin dropped. "He said he'd been seeing a woman flying in spirit form in his sleep. Then he met this art student in the museum where he was working who had a photo of one of Clarice's paintings that was identical to his dream. He was called by God, John, called to defeat that black legion from hell." John was silent a while and fingered the chipped laminate on the table.

Just thinking of Clarice that way, flying around in spirit, made his blood boil. If circumstances were different, he'd be sitting in a confessional at Saint Elizabeth's Church and talking about it with Father. He needed to confide in someone. Chin down John uttered, "Father, that's just it. I—I can't seem to get past her lies." His fingers on the table clenched. "It's like our marriage is...was a sham."

Father Tom's head came up. He waited till John looked at him then spoke softly. "John, you know Clarice confided in me about her past, about her parents."

"Yeah, her dad died of cancer, her mom of early Alzheimer's," John answered blankly.

"She had to take care of both of them all through high school. They both died so young—"

"Father, I can't see what that has to do with her deceit," John said, choking on the hurt and anger as if it were a live thing in his throat.

"Well, I can't really speak for what is in your wife's heart. But I think it does matter, John, it does. Don't you see she lost her whole family? She had no one till Jackson was born then you came into their lives. That made a whole, brand new family—"

"I still don't see—"

"Perhaps she was afraid. It would be natural, wouldn't it for her to be afraid of losing you, of messing that up. John, as I said, I can't know, I mean in the short time I had to speak with her…. I've only been a priest for so long, even so, it's been my experience counseling couples that emotional scars such as the loss of a parent can create trust issues, she—"

"She couldn't trust me?" John jerked his chin down, leaning closer and keeping his voice low, "She couldn't in six years find a way to say, 'Oh, by the way, I can slip out of my body and fly around and see angels and devils. And oh yeah, I think our son can, too.'" His voice cracked with emotions bigger than himself—a man who could count on one hand the number of times he'd ever cried, a man who never ever had a problem forgiving or loving. He absolutely felt betrayed. His wife had hidden a huge, huge part of herself from him and locked him out.

"John," the priest's voice was overly calm, "listen to how fantastic it sounds. I can't really speak for Clarice, I mean I don't know her mind or heart, don't you think it's possible your wife was in constant denial of the things she experienced? Even when Father Simeon and I visited that first time, I believe we both saw that. We even discussed it on our way back to the hermitage. Father Simeon thought it likely she blamed God for the loss of her parents and for, well, as she saw it, her affliction. The last thing in the world she probably wanted to do was admit she was seeing good and evil entities. She may even have convinced herself she was crazy. It's possible Clarice never understood why she could see the spiritual world—never understood God's plan."

"I'm not sure I understand God's plan," John jumped at the chance to change the subject and get off Clarice. Father's words pricked his conscience, made him uncomfortable. He wasn't ready to listen to excuses or explanations for Clarice's omissions. It should never ever have been that way with them. Secrets and lies! The one thing he treasured most in her was her sincerity and honesty. It hurt, damn it; he'd thought they were so close.

Again, the two lapsed into silence and John suspected the priest was praying for his hard heart. At last, he brought up Jackson.

"Father, I believe . . . I have faith, but . . . I just—what will happen to our son? What is his mission really?"

"John," Tom whispered, "remember what Father Simeon told us. Jackson is a gift from God to a world in sin. One day he will emerge from the Glen to prepare the world, and many in the world will listen to his message. I don't pretend to know much beyond that, but we all understand how unsafe it was for him. Pure evil sought his destruction. That should tell us something of how powerful is his mission."

"Time." The prison guard stood in the open doorway, waiting.

Tom gave a polite grin to the guard and stood, pushing his chair back with his legs. The chain on his handcuffs clinked on the table. "I can't wait to get back to my pulpit. This has changed me forever, John. I feel as if I'm meant to help prepare the faithful for what's to come."

"Okay, Father," John stood. Tom reached the door and the guard took hold of his elbow. "Pray for us, alright?" John called out weakly as the orange clad prisoner disappeared from sight.

6

What Cars?

Sergio came back to the motel room, a six-pack of beer and a bucket of KFC in his hands. He threw his keys on the bed and flipped on the TV, which blasted something about the Fairview Inn of Albany. He changed the channel to Cable News. It had been a week of the kid's picture plastered all over the set with the Miller's whining for his return. He popped open a beer and kicked off his loafers. Man, he needed clothes; his shirt had been ripe for days. Pulling some pillows over to one side, he stripped off his shirt and got comfortable on the bed. Smells of KFC filled the room, and Sergio dove into a crispy leg. The station went from weather to politics to Washington. It would return to national news after that.

Half-asleep with a can balanced on his belly, the sound of sirens snapped Sergio awake. Beer sloshed on his stomach. It was the TV. He pulled a sticky napkin from the nightstand to mop up the drips, keeping one eye on the set. A helicopter was filming a dozen cop cars speeding up a dirt road. They had found the Ranch. Sergio sat up straight, deposited his beer on the nightstand without looking. Cameras zoomed in on the black Cadillac Deville. So, they knew the plates, alright. He swung out of bed looking for the yellow bug. Where was the Volkswagen? It was right next to the Caddy. Who moved the bug? In the corner of the screen was a picture of a girl, and the announcer was talking about someone named Jessie Fuhlible.

"Oh *merda*!" He remembered now; there was still one in the house. She was upstairs. He totally forgot about the pregnant chick. "*Porca Vacca*!" The yellow bug showed up on the screen, and Sergio froze to listen.

Jessica Fuhlible was stopped earlier today driving this Volkswagen Beetle, in the town of Andover, Ohio. The car is registered to a Roxanne Cassan, a reporter at the Binghamton Journal who was found brutally murdered last week at Macromania, a health food store in Binghamton, NY. Police gained information from Miss Fuhlible, who is at least six months pregnant. That information led them to this property in Cobleskill, NY where Miss Fuhlible claims she escaped, and scores of other women were being held against their will by a satanic cult.

The murder of Miss Cassan has been connected to the kidnapping of six-year-old Jackson Miller. Cassan and Clarice Miller, the boy's mother worked together at the Journal before the Millers moved to Ithaca, NY some months ago. Chopper 4 and WYNA were first on the scene today via our helicopter broadcast. We have been trying all day to gain as much information as possible for you, but police and authorities are keeping the media far outside the compound…

The screen returned to the helicopter view of the Ranch, and as it panned the area, he saw the big, empty field. He watched for a second before it sunk in. Then he spun around in confusion, knocking the bucket of chicken to the floor.

"Where are the cars? Where the hell are the cars?" he yelled at the screen. His hands tore through his hair, and he paced the room in shock. "*Porco mondo*! Nooo, no way!" Mamma Mia, every car was gone. They got out! Every last worshipper escaped the cave. And everyone of them knew he and Mark had left them there to rot. He was dead. He was a dead man. It was only a matter of time.

He had to get out now, like right now! Leave the country, fly somewhere, start over. At the dresser, Sergio dumped the contents of the plastic bag out. Plenty of cash for a plane ticket, hotels and food, but that wouldn't last long. His own account had practically nothing in it. He turned the black velvet sack upside down spilling a few pieces of jewelry and a yellowed notepaper on the dresser. He pulled the jewelry apart and held the necklace up to the light. The gold looked antique and the crystals had weird colors. He didn't know much about gems, but these didn't appear to meet the bill. Unfolding the old paper, he read:

> *October 17, 1945*
>
> *Dearest Christian, This jewelry belonged to your great grandmother in Austria. I had always thought I would be handing them onto a daughter, but as your father and I were blessed with but a single heir, I am leaving these to you in hopes that perhaps if you should one day marry you would give them to your bride. Alas, with your father gone, and my terminal condition, we are not likely meant to see that happy day, but I pray you will think of us whenever you see your beloved don these heirlooms.*
>
> *With deepest love,*
>
> *Your Mother.*

"Menger, you seed of the devil!" Sergio spit. This was too much. That guy had a mother, a mother who cared even, a mother who probably loved him. Oh, what Sergio would have given to have a letter like this in his name! He thought of his life as a foster child, bounced around in a system devoid of love and stability. How many fake mothers had he had? Life was never fair. Never! His anger mingled with that familiar taste of deprivation and loss—a little boy hurt that would not heal. For most of his childhood, Sergio had dreamed of having a mother—his mother to love and to be loved and cherished as all little boys ought, and this man had thrown it all away, and for what? For whom—Satan? Sergio shoved the note and jewelry back in the bag, shoving his emotion in with it. Maybe an antique dealer would give him something for them.

Calming himself, which was something akin to throwing ice on a hot pan, Sergio opened the first manila envelope. On an otherwise blank sheet of paper, he found several account numbers, dates and balances, all in the master's slanted script. Rounding each amount, he quickly tried to add the numbers in his head. How many zeros are in a million? Is it five or six? *Mannaggia*, I'm dense. He went over the place values like he was back in school, tens, hundreds, thousands, holding up his finger for every place. "YES!" he cried out. Maybe one and half million in these accounts. The sheet had no other information, no banks, no names, nothing else on the paper. How could he transfer money if he had no idea what banks held these accounts. They could even be in foreign banks.

He scowled tearing into the next envelope. It contained two deeds, one to the Ranch and one to a house owned by Todd and Emily Menger. Sergio shook his head. The master had a childhood home, real parents, real love it looked like, and still that prig became whatever it was he was. Evil, that was for sure. If possible, he hated the master even more now, seeing what he had and threw away. To Sergio whatever he had become himself, he felt sure he would not have made the bad choices he made if he'd had any kind of real family or upbringing. He looked at the deed, which was to a house in Gary, Indiana. Gary? He thought he remembered that house in the sticks, a tiny blue farmhouse with boarded up windows. He had flown to Indiana with the master, without knowing why they were there. Deserted, the place had no pictures or personal stuff, only a few pieces of sheet-covered furniture. He thought back to the day, recalling the odd list of chores he'd done there and one task in particular. It was odd, too. He'd packed a cardboard box with things from a desk, and to it, Sergio thought he'd added paperwork from his briefcase. After the box was packed, the master had Sergio hoist it up to the attic, place it between two joists and lay insulation over the top. If that box had paperwork, there was at least some chance it could contain the names of the banks Menger used. One thing for sure, he couldn't look for any information back at the Ranch.

Sergio picked up the passport and opened it. Christian glowered back at him. Glancing in the mirror, he studied his own Italian features. He was barely thirty-five, olive skin, high cheekbones, deep, dark eyes, and long, wavy black hair. He was almost as tall as Menger, who was 6'1, but Sergio was broad shouldered and solid-bodied, his muscles well developed. For a split second, he tried to picture himself in the disguise of Christian Menger. That was nuts. The guy was like eighty years old, pasty and emaciated. The passport was worthless, especially now with how close they check after 9/11. Getting his own seemed iffy. He'd need his birth certificate and social security, proof of residence, besides his license. Then there was his criminal record, he'd done time. Do they even let you get a passport after that?

Topping it all off was the expungement. He was never too sure about that since Menger was involved. Was the record really wiped out as he'd promised? Couldn't trust that SOB, dead or alive.

Had to get out of the country. People knew what he looked like, that couple, what was their name? The Miller's, they knew, and that girl on the news that led them to the ranch, she would recognize his picture too. He had no idea how widespread the cult was. No matter what, he had to try to get the money in those accounts. With that kind of money, he could buy his way anywhere. Sergio ran his fingers through his long hair gripping a handful. Have to change that right away. Holding his shirt and room key, he flew out the door.

* * *

Tuesday morning, puffed up and proud, Mark pulled into the Castle Creek diner in the Jaguar Coupe. He looked good in this Jag, and his new clothes didn't hurt either. The black jeans and snug shirt fresh from the men's store showed off his muscular frame. Pulling off his new shades, he twisted the mirror towards him and ran a hand over his smooth jaw and then through his crew cut. He looked like, he decided, a pro-football player or somebody important in this hot car.

The diner was two blocks from his old house, but his parents didn't live there anymore. After his brother died, they moved to Florida. They couldn't prove it was Mark, but his folks knew. In fact, besides the Master, they were the only people on earth who could have proved it was him. He'd used a tire iron right from Tim's own car. He used to see poor Tim's skull bashed in, used to picture the day, the moment, wishing he could take it back. But that was long ago, before the master. Timmy should have known. Of all people, his own brother knew his temper. He couldn't help it; he just got so mad at stuff, at people. Now, he felt nothing. Regrets had dried up, hardened like gum under a school desk.

Right after it happened, the Master had been there. For the life of him, Mark never could figure out where he was located, how he could have seen him commit the murder. But he knew stuff, the Master, like where the crowbar was stashed, and exactly what Tom and he had argued about. The Master helped him get away from police, gave him lots of money, and all the drugs and whores he wanted. It wasn't bad in the beginning, a few jobs here and there. But by the time the

55

Master was calling him Cain, he hated him. Hated that guy with all he had, and it didn't matter one bit to the man they said was called Menger. He was just about convinced the Master was the devil in the flesh. He sure as hell had powers, all kinds. Now, he was as dead as anyone, as dead as Mark's brother, Tim, as dead as all them girls, as dead as all those sick worshippers in the cave. Dead, dead, dead! And he was free. Life would be sweet again.

Mark parked in the handicapped spot right in front of the diner. His girth and the car being so close to the ground made it awkward to exit. Jingling the keys, he lumbered out of the racecar, smiling at the waitress in the window. She was impressed; he could tell. He ran a hand over the Jag's hood, had to be worth over a hundred K. Chicks love that stuff.

This early in the morning, he had his pick of booths since most blue collars had already come and gone. Choosing a booth, he ran the palm of his hand up the length of his nose and sat down. He looked at his watch—almost nine. He should probably check out the news or something. It had been a week since he and Sergio left the ranch, and so far so good, just a lot of shots of the missing kid, teary parents, and all the dead people. The master, that priest they saw in the Miller's front yard, and that Jewish guy who ran into the woods with the kid. He wondered where the kid went. If the Jew was dead, and the parents don't have him, and Menger is dead, and all the elders were trapped in the cave with the worshippers, then who has the kid? Aaach, what's the difference? So far, the cop drawings of him and Sergio looked nothing like them; least he didn't think so. Still he hadn't watched the news or even listened to it on the radio since yesterday morning. Could ask the waitress to flip channels on the set behind the counter. Naw, she'd think he was a loser who watches news.

"Can I help you?"

He studied her face, following the strands of her shorn black hair, which curved inward on full cheeks and pointed to her upturned nose. She was only a little chunky; he could do her. He ordered four eggs, bacon, toast, and hash browns. She came back a second later to fill his coffee.

"That your Jag?"

Oh yeah, she's into cars.

"Yup, '93 XJ220. Sweet, huh?"

"I love old cars." She smiled nervously.

Probably shy, Mark figured. He'd talk her up after breakfast. He watched her as she went back behind the counter. Her bottom was wide through the old-fashioned uniform but still appealing. She made a phone call turning her back to him while she talked. A couple minutes later, she returned holding a pot of coffee. Pouring his cup, she almost jumped out of her pink dress when he touched her hand. She was a shaky thing, but that was okay. She was definitely interested, especially the way she kept looking at him and then outside like she couldn't get enough of his car. His eggs and toast appeared quickly, and she zipped away before he knew what happened. While he was eating, he watched her talking with her hand over her mouth to the cook. It was like being back in high school when she pointed to him and then the car.

Mark slugged the last of his coffee down and glanced up at the TV behind the counter. There was a huge picture of a British green XZ220 Jaguar. Just like his jag! The waitress banged her hand on the set, and it went blank. Why'd she do that? It didn't matter; the cutie would have to wait. He whipped a ten out of his wallet, slapped it on the table, and rose to leave.

Mark heard the sirens before he reached the front door. He watched fascinated while three patrol cars zoomed into the lot from three different directions surrounding his car. He finally put two and two together and cast a look back at the waitress. Her hand flew up to her mouth, and her horror-struck look revealed her betrayal. Rubbing his hand across his nose, he watched as twenty cops came out of nowhere all pointing their weapons at him and yelling, "Freeze!"

* * *

Ten minutes to noon, hot and sticky, Sergio came in whipping the Mets cap off his head. Late last night he'd bombed out looking for a barber and went out early this morning instead. He threw the clothes bag from Colonie Center mall on the bed, cranked the AC, and went to the mirror to look at his shocking head. With his hands on the dresser, he leaned in. He'd never ever seen his head shaved. The skull looked round and weird, his dark features almost haunting. This was going to take some getting used to. Sergio closed his eyes to think. *Plip, plip, plip*, three loud drops reverberating in the porcelain sink in the bathroom. He waited.

Silence.

Plip, plip, plip.

Silence.

The hotel was thickly quiet, he strained to hear any other sound, no cars whizzing by, no TV's humming, no babies or yelling, so completely void of . . .

Plip, Plip, PLOP.

The ominous sound vibrated in his ear. Sergio sensed he was being watched. He popped his eyes open.

Staring back at him was the crinkled face of the Master. "*Aaahhh,*" he screamed at the mirror. The master's black eyes bore into him; high cheekbones, sunken cheeks, and yellow skin were right there in front of him. Sergio jumped back two feet, tripped over his shoes, and knocked into the bed, his heart racing against his chest.

"What the …!"

He righted himself. He was just tired. Tired and hot, that was all. Sergio glanced at his refection on his way to the bathroom to splash cold water on his face. He watched the faucet, remembering the dripping. Nothing happened. He reached down, felt with his fingers. Not a drip, sink was even dry. Must be the tub then. He reached behind the shower curtain. Nope, that was dry too, and so was the showerhead. *Oofah!* Was he hearing things as well as seeing things? Guido, get it together! He smooshed his palms into his eye sockets and rubbed. All he needed was a shower and some Zs. He turned the handle in the shower and went to get a pair of new boxers from the Macys' bag. He clicked on the noon news, and there was Mark, handcuffed, standing by that ridiculously, recognizable Jag.

"Castle Creek!" Sergio shouted at the TV shaking his head. "Mark you 'chooch', you went back home? Man, what a friggin' stunad!"

After his shower, Sergio Valenti fell asleep wondering if Mark would rat him out, if the elders would find him, or if Hell had other plans for him.

7

Angela

Angela Miller awoke to the jab of a pointy boot slamming into her thigh. Pain was immediate.

"Get up, bitch, make me some coffee."

"Ok, already. You have to be so friggin mean bout everything?"

He tore the sheet off and punched her hard in the back. Angela swallowed a yelp, thinking she'd asked for that one. She rolled over and waited looking down at his snakeskin boots. Would he move? He stood there, feet apart, braced and ready. He enjoyed this, her fear hanging in the air, so real you could frame it. If she moved while he remained there, it was sure he'd clip her. If she waited too long without obeying, he'd lay into her as well. Lose, lose. Man, he enjoyed the power! He finally grinned and stepped away towards the can.

Eddy was one mean-ass boyfriend and pimp. Hitler would be the Dali Lama next to him. Angie got up, holding her backside, wondering how bad the bruise would be. He never hit her in the face or anywhere in front. She picked a trail over the carpet, invisible under a pile of clothes, beer cans, liquor bottles, and encrusted takeout containers. She went to the counter behind the threadbare black velvet couch in her cramped apartment to fill the coffee maker. At least it had been her studio till Eddy moved in to *protect* her. What a joke!

She reached on the shelf between a box of cereal and an open package of stale cookies for a coffee filter and the can of coffee. The smell of sweat and his dirty sneakers hung in the air, insulting and rank. It stunk in here ever since he came. She gave the handle by the window half a dozen cranks, knowing full well Eddy would let her have it for wasting the AC, but dammit, it reeked in here. The open window barely brought relief as faint sounds of the strip drifted in. Sin City, she thought, what happens in Vegas, stays in Vegas. A saying that made it easy for tourists to sin and to imagine they could leave their sin behind. Angela had no such delusions. Her sins would follow her, had followed her wherever she went. She had the life she deserved, the one she'd earned. Vegas with its endless lights, gambling, shows, and sights was an escape for tourists; for her, there was no escape.

The city of Las Vegas, founded in 1911, saw its first casino, El Rancho built by Thomas Hull in 1941, and the birth of organized gambling. Here too, was born perhaps Las Vegas' greatest cultural contribution: the all-you-can-eat buffet. With the decadent combination of wanton gambling, drinking, and eating, prostitution was not far behind. Despite its legality in brothels only sixty miles away, and continual efforts by law enforcement to keep it out of Clark County, the sale of human flesh thrived in Vegas. Whether toothless and scarred or fresh off the bus, whether high on crack or part-time students, the women of the night here sell themselves every hour of the day. And none of them, Angela thought, none want to be here. It would take a team of psychologists and drug counselors to figure out how she got here and why she stayed. It felt as if her life was over, but she was in her twenties for crying out loud. How could life end in this toilet bowl, this wasteland of sin?

Angela turned from the open window, to the sink where she stood running water in the coffeepot. On the half wall in front of her sat a stainless steel toaster, throwing back a smeared reflection of thick, unruly blond hair, ugly shadows haunted her deep-set eyes, and sallow cheeks. A fresh wave of self-pity washed over her.

Enough already. She looked down at the running water absently watching its clear stream. Almost immediately she saw him, a child in a beautiful sylvan paradise of ancient towering trees, lush foliage, and a crystal stream with moss covered banks. The kid was always playing in his little waterfall, running after some light beam, or sitting quietly against a wide trunk surrounded by prehistoric looking flora. She decided it was a boy since he wore no shirt. Like a lonely, but happy young Tarzan, living on his own in the wild. Only this forest seemed nurturing not dangerous.

Wham! Angela's hips slammed forward into the counter when Eddy delivered a kick from behind. The drawer handle jammed in her pelvis, and her hands instinctively grabbed the counter ready for the next blow.

"I see you up, but I don't see you moving, Angie. I need smokes."

She released the counter and slowly walked back to her bed. Tears sprang from her eyes, as she eased jean shorts over her newly bruised hip. She spied her shirt across the bed but too close to Eddy, so she didn't bother to cover her tank top. Snagging a ten from the table and her platform heels off the chair, Angela hurried out the door, wondering if he was finally going to kill her one of these days and whether she would welcome the relief.

8

Cleaning Up

Clyde finished washing his hands in the casino lavatory and glanced in the mirror with disappointment. It seemed disrespectful that his work pants were so worn that the blue color was fading right off the thighs and knees. Now his matching work shirt had a tear. The new yellow nametag had caught on a dresser he was moving. He read the crisp black letters: Clyde Stoltz, Janitorial. The tag seemed unnecessary. Everyone, who cared to, knew him as Clyde, and the work clothes, mops and buckets said janitor well enough, he guessed. He wet his straight brown hair and whipped out a comb to slick it back into place. For no reason, he felt smaller than usual today; even his features seemed smaller. Must be losing weight again. He was only 5'2", and still he had trouble keeping his weight at 130.

Clyde picked up his brown lunch bag and thermos and left the bathroom, taking a shortcut across the casino floor to get to the boiler room. If he stayed by the slots, he wouldn't be noticed. Janitors were expected to be invisible. He wasn't supposed to cut through the gaming area, but if he went all the way around, past the shops and lobbies to get to the other side, too much of his lunch break would be wasted. It was just noon as he cut a path through rows of empty slot machines. Here and there were the diehard players, mostly overweight people, sitting on their cans, holding wide-mouthed plastic cups of coins, and pulling levers. They did it all day, everyday some of them. Where they came from, he always wondered. Where do they live? Every face looked blank, so lost and bored. Sure, he sometimes saw a happy new face, probably here for the first time or just here for a good time with friends. For the most part though, the slot players had this vacuous, unsatisfied look. Clyde couldn't see why, but one thing was for sure, they were not happy. He liked to study people, quietly watch their faces and imagine their lives. So, he knew happy, he knew sad, and he knew bored, and tired and he knew undirected, misdirected and unfulfilled, he knew hope and he knew despair. Clyde knew people on the inside.

A heavy, dyed blond, sitting alone at the end of a row of empty slot machines, gave him a weak smile. Her tiny eyes, swallowed up in a fleshy face, were slathered in blue eye shadow and tarantula lashes that did nothing to help the tiny slits. Clyde acknowledged her with the same pity he always had for such slaves of the slots. The tiny slits glazed back over, when whatever light his presence had awakened passed, and her fat arm covered in bangle bracelets went right back to the lever.

Clyde Stoltz liked watching people, at least when he wasn't in one of those states. He never tried to figure those out, just accepted that there was some kind of hidden world all around him. Clyde would occasionally buzz out and see people as if they were spirits with good and bad light around them or even in them. When he was little, he'd asked his mother about it, and her simple explanation had satisfied him for most of his forty years on earth.

"Clyde," she'd said, "don't you worry none about what you see; them shapes won't hurt you. It's just a peek beyond, Clydey, a peek at the good and the bad. Some reason you got the knack. Maybe one day you'll know why."

He crossed a shiny hall and reached the door, descending to the boiler room. With no office, Clyde liked to think of this place as his own. Even though he had to sort of hide down here. It was his hangout, all his. Other workers ate in the breakroom, loud, laughing, cracking jokes, and arguing. With the casino teeming with noise, he'd think they'd just want peace and quiet like him. But his coworkers seemed to need the camaraderie of company and visiting, he guessed. He needed the quiet, so he came here, and for almost a year, or thereabouts, his hideout remained undiscovered. Course he took precautions, like he sat on the floor behind the boiler furnace in the summer months. He'd cleaned the cubbyhole out, laid a soft blanket there, even rigged a tiny light behind him to read his stack of magazines and books. Others would have found his lunch habit bizarre, but for him it was a mini retreat.

Clyde was special, that's what people called him, sometimes even to his face. He always felt different, but he never understood the term "special." Maybe if they knew about the stuff he could see they could call him that, but he never told anybody but his Mom about that stuff. It was after high school really that Clyde figured out what they meant by special. He was slow, slower than most at every subject, slower at conversations, slower at thinking. Still, he figured he knew a sight more than most people, though he could never explain it 'cept to his Ma. In school, they always stuck him with Downs or handicapped kids. He never minded much, they were the best people anyway, rarely mean or unhappy, smiling, willing. After school, he learned a trade cleaning just as his mother had when she needed extra money for them. He wasn't slow at work, careful though, not slow. Better to be careful than sloppy like some, Clyde thought, settling himself and unwrapping the wax paper on his cheese sandwich.

A few minutes later, turning a page in his paperback book and munching a bite of sandwich, Clyde heard noise on the stairs and froze. Several pairs of feet were clicking and clomping down the concrete steps. Shoot! A maintenance crew? They could be checking the furnace. He'd have to explain himself. It would be embarrassing as all get out. He peeked between the boilers to see if he knew any of them. The noisy feet turned left at the bottom of the stairs and crossed directly in front of Clyde's cubby area, passing by him not five feet away. He watched a parade of suits, five to be precise, and very expensive if Clyde knew anything about suits in Casinos. Four were men and one was an old, but dignified lady. The five continued walking over to a corner by some stock boxes. That section of the basement was full of crates, broken furniture, and empty file cabinets. Maintenance tended to pile junk in that area, stuff they were supposed to fix, or stuff left over from those kits of Sauder furniture units used throughout the hotel.

Crouching, Clyde inched his way to another position between one of the blue furnaces and a tan water softener unit where he could watch the five intruders and remain hidden. It was super uncomfortable, worth it though if he heard something exciting, maybe a casino scam or criminal talk. The old lady leaned coolly against a tall, grey file cabinet. Clyde studied her fascinated by her looks and mannerisms. Her grayish brown hair was flipped and styled in an old-fashioned doo of the forties. She was petite and bony, but elegant in a navy pinstriped skirt and jacket, a red silk scarf and red patent leather pumps. It must have been her heels that made the clicking sound he'd heard on the steps. Clyde, an old movie buff, was reminded of Bette Davis as she held a long cigarette out to the huge, dark haired man behind her, expecting a light. He stood at least six foot seven, as solid as a tree trunk and large all the way around. He had to bow low in order to light her fag, and the match illuminated his giant features and very square jaw. Most curious was a long, earthworm scar that stretched from his chin to his temple. She patted the enormous face and smiled sweetly as if he were a favored toy. He was maybe forty-five to her seventy-five. They made an odd looking pair, Clyde decided.

The Goliath man straightened and stood protectively near her, throwing a threatening look to the other three men. Two of whom now had their backs to Clyde as they half sat on some boxes. The heaviest one was downright obese, short with stubby gray hair on a mostly bald head. His suit like all the other men was dark, navy, or black. On the box next to the fat guy, sat another middle-aged man, an inch or so taller than Clyde, not fat but thicker like once upon a time he might have lifted weights. He had longish sandy hair slicked back against a receding hairline.

The last figure in the room was as distinctively stylish as the woman, though far younger. He stood facing the two on the cardboard boxes and kitty-corner to the odd couple. He was about five foot ten or eleven, trim build, peppered gray hair, and a handsome aquiline nose. With princely features and coiffed dark hair, he looked as if he'd stepped out of an issue of *GQ* for men over fifty. Indeed his suit even stood out among the rest, a dark gray with coral pinstripe, perfectly accenting his hair. Clyde guessed he was vain. He liked studying people, watching them not to judge them he hoped, that'd be wrong. Just that he was fair at figuring folks out. The immense one, whose flabby left cheek hung grossly askew on the box he was crushing, was addressing the handsome one now.

"Emmett, this is highly uncomfortable, why don't we move to your suite?"

The blond on the other box jerked his chin, revealing a goatee. Those always made Clyde want to laugh. "He doesn't trust us, Philip, that's why. Emmett thinks we'll off him in his sleep if we know where he lays his head."

"Ha," the old woman said blowing out a long trail of smoke, the cigarette poised in her left hand. She stood off to the side in front of abandoned file cabinets. Her left arm lay across her waist, it's wrist supporting her smoker's elbow. Polished red nails drummed slowly in the air as the others waited on her words. "Par—anoia is not ex—actly an unhealthy trait a—mong El—ders." Her smoky voice, punching syllables and jabbing consonants as if she were a boxing linguist, made the resemblance to Bette Davis uncanny.

Silence followed her comment. Each suit seemed to be sizing up the others. The one called Emmett played with the ring on his manicured finger, stealing looks at the woman, but boldly staring down the goatee guy and the fat man. Clyde studied the ring he was twisting. Highly unusual, it seemed to be made of black onyx. Rather than the black gem being laid as a stone in a setting, the ring itself seemed to be carved of solid onyx. Embedded in the glistening black stone on the flattened surface were, he guessed, tiny rubies laid in a pattern unfamiliar to Clyde but reminding him of Egyptian hieroglyphics.

"Vera is right," the dapper one finally said. "I'd be a fool to trust anyone too far, when we have no leader at present."

"It's Mizzz. Wheaton," the old woman said, "show some respect Misss-ter Pierce." The giant behind her made a step forward, but the woman swung her arm out across his belly. "Quite alright, Worm."

"Deepest apology, my dear," the one called Emmett said with some exaggeration. "I meant no disrespect." He tensed but seemed to recover quickly. "Perhaps it is a generational divide; I tend to use first names among equals. As for me, please feel free to call me Emmett, Ms. Wheaton."

Every one of them tensed. This was no meeting of friends, Clyde decided. He looked over at the Neanderthalic man she called Worm, evidently nicknamed for the long raised scar on his face. It was hard to believe he would like being reminded of it, and Clyde, almost as small as the tiny woman, found it mind-boggling that she dared call him that. Obviously, he was completely enamored and fiercely loyal to her.

"What about my car?" The fat one with the buzz cut whined. He sat with his bottom half on a crate, one short leg extended to help support his weight, his stubby arms trying to rest on some part of his legs, but his wide middle pushing them out from his side.

"Oh, do shut up about your precious BMW, Philip!"

"Easy for you to say, Scoootttt. They didn't take your car, just mine and some lesser's Jag. He will pay."

"Bloody hell, Phil—"

"Enough," Emmett yipped, "Of course he'll pay. They'll both pay. They left us buried alive in the cave, didn't they?"

"Are you aware, Emmett, that the bodyguard Mark has been caught," the woman called Vera said, dropping her spent butt on the cement floor and with pointed toe, ground the filter in a slow exaggerated motion. "Highly inconvenient, and the other one . . . Valenti, the one known as Judas—"

"I know," Emmett said, glaring at Vera. Clyde could see the rivalry, some sort of tussle for control of the group. "Mark is a hiccup. We'll see he won't last long enough to do any damage. He's in jail. We have more than enough lessers on the force. Scott, you'll see to that detail, won't you?" Emmett tilted his gaze to the blond man scratching his goatee.

Suddenly lightheaded, his circulation cut off in the crouched position, Clyde shifted his weight. He sat back, careful and quiet, unscrunching his knees and stretching his legs. He couldn't see them from this position, but he could still listen to the conversation as he waited for the feeling to return to his limbs. Rubbing his calves through his blue workpants, Clyde refocused his attention, realizing he'd missed something for the topic had changed.

"So, now what?" It sounded like the longhaired one named Scott, "Choose a new leader, or do we wait to be shown who it will be?"

"Several things must be done first," the old lady's gruff voice cut in.

"I say you should be the new Master." The obese one called Philip said, but Clyde couldn't see to whom the remark was addressed.

"Flattering to be sure, Philip, but I may be too old."

So it was the sharp looking one in the gray suit speaking. Clyde pictured him, the one called Emmett, prissy, stylish, his fancy suit, cufflinks, shoes—everything designer if Clyde knew anything. This was rather an exciting lunch, he thought, for a people watcher like himself.

"Menger was our leader for fifty years," Emmett said, "barely thirty when he took over."

Clyde could easily tell this remark was aimed at the old lady. He wished he could see, darn it. It was like going from a TV to a radio.

"I would not presume, Emmett that age will be such a factor as all that. This era may be drawing to a close." The old lady threw her hat in the ring for whatever position of leadership they were talking about. "We must arrange a high coven to decide the matter. By the by, Emmett, do you really think it wise that you sport the master's ring so brazenly. I mean really, doesn't it strike you as presumptuous—"

"My dear Ve—Ms. Wheaton," Emmett said, and Clyde tried to remember the distinctive ring. "I was merely the one who managed to acquire the ring from his finger in the city morgue. Had I not taken the initiative, we might have been reduced to sending a crew of lessers out with shovels in the night, like common grave robbers."

"Still Emmett, I should wonder why you don't place it in a safe or safe deposit box until a new elder is honored to house the Legion and lead the coven."

"It is merely a convenience, I assure you all. I haven't a safer place to keep the treasure for the time being. I believe we have more pressing matters, haven't we?" Emmett's voice hurried on. "Unless of course you have located the Coven's safe deposit box and all its assets. Besides silencing Mark, moreover, we must locate the other bodyguard, Valenti."

"That Judas, he has my car, that pompous thug. He better not hurt the seats or scratch it."

"Will you just—" the one named Scott complained to the flabby one, who simultaneously yelled, "Oh yeah, easy for you, easy for you, you're—"

"Enough!"Both were cut short by the guy in the expensive suit,

Everyone was silent. Clyde was dying for another look. Quiet as a mouse, he pushed himself back into the crouched position. Too late did he realize his wooziness this time had nothing whatsoever to do with his circulation and everything to do with entering that other reality.

"We agree a high coven must be called."

Clyde's heart leapt to his throat, looking towards the voice known as Emmett in the gray suit. What he saw paralyzed him. Where stood a man before, now stood a creature covered in slime, its grotesque rust colored body, a cross between a boar and a hyena. Its flattened nose had three holes, and something oozed from its mouth of pointy opossum teeth dripping down a curved yellow tusk. The shorthaired body of this hyena-pig stood on stunted limbs ending in cloven hooves. Clyde looked from one spot to another, which only seconds before held the forms of human beings. His hand flew to his mouth stifling his gasp, tears sprung to his eyes, his skin crawled with his own sweat, and something let loose between his legs. Clyde's terror was complete, but his instinct for survival as keen. He forced himself to watch and listen as the one who used to be the woman spoke.

"The Miller child is obviously the new John, and seemingly untouchable in his sanctuary. The high one will be furious with us for losing him." The red eyes of the beast glowed. "But we must remain calm. He needs us, he will always need us."

But it was too much for poor Clyde, who missed the rest of the meeting, having mercifully passed out on the brown lunch bag atop his ratty blanket behind the boiler in the basement of Four Kings Casino.

9

Child of the Sun

SPRING OF 1992

Angela slammed her locker and gave it a wiggle to make sure it was locked. A sea of kids streamed by on her left and her right. She smiled at a few faces, not a one smiled back. High school sucked. Everybody was so stuck-up and unreal. Friendliness was a disease. The less of it you showed the cooler you were. Well hell, she felt like smiling, so what? Big whoop.

She pushed against the bathroom door and headed for a stall. Two seconds later, lit cigarette in her lips, she heard a bang on her stall door and froze. She crouched slowly to peek at the feet, her smoke poised over the bowl for quick dousing—red platforms.

"Lisa, you dweeb!" Angela pounded the stall door hard.

"Hey!" Her best friend Lisa caught the swinging door an inch from her face. "That's what you get for smokin' like the Lone Ranger. Supposed to be a social habit, Angie," she said, lighting up her own stick.

Lisa plunked herself on the edge of the sink, her short little body fitting easily. Though she was a bit chunky, Angela might have traded places with her. Short girls just look cute, she thought. Being tall is like, never cute. Even Lisa's overalls, with one side latched and the other flopping down, looked better on short girls. Angela didn't care for Lisa's black hair, but the punk style with a red streak did match her personality.

"Angie, fix yer hair, girl. It's pretty sad."

Without argument, Angela moved to the mirror and plucked off her skullcap, which had done its job of keeping at least half her hair calmed down after her shower. She pushed her fingers through the thick, unruly hair, pulling and tugging the knots. Underneath the fuzzy top layer lay silky curls. When she bothered with a half ponytail or used a clip, that hair underneath actually looked pretty decent, full of ringlets and soft waves.

"My version of a pick," Angela said, wiggling digits at Lisa. "Look at this excuse for blond. Is un-sunny a word?"

"Ya could color it, you know." Lisa swung her legs to and fro.

Angela ignored her friend and looked at herself. She never felt pretty; usually she just felt awkward. She grew too tall, too fast. Other girls were a perfect 5'5" or 5'6", and she a lanky 5'9". Her nose was too long as well, no matter what her mom said. Her eyes were these dark, deep-set orbs of blue, and her lips too full for her narrow face. Looking over the rest of her, she had to admit she had a good figure, and she liked the grunge look. The *501*'s were perfect for her long legs, and the ripped t-shirt accented her small waist. Plus the flannel shirt kinda hid her barely-B chest. Angela flicked her ashes in the sink and finished forcing her fingers through her hair.

"Hey, guess what? We're going to a house party tonight!" Lisa hopped off the sink and doused her cigarette in the basin.

Angela gave hers another drag. "Whose party?"

"No one we know. It's one I heard of, and we—are—going." She tapped a pointed finger on Angela's nose.

"How?" Angela knew Lisa probably had something all cooked up including rides and stories for prying parents. She loved Friday nights and Lisa.

Later at home, the Miller's sat around their kitchen table. Dinner was loudly quiet, that silverware hitting and scraping the plates quiet. These awkward moments perplexed Angela, herself a fairly happy, outgoing personality. With the four older boys all gone to college or married, dinners these days possessed a calm unfamiliar to the previously large family. Mom only cooked three or four times a week and half the time her brother John, in his fourth year of college, or herself were absent. She preferred not to be here most of the time since the shrinking household only emphasized the problems she had with her dad.

She looked at her balding dad with his squarish frame, dress shirt, glasses, and hard mouth. Her mom the picture of perfection in her silk blouse and styled hair, sat arrow straight like a rod was rammed up her spine. John sat at the other end of the table, opposite her dad in every way, tall, full head of brown hair, football star good looks. Tonight, excited about the party and anxious to share some news, Angela decided to push a little, to shake it up, and try again to make him care about her. Amidst the clanking forks and knives working on pork chops or plucking salad, Angela spoke up.

"I got an A on a Math test today." That should impress him. He knew how she sucked in math. She looked right at him. Nothing. His eating continued as if the air had not been disturbed with good news.

"An A, huh, squirt. Didn't think you liked math." John piped in, always her savior.

"I don't. Just got lucky, I guess. And John, I'm like 5'9". You're the only person in the world who calls me squirt."

"So grow half a foot, and I'll consider changing your name. You'll always be squirt to me." She flicked a pea at him. "Hey!"

It was quiet again, clinking and chinking sounds moved back in as if they'd never stopped.

"Dad, I'm thinking of taking shop next year." He loved wood and building things. He should care about this bomb. She paused, got nothing and plowed on, "I talked to Guidance, and they said plenty of girls take it." Her dad just stared at his food. It was embarrassing. Angela's stomach knotted.

"Bob," her mom nudged him, "shop class, what do you think of that?"

He grunted.

"Dad they make all kinds of stuff. I was thinking I'd make that wooden base for the TV in yours and Mom's room.

"What for?" He finally spoke, but he knew damn well what for.

"The VCR would go under it; give you more room on your dresser."

Mom waved her fork with a piece of meat on the end. "Well, you've been asking for that for a long time. Wouldn't that be great if

73

Angie made one?" She tilted her head to her. "Daddy could help you. You could do it together."

"Not gonna wait a whole year for that," Dad grumbled, "might as well buy one." At least he was listening.

"I can make something else." She just couldn't give up. John gave her a pathetic look of sympathy, which she chose to ignore because what mom said gave her hope. She could do shop class. She could interest her dad out in the garage in his workshop, and they could spend time together under the guise of him helping her with school.

Angela got up, walked her dish to the sink. Suddenly, hope sprang up in her, and it seemed a great idea to hug her dad, kind of force the love out of him. It would always be awkward with him, but she could just hug him. She could push the envelope a little, and maybe things would change. Angela leaned to hug him with her arms out, prepared to dive in and push away the years of indifference with one good squeeze, and he pushed her away—literally pushed!

"What are you doing?" He snapped.

Red-hot waves of embarrassment rolled over her. "It's called a hug, Dad." Humiliated, she ran from the room, but not before seeing him reach for the stupid newspaper by his plate.

Upstairs on her bed, her face smooched into her pillow, smelling faintly of Clorox and detergent, she cried till she thought her head would explode. I hate him. I hate him. I hate him. I hate him. I hate him. What did I ever do to him? Why is he like that? I hate him. I hate him. Her chest tightened and burned, full of self-pity and doubt.

Later she heard a tap at the door. John didn't wait for an answer, but came in wiggling his car keys. He had class tonight.

"He doesn't mean anything by it, Angie." He sat on her bed while she rubbed her eyes willing them to stop leaking. "It's not like he hates you or something." Sincere, her brother's eyes pleaded with hers, but she could tell he never knew how to explain their dad's obvious rejection of his only daughter. The stunt she pulled was stupid, and she should have known it would go as it did, but it hurt like hell anyway.

"He pushed me, John! Pushed me away! It was a hug, a frickin hug. He's all, 'What are you doing?'" The words came out in gasping

74

sobs. "What —are you—doin, like, like—I'm attacking him. Why's he gotta to be like that?"

"Oh Angela, stop being so dramatic." Her mom stood in the doorway, a dishtowel in her hand. "Your father is your father. You can't change him. You expect too much." Her well-bred voice was sing-songy with a rational distance.

It was pointless to argue with her mom especially on this subject. John gave her a hug and kissed the top of her head before leaving for class. Angela brushed past her mom without a word to go to the bathroom and wash her face.

An hour later, she checked herself out in the mirror. The curling iron had calmed her hair making it more manageable, a bit of blush on her high cheekbones, and the dab of lip gloss transformed her. She wasn't bad looking actually, maybe even pretty. Whatever! Tonight she was going out. Screw school, screw her dad, she was going out.

"Lisa! It's like five miles downtown!"

"Don't go all postal on me. We'll get a ride back with someone. We only have to walk there. Let's roll."

It was a perfect night in May, dry and warm at 72°. She had her hands shoved in hoodie as they walked. Lisa stopped to light up, so Angela joined her. Cigarettes were their outlet. More than a rebellion, it was a pressure relief valve for stress. Every drag, hooked up with some problem or grievance that drifted away in an exhale of smoke. They cut through neighborhoods, concentrating on the work of the walk. As they got closer to town, they followed Main Street, a road that began and ended as a highway on either side of the city. They'd been walking single file, and Angela found herself brooding when the sidewalk reappeared and the two walked side by side again.

"You know, Leese, my dad always spends time with my brothers. They come home from college, and he can't stop laughing and slapping them on the back. I walk into a room, and I'm all invisible. John so much as passes in the hall, and my dad calls him in to ask all about his life. He plays football with them, baseball, any ball; you name it. I can't even catch a ball, so I like don't exist. Do you know he gets up and leaves the room sometimes right while I'm talking to him?

No, serious, he does that." Lisa was silent; she'd heard this before. She was the bomb though, letting Angela unload.

"I love your brothers. They're wicked hotties, and they're always cracking jokes."

"I know. They're just so much older than me. Even John's like seven years older than me. Lisa, I think my dad never wanted another kid, four was too many." Angela heard her voice tremor and crack, unable to control the emotional hurt bubbling up. He probably thought mom was done having kids, and then she gets all pregnant. I think he's been mad ever since I was born."

"We're here, Angie, chill out. We'll get blazed; you'll feel better.

Lisa had turned down a side street and then up another. It seemed amazing how she could weave her way to a perfect stranger's house based on sketchy info from some guy at school, when Angela herself couldn't navigate her way out of a paper bag. But that was how they met, Angela remembered. Freshmen year, third day of classes, standing in the hall completely lost in the big new school. Big compared to St. John's, her grade school with eight nuns, one principal, eight classrooms and one cafeteria that served as just about everything else, except gym which took place in the parking lot or the church basement. Public high school had been more than a culture shock for her. Lisa had pretty much adopted her that day out of pity leading her around. She was so different and had that touch of rebel for which Angela yearned. Letting that side of herself out, always felt good.

Lisa sang in a stupid voice, "Party, party, par–teeeee."

Angela stomped out her third cigarette, swiped her hand across her nose, and stuck her chin out.

"Jeesh, Angie, I'd tell ya to wipe your runny mascara, but you're not wearing any are you? And you think you're not gorgeous. You could be Rosanna Arquette. I'd kill for those lashes and blue eyes.

"Oh puul-ease, what are you kissin' my arse for?" Angela laughed and hugged Lisa, she was the best friend ever. She clung to her best friend another second then let go and looked down on the full face and maroon lipstick that matched Lisa's hair. "You're all that, you know? Let's par-teeee."

They'd reached a run-down house where the party was obviously going strong. Even from outside on the sidewalk, the thump of the bass on the stereo was loud enough to both hear and feel. Lisa led the way to the back door. The two walked down a crumbly cement walk running between the homes, which were so close neighbors could shake hands and never leave their house. The dirtbags in the kitchen definitely looked like their kinda crowd, but older, much older. Angela stepped inside noting a couple necking by the stove. "Sure why not let all the juvies in," the chick said, giving she and Lisa an up down before returning to her boyfriend's face. Hard rock blared, and thick, pungent smoke hung in the air like smog. People in the kitchen were drinking something the color of tea out of huge plastic cups. One of them offered Angela a drink, which she accepted and kept walking. It tasted sweet like tea.

"What is it?" she yelled behind her to Lisa.

"I think they call it Long Island Iced Tea. It's mad good, huh."

In the next room, people were all over the floor and the couch. Angela watched fascinated as they took turns on a giant bong. She hunched in a deep-knee bend, letting her bottom hit the floor, her long legs high on each side of her face. It wasn't a minute before she was invited to take a hit, and only a moment more before she thought what the hell and accepted the long tube. It burned her throat like crazy. She chugged the rest of her drink, which didn't really help. In no time, she was cranked—a little scared too as she felt herself losing control. After her turn and Lisa's, who practically grabbed the bong from Angela, the two sat against the wall on the floor for a while, listening to music and enjoying the high. A couple guys came up and slid down beside them, one on each side. When Angela turned from the older boy talking to her, Lisa had disappeared. Woozy, and ignoring the boy, she got up to look for her. She followed a narrow hall past a tiny bathroom. At the end of the short passage, a bedroom door stood open where a half dozen people sat on the bed, passing around a mirror with fluffy coke lines. A girl with stark white skin and dark, heavily made up eyes held a straw out to Angela. They were sucking that powder right up their nose. That can't be good, she thought, a little freaked. Besides she was high enough anyway. This party had pot and coke heads—out of control.

Angela smiled, hiding her fear. "No, thanks, I'm just looking for my friend."

She turned to find Lisa, finally locating her in an upstairs bedroom with a bunch of people chilling to some music. Judging by the look of the rooms, the house seemed to belong to or more likely being rented by college kids, or hippies, or something. No way was this a house of some kid's parents, which was usually the case at the parties her crowd found. Lisa was sitting on top of a desk in the corner with some guy. Angela crossed the room and leaned in, speaking right in her ear over the music.

"Not yet, Angie, we just got here. Mike is gonna drive us home in another hour, k?" She turned to some guy with wicked long hair next to her, "Zat right, Mike-ster? One hour, right?"

A glassy eyed Mike uttered, "Word."

Angela made her way back through the house, squeezing between people and stepping over others. She passed through the kitchen and out to the back porch stoop where she sat. The coke had scared her. The dope in a bong she'd seen a couple times before; half the kids in school did that stuff, but coke? That was a whole 'nother level.

Out of her black zippered hoodie, she pulled her pack of cigs and lighter. Angela clicked the torch five times with no success.

"Wanna light?"

She looked up at a handsome full-bearded face. His long hair fell in soft brown waves ending at his shoulders. He sat down on the stoop beside her offering his lit cigarette. Angela put down her failed Zippo and used his end to light her Marlboro. Silently puffing, the two sat their thighs just inches from each other. She noticed his long legs clad in soft worn jeans, bare feet in moccasins. Out of the corner of her eye, she caught the rest of his attire, a black T-shirt under an old blue flannel shirt that looked as soft and worn as the jeans. Funny, how it didn't feel odd not talking. There was a peaceful vibe coming from this older guy.

"You like this?" he finally spoke, pointing backward to the house. Angela quickly decided whether he meant the party or the music.

"Nirvana? They're all right." She listened. It was new, *Smells like Teen Spirit.*

78

"Oh, I thought maybe you were out here to escape. Guess this isn't so bad, but the stuff earlier man, not my idea of music. You ever heard the Dead?

"Grateful Dead? Sure, they're fresh. I don't hear 'em much, though."

"Woe, you should try a concert, nothin' like it in the world, the whole crazy world." He went silent, leaning back on both elbows. He took a slow drag, and again they each smoked all natural like. She looked at him, a look he caught and held. "I'm Reef." He smiled warmly in her eyes, it seemed with no expectation of a reciprocal exchange.

"I'm Angela, people call me Angie."

"Cool," he said, and looked away comfortably releasing a stream of smoke. "Angela, Angie," he whispered like he was trying the name on for size, "that's real fine." Reef was easily in his thirties, maybe even late thirties, still an attraction for him was building. He was so different, relaxed and easy going. Several more stolen glances revealed a handsome face, kind eyes, and a nice build, like he did some manual labor of some sort.

They got up after a few minutes, and Reef turned to her, "You goin' back?"

"Yeah," she answered then followed him back inside no longer scared. He was just tall enough, maybe 5'11, she thought, sizing him up against her lanky 5'9".

"Hey Boner, change this jam up, wouldja?" Reef slapped some skinny guy on one of the couches. "Play some Dead man; us Heads are dyin' here." Boner got up and moved nimbly over half a dozen prone bodies to the stereo so that Angela guessed he wasn't stoned, or if he was, he functioned regardless. The air was so thick with pot the second hand stuff could make a tree fly. Angela looked for a clock half-wondering if she really cared what time it was. She could sneak in unnoticed except for John, but there was always a way to sneak in Lisa's. Their middle-aged parents crashed so early and slept so sound, they almost never got caught. She wanted to spend more time with Reef, and sitting in a just vacated spot on the couch, she tried to figure out if she would accept another hit on the bong if offered.

It was getting late. Younger kids began leaving soon after they started playing the Dead. As the house emptied, the remnants of partiers gathered in the living room and Lisa showed up attached to the Mike guy. Buzzed, Lisa slumped on the floor, propped against her new red-eyed friend. Reef talked quietly to Angela on the couch, about his life in a real live commune on the edge of the Redwood Forest. They were Deadheads he said who shared everything.

"It's all about the love Angie, all about the good love. Everyone's in this world together. We need each other, and Sun kids live the beautiful truth, man. But it's all good. Everyone's good. Everyone's gotta be true to themselves. Love's all around us, Ange. The Dead they capture it, they free it in the people. You'd be blown away at a Dead fest, blown—a—way."

They talked into the night. Reef listened, like no one before, to Angela's troubles. She found herself unloading all kinds of pent up insecurities, hurts, and disappointments. His brown eyes stared into hers with such compassion, as if he was holding her even though he kept his hands to himself. She caught herself wanting to fall into his arms and experience the caress his eyes suggested. Reef opened up too, telling her all about the Children of the Sun and their spirituality. They had no leader, which he described as the ultimate in commune life.

"How'd it start?" Angela pushed the bong back across the coffee table to the group on the floor. "I mean, how'd you join?" Someone called out, "It's Uncle John, crank it up." Reef moved in closer to speak in her ear; a ripple of excitement tingled her spine. She might be falling for this guy, no matter how old he was.

"A friend of mine and I, we visited this huge commune and saw some stuff we liked, and some we didn't. Like their guru leader was dishing out orders and rules as bad as *the man* out here, you know?" The music pounded, and Angela had a little trouble hearing and following, especially his talk of *the man*. "Anyway," Reef continued, "we decided we'd live as Deadheads full time, and help others do it too. We cashed out, bought twenty acres in Humboldt County, California, right on the edge of the Redwood Forest." Reef's hands swooped out and his face became animated. "Gorgeous spot, Ange. Nowhere on earth like it out there.. You know Ansel Adams?" Angela shook her head. "He's a famous photographer, travelled all over the world, but he said he never needed to leave the West Coast because all the beauty in the world was there, right there man. So like I said, we bought two used trailers and invited a bunch of Heads to join us. The only two rules," he said holding up two fingers, "share whatever you have and work when we need you to. Everything goes in a pot."

He paused and tapped his hand to *Uncle John's Band* for a bit. Angela wanted to know more. "Sounds awesome," She spoke over the music then leaned closer placing her shoulder to his. "How many people live with you?"

"*Shoo,* people come and go. We got about fifteen Heads right now." Reef was so close his breath tickled her ear. The closeness against the music felt comfortable, like they were in their own little world but still a part of the group. "We got this garden, and we grow all kinds a junk. We eat some and sell some. A few of the girls make jewelry and sell it to tourists. We bring it to concerts too. Sometimes I go work for the man outside, you know, make some money to keep it together. I was a suit, Angie, can you believe that?" She couldn't. She tried to envision him in a business suit.

"What'd you do in suit?"

"Not in a suit, Angie. They call me a geologist. I tell the oil companies where to drill. I only do it when the kids are real bad off." Now she wondered if he meant he had actual kids, or was he calling the Deadheads kids. Too shy to ask, she thought of something else to say, and the night disappeared this way, all mellow like with talking and music.

Each of the Deadheads, these Sun-children, exuded some indecipherable quality of profound tolerance that almost saturated the very air. They took each other as is and seemed ready to accept each new soul they encountered with that same I'm okay, you're okay acceptance. It was nearly a religion by itself among them. Except for John and Lisa, Angela had never experienced such acceptance, and the feeling it gave her was exhilarating. In one night, it seemed to her, she felt more acceptance and love than she had felt in her whole life. Her soul screamed for both. After meeting up with them three more times that week, clothes crammed in two backpacks, Angela Miller took off to be a full-fledged Child of the Sun and a full time Deadhead.

10

The Parking Lot Scene

JULY 9, 1995

Just as thousands of new youth discovered the Grateful Dead band and flocked to the parking lot scene, fueled by myths of hippie love, easy drugs, and transcendental music, the light that was Jerry Garcia was nearly extinguished despite his last ditch effort to fight his heroin addiction. The music, the band, and the parking lot were as symbolic to these new fans as they had been to the hippies before them. It was their chance to rebel against a society focused on the almighty dollar, on designer clothes and Hollywood icons. Touring with the band, absorbed in mellow music and the total acceptance of individual expression, the youth of the early 90's embraced the old message of love, peace, and brotherhood. Getting high and feeling good, fellow Deadheads enjoyed the ecstasy of the spiritual release known as the Grateful Dead. Then as suddenly, as it was rediscovered, Jerry Garcia would die, and the 60's would be over again.

Soldier's Field, Chicago, July 9, 1995, the Grateful Dead performed for the last time on the tour from hell. The flawless night watched the sun sink over the lake and throw its reflection back in a fond farewell. Everyone listened as a fading Jerry Garcia issued his final goodbye, real and imagined, in Black Muddy River. Decades of the most unique subculture America has ever seen would come to at least a partial close. But for Deadheads pulling into the parking lot scene that warm July night there was only the typical expectation and joy.

Angela looked out at the parking lot awash in cars and easy going Heads, vendors and propped tarps. The community buzzed with the usual soloists giving mini concerts on guitars or bongos while aging women disguised as spirited girls twirled and danced freely getting in the mood for the great show to come. The Grateful Dead music would raise some of them to a higher consciousness, some to a marvelous peace, and most, simply to joy. Angela loved the parking lot before the show when the family bonded with fellow Deadheads. For her the ideals of the sixties lived on in every parking lot of every show that the Grateful Dead would ever perform.

She wandered with fellow Deadheads in and out the sea of cars, vans, and open hatchbacks in search of food, drinks, maybe drugs, and definitely camaraderie. Food was easy enough and usually cheap enough for any Head. Her dollar would buy a grilled cheese sandwich sold out of dreadlock Jimmy's Volkswagen Bus, or a homemade burrito from Crazy Cal's Chevy Van.

A girl held out a worn-out sign with a hopeful look toward Angela. She smiled piteously at the words, "Looking for a M I R A C L E," and held empty hands up apologetically. Her family had no ticket to share tonight, but the girl's hopes were far from unfounded. The generosity of Deadheads never ceased to amaze Angela. Stories abounded of ticket-less fans looking for a miracle and receiving one. Who but Heads would buy extra tickets just for the sheer pleasure of seeing that joy on the receiver's face? Angela wished the girl luck and continued her search for Jimmy's blue bus.

She noticed the mood was a little off tonight. The wound of the Deer Creek debacle just one week earlier was still fresh. At that concert, hundreds of gatecrashers in Noblesville, IN, broke through the fence to the cheers of misguided Heads inside. The disappointed band wrote to fans, begging them to act like Deadheads and not maniacs. "We're all about higher consciousness," they pleaded in the letter, "not drunken stupidity." The next day's show was cancelled after death threats to Jerry. The Sun Children and other loyal fans denounced the violence and behavior of non-ticket holders. But the riot, complete with police, gas and dogs, along with the aging and sickly Garcia, may have signaled the end of the end.

Angela passed a row of tents selling Tie-Dye shirts and glimpsed a plastic baggie of LSD pills and a blotter paper quickly pass hands. Drugs remained a huge part of the experience for some fans: LSD, marijuana, mushrooms, and even nitrous oxide sold in giant balloons. Whatever the psychedelic drug of choice for those who enjoyed the music this way, it was meant to enhance their experience and bring them to another level of consciousness. Angela never judged them, although she rarely partook beyond a little pot and occasional shrooms. Course the Dwarf Rats were a big presence these days, and did more than their part to dissuade the drug users. She'd seen them earlier setting up their booth festooned in yellow balloons. Dwarf Rats were recovering users, who preached against the drugs, encouraging a pure experience of the Dead's music.

Happy as she walked, Angela looked this way and that with her usual open smile. A tanned older woman stopped her in front of a card table of handmade jewelry, which Angela charitably looked over.

"Sorry, I only have a buck and I gotta eat," she told the aging Head.

"So-k sweetie, I hear ya."

She passed a couple of young shirtless guys playing Hacky Sack, dodged a Frisbee flying overhead, and nearly bumped into another tie-dye seller. Finally, she spied Jimmy's rusting blue Volkswagen bus, wondering how he kept it on the road, and how he managed to get to so many of these concerts. It was near impossible for most Dead Heads to hit so many. Angela felt lucky; that's all her family did.

Tour Heads followed the band full time. Tonight they were camping just outside of Chicago. Sometimes they rented a rundown farmhouse, and if possible, they just squatted somewhere. That was best, cause then all the money went to food and tickets. Some in the family made bracelets, and hair decorations, others actually worked, like real work—but mostly under the table. A couple of wannabes, who joined them when possible, would send the family money from time to time. Reef kept the money, bought tickets, gas, and food. He was the one who gave her the buck for food.

"Angel, cool!" Jimmy came around the other side of his mini gas grill to give her a hug. She loved Jimmy, tall, handsome, and always welcoming, the epitome of a cool Head. He was the only soul in the world who called her Angel. His long brown hair was trapped in dreadlocks, which never looked out of place on his smiling white face. He gave her a big hug then wrapped his long arm around her shoulder reminding her of her brother John. God, she did miss John sometimes.

"How's your tour feeling, girl? You got any bets on the first song?"

"Naw, well maybe Jack Straw?"

"I dunno, Angel. But if you want it, your good vibes are gonna bring it on, right? What can I do ya for?

"Just one, Jimmy," she waved her dollar, and frowned.

"Hey, skinny, I'm gonna make it my famous double-decker, no extra charge. Can't have Angel's growling stomach interrupting the show, eh." Jimmy was sweet, and she was mad hungry.

Angela headed back to the two Sun vans, eating her sandwich on the way. As hungry as she was, she only managed to eat half the sandwich before feeling nauseous. Damn! It was getting unreal, how often she felt like throwing up. She found Reef sitting on a folding chair under the tarp, which was slung out over the open van doors. Two of her sisters stood behind the table of leather jewelry they'd made to support the family.

"Reef, you got a baggie I can save this in?"

"Why not eat it, bones?"

"Aw, c'mon. Anyways I feel kinda sick"

"Amy's doin' kitchen; ask her." Angela continued past him to the other van and called to her sister Amy.

Amy appeared, her stringy blond hair falling forward as she stood hunched over in the doorway of the seat-less van. "Sup, Angie?"

"You got anything to put this in?"

Amy, twice her age looked at her sympathetically, "Baby, you sick again? You're gonna melt away and disappear at this rate."

"I know. What's up with that? Everything makes me sick even that weed stink in the van. What the frick is wrong with me?"

Angela had been with the family three years. The health food wasn't all that great, but she'd gotten used to it. She'd never been sick once either.

"Girl, you preggos?"

86

"What?"

"Pregnant, stupid. Maybe you're pregnant."

Angela scrunched up her face, unable even to begin to process the idea. Reef and her were more like friends. He never pushed for that kind of thing, and she and he didn't really do it very often. Mostly it sort of just happened as a result of a comfortable closeness they felt. Like last time, a few family members had dropped a little acid and were chilling in Reef's tent. She'd had a joint and a Bud. She was lying sandwiched against Reef while everyone talked. They fell asleep that way, and at some point in the night, they made lazy comfortable love. How long ago was that? The Daytona concert—that was like three months ago!

"Is it Reef's?" Amy sat down her legs hanging out of the van. She patted the spot next to her inviting Angela to sit.

Angela sat studying her half-sandwich. "Well it has to be. I don't do it with anyone else. But Reef, he's like forty."

"Duh, guys can plant it when they're eighty. Jeesh, you really are naïve."

Angela scooped her legs up and wrapped her arms around her knees still holding Jimmy's double-decker. "How will I find out if I'm pregnant?"

"You pee on a stick, sweetie. I'll get Reef to give me a ten and buy it tomorrow. You shouldn't tell him till you know. I'm pretty sure Reef don't want a real kid. The family is his kids, and we barely feed ourselves, you know?"

Amy jumped down then bumped her forehead to Angela's, plopping her wrists on her shoulders. "Don't worry about it. Clinics are free now, especially for abortion." Amy's hands moved to Angela's untamed locks, smoothing and petting them. "It's quick and easy. No worries, kay? I'm gonna twirl for a bit. You wanna come with?"

Later inside the concert, the air was thick with the pungent aroma of marijuana and Deadheads twirled, and waved and cheered their beloved band and its leader struggling to perform. Angela joined the sea of wiggling bodies, bobbing heads, and raised hands, clapping and swaying overhead, but all she could think about was a baby in her tummy, Reef's baby, her baby, a new life.

87

11

No Children Allowed

AUGUST 9, 1995

They drove up to what looked like an old apartment house in Arcata, just a half hour from the Sun's home. Angela had passed it a dozen times before and never suspected it was an abortion clinic. Reef pulled up to the curb and looked straight ahead as he spoke. "You goin' in with her, Amy?"

"Well a course, Reef. Whaddaya think I came for?" Reef had changed since she told him a few weeks ago. He acted strange whenever they were together, like their decision, his decision, had killed their friendship. It had all been decided very matter of fact. Angela had no income to speak of, and the family was struggling. Reef didn't want to play daddy, and how could she possibly play mommy? They headed back after the Chicago concert, which was the last on the tour anyway. They heard Garcia had checked himself into another rehab trying again to beat the heroin. Good for Jerry, she thought. Angela felt sick all the time and sympathized with him.

After Amy and she were buzzed in, Amy led the way through a door with a "NO CHILDREN ALLOWED" sign on it. Angela tried not to focus on the word children. Inside the receptionist handed her a clipboard and a pen.

August ninth . . . She estimated she was about four months pregnant. There were these butterfly movements in her stomach now, rather than the nausea. She guessed they belonged to the baby inside her. How can a blob move like that? What did it look like anyway?

There was no use thinking about it. The decision—the only practical decision—had been made. Angela's eyes welled up as she strained to focus on the paperwork on her lap. When Amy asked if she was done, she nodded and handed her the clipboard to give to someone at the desk.

Forty-five minutes later, a stern looking woman led Angela to a cramped office and began explaining the procedures. She asked her if she was sure she wanted to do this. Angela nodded, but inside something screamed, "No, no you don't." It seemed too late to listen to tiny inward voices, so she meekly continued the interview. Before the ultrasound, she asked about hearing a heartbeat, but the nurse said the sound would be off, and she shouldn't worry. After that she peed in a cup and went back to the waiting room. A nurse came out to explain two different ways to handle it at this phase. The series of pills sounded easiest, but there was a chance it might not work. If she chose the surgery, the nurse said the doctor had an opening in one hour, and they could just wait.

"Makes the most sense, Angie," Amy said. How many times was she going to hear this decision reduced to those practical terms? Absolutely terrified, feeling alone and sick, her glassy eyes stared at a lame magazine of houses and food while Amy strung beads on leather straps she'd brought in her giant homemade cloth purse.

After the longest hour in her life, the nurse came and handed her what looked like a giant folded paper towel. They walked down a long hall that stretched as far as her indecision. The nurse told her to put on the gown, (really just a piece of paper with holes in it), and wait for the doctor. After forever, the doctor finally came in. He told her in a robotic tone what to expect, brusquely examined her and left. A few minutes later, the nurse returned, leading Angela down another long hall of doubt. She held her clothes with one hand while the other held the paper gown closed in the back. She left her dignity behind as she entered a big room where she sat on a metal table and received a shot. The doctor told her that she wouldn't feel anything—that she'd go to sleep while counting to a hundred, but the shot never put her to sleep. She was too weak to move, still feeling pain, and wide awake when they gave her the shots in her cervix to open it up. She cried as he performed the abortion and finally blacked out from pain.

Angela woke up in the same room; it couldn't have been long. The doctor was gone. The nurse stood at a table moving jars of something. Pain wrenched her gut. Angela turned her head from the woman, stared at the giant cold light on the ceiling, gripping her abdomen. Her thoughts were foggy, but one was distinct—the baby was gone. There was a baby—the baby was gone—now there was nothing left but pain. She gasped and found herself struggling for breath as the nurse approached with the stretcher. She announced her respiration was thirty-four per minute. Angela wondered what the heck it was supposed to be. The nurse handed her a cup of pills and ice water, which she mostly spilled on herself. Angela lay back wincing, unable to move as if a metal blade was shoved up her bottom.

"Rectal pain is normal, honey," the nurse said taking the cup back. "It's okay."

Okay? She had Reef's baby, and now she had nothing, nothing but a blade shoved up her bottom. How is that okay?

The nurse called Amy, who had gone back to the Sun's since she was told Angela would have to stay till 6:00. Amy came soon after and was quiet as she helped Angela dress, and even though it may have been nothing more than not knowing what to say, the nothing seemed more like a pounding condemnation. Angela had absolutely no control over the tears spilling from her eyes as she gingerly lifted herself into the waiting van. Reef wouldn't even look at her. He said nothing; Amy said nothing—very loud nothings. Angela stifled her cries and the chest that wanted to heave, feeling the imaginary knife in her rectum the whole ride home.

The next day the news was everywhere; Jerry Garcia was dead. He was gone, just like her baby. The family was devastated. Jerry died August 9, same as Reef's baby. Angela's bursts of torturous physical pain, guilt, and regret were intensified, as her family in mourning wandered about the property not talking. Everyday grew worse. The family was lost; the love was gone. Angela received nothing from anyone, no affection, no support. And whether real or imagined, their judgment mingled with her own self-reproach, a bilious poison that filled her soul.

It was hard to tell when the physical pain ended; it was so thoroughly replaced by an aching emptiness. Her action went against her upbringing and her conscience. She had betrayed her very soul. Right or wrong didn't really register now, any more than before the abortion. What did matter was that she'd gone against what was right *for her*. She hadn't been true to herself. She had all those doubts, but didn't listen to them. She had placed the family ahead of her own flesh and blood. She couldn't look anyone in the eye. Everyone knew what she'd done. Every pair of eyes, especially her own, could see her sin and her betrayal. Angela literally kept her head down so much now, her neck hurt.

Over the next few months, everything and everyone changed. Reef left to return to his job as a geologist. He told everyone he hated working for the man, but he had to get out. Everything changed for him when Garcia died. All his talk of peace, love, and real living ended with one man's heartbeat. More and more Heads moved out to return to their former lives or forge new ones. Angela soon availed herself of the myriad of stronger drugs they left behind. During her three years with the family, she had only drank and smoked occasionally. Now, desperate to numb the pain and quiet the demons, she searched for harder and harder drugs. But there was no peace for her, and soon no sleep without the drugs.

Three months after the abortion, the eviction notice arrived and the last three Children of the Sun hit the road. The middle-aged couple, who'd always treated her decently, invited her to stay with them. Takoda said they were heading to New Mexico, hoping to live on a reservation. They had both taken Indian names when they became Sun Kids. Takoda means friend of all, and Satinka, magic dancer. Satinka was the one who taught Angela how to twirl. But how could she make them live with her sin? She would instead hit the streets. In the streets, Angela decided she would accept all the hardships that nature could deal her. She deserved it, her punishment for what she'd done.

12

C'mout, C'mout, Wherever You Are

September, 2006

"Mr. Valenti, open up!"

In the dark, lying on the bed in just his jeans, Sergio tried to process the demand. The clock glowed 6:05. It was still dark outside, and it would be for another forty minutes. Who would be—

The knock turned to pounding, and he swung his legs to sit up. The pounding became a full-fledged slam, shaking the wall. "State Police! Open up!"

Mannaggia, the beamer! Sergio's mind kicked into gear. The elder must have reported the car stolen. Throwing on sneaks, his eyes darted wildly about the room—nothing to use for a weapon and no escape. The bathroom window was smaller than a pizza box. No time to think, either. Can't get caught, he'd never see the light of day. Desperate he jerked the door open fast and barreled straight past the two bodies in his way. They fell like bowling pins, taken completely by surprise. Sergio vaulted over the second story rail, landing on his feet like a cat. The two cops, both in plain clothes, tore down the cement stairs after him. Morning air cut across his bare chest as he shot through two rows of parked cars then blindly out into the four lanes of traffic on Wolfe Road, which even at six am on a Sunday morning had a few cars going both ways. One car slammed on its brakes and another swerved to miss him, angrily laying on the horn. Gaining the other side, Sergio stole a look at his pursuers satisfied to see both just finishing the stairs.

Mamma mia, no, no! It suddenly struck him that the cops knew his name. It would only be a matter of time before they littered his picture on the airwaves. He crossed an empty parking lot, quickly deciding to go right toward a small strip mall. He ran like hell down the sidewalk along the row of closed stores. Coming to the end of the walkway, he rounded the corner of the building catching a peek at the two undercover cops. A flash of steel glinted in the hand of one who looked Asian. Something was familiar about him. These were no cops. Panicked, he wracked his brain to remember where he'd seen the guy before.

Behind the stores, Sergio ducked into the first doorway deep enough to hide him and flattened his bare back against the cold metal. One of the fake cops yelled, "Which way?" obviously, unsure whether he'd gone behind the stores or the gas station next door. Then it hit him—these were lessers, coven members sent after him. Both men were smaller than him, one was tall and lanky, a regular Slim Jim, and the Asian looked fit but short, not much of a build. He could take them in a fair fight, he decided.

Sergio readied himself. One of the guys was coming this way. The other must be checking the gas station. He heard steps heading in his direction maybe ten feet away. He was a sitting duck. If this was the Asian, he could wrestle him for the blade, but he wanted the upper hand. He shot out at a sprint, making a beeline for a dumpster. A loud crack split the air, followed by another, the two shots whizzing over his head. They had a piece and a silencer, boosterless, but still cutting the noise and echo of the gunshot to a degree where these two might be gutsy shooting in public. Sergio ran across the weeds into a tiny yard, knocking over a charcoal grill, which clanged loudly on a small, cement patio. He cursed; last thing he needed was to wake up the sleeping neighborhood.

"He's over here. Over here Hui!" the Slim Jim called to the Asian.

They were following him again. His long, muscular legs could outrun them in the short race but not a long one. Both of them had less mass to lug around for the chase. He needed to double back, get his stuff from the inn, and escape with his car. Sergio passed his seventh yard, coming to a redwood fence, leaping without pause and practically knocking it over. Hurdling the other side, a pointy picket jammed his ribcage. Ignoring the sting and still running like hell, a six-foot cement wall presented itself. *Crack*!

A bullet grazed his calf and planted itself in the wall. Sergio turned and ran along the side of the brick house as a light clicked on in one of the rooms. Cutting across the yard to a sidewalk along Sand Creek Road and paying no heed to the bite out of his calf, he felt every inch of yesterday's workout and cursed the extra squats. He raced two blocks on the quiet street, hearing the footfall of both men behind him. Another four blocks, and his side would to split open. His lungs burned for relief; he couldn't keep this up.

Ahead, a giant yellow sign on wheels read, "Closed Sun.& Mon." He blasted across lot, jammed his foot between the links, and scrambled up the fence dropping down on the other side. It was some kind of memorial business with a mess of headstones, grave markers, granite monuments, and statues. Sergio slunk behind a huge pink granite and pulled his black jeans over the winged calf. It was superficial. The chain link fence rattled followed by two thuds.

"Hey Valent—eee! C'mout, c'mout wherever you are. You had to know Tri-O would find you."

"I'm out, you hear me? Out of the coven, *finito*! Take the stuff I found. Keep it, give it back, I don't give a rat's A, just back off. Leave me out, *capisce*?"

"You're kidding, right," the tall one cried, and a shot hit the top of the stone in front of Sergio, raining flakes of marble on his head and shirt.

Che palle! Sitting duck again! Sergio dove close to the ground between a tall monument and a giant statue of Saint Michael the angel, its face looking down on him pitifully. He had some vague remembrance of that angel as an avenger of some sort. He pictured the great warrior squashing his wicked life like a vile bug, but he remembered angels were supposed to be protectors, too. Feeling superstitious, he touched the angel's foot before plunging behind another piece. Slim seemed to have lost track of him and took a pot shot to the center area decapitating a Saint Anthony statue. It crashed down, coming to a stop, the stone face lolling to the side, looking at Serge accusingly.

Continuing at a crouch, he came to the left corner of the yard where markers were decidedly shorter—the least likely area to try and remain hidden. Sergio inched like a worm, hearing the men knock over stones on the other side of the yard. If he could make it over the fence without them seeing him, he might get away. He kept track of the direction of their racket, passing a full minute behind each stone before he would dare move. Inching backward, his foot thumped into a warm thickness. It was the Asian, Hui.

"*Porca Miseria,*" Serge yelled. Hui delivered a tight kick to Sergio's lower back. Serge ignored the blinding pain in his tailbone as well as the instinct to move away. Instead, he spun fast in the direction of the kick, locking an iron grip on Hui's leg and pulling him in hard. Hui's kick was trained. Sergio knew any one-on-one better be up close and personal. Sergio seized an arm and delivered a head butt. Hui squirmed trying to free himself, but Sergio slipped him into a head hold—a move from his days of High School wrestling. His weighty thigh whipped over both of Hui's, trapping the weapons.

Another shot from the nine millimeter cracked and sent a shower of cement shards down on them. In a blink, the Asian was standing. He spun fast, aiming a deadly kick toward Sergio's head. It clipped his left ear with incredible speed, and pain reverberated in his skull. Still on his knees, Sergio dove for Hui's legs. The Asian jumped causing Sergio's arms to grasp nothing but air. Hui had him trapped against a tombstone, and Sergio braced for the kick heading right to his face determined to capture the assaulting foot. He made contact a second later and pulled Hui's leg, bringing the Asian down on top of him.

Once again, they were close enough for Sergio to have the advantage of strength, but he completely forgot the knife in his opponent's hand. Swiftly, the blade sliced a lightning bolt across Sergio's forehead. It cut deep to his skull; the pain served only to boost his resolve to arrest the knife from his opponent's hand. Sergio threw a heavy leg over Hui's thighs shoving his other leg underneath and squeezing hard pinning him in a classic scissor. He reached for the Asians wrist, holding the knife away when out of the corner of his eye, he spied Slim Jim taking aim from the shelter of the huge Archangel. The last thing he saw was the angel's face, and for a split second, he begged for help before flipping himself onto his back still holding the Asian tight.

The shot popped, and warm blood gushed over Sergio's bare chest and his jeans. He was stunned for a moment before Hui went limp. He was about to throw the body off, when he thought better of it, realizing the corpse was the only thing between him and the nine millimeter Glock. He managed to hold the carcass as he got up, using it as a shield and backing behind another gravestone.

"You stinking wop!" Slim bawled. "You're gonna pay for that. Hui and I were tight."

Sergio threw the body and took off in a crouch. He needed time to make it over the fence. Another shot cracked. Not even close. That was hopeful. Occasional and ironically helpful shots rang over his head in a lame attempt to flush him out. He worked his way across the yard. Hurling a rock in the direction Slim had last fired, he listened as blood from his skull dripped over his eye and nose. He stole a look at Slim, who was tiptoeing a hundred and eighty degrees in the opposite direction.

"You're trapped like a pig in a pen. It's slaughter day, Valenti. Give up now; I might show you mercy."

Sergio took two giant, silent steps, stuck his foot in the chain weave, and began to climb. The metal rattled against the morning stillness, and Serge knew he was made as a shot bit the chain link by him. Two more ripped out before he was half way across the backyard. The fence jangled as Slim began his ascent. Sergio kept to the back yards, without the head start he had before, but this time, prepared for obstacles and fences. He ran at them, even welcoming them, hoping Slim wasn't as agile as himself since the guy had that Glock at the ready, leaving one less hand to climb over barriers. Over the course of the six blocks back to Wolfe Road, Slim was still nipping his heels. Sergio quit the last yard, ran across the weedy area, and came out behind the Speedy Fill station.

Lungs burning and close to throwing up, Sergio jiggled a door to the gas station bathroom—locked. Slim hollered something unintelligible crossing the weeds. Serge tore around the building towards the set of pumps. Over his shoulder, he saw the attendant in the window, his back turned as he stocked sodas. Sergio was a second from continuing across the street to the Fairview Inn, before he realized Slim would have a clear shot at him so instead, he hunched behind a pump. Whipping a credit card from his wallet, he swiped it, reached for the gas handle, and flipped up the lever. As Slim came around the pump island, Sergio leapt out squeezing the handle till it locked. A stream of gas waved over Slim, who shut his eyes against the assault. Sergio ran for the street throwing the handle down, gas still gushing.

Slim opened his eyes a full three seconds later to see his prey slipping away. Angry as hell, too angry in fact to consider the possible danger he was risking in pulling his gun—a costly mistake for Slim surrounded by invisible gas fumes—he snapped off a shot, the spark and static of which easily ignited the vapors. A huge flare exploded around him. The flames quickly caught his gas soaked clothes and ran down his long body. Uniting with the ground vapors, the blaze flashed upward in an incredible red and yellow plume.

Sergio tore across the highway, hearing the explosion behind him and refusing to look back. Taking the steps two at a time, he fumbled for the key card to his room. His eyes darted to as many windows as he could, most with closed drapes and others, dark with no faces he could see. It would be impossible to get out of this if anyone saw him covered in blood and dirt and coming directly from the fiery mayhem. He let himself in his room, careful not to make a sound and looked out the crack in his closed drapery to an enormous column of fire rising into the sky. Slim's body—his legs at least—were sticking out from the pump station. *Not my fault, I just wanted out; God I just wanted out!* He watched only second more, and saw the kid who'd been stocking coke talking on his cell and running across the street. Sergio's hand gripped the curtain, processing the loss of life, feeling a mix of remorse and relief. He stepped away from the window, pacing the room before he headed to the bathroom. Dousing a washcloth with cold water, he dabbed his head. Why hadn't they just let him go. That was all he wanted . . . if they had just taken the money and let him go. *Damn the coven; damn it all!*

The knife wound, which bled profusely but had slowed and begun to clot, was open again. Patting the cloth over it, the line revealed itself, half in his shaved hairline, half on his forehead. It was a clean slice, though deep. It needed stitches. No way could he go to a clinic and get it sewn up. What the hell was he going to do about it. For now, he had to stop the bleeding, clean himself up. Figure out a way out of here that wouldn't look like he was running away. Using his jackknife, he cut a long strip out of one of the motel towels. He made a few more for when the wound would need changing. Wincing, he tied it like a bandana and tightened it down before stepping into the shower. The jeans, his boxers, and bloody towel went in the motel's plastic garbage bag.

As he dressed, sirens blared and the view of the Speedy Fill was blocked by two fire engines, a pumper, an emergency medivan, and a half dozen cop cars. He knew there were a couple of convenience stores not a block up on his side of the street. Something had to be open. But would it be safer to walk it or drive? He'd just be a car pulling out of the motel or a pedestrian walking. The point was moot anyway, he realized as he exited his room smelling gas and smoke and shoving the towel tourniquet beneath his Mets cap. The police were blocking traffic north and south on Wolfe as well as the turn down Sand Creek. Pockets of half-dressed, pajama and bathrobe clad curious bystanders lined the sidewalk. He made his way toward the stores after tossing the plastic garbage in the motel dumpster.

Not much was open, but Serge managed to get everything he needed at a small drugstore, including a couple bandanas. He used the store's bathroom and redressed the wound with antibiotic and a couple butterfly closure strips. His leg too was patched up with gauze and sport's tape. He buried the bloody towel strip in the bottom of the trash, and gave himself a quick once over in the cloudy mirror. The red and blue bandana actually looked right on his shaved head, and the ball cap, kind of redundant. But he worried about the head wound opening, so he kept the cap to help hold everything. He shoved all the papers and wrappings in the plastic store bag and headed back to the Fairview. The excited crowds had grown as the incredible conflagration still raged. Passing through a glut of cackling women, a few keyed-up teens, and a fat man in a wife-beater tee, his beer gut pushing the tee up and revealing a hairy belly, Sergio heard something about Sand Creek road and wondered if they found the Asian guy.

"What about Sand Creek?" he asked a skinny lady waving a long cigarette.

"Nothing just I heard some old guy tellin' the cops he saw two guys running through his backyard after he heard a bunch of what he thought were gunshots. I guess cops are combing Sand Creek asking neighbors if they heard or saw anything."

"Jumping Jehovah's, Gail, I better head home then," said a woman with way too tight jeans and a tank top.

"They'll be crawlin' through your yard, sweetie, if I know anything 'bout bacon. You better pull your weed inside for a while."

"Shoot, I'll take it off your hands," yelled one of the teens.

Serge moved away and continued back to his motel room. They would find Hui's body. He wondered too if he had dripped any blood back this way. How could he not. Although by the time he reached the room most of the blood had congealed, and miraculously none was on his sneaks. Still holding the bag, Sergio collapsed on the bed, closing his eyes trying to think of a plan, where instead, his body exhausted, he fell asleep.

Bang, bang, bang.

Three knocks woke Sergio up an hour later.

"Police sir can we have a word with you."

Sergio froze; it was just like this morning.

"Mr. Valenti?" The knock came again. Probably real this time, he thought. Sergio sidled up to the door, preparing himself for anything. He heard them talking outside. "Manager said this one was here, car and all. Lieutenant said we gotta talk to all of 'em." They pounded again.

"Uh, just a minute," Sergio said, going to the mirror and checking his bandana, which had dried blood on it. He whipped it off, threw it in a drawer, and tied a second one over the butterfly bandages, which had held even though blood had oozed past them. He returned to the door, opening it only to the chain. Two uniformed cops stood outside.

"Sir, we just have a few questions about the explosion."

"The what?" Sergio played dumb, taking the latch off and leaning on the door, his eyes squinting in the light. He wiped them hoping to emphasize his having been asleep.

"The gas station across the street, you couldn't have slept through it." Sergio gave him an even dumber look. "The Speedy Fill station blew up, not two hours ago, right over there, practically at your doorstep," he said incredulous while his partner eyed him suspiciously.

"*Boh!* Whaddaya talkin'? Where?" Sergio leaned his head out the door, squinting and blinking, like he'd never laid eyes on daylight before and making a show of looking for the gas station. He whistled then pulled his head back in. "Wha— happened? Some stunad drop a cigarette?"

"A lot more than that," the taller cop said. "Where were you at six this morning?"

"Me? Here. I was out all night; I tied one on, major." He looked at their dubious expressions. Sergio yawned and scratched his chest, trying to look unconcerned. "My girlfriend always says I sleep like a rock."

"So you didn't see or hear anything till we knocked?" The cop's voice went up.

"That's right." Sergio smacked his lips. "Look if I have to stand here letting my head get all big like, I'm gonna require a drink, eh? Can I get a beer while you jaw at me?"

"Never mind," his partner said, pulling the other cop's arm, "C'mon we got like two hundred more doors to hit."

"Fine, hit the sack guy, you're in no shape for more booze.

"Yeah, whatever." Sergio boldly shut the door in their faces. Inside, he found himself shaking like a leaf. Damn that was close. He had to get a plan and soon. But he couldn't check out till all the pigs cleared out. Anyway, in some way, it was the safest place to be right now, at least as far as the coven was concerned. The beer sounded good. Damn good. He headed to the mini fridge, snagged one, flipped on the TV, and sat heavily on the edge of the bed.

13

The Strip

Her platform heel wobbling back and forth, Angela stared at the rows of prophylactics and pregnancy tests. There were a lot of them. *Oh God*, she could hardly believe she might be pregnant again after all these years. It was eleven years and three months since that awful day, and the roller coaster of drugs, homelessness, prostitution, and rehabs hadn't erased it. At least till now it had been buried so deep it seemed to belong to a different person. Pushing a strand of frizz from her face, she stared at the boxes on the shelf, all of them fifteen to twenty dollars. She couldn't ask Eddy, and even if she used his cig money, she wouldn't have enough to buy a kit. Shoot. Was her whole life going to revolve around these kinds of choices? Stealing it was the only way. She had nothing on but shorts and a tank top. Great, where was she supposed to put it? All she needed was the stick inside the package, and that could fit in her pocket. She emptied a box, quickly shoved the wrapped popsicle-size stick in her back pocket, and then headed to the register.

"'Shwing', sweet thing," a big black guy said while humping midair. "Mama, you know you wanna roll with this!" The guy with him made a grab for her butt. Angela pushed forward dodging the free feel. She looked like crud, and still these "wangstas" hit on her. She squeezed herself in front of some harmless tourist in a zipper jacket listening to the end of the hood's spiel. "You missing a fine time, baby doll," he called to her. "Once you roll black you never go back."

Angela turned to look over her shoulder on the verge of sassing him with, *Hey Black Jack, you don't pay; you don't play*. But her eyes met the mild looking middle-class tourist behind her in line, and somehow she cared what he would think. he looked like a high school English teacher with his Members Only jacket and JC Penney slacks, plastic rimmed glasses perched on the tip of his nose. He smelled of clean aftershave. She turned back around, ignoring the catcalls.

It was her turn, and she pointed to the pack of Camels, Eddy's brand. The clerk, with a funny look on his fat face, crooked his finger to another worker, a huge smirk crossing his thin lips.

"What about this, whore?" The other worker sidled up next to her, waving the empty box of the pregnancy test kit.

"You paying for it, or we calling the cops?"

Blood rushed to her cheeks. Everyone in line stared at her. The other clerk, big and wide as a football player, blocked her from running. Boldly he reached around to her back pocket, pulling the stick out.

"We usually keep them in the box when we ring them up," he said, sniggering.

Angela wanted to cry. The whole world was against her again. Would nothing ever change? "Oh, I, ah, I ah . . ," What the hell could she say, caught red faced and red-handed. *Oh, God!* The man behind her shifted. She could only imagine what a decent person like him must think of her. He stepped forward to put his things on the counter. *Oh man, I'm like holding him up, too.*

"Ring it up with these."

The clerk scowled, "You don't have to do that, sir. She's nothing but a filthy—"

"Add the camels, too," the man commanded with a stern look.

Angela was absolutely blown away. Walking out with the man, it hit her two seconds later, that even this middle-aged, clean-cut, sightseer probably wanted something to pay for the favor. He turned and handed her the bag with the pregnancy test and cigarettes.

"Look," she started, prepared to set him straight, "I appreciate this and everything, but—"

He held a hand up for her to stop. "You look like my niece, that's all. I know your life is probably hard. I just wanted to help. That's all, I swear. If you are pregnant, I hope you'll find some help. I'll say a prayer for you."

He turned and disappeared quickly around the corner. Just like that, a random act of kindness from a total stranger. Never, not since she left home, not even when her old friend Lisa would listen to her, never, had she heard those words; "I know your life is hard." Oh God, how could a total stranger, a good, honest person like that have sympathy for her and her life? His understanding, his sympathy, and pity . . . it was too much to bear. Her cheeks flared anew. Angela clutched the bag and ran all the way back to the apartment, letting the air dry the tears. Outside the rundown building, she threw the box away and pushed the stick in her back pocket. The metal stairs, littered in discarded beer cans, wrappers and a filthy pair of abandoned underwear, shook as she climbed them. What a hole!

Angela lived in an apartment complex on one side of what was known as Crack Alley. The place was alive all hours with the comings and goings of those doing "business." They came in and out of the apartments, hung out in alleys and walkways between the buildings, sat on stairs or paced the sidewalks looking to hook up or to be hooked up. Pushing, pumping, touting, or running (for it had many names)— whatever you call it, people were working it. She passed a trio leaning against the wall, one saying, "Uh-huh," as she walked by them. Angela was known and mostly unharassed here. Eddy Platzmann was a dealer; they were users, and she was his. Her steps slowed near the grey apartment door, hoping Eddy wouldn't notice how long she'd taken.

"Eddy, I got your cigs," she called, scared. "Eddy?" Only the sounds of the complex, the boom-boom of music and random yelling, greeted her through the tiny open window. Relieved, she threw the Camels on the table and went straight to the bathroom to pee on the stick. Afterward, she put it on the back of the toilet and undressed to shower.

She washed, thinking what it would mean if she were actually pregnant. She'd punished herself for years for not keeping Reef's baby. Becoming a crack whore was just another nail in her self-made coffin. Back then, after parting with Takoda and Satinka on the road, she'd wandered into town looking for under-the-table work. Arcata was nothing but a college town for Humboldt University with slim pickings for work of any kind. The memories of the abortion had

105

been too fresh to stay there long. The town turned out to be a tough training ground for street living.

Tired of being chased from hiding places in the plaza, a few stairwells, and a Victorian house under renovation, Angela took to the Arcata Marsh. The Marsh, really a wastewater management system of ponds and wetlands, attracted cyclists, joggers and transients alike. She'd spent most of the fall there, but winter months were too cold. One day in January, a gang of guys promised her food, drugs and a ride if she'd roll with them. It was her first time trading sex for anything, but she was desperate to leave, hungry, and even more desperate for drugs. Looking back, she knew she was lonely, too, aching to fill some gaping hole left by Reef—no, left by her father. The driving need for shelter and food, they were catalysts, sure, but the need for male affection and approval, that ran much, much deeper. A few more towns and a couple more years and she'd landed in Vegas, a hardened prostitute. For a long, long time, Angela accepted each suffering and every heartache as something deserved. Slowly, her guilt was buried under a pile of misery. The abortion, a lifetime ago, while not forgiven, had at least been allowed to be forgotten.

The hot stream of rusty hard water beat down on her head, as Angela cried slumping to the floor of the shower. What would it mean if she were pregnant, if this was another baby? A second chance... a chance to do right? She could protect this new life, accept this baby and redeem herself. Was this a test? The very thought made Angela wail harder. Unworthy and afraid to hope, she curled into a ball pulling her knees to her chest, and for the first time in a decade, she dared speak to a higher power.

"Oh God, God, I know I shouldn't of done it," she said, looking up and tasting rusty water running into her mouth. "I went against my own conscience. You . . . you wanted me to keep it, but I swear, God, I swear if this is a baby I'll protect it. I'll call John. I'll go home. I'll do anything."

Her life was so dead now, so unredeemable, it seemed impossible that two blue lines on a stick would be a sign from God. Yet, that's exactly how she would view those little strips of blue. If the test was positive; it would mean God was giving her another chance, if not at another life then at least at a chance to make up for that one bad choice. Squatting on the shower floor, water dribbled from her bent head, rolling down her brow and nose and joining the tiny stream swirling to the rusty drain, and with it. . ., stirring something in her heart. The tiniest drop of hope passed between her and her Creator. She saw the waterfall and jungle boy, his back to her, asking how it was she dared to assume her sin was greater than God's mercy. Had she ever given God a chance to forgive her or help her? Had she ever tried to talk to him? She had assumed her sin was unforgiveable.... Each new low of addiction, prostitution, or homelessness drove her further and further away from God. In her mind, every fall from grace had left her less and less worthy of his friendship—of any friendship. That's how it had been for the last ten years. She had assumed her sin was unforgiveable, and in many ways until she could forgive herself, it was. Now some microscopic thread stretched from the Universe to her pained heart and whispered her mistake. Not the sin for which she so often punished herself, but her blindness to God's love. He was telling her she'd been wrong about *Him*.

Angela stood. Could a body as used and abused as hers even get pregnant? She'd been pretty clean the last year, the result of some rehab program that managed to awaken a vein of self-preservation. To top it off, she hadn't so much as had a joint since those dreams started months ago. Were those dreams of this baby kind of grown up? Was Jungle boy her kid? Angela turned off the shower and wrapped her hair in one towel and her body in another. With a deep breath, she lifted the stick and held it out.

"Oh God!" Two blue lines shone clear as day in the little window. *A baby!* A baby was inside her again. She raised the stick a second time, held it under the light. No mistake, both lines were sharp and true. She stared at it. The initial shock gave way to racing thoughts. When? How far along was she? Two months, maybe... Her fingers counted August, September... *Oh my God, August!* Had she conceived the very month she lost her first baby.

She had to leave. She and this new baby had to leave, to get away from Eddy, get out of Vegas. Her thoughts spun with the reality of it all. She would stay clean. She'd eat right too, maybe find one of those clinics with free doctors. There might be pills or something the baby needed. She would make sure this baby had a chance. Maybe she should give the baby up to some nice childless couple. She heard John was married. Maybe he and his new wife, Clarice would want the baby. She wasn't good enough to be a mom. No, there were no delusions there, but she could make sure the baby saw the light of day and a healthy light at that.

She walked into the other room, past the seedy black couch, to the tall dresser in the corner. Clothes were strewn everywhere. Eddy's were mostly on the floor and bed, but hers were piled in and around the old dresser. Opening the top drawer, Angela regarded the stick one more time in disbelief of the hope it gave her. She placed it beneath her undies, pushing it to the back of the drawer. Eddy can't know. He can't find it, yet she couldn't throw it away, the stick represented a second chance at life.

She dressed tingling with new hope and figuring out the best way to leave Eddy.

14

John & Clarice

Their steps crackled on the forest floor, the only sound between John and Clarice as they walked. The woods were lush with green, but the leaves were just beginning to turn on the oldest trees tinged with bright gold, orange, and blood crimsons. Clarice inhaled deeply, a forced effort drawing in a heady scent of wet earth and leaves. Despite the beauty of the woods, their hearts lay heavy with the emotions bottled inside them. They needed this walk just as Sergeant Blaine had suggested when he more than hinted at the obvious tension between them. "You two are a clogged drain waiting to be plunged," he'd said before ordering them to go for a walk.

Clarice had come to like Blaine. He spent so much time with them; he seemed at least 75 percent convinced they weren't involved in their son's disappearance. Blaine was leaving today; his assignment at the house was over. Authorities and the FBI concluded that a ransom note or call would have appeared if the intent of his kidnappers had been to extort money. It had been over six weeks, and although they never put it bluntly, in their book, no ransom demand meant he was dead. The bodyguard named, Mark Schmidt had been arrested and admitted his part in the murder and kidnappings of the girls. Naturally, he claimed to know nothing of Jackson's whereabouts. He was found hung in his cell less than twenty-four hours after his arrest. For John and Clarice, it was a relief he could say no more, but with his death came the shocking realization that cult members must be everywhere, even amongst the police. They were investigating the death of course, but no matter what they found, Clarice was convinced the guy had been killed to shut him up. She wondered how many others were still out there plotting to kill her son. Thank God, he was safe and hidden in the Glen.

Clarice hugged her fleece a little closer, even though it wasn't at all cold today. It was the silence between John and her that felt chilly. She thought of something to say. Perhaps how great it was that the phone company had finally put in all the lines. They'd had poles up for months, but till last week, they hadn't connected anything. John had already put the new number on Miller Construction's answering machine. Their cells had been so sketchy up here; it was a relief to have a landline again. They had internet too through the phone line. But a conversation about that wouldn't help anything. They needed to talk. She decided John should open the conversation, and she had no idea what he was thinking. She'd hurt him; he had to express his anger before she could explain herself. Thinking of that betrayal, Clarice reached out to grasp John's hand as they ambled towards the deeper woods. The action triggered a slight flood.

"I just don't get it," John blurted. He continued to walk allowing her to hold his hand but in no way holding hers back. "I feel like you never really loved me."

His words cut deep. John was a man who never spoke lightly. "How can you say that?" Clarice squeezed his hand. She knew she owed him more, but he was the one who had to be drawn out. She'd been walking on eggshells around him for a month, and the tension was destroying their relationship.

"How could you hide so much from me? It's like finding out you're a spy or something. And even if . . . even if you—" He freed his hand, too frustrated for the contact, and he ran it through his wavy hair. The pain on his unshaven face was killing her, and now he wouldn't even touch her hand.

"John, I love you more than life. I never wanted to…" Clarice's voice fell away. That wasn't what he needed to hear. He needed to understand what she'd felt since they were married—felt for her whole life for that matter. A mammoth fallen pine lay ahead. "Can we sit?" He shrugged, and they left the path. They sat on the prone trunk;

her legs, so much shorter than his, swung freely in front of her. She played with the giant leaf she'd plucked. "John, for you to understand, I have to start way back. I mean like when I was a kid." She peeked at his face, but the expression was blank, gazing straight ahead. "The first time I had an experience I was about seven. It was my birthday, and my mom and dad threw a party in the yard behind our apartment building. I remember feeling so happy. I never had a party like that. Anyway, while we were running around playing tag, I felt this whoosh in my stomach like when you're falling." Clarice's legs stopped swinging as she concentrated on the memory. The giant leaf fell from her hand and wafted to a log. "I stood still and watched the whole backyard fading. Like it was there, but sort of see through. And around all the kids were these light forms, really pretty and twinkling. They seemed protective and warm. But then there were these dark clouds too, so malicious and ominous. They seemed to be trying to get at the kids. Those scared the hell out of me." Clarice looked up at John, trying to read his reaction.

"So? Why couldn't you tell me that?" His boot kicked a stick.

Her eyes followed the kicked stick to the base of a pine tree, and they both stared at the rutted trunk, rather than at each other. "When I was a kid, I never believed any of that stuff I saw was real. I had more incidents, but after a while, I figured out how to sort of snap out of it when that falling sensation would start. Except for eighth grade once. I let it happen again. It was Mr. Evans, my math teacher. I was bored with the lesson. I felt the feeling and just let it come, didn't fight it. I saw him, how he wasn't human. He was this huge horrible creature." Clarice squeezed her arms in tight between her legs, and humped over looking at the forest floor. "John, it was scary as hell. You can't imagine what they look like. I saw more of them in that cave where they threw Jackson."

"The cave in Cobleskill?" John said, sounding pissed. "That's like three hours away. You were in a cave while your body lay in my arms in the Glen!" John was such an incredibly forthright, honest man. Deception, omissions, none of it made any sense to him. She had to make him see her point of view.

"John," her voice croaked, "I spent my whole life hiding from that stuff not flying around like some spirit. I wasn't just scared of it; I

111

really thought I was crazy. You know how my mom had dementia. I was afraid I was just like her, and these things I saw.. they were just proof. How could I...how..." Her words broke into faltering sobs and trailed off. All the frustration, all those years hiding herself, hiding from herself, she knew it was wrong. John and she shared everything, everything but that part of herself. They had the perfect marriage, the perfect union. She rubbed a wet eye with the back of her hand and dragged her sleeve across her wet nose. She spoke again very low. "Why would I . . . how could I tell you about something that I didn't believe myself? I didn't want to ruin what we had. I was afraid."

"You didn't trust me, Reece! Do you know how that hurts?. You held all this inside, and you didn't trust my love!"

"It wasn't that exactly," she pulled her hand to her nose about to drip, just when John handed her his handkerchief without so much as a side-glance. He always had one on hand when he'd been on a construction site. This morning he'd left Mike Barrie alone to handle everything at Miller Construction. He seemed to be spending less and less time at work. At least he was here with her, and they were finally talking. The hanky smelled of sawdust and Aqua-Velva; it smelled like him. Her gut knotted. This was threatening to turn into everything she feared. Only, it was happening because she'd delayed telling him the truth, instead of happening because she told the truth. She wiped her nose back and forth thinking. She wanted to throw herself in his arms, but he felt stiff beside her. Other than handing her a hankie, he made no moves to console her.

"John, say something, please. Ask me something, anything."

"Fine, I have a million," he said, breaking a chunk of bark off the log and chucking it at a tree, still not looking at her. The painting you gave me for our first anniversary, the one in my office, did you know that's what brought Gabe Katz from Boston? It was a picture of your painting. He told Father Tom he'd dreamed of it, of you."

He was talking about the painting of her spirit flying for the first time, her first painting, painted before she even met him. The experience had been exhilarating; she'd wanted to capture it permanently. She'd tried her hand at oils, and it turned out she was a damn good artist. The painting depicted a gauzy translucent spirit flying over a meadow—just as her spirit had that first time. When

112

they'd married, she'd hidden the painting, but later decided to give it to John on their first anniversary without any explanation of its meaning. This was one of many things she had yet to explain. So many things she realized.

"I didn't know about Rabbi Katz seeing the painting or dreaming of it. I had this intense experience when I was pregnant with Jax. I painted it months after it happened before Jax was born... before we even met you." She paused, playing with the edge of the hanky and wondering where to begin. John remained silent, picking at the bark on their makeshift bench. She snuck a sideways glance at him; his jaw was clenched, his look firm and unbending. "I left my body that time. It was when I was pregnant with Jackson. One morning I was nauseous and went outside on my balcony for air. I was so queasy; I guess I was powerless to stop it when the feeling came. I felt myself kind of rising up and up . . . " The memory of that morning stimulated her as always. Her eyes lifted, her body straightened, and Clarice took a long controlled breath. "It was soooo beautiful, flying free and weightless. The air flowed around me and through me—you have no idea! But . . . while I was gone this presence—something black and evil threatened my body back on the porch. I figured out it was trying to get the baby." The sudden realization hit her like a mini epiphany, and her voice dropped to a reverent whisper. "Even then something was trying to destroy Jackson." She shook her head at her own prior blindness. "When my spirit returned to my body, I found I was balancing on the wrought iron rail. I could have fallen two stories." Clarice clenched the handkerchief feeling the same age-old guilt. "Oh John, I thought I'd had a— I don't know,. . . some crazy break with reality and that I'd almost killed my child. Don't you see? I was in denial about every part of the spirit world I saw." She stopped, John was silent, taking in her words, wrestling no doubt with the idea of her being able to leave her body and fly as a spirit. She clutched the hanky like it was a part of him. It was a good two minutes before he spoke, two long heartbreaking minutes. But she had to let him work this out.

"What about at Nicey's funeral when that ball of light slammed into you? You weren't the same after that. I swear after what we all saw—" John stopped, hopped off the log. He turned to face her but kept his distance, crossing his arms and squaring his shoulders. He was still mad, but finally looking at her, though not the look for which she longed. "When you were unconscious," John choked, "in the graveyard and at the hospital . . . they did all those tests—I thought, God, Clarice, I was worried out of my mind. And when you came to, you were holding something back, not telling me what you knew, or what was going on inside you." His voice rose and sounded disgusted. "That was bull, Reece. It wasn't fair; we were supposed to be a team. I thought . . . "

She looked down at the white handkerchief away from him, his pain, too much to watch. She blew her nose and spoke still wiping it. "It's hard to describe what happened at Mrs. Nicestrum's funeral. I didn't understand it, couldn't explain it. Probably still can't..but I think it was some power from Mrs. Nicestrum, that ball of light from her casket. I . . . I had no idea any of you were seeing what I saw. Then I heard Nicey's voice. Did you hear—?

"No," John cut her off. He walked over to a hanging snag, sticking out from a pine like a boney arm pointing at something. He snapped the dead branch and cracked pieces from it as he spoke, avoiding looking at her again. "We saw the light. It rushed into you and knocked you out cold."

She nodded. "When I woke up in the hospital, I—I don't know it was like there was this invader in my soul. I could feel it, almost see it inside me . . . I didn't want it there, John," —she dared to search his eyes—I didn't want to listen to it. I used every ounce of my will to keep it at bay. It was sapping all my strength. Just talking to you was a feat." Her head lowered in shame. "I was fighting it, even though I knew it was something good. I fought it. I can't believe my stubbornness. . . Then Jackson he spoke to me in my head, telling me to open myself to the light."

"In your head?" John snapped. "What the hell does that mean?"

Clarice looked at him meekly and all but whispered, "He spoke to me telepathically."

"What! Are you kidding? Great, that's just great. And NONE of this struck you as anything to share with me. Our son was having these catatonic trances, we're worried half out of our minds, and you,

you're talking to him telepathically! And still you tell me nothing. Why? Why!"

"John!" Crying she pushed herself off the fallen tree trunk and went up to him to force a hug. He took her hands, roughly throwing them off himself like they were dirty. He brushed past her and began walking fast down the path.

"I can't talk anymore. It's too much, Clarice, or maybe it's too little too late. I need to think."

"John," she called but didn't follow him. He had enormous resentment to work out. She watched his strong back disappear and whispered murmured, "I'm sorry, so sorry. . ."

Clarice listened to his receding steps on the forest floor. She had no idea that his hurt was this deep over her secrecy, but it made sense. Who did she marry? Not some macho, self-centered business tycoon, this was John. John who wore his integrity like a second skin. He married her to share their life together, everything together. It was true she hadn't trusted him, and there was nothing, nothing she regretted more. He deserved all of her. Their marriage was so perfect, but the perfection was a charade without honesty. She knew that's how he saw it, but it wasn't exactly how it was; was it? She hadn't believed these things were happening when they happened. She spent long hours denying them or making up plausible explanations for them. How can he understand her silence was a self-protection mechanism? If she'd talked about it, somehow, it would have made it all real, and she hadn't been ready to accept any of it.

She collapsed against a wide maple. *Oh God, I love him. What a mess this is!* And there was still so much more to tell him. What about the night Nicey died and the incident in the park last year? Oh Lord, how can I tell him all that? She had to tell him, she promised no more secrets. But not now, not when he's like this. They just had to keep trying. *Please God, don't let him give up on me, on us. Don't let this ruin us, not now, not on top of losing Jackson.* I beg you. She cried, pressing her head into the tree trunk.

After a time, she lifted her head trying to sense the Glen. She was not surprised when she felt nothing. She knew she wouldn't, knew she shouldn't, too. The mystical sanctuary no longer called to her spirit as it once had. Her son was here somewhere on this mountain hidden and safe. That had to be enough. With one wistful look down the path the way John had gone, she turned the opposite direction and followed the trail uphill.

A few minutes later, Clarice left the path and cut across to the big oak tree. The police tape had been removed, and recent rains had washed much of the blood away from the tree. She ran her fingers over the words, "THOU WIN." She fell to her knees, feeling the rutted ground poke through her jeans. Clarice spoke to Rabbi Katz and Mrs. Nicestrum, her son's protectors, as if they could hear her. Somehow, she found comfort; whether it was from their beautiful spirits or just the words her son had carved. The Glen was near; her son was safe. God would have mercy, and He would make good come from bad. Even her fledgling faith, as new as the morning dew, knew to hope for that. God always wins. "Thou win," she whispered.

* * *

Weeks later, she stood in her studio debating. The sun had long since passed the picture windows of the room in the East Wing. The French door behind her led to the right side of the wide front porch, and Clarice considered sketching on the settee outside. Despite the warm sun, she decided she would feel too chilly in the crisp, autumn air in the sleeveless sweater, so instead, she slid her apron over her neck, snagged a fresh charcoal off the desk, and took up her pad. Her eyes scanned the airy space she shared with John. Filled with light, the long room lent itself to their duo needs. John's chestnut desk dominated the office space at the end of the room, and the window behind it framed the distant woods. Her end of the sunny space with paints, jars of brushes, easels of works in progress, and the drafting table where she now sat, looked like any artist's studio with the exception of a pricey ventilation system John installed to cut the smell of turpentine.

Clarice's charcoal skimmed carefully here and there on the sketchpad, and in a short time, an image of John appeared against a forest setting. The lines of pain in his face stared at her just as they had weeks ago. Her emotions were always the catalyst to her work or at least her best work. Whether sad or ecstatic, frightened or gay, the image sprang to life and made her compositions sing with a unique vibrancy. She worked now to alter the features, making the nose wider

116

and the cheeks sallow. The pain in his eyes would remain, but the telling characteristics that make this face John's had to be removed for it would be wrong to immortalize his personal anguish. Besides no matter how much she modified it, she would always know it was John. She sketched making a silent vow to herself that the eventual painting would be a constant reminder of her mistake, keeping her sin before her so that she would never forget the pain her secrets had caused him.

As Clarice reworked the high forehead, even John's resemblance to a young Mel Gibson disappeared. *Oh John,* she held the pad out, thinking of how distant he had been, barely speaking to her except to mention a few practicalities like picking up milk or dinner, or reporting where he was going to be in matter of fact tones like, "I'll be at the office till nine then at the Leitman house." Stuff like that.

A door shut, echoing in the enormous house now practically empty of life. Straightening up, she ran a smoothing hand over her hair and frowned at the smeared apron hiding her soft pink sweater and the scoop neck that showed off her figure. Would he look for her? Should she wander out casually and try to talk about something? It was like going back to dating days, worrying about how she looked, how she dressed around him, wanting him to see her, to want her again. What could she say? She strained to listen and was met with the unruffled quiet of the house. Without Sergeant Blaine here, the constant hum of the TV, or occasional polite conversations, the place was morgue, mocking their pain and the loss of Jackson. It would be Halloween in a week or so. Last year at this time, the house was being framed. Jackson was five and had started homeschooling with Nicey. It was so important that he have a good costume and trick-or-treat with the kids he'd known at preschool. She remembered him helping to wind the soft yarn around the mouse tail she'd made. He was so cute...

God, no, I can't think about my baby. Too late, her mind went to her beautiful boy, his curly blond hair, his smell, big green eyes behind Poindexter glasses—what if he broke his glasses out there in the Glen! Does he need his glasses there? Maybe the Glen heals eyes just as it heals wounds. She pictured her hand on his cherub cheek, and his soft little hand reaching to caress hers like he so often did. *Oh*

God! She gripped her apron at the chest, squeezing the fabric in a bunch. *NO! Don't do this!* Clarice took a trembling breath. She didn't want John to find her with red eyes or sobbing again. Yet, John must feel the same way. John, I need you. She released the apron, seeing the black where the charcoal had been crushed in to the folds. Feeling defeated, Clarice turned back to her sketchpad. After so much, trying to deal with the pain of their loss, the stress of the police and FBI, and John's hurt, she was exhausted. She repositioned the sketch, and traced John's deep-set eyes full of expressive pain.

The phone rang, shattering the wall of thick quiet. Clarice paused, charcoal poised over the pad to see if John would pick up. It rang again. Could be John's work or that art dealer Gretchen something or other from Ithaca. She had called a few days ago asking to view Clarice's paintings. She said she deals with twenty-three studios, from across New York and as far as Montreal. It sounded impressive. Nevertheless, Clarice got the idea the woman wanted to capitalize on their pain somehow. The sharks were in the water, coming from every direction since the murders and so called kidnapping. They followed the trail of blood and guts like sprinkled chum in the water, hoping to feast and grow fat off someone else's misery. It made her sick, but in the art world, this lady was someone important, and Clarice would have to give her more than a cursory nod. It would open doors, and in the back of her mind, Clarice admitted at least this way her work could be appreciated.

She flipped the pad over on the drafting table, hopped off the stool, and strode across the room to John's desk. Sitting on the edge, she picked up on the fourth ring, at the same time hearing John's business-like "Yeah?" on the kitchen phone. His deep voice was slightly stereo coming from both the line in her ear and from the kitchen. She held on quietly just to see if the call was going to be for her. Having a landline was convenient, but John's and her calls were now mixed.

"Johnny, is that you?" A small, tremulous voice came over the phone. "It's me, Angie."

"What? Who?" John said.

"It's me Angela."

"Angela? Who is this?"

118

"John, it's me. Your sister.

"You're alive! It can't be...you're . . . Is it really you?"

Clarice replaced the receiver. Something banged, and John's voice rose. She tossed aside the apron and hurried to the kitchen. Angela was John's sister. He rarely talked about her. The whole family assumed she was dead. She'd run away at sixteen and was never heard from again. For years, they'd searched records, social security, and death certificates without turning up anything. John never wanted to talk about her or why she'd run off, and Clarice never pushed him. John stood by the island phone next to the stool he'd knocked over. She righted the stool and stood a little behind him.

"Calm down, Angie. Calm down." John yelled into the phone. "He hit you?" John glanced over his shoulder noticing Clarice, a look of terror in his eyes.

"Listen.. just listen. Tell me where you are." He tried several times to get Angela to answer and calm down. It was clear John's baby sister was in some kind of trouble, danger even. Unsure how to help John, Clarice moved a step closer to his side.

"Get out, Angie! Get out of there now and call me from somewhere safe. I'll come get you. Where are you?" Clarice heard mumbled crying.

"A shelter, John," Clarice piped in, thinking it needed saying.

"Yes, a shelter," John echoed. His deep voice took on that calm, authoritative tone. "Angie, find a shelter for women. The numbers are everywhere. Call 911—"

Clarice moved even closer. His acceptance of her words gave her the idea it would be ok for contact, and she placed a hand on John's shoulder. She was close enough to hear the frightened voice on the other end, but couldn't make out any words.

"Then get out this second! Leave now if he's coming back." There was a moment of silence. "Ange, I love you squirt. Everything's gonna be okay, you hear me? I Love you. We'll help. Now GO! Go!"

His sister hung up, and John stared at the tiny caller ID screen before clicking it off. All it said was unknown caller. John stood there in shock, his hand still on the phone after laying it on the receiver. Clarice's hand slid off his shoulder to his forearm, giving it a good

119

squeeze. He let go of the phone and tore his fingers through his thick brown waves.

"She's alive! I can't believe it. From what I can tell, she was beaten, and bad." John knit his brow shaking his head back and forth in disbelief. "She said he'd done it lots of times just never this bad. And she said something about how it didn't matter before cause it was just her. She said it mattered now, and that he'd kill us. I don't get what she was talking about. She was pretty upset, it was really hard to hear her."

"She could be with other girls…or maybe she's got a kid?" Clarice offered. Puzzled John thought about the suggestion.

"Maybe, but why would she say the other times didn't matter. Why would she let some guy beat her up on a regular basis? Shoot! Oh God, help me! I don't even know what town she's in. Oh man, not even the state. There wasn't time she…she didn't say or I didn't ask. I don't know; it all happened so fast . . . I don't know what she said—"

"John, stop. It's alright."

John turned to her. "Clarice!" He caught her and pulled her to himself. She threw her arms around his waist, and they embraced. He needed her, wanted her, and she wanted to be there for him one-hundred percent. They finally released, and Clarice led him to one of the large leather couches in the family room, facing the monstrous floor to ceiling stone fireplace. Still in shock, he was quiet, and they stared ahead at the fieldstones of the giant hearth. Each stone had been carefully selected by both of them. They were proud of the project. One they'd done together. They always worked as a team, as they would work now through this crisis with John's sister.

"This is bittersweet you know?" he finally spoke, barely controlling his voice, "The last we heard she'd joined some group of hippies that followed the Grateful Dead. But we didn't find that out till '95, same year Garcia died. Lots of Deadheads, that's what they call them, just dispersed. We thought she might come home, but she . . . she never did. She just disappeared without a trace. You know how many concerts my brother's and I went to holding up signs asking if anyone knew Angela Miller." He spoke staring straight ahead while she looked intently on his profile. "Nothing, we never found a trace. And now, now . . .," John's voice broke, and his eyes pooled.

Clarice picked his arm up and nuzzled under it smelling wood from a work site mixed with a hint of that sweet and stale sweat of a hard day's work. God she missed that smell. She missed every inch of him. She took his rough chin in her hand turning his face to meet her gaze. "I love you, John." She said it tenderly then made her voice firm, "Now, you listen to me, John Miller. Angela will be safe. She may have a reason now, someone outside herself to live for. She'll find a shelter, and she *will* call us again. You hear me? She will!" He searched her eyes like a man overboard looking for a life ring. And in his panicked eyes, she saw his pain, the old pain of Angela mingled with his new pain over the loss of their son and his sense of her betrayal. She couldn't look. She wanted to erase his anguish with love and closeness. She buried her head on his sturdy chest, and the two sat close in the empty house, allowing its stony silence to envelop them once again.

15

Plip…Plip….PLOP

8:00 PM and Sergio turned onto Wolfe Road from Albany Shaker in Colony. Wolfe was a five-lane road with two-way traffic. The center lane was a shared lane for turning left. The burger joint came too fast on his left to do any good, and Ted's Fish Fry sounded like a shack. He continued searching for fast food and thinking about the best way to get a new car and a passport. He was starved—should have come out sooner. He'd been living off beer and peanuts for days and wanted real food. A doughnut shop came and went as did the pizzeria, but he wasn't feeling it. "Move Along" by All American Reject's was playing with Sergio rocking in his seat and tapping the wheel like a drummer. The headlights of busy traffic on the five-lane road competed with the lights of businesses and restaurants lining the parkway, their neon signs waving at him like kids in a gym class yelling "pick me, pick me." He passed lots of strip mallish stores, but too far in to tell if there were any restaurants. Plenty of places to eat. He wondered if he had that picky hunger now, like he went too long and now it seemed so important he pick the right food. Sergio kept his car in the left lane next to the turning lane in case he saw something on the left.

Out of nowhere, the music on the radio turned to classical jazz. *Huh?* He looked at the station, which had in fact changed. Sergio pressed the Seek button on the steering wheel, returning to the rock station. *Uffa*, he thought, realizing he'd passed a Taco Bar—*coulda gone for a pile of Gorditas and Quesadillas and those cheese potato things.* He continued looking. A second later the hard twang and thrum of the guitar suspended, and the eerie and long drawn-out tones of a clarinet filled the car. *Mannaggia, again?* Sergio changed the station, this time leaning over to use the radio controls on the dash. Sitting back up, he glimpsed the bright orange letters of Mike Hooligan's Bar & Grill, mocking him as he whizzed by. Maybe he should turn around . . . *naw*, five lanes would make that a pain in the butt. Wolfe road was long and swimming with choices anyway, he'd keep going. He drove quite a bit of it before noting his choices on this side of the road were quickly disappearing. He would soon meet Central, which connected to the highways. Colony Central strip mall lay ahead, but he'd need to make a left and double back to it.

The DJ promised Gnarl Barkley's "Crazy" when for a third time, the radio changed, and the air swam in the dark reedy sounds of a clarinet. Pissed, Sergio looked down at the steering wheel for the Seek button, thinking what a piece of work was this BMW, when all at once in place of his own hands he saw the hands of the master holding the wheel. The same crinkled skin, bony fingers with long yellow nails, the familiar ring, every inch of those hands he'd studied for years.

Aghhhh!

He yanked his hands off the wheel and stared at them as the car began to veer into the center left-turning lane. Cat-like notes of the Clarinet pierced the air, and Sergio, oblivious of the traffic, vigorously shook his arms trying to make the hideous specter disappear. The car swerved into the left lane cutting off another vehicle, which blasted its horn in protest, causing Sergio to look up from the bony apparition into the oncoming headlights of another car. In a knee jerk reaction, he yanked the wheel sharply to the right, but again his eyes caught the sight of heinous hands not his own, and he stared in disbelief as he unconsciously pressed on the gas. The car continued drifting left again—nearly half of it in the opposite traffic lane—cars swerving around him laying on their horns as he gaped at the master's hands.

The center guardrail came out of nowhere for it was at this juncture of the road that the lane split in two before the highways. The screeching sound of metal on metal jarred him back to reality as the beamer rammed against a guardrail, scraping and squealing the length of it. Sergio forced the ancient hands to take the wheel while his foot smashed on the brake. The car came to a full stop on Wolfe just before crossing Central Ave. It's once perfect, gray hull bowed in hugging the metal guardrail like a new friend. It had travelled the eight feet of metal rail, down the thirty-foot length of cement dividers, and stopped on another and final eight feet of metal rail just inches from a major four-way intersection where Wolfe had opened to seven lanes.

Sergio's eyes shut against the vision of Menger's hand. Silky Jazz and the notes of the taunting clarinet floated around the plush interior. He quickly reached out to slap the dial and silence the lingering sound. Peeking as he did, he saw hands that were his own. Even so, his heart rolled in his chest; his empty stomach threatened to heave whatever it could resurrect of this morning's peanuts and beer. He threw the car in Park, twisted the key off, and wiped beads of sweat from his shaved head with his forearm.

Minutes later, spinning red and blue lights appeared in his rearview accompanied by a single whoop from a siren. *Great, just great!* The blue and white pulled up behind him. Both cars sat in the far left center lane of the two-way road with the mangled guardrail on their left still attached to the BMW's back end. A stubby figure crawled out of the squad car and walked around to the passenger side window of the BMW, which Sergio rolled down with a shaky finger. The guy had one of those thick constructions; the kind of body that looked like it could be squished downward making a perfect troll. A sloop of puffy blond hair stuck out from his cap like it was saluting. His mushed face was pocked up with craters and lumps. A pig this butt ugly was bound to be hard on him.

"You have a little trouble there, sir?" The word sir sounded condescending. The pig held his Maglite on his face then shined it around the inside of the car. "Are you hurt?" Sergio shook his head. "You, uh, been drinking or doing drugs?"

"No, no it's nothing like that. I just . . . I lost control of the car, I—"

"License and registration, sir."

Sergio thought fast and spoke while leaning over to release the dash drawer, keeping his eyes away from his own hands lest they morph into the master's. "See, only thing is, I left the hotel without my wallet. I just grabbed cash for some quick food. See, the radio, it's broke and I kept trying to get my station. My head hurts, and the music was wrong, all wrong. I hate jazz, I can't . . . I wanted the guitar,

125

the rock station. I . . . I haven't been sleeping." Sergio knew he wasn't making much sense. Handing the registration to the cop, he wondered if this would be it. Even if the elder hadn't reported the car stolen, the cop might push to follow him back to the motel to get his ID, which of course was not going to match the elder's registration.

The policeman scanned the paperwork without a word then walked importantly around the car sweeping light on the damaged side. Finally, he came back still holding the registration. He leaned in the passenger window, shining the mag in Sergio's eyes. "Tell you what, I deal with addicts every day, but you...you got a different look. Looks like you haven't slept in a week, that's what. You're a mess. You might hurt someone else next time." Sergio tried to examine the guy's pockmarked face to judge his expression. As unlikely as it seemed, the cop's voice sounded like he cared, making his face automatically less porkish. "Where you staying," he glanced at the registration before finishing, "Mr. Henderson?"

"Fairview Inn," Sergio spoke without a sliver of hesitation. Anything but a forthright response would raise a flag for any but the dullest pig.

"Oh! You're across from that inferno. J'ou see that thing? He whistled and went on not pausing for an answer. "Yeah, I got the call just after my shift; only I'd already turned in my squad car. Yeah, I had ta find a ride to hitch over there. Shoulda just taken my Camry, but I wouldn't a been allowed close without an official vehicle. You know?"—again barely a pause—"Two of my boys were..." The cop continued talking, and Sergio wondered what is it about accidents that make everyone that witnessed one feel so damn important or involved? He missed some of what the cop said when the air went dead between them. "So, you see it?"

"Uh, no actually. I was kinda passed out asleep" Sergio leaned his head slightly and stretched his fingers over his brow.

"Heh guy, you gonna be ok?"

"Yeah, I'll be fine. It's work and stress, that's all."

"Welp," he stepped back and swept the flashlight over the guardrail, "I guess this rail's met a few cars. You need some sleep, buddy. No job is worth it." The cop handed the registration back to Sergio.

126

"That's it?" Sergio asked in disbelief.

"What the hell," the cop grinned, "I gotta figure fixing this beauty will be punishment enough." He shined the light in his eyes again and deepened his voice. "Straight back to the hotel, you hear?"

Sergio nodded watching in his side mirror while the squat figure returned to the patrol car. Pulling out slowly, the side made a freakishly loud scraping sound as the car separated from the rail. The cop stayed put, his lights still spinning, and Sergio wondered if he was running the plates again. For some reason, the car hadn't as yet been reported stolen. Maybe the elder was killed in the cave-in. Sergio glanced in the mirror, his eyes haunted with dark circles and a look of terror. No wonder the cop let him go; it was that or the psych ward.

A fleshy fright crept over him making Sergio look away before the face in the mirror could turn into the master's face. Being afraid was weak and that ticked him off. He stiffened his back, stuck out his chin and defiantly looked in the mirror. All this crap—real or imagined— who gives a flip? Hear that, you dead wrinkled piece of carcass! Diavlo slime," Sergio spit, "you're dead."

The tiny show of bravado buoyed him. He was tough not weak. Life as a foster child deprived of affection left him hard-boiled. Whenever he felt vulnerable, he'd slip into its legacy of hostility and bitter cynicism like a comfortable bathrobe. A bastard child with almost no memory of the mother who was labeled unfit before he turned five, he'd lived in at least six homes growing up. It was the second foster home that held the only mother he ever knew and the only human being who had ever truly loved him. Her name was Mrs. Lasky, but Sergio knew her simply as "Ma".

Still driving slow and keeping one hand on the wheel, he reached for his wallet to view the solitary picture he had in it. Opposite his license, Ma's sweet face smiled at him. She looked like that lady on the old TV show; he shook his head, half his lip curling up, man, almost any show from the fifties. What was that lady's name? … Yeah, Mary Tyler Moore. He used to kid her about it. When she'd tuck him in at night, she'd call him Richie. Ma was good to him, always loved him. Then she got MS (Multiple Sclerosis) and the day after his eighth birthday, they removed him from her home. Now, that was a bad day. That had to be the worst day of his life. He cried, she cried, hell, the social worker cried. By the fifth foster home, he didn't need to slip into the bathrobe of hate; it was fully sewn to him as tight as Peter Pan's shadow. Sergio was completely embittered.

In that last home, he was one of six—frickin' six kids—in the care of two, fat, money-grubbing, women who hated kids. Supposedly, they "specialized" in older foster kids. Made him sick once when he heard them bragging about their willingness to take in the hard cases. They only did that so they would never have to get off their lazy asses to do anything. Older kids could be ordered around, and when they ran off, they could just keep collecting money for them. He was fourteen then. That's where he met Vinnie, who taught him how to ease the hurt inside with alcohol and drugs. Vinnie, his goomba, was Sergio's first link to his Italian American heritage. With Vin and his gang, Sergio belonged. His name, Sergio Valenti and his pure Italian features, endeared him pretty quickly to the group that made being Italian American a real club; only this club was a gang and admittance involved drugs, robbery and for some, murder. Sergio soon learned dealing the drugs was safer than using and way more profitable.

Ma wouldn't a liked that. Sergio looked longingly at her picture as he waited at a red light just before the motel. He wouldn't have had to do it if he could have stayed with her. No use thinking how it could have been, though. Getting out at Fairview, he slammed the door to the beamer and considered chucking the keys in the bushes. Instead, he shoved them in his pocket and fished for his room card. As he climbed the stairs two at a time, he thought of one thing—he had no plan. He needed one fast. That close call with a cop, the creepy stuff he was imagining, he had to get it together and quick before he ended up dead like Mark. How long did Mark last, like less than twenty-four hours after being caught? That had to be the elder's handiwork. They had connections all over the country.

A little after 9:00 and still hungry, Sergio let himself in his room. The cash from the Ranch and the deposit box would pay for hotel rooms, food, and maybe plane tickets, but it wouldn't last. He had to get the money out of those accounts then find a way out of the country. He'd disappear and put all this crap behind him. A trip to Menger's boyhood home in Indiana to unearth that box made sense. Hopefully he'd find the names of the banks and who knew what else.

128

Standing by the bed, Sergio made two calls. He called the pizza place listed on the motel's brochure, and then he called an old friend, Joey. Joey had been with him in his earliest days selling drugs. He was a chipmunk who talked faster than a pair of ears could listen, but Joey knew everybody's business.

"What up? Talk fast before I lose interest."

"It's me, Joey, Sergio." He coughed on the caught breath he was unconsciously holding.

"Valenti? That you?"

"Yeah, Joe"

Joey swore, sounding more than surprised. "Madonn, what the hell happened to you man? Last I knew you were in hot oil after selling out Gino—and what the fu-- was that anyway? Then's all I know is, Gino's dead, his neck snapped like a chicken and his eyes bugged out like a zombie. Fu--ing *stugats* for brains." Joey ran on in the old way. "You got balls callin' me, you know? There's no one would nada kilt you on the friggin' spot after that!"

"I know Joey, but there's more to it than that. Come on, you and me, we were tight once. We're *paesano*, Joey. Same hood, brothers, eh?" His shoulders shrugged, and he fell into the familiar Italian slang they lived and breathed back in the day. For Sergio, it was like a faucet he could turn on or off depending on who he was with or how he felt. He guessed it was cause he came to it late in his teens, not growing up with it in a family like the others.

"*Va fongool,*" Joey cursed him.

Sergio humbled his voice. "C'mon Joe, *prego*. We're not like that, you and me. Ya don't gotta be like that. I always got you good scores. Didn't I watch your back? And I didn't mess wit-chu. Not me . . .not you, I didn't. What happened with Gino, that was just cops and deals and all. I had no choice. Straight up Joe, none, swear to Go—"

"You are so much bull, Serge. You know that?" There was silence. Serge waited scuffing his shoes back and forth on the carpet, his free hand making circles on the nightstand. Joey and him went way back, back to Vinnie days in Jersey. They'd been through plenty, and up until snitching on Gino, Sergio had been known as a stand-up guy. He could only hope Joey would remember that.

129

"F— you, Serge." Silence. "I don't screw nobody who helped me, capisce? You got like ten seconds to tell me what you want."

"I need ID,"—Sergio stifled a sigh of relief and began pacing the room—"and a way out of the country. I'm in deep, Joe, cops and worse all over me. I gotta have like a clean driver's license and a passport."

"Whaddaya talkin? Where the hell you gonna go?"

"Word is Vinnie's moving heroin through Panama. I could hook up with him. He'd help me, I think." Joey was silent again, Sergio landed by the window holding the curtain out to peek outside.

"It's gonna friggin' cost ya, dago" he finally said. Good old Joey —money always talks. "You got chips Serge, I give ya that."

"Yeah, yeah, Joey." Sergio scribbled down some names and contacts on the motel notepad.

"This evens us Valenti, we're done. I don't owe you a G-D thing. I see you round after this, I kick your ass same as anyone else here. You got that?"

"Yeah, yeah I got it, Joey, fuhgetaboutit. *Capisco. Grazie, ciao.*" Sergio hung up. Joey couldn't kick the nuts on a spider monkey, *mezzo finnochio*. Still, he got what Joey was saying. In fact, echoes of the master seem to have been whispering "Judas" in his ear the whole phone call. He really had betrayed Gino, who had been so close to him, and when Gino was brought down, they busted a mess of his other friends too. He had no real brothers. How could he have treated them that way? The whole thing had just snowballed. He remembered the cops grilling him, threatening one minute cajoling the next. They had a butt load of evidence against him. He was going down for a good ten to twenty. No lie, they had him dead to rights, but they wanted bigger fish and Gino was the only one Serge had worth trading.

The only thing Sergio remembered thinking was how he could not do time again. He'd spent almost a year in State for possession and dealing . . . practically a kid. Before he could figure out how it worked on the inside, he'd been raped once and beaten several times. *Those sick pricks* . . . Sergio's fist clenched so tight his own nails could have drawn blood. On the inside, he lifted weights, worked his tail off, eating every ounce of food he could get, building as much brawn as he could, and becoming crazy mean. No one was gonna mess with him again. His fist shot out into the wall, leaving a neat hole and a flap of chalky wallboard hanging down like the tongue on an old dog. He'd do anything, any imaginable thing to stay out of prison then and now. But he never wanted to be like this, never saw himself as a snitch or worse a murderer.

All those girls . . . Oh God. Sergio buried his head in his hands.

The master, it was the master… Menger… if he'd never met him, never agreed to work for him… should have let the gang kill him in that parking garage. Sergio dwelled on the painful memories oblivious of the tears welling in his eyes. After the cops offered him full immunity and a total expungement of his record, he squawked like a flippin' hen in heat. Not only did they nail Gino, but half a dozen others too. The cops promised no one would know it was him. Damn, they were so convincing, but within a month, word was out. Maybe someone in the DA's office leaked it. Maybe one of Menger's people, it didn't matter. He was dead meat after that. Every stinking stooge on the street was after him.

Then one night a slew of them cornered him in an empty parking garage under M & S Bank. He wasn't doing too bad. He was able to fight them off for a while, but there were too many. Finally, they laid a good hold on him. Bean and Nick held him against the steel beam while the others took turns belting him. They were like rabid dogs in a frenzy. He'd seen others pummeled to within an inch of their life, even to death. He was so close. Out of his swollen eyes, he remembered seeing the tall, dark figure in black with his grey hair and skunk-like black streak. One wave of his wrinkled hand, and they released him. He noted the unusual power the tall stranger held over the maddened mob just before he passed out.

When he came to he found himself at the Ranch. A perfect mark for the master's mind games, Menger knew everything about him, his crimes, his time, even the prison rape. At that time, as he was nursed back to health, he'd felt grateful to him for saving him. In the beginning, he was wooed, every passion fed and fed well while he blindly fell further and further under the master's total control. Was it blindness… or was it just convenient and safe. By the time they were kidnapping young girls and dumping them in the barns, Sergio

Valenti had become a blanket of numbness, a dead soul in a living body with no way out from under the master's iron grip... till Menger died that is.

A knock at the motel door brought the deep-dish pizza. He ate the entire thing washing it down with two beers then crashed in the bed falling asleep to an episode of *Cops* on Fox.

Plip . . . plip . . . plip.

Plip . . . plip . . . plip.

Sergio woke to the reverberating triple sound. Goosebumps swam across his bare arms. He waited listening... lying perfectly still. Wait...wait...

Plip . . . plip . . . plip.

Three more thunderous claps slapped the stagnant air. The silence reformed itself, closing around him again, draping him in a noiseless curtain. Wait, listen.

Plip . . . plip. . . . .PLOP.

Again, giant sounding drips spanked the quiet. The more he tried to ignore it, the louder it grew. Sergio lay unmoving, painfully aware of every breath, listening for the next series of drips from a faucet he knew was dry. As he waited, it became difficult to tell if he was awake or asleep. The quiet filling the room had an almost tactile quality. What about that, anyway? He knew he left the TV on but heard nothing. Too petrified to open his eyes, he lay there wholly inert, waiting . . .

PLOP. . . . PLOP. . . . PLOP...

Three drips huge against the thick silence, a silence that laid on him like a heavy blanket. It seemed as if the giant plopping drops were landing on that blanket of thick quiet. Paralyzing and heavy, the quilt of quiet pinned him down, leaving him powerless to move or throw it off him. Waiting . . . waiting. His heart became a live, thrumming thing, running faster and faster, like a cook beating batter in the bowl. So fast, it threatened to spill right out of him...

PLOP.

Slow and hard.

P L O P.

132

Hitting him solid and long, impossible to escape.

Plip.

Always three, exactly three. . . Now the waiting...waiting...

Something tickled his legs under the sheet. Beneath the heavy and pitiless imaginary quilt, his limbs were alive with tingling; a crawling sensation slithered up and down each leg.. . .Can't move the legs; can't. . . move. Swarming tiny brushes of microscopic stimulation crept up and down his limbs, slow and featherlike. He tried to move, needed to move, but couldn't. The invisible, heavy weight fixed him firmly where he lay. If he could—just—move—m a k e himself m o v e! STOP feeling. STOP listening. STOP wait—

In one sudden movement, Sergio snapped his lids open and flung the sheet off his limbs. Whatever he had hoped not to see, whatever he hoped his imagination had been cooking up—it was nowhere near the horror he now saw engulfing his limbs. Bugs everywhere, red ants making paths through his leg hair, green horse flies lightly walking, black spiders tapping multi legs across his knee, beetles waddling back and forth and even a few writhing pus-colored maggots. He watched in disbelief. They crawled up and down busily chomping where his flesh lay open in cavernous sores as if they had been munching all night. The phantasm of what he was seeing had a paralyzing fascination. As he gawked, they moved, biting, sliming, and squirming.

All at once, a vile laughter rang in the air. Sergio would recognize that voice anywhere. He fully expected to spend eternity in hell with that very sound in his ear. *Oh God! Madonna Mia!*—not another second, not one more second of this torture. With every ounce of will in him, Sergio forced a sound from his chest, yelling no.

"Noooooooooo!"

His voice seemed to release the restraining impalpable blanket; his trapped limbs were his own again. Vaulting from the bed, Sergio beat his hands across his thighs, sloughing his legs, pushing invisible insects (or the memory of them) off his skin. For, although it would be some minutes before he would know it, the bugs were gone, the dripping was gone, even the voice was gone. Only the sound of a Levis commercial playing "Very Superstitious" could be heard in the room.

133

Minutes on end, Sergio danced up and down, raising his knees one after the other, shaking and running in circles, stopping now and again to scrape his hands roughly over his bare thighs and hairy calves—over and over. *America's Most Wanted* buzzed in the background. He knew the nightmare was over, still his body refused to quit seeing and feeling it. He continued to run a reassuring hand over his legs, choosing to sit in a chair by the cheap table, through *America's Most Wanted*, through *Mad TV* until he finally nodded off to Spike Ferestein.

16

Tennessee

Cooper stood behind his black and white Crown Victoria watching as cars pulled in the open field. So they were back—his jaw clenched, his head gave an imperceptible wag—and he was working for them once again. Turned out Jean meant more to him than he ever imagined. Well, he knew that. His vow to be done with this evil cult had been broken as soon as they threatened again to reveal his one-time affair with that slut, a total stranger. Not only Jean, they promised to smear his name all over the Tennessee Highway Patrol, killing his chance for promotion. When he accused the old witch, Vera of orchestrating the whole thing, she laughed. He asked how else the organization could have photos of him and that whore. Then she all but admitted it, saying it didn't matter did it? That he'd done what he'd done, and he was just as free to ignore their request in this illegal use of state land as he had been free not to commit adultery with that woman. "It's all about free will," she had sneered at him. She was crooked as a dog's hind leg, but she was right enough in that.

Coop leaned against the back of his patrol unit chewing a blade of hay and watching the coven members arrive in all manner of cars with license plates from around the country. They looked normal, really nothing out of the ordinary, couples, singles, old and young, like a crowd arriving at a rally or event. Some of them donned their black robes right away, likely feeling the chill in the air. None of them were stripping to put them on as they had in June. At least these freaks were dressed underneath their robes this time. Seeing them dance naked in the moonlight was about the most disturbing thing he'd ever witnessed. Part of him naturally wanted to gawk at the nakedness of the younger women. He saw a few breasts and buttocks that began to excite him, but that was spoiled pretty damn quick. The way they moved and danced, and carried on, it felt evil, it did, wicked as the day is long. So why was he cooperating with them, letting them use state land, setting up roadblocks and keeping guard for them? He'd asked himself a thousand times, and it always led back to Jean.

Damn, how he loved her! He could see her now standing in the kitchen in that tired checked robe doing the crossword puzzle. She no longer had a good figure, no longer had a pretty face, but her heart was pure. She was his Jean, and he loved growing old with her. Why had he let one night, one stinking night, threaten all that? So here he was, and here he may be again. Cooper would do just about anything now to protect Jean, and he guessed Vera knew it.

Several pickup trucks came in loaded with firewood under tarps. Men were unloading these, and most of those arriving went to one of the trucks to receive pieces of firewood to carry. Vehicles couldn't travel the footpaths. All was done in silence. No directions were given, yet these people moved in a highly organized fashion. This meeting seemed different to Coop with folks more sober, more silent. He stared at half dozen of them by a new truck, arms out accepting logs. Two goons in the flatbed went mindlessly back and forth unstacking firewood and loading arms. Wondering at their wordless work, Coop was jarred by an engine's roar and looked to the road.

A red Ferrari zoomed past half a dozen cars and pulled directly in front of Cooper who was still leaning against his trunk. He recognized the huge man getting out right away. If his thick size, towering height, and shiny black hair didn't give him away, there would be no mistaking that ugly scar stretched across his square mug. The old lady called that one Worm—for the raised scar, no doubt. Worm shot Cooper a menacing look, and walked to the passenger door of the Ferrari opening it for Vera Wheaton. An old but delicate hand slipped into a baseball-glove paw as Worm helped her out of the car. Cooper knew little about her and what little he knew, he'd used the department resources to learn. She was born 1926 in Massachusetts to well-to-do parents. In 1936, she was sent to a religious boarding school at the same time her father mysteriously disappeared. The school was shut down in 1948 following a scandal involving child

136

abuse and oddly, animal sacrifice, but Wheaton was gone five years by then. He found no other record on her—no marriage, no births, no living relatives. Her mother was found dead in her bathtub in 1945, victim of an accidental electrocution when a reading lamp fell in the tub. He knew nothing more of Vera Wheaton.

Even here in the woods, he noted, the old cat dressed smartly in a tailored red suit. A low-heeled shoe was the only nod she gave to the sylvan setting. He speculated what she would have done if the paths had been muddy. Worm smiled down adoringly into her face—the goon would've carried her, Coop decided. She patted his chin like a beloved pet. Then her hand flung out palm up, waiting for Worm to perform some unknown action. The ox reached beyond her, leaning awkwardly into the car and producing a gold cigarette case. Who used those anymore? Her movements were so precise and dramatic as she withdrew a long cigarette and held it to pursed red lips.

Wheaton took two long drags on the slim stick and finally looked at Coop, who felt sure she could sense his pure hatred for her and this whole stinking group. Cold fingers played a tune on his spine, and he stubbornly resisted the urge to stand up, still leaning on his trunk acting casual. She sauntered over to him, Worm protectively close behind. Her gait too had a singular swing and strut to it. As she neared with such cosmopolitan authority, Coop caved, stopped leaning on his trunk, and stood erect eyeing Worm's looming figure. He wondered if the big galoot ever talked, and if so, what his voice must be like.

"Mr. Putrino," amazing eyes met his, wide and beautiful despite the aging face, "have you placed blocks on each of the roads that we discussed?"

"Everything is in order just as y'all asked, Ms. Wheaton."

"See dar-ling, here is a man who knows his place." She glanced up at Worm then back at Cooper. Every word of her staccato speech delivered like a punch. "Might I su-ggest you guard the main paths from here this eve-ning. There will be no dan-ger of anyone leaving tonight, but once the coven convenes none shall be a-llowed to enter." The cigarette flourished as she dramatically flicked ashes from its end. His eyes followed the cinders when a white Lamborghini swung by, parking on the other side of Cooper's patrol car. A slick looking graying man of about 55 got out of the car. He dressed neatly but practically in khakis, polo shirt, and navy zippered jacket. Coop could imagine this one in some sort of boating attire aboard a yacht. He looked high in cotton, that one. His salt and pepper hair was expertly coifed, and Coop would bet his last dollar those nails had a manicure. The man threw back trim shoulders in a dignified stretch while sucking in a cavernous breath. The passenger door opened, and a corpulent, stunted figure struggled out of the racecar. This one gave a disgusted look to the driver and said, "Really, Emmett, was it necessary to race the entire way. Honestly, you're like a teenage boy with his first car." Podgy arms reached up to rub his balding scalp then went back down to hoist his pants from the valley of fat under his belt. The two came from around their car to join Cooper, Vera and Worm. Coop had never met these two. He'd dealt strictly with Vera and that other ancient man. Thinking of that dark old one, he wondered where he was. Last time he showed up first and ran the whole show.

"Em-mett, Philip," she nodded, "nice of you to join us." Wheaton turned back to Cooper. "As I say, you will guard this entrance and see that none pass once the co-ven convenes, and that—

"Will be at Sunset," the yacht skipper said, wedging himself between Coop and the woman. "That will be at precisely 6:36 this evening."

"By all means, Em-mett," she waved the cigarette nonplussed, "instruct away, but do recall moonrise is the official opening of a sacred coven. 6:53 Mr. Putrino."

Cooper looked from one to the other, feeling like some ball caught in a tennis match. The rivalry between the two was electric.

"Humph, it hardly matters to uh...this guard here." Emmett coughed. "I mean so long as the wishes of the elders are carried out."

"Exactly," the fat one chimed, looking uncomfortable beyond the continual discomfiture of his bulk, which shifted and leaned as if it would collapse under its own weight. "Er...there are details to be seen to aren't there," he said trying to break the magnetic glare between Vera and Emmett.

The four of them finally left Cooper alone, when they went to greet two more so-called elders who'd arrived in an obnoxious hummer. Coop squinted into the waning sun to get a look at them. The driver was about 5'10. His long hair, a light color, was greased back, too short to end in ponytail but ending in the back of his head as if there were one. A couple of gold chains on his neck glinted back at Coop, and when he turned in profile, Coop clearly saw the goatee. His passenger coming around the side of the square black vehicle at this distance reminded him of a bookworm girl with her giant glasses and short flat hair. The elders continued in conversation walking two by two and disappearing down the wooded path.

Coop passed the time watching the others finish their work and follow the elders. The forest grew incredibly dark and the sun set at 6:36 just as Emmett promised. Coop hadn't seen a car in half an hour, the log trucks were empty, and all the coven members had gone to the clearing. Feeling chilled, he retreated to his car turning the heat on and the radio low. From beneath his seat, he fished out his latest copy of Penthouse and munched on a bag of trail mix. An hour later, he grew bored with the photos, and despite his disgust with his own weakness, he found himself daydreaming of the writhing naked bodies he'd seen that night. Instead of the unsettling, demonic, and possessed movements he should have remembered, in his mind's eye, Copper saw only flashes of smooth skin, tight thighs, buttocks, and breasts, wriggling, twisting and stretching across his vision. He wondered if they were at that part in their sick ceremonies. He could just watch a little, check them out, see enough to stave off his boredom, come back here before they even knew he was there.

Making up his mind, Coop rolled the Penthouse, tucked it under his seat, and turned off the car. With his jacket and torch, he headed for the path to the clearing. His long beam cut a decent swath in front of him revealing sticks and dead roots, dry and crunching under his feet. These woods were deader'n road kill. There didn't seem to be an explanation either. It was not as if a swamp had moved in, or as if a fire had swept through choking the life of the trees. Why so dead? What killed everything here?

As he walked his thoughts jostled around between excitement and guilt, and somewhere in the recesses of his mind, he knew both feelings were of a boyish variety. His schoolyard desire to see a bunch of random female body parts was playing against his church-school upbringing rejecting impure thoughts.

A hum of mumbling ahead made him slow his step and drop his beam to just in front of his feet. Through the dead branches, he saw the bonfire going full force in the middle of the clearing. Coop doused his torch before coming to the end of the path, and crept up to a giant tree trunk where he could watch unseen. Half relieved and half disappointed, he noted the members were all clothed. The sea of black robes swayed and chanted like a club of drunk crows. Looked like 200 of them, even though he knew there were only 72. Not only had he been told to expect exactly 72, but he'd counted them as they arrived. They held candles, standing around the blazing fire chanting in unison. Trooper Putrino watched fascinated trying to make out the chant, which at first seemed unintelligible but eventually began to sound like, "*Adveho oh valde unus, adveho.*" Definitely Latin, he thought. Cooper had learned a lot of Latin in choir and because of it had taken two years in High school to fulfill his language requirement. Also his mom had convinced him that taking Latin would help him ace the SAT's—it didn't, and he never, never tried to retain any of it. So now as he hunched beside the rotting tree listening and watching, he screwed up his face trying to retrieve the translation. *Adveho, adveho*…sounds like advent—what was that? Come! It came to him. Come oh *valde* one, come. *Valde, valde*…what was *valde*? Shoot, he had nothing on that one. Come oh something, come, over and over they chanted.

A row of figures stood closer to the blaze, and Cooper could make out the six elders who had come tonight. They stood out, decidedly not swaying against the waving black crows. They formed a semicircle, their arms wide open, and palms out. They chanted as well but a different phrase, their voices unnaturally loud and deeper than all the other 72. Now he focused his attention on the deeper intonation of the elders, hearing, "*Desumo vestri vernula.*" *Desumo* was easy—it meant to choose. *Vestri* and *vernula*… he hated *V*'s. He had no clue.

The fire danced and leapt like a living thing. It didn't take much to forget his aspirations as a peeping Tom, lost in the secret and solemn ritual ahead of him. As he gaped mesmerized, it began to dawn on him what this more solemn gathering might be about. No way would the old man, who was such a presence, and obviously their leader, miss this kind of ceremony. And the rivalry between Wheaton and the Skipper could only mean one thing; they were choosing a new leader. Either he died, or...maybe they killed him. Cooper put nothing beyond this group.

"*Adveho oh valde unus, adveho,*" Softly the outer circle droned like an army of bestial bees.

"*Desumo vestri vernula,*" the inner circle answered in a deep thundering, a rumbling, full of power and demand.

Against the background of a mammoth full moon in a pitch-dark sky, the black robes chanted Latin, humming and thrumming like a maniacal machine. The large bonfire seemed to burn without burning up with no crackling or snapping embers and no tiny sparks escaping, and, suddenly Coop realized, not even any smoke. It moved like it was alive. In just seconds, it became apparent who was being singled out as several distinct flames separated from the bonfire and flew towards the smaller figure of Vera, dancing before her face and about her head.

"Yes," she screamed out, "yes, my friends, *adveho.* Come! Come!"

At least a dozen flames, Cooper lost count, hovered around her while the other five elders, one after another dropped their arms. Like blasts of tiny bolts of lightning, each flame shot into Wheaton jolting her petite body. Her eyes closed and her arms flung out in welcoming ecstasy; she looked like electric joy as she embraced whatever just entered her. Emmett, whose profile was clearly visible from Coop's place beside the tree, looked on with a fiercely jealous glare. The chanting ceased, the swinging robes stopped and 72 candles fell to the ground as everyone watched the spectacle. Vera Wheaton's eyes popped open.

"*Qua est vinco, diabolus?*" (But where is my master, Prince of Evil?)

In answer to her plea, something dark stirred in the very center of the raging pile of fire. The darkness rose and began to take a shape, one with arms and limbs, but nothing that could be termed human. A black figure materialized against the red and yellow flames and walked out of the fire, appearing to take every ounce of the blazing

141

flame with it. By the time it fully separated, the burning shape towered before Vera, twice her size.

"*Etiam meus Vinco, exspectata, exspectata, valde unus.*" (Yes, my master, welcome, welcome great one.)

The fiery figure rushed forward slamming into Vera's chest. Her body, engulfed in flames that refused to burn her, lifted off the ground; her back arched, her head fell back, and she hung suspended in the air like a limp ragdoll. More flames danced around her in a wild circle of hot adoration. The worshippers imitated the flames, forming a circle around Vera, whose body continued to float above them. Black robes circled her, and 144 arms rose up like charismatics in a gospel mission. Their voices rose as one and echoed.

"Hail Vera! Hail, house of the great one, home of our legion!" Others took up the chant bowing and worshipping.

Finally, Cooper could take no more of the unholy sight and instinctively ducked behind the tree with no thought of the stir his movement made. The motion caught the attention of a pair of women on the outskirts of the crowd, who pointed and screamed to two men. Coop was made. He scrambled to stand, finding his legs stiff from having crouched so long. His right calf tingled, fully asleep. Despite the moon, he could not see the path. He heard them behind him as he ran from tree to tree and worked to unleash his Maglite. It stubbornly clung to its strap as he jerked it in the wrong direction. He kept moving but trees were closing in on him. At last, he freed the mag, clicking it on and swinging it wildly looking for the path. It had been to his right, he thought. He swept the area behind him where the sound of running feet followed. Four figures were rushing towards him, their black robes flapping like bat wings. Coop turned in a gush of panic and leapt forward tripping on a root. He caught himself before falling, but not before a large branch whacked his wrist causing him to drop the mag. There was the path; he made it! He reclaimed the light in his left hand and kept it on the ground looking for roots, all the while, his right wrist throbbed—probably broken.

A fist out of nowhere slammed his left cheek. Coop turned to fight, using the Mag as a weapon. He jabbed at the guy's head and connected but without much power. He never was any good with his left jab. The scrawny kid threw himself forward, and Coop jumped

142

back, just as something seized his neck—a girl. He flung her off while kicking out at the kid to keep him off. The girl landed with a thud against a tree, and on instinct, Coop twisted to see if he'd hurt her. A third black robe caught his right wrist, and Cooper screamed as searing pain shot up his arm and shoulder. Another yank from behind, and he was down.

The next thing Trooper Putrino knew, he was being dragged into the clearing. On his back, he held his broken wrist, and squirmed and kicked at the men pulling each of his legs. For no apparent reason, they suddenly dropped his legs. Coop wasted no time in standing up, and although he was one hundred percent sure which direction he wanted to go, he was amazed to find himself heading instead directly towards the center of the black crows. As if his legs were not his own, they plodded in a zombie gait on the barren ground. The two women, who'd first discovered him spying by the tree, were giggling, following alongside, jumping in his face, sneering, and laughing like crazed mental puppies. The bonfire had returned to normal, popping and cracking like any blaze at a homecoming football game. The many crows bounced and laughed around him, bobbing in and out of his path, and taunting, although none actually touched him or impeded his progress. Vera Wheaton stood directly in front of him, and Cooper realized with a sinking heart, it was she, who was pulling him forward with her eyes—those amazing eyes, now as red as if she were a living photo. She laughed as she drew him.

"Officer Putrino, have you enjoyed yourself?" she said, as his legs stopped two feet in front of her. The effect of the coven members biting and snarling at his heels like feral dogs, Vera's alien-red eyes, and everything he'd witnessed rolled together into an incredible seizing fear, which began somewhere in his chest but ended decidedly down his right leg in a stream of warm urine.

"You have seen what no one but the high-est coven mem-bers have ever seen," Vera said in her signature Betty Davis voice. "Your insolence will be rewarded and your curi-osity more than satisfied. It's re-ally quite a-ccommo-dating of you, you see. I wish to offer the great one a token of my gratitude for his gifts. Come Trooper Putrino, your service is at an end."

143

Again, Cooper was drawn against his feeble will. For a second, he dwelt on his wet pants and still searing wrist before the horrifying reality of where he was being pulled wiped out every other thought. Officer Cooper Putrino was walking directly towards the leaping flames.

"No!" he yelled.

"Silence!" she ordered, and he was immediately mute. Legs not his own walked closer and closer to the fire. The coven members squealed in delight. Out of his peripheral vision, he saw one after another whom he'd seen drive in looking like ordinary people, getting their logs, and walking to the clearing. There was the middle-aged lady, who looked like his Aunt Joy. There was the chubby girl, who'd actually nodded hello to him as she passed his patrol car, and the tall gangly man, who picked up the fallen log from an old woman then gallantly added her load to his. Now they looked like wild animals whipped into a feeding frenzy. And as they whooped and howled, laughed and slapped each other, and as one strange foot of his followed after another approaching the fire, Cooper thought of Jean. What had he done? How had he gotten involved with these evil maniacs?

The heat was intense. It was insane to be so close, but even as every instinct in his body fought to draw back, his boot lifted again and came down square on a burning log. His eyebrows and the hair on his head sizzled and shriveled under the heat. Cooper screamed and looked over at Vera pleading. "No, I don't want to die. I'll do anything."

Vera merely laughed. "Hear him children? Why do they always regret their action when it's time to pay the piper?"

"Please no, nooooo!" he yowled as flames licked his pants and raced up his leg still lifting to take yet another step into the raging conflagration. The fire hungrily devoured his uniform, searing the cloth to his skin while two more steps brought him to the inferno's center. His body turned one last time to face Vera, the elders and the worshipers, every one of which had a smile as hungry as the flames greedily eating his flesh. He recognized his own screams in the last seconds, and out of them one last desperate thought. "Forgive me God. Forgive me Jean, my Jean…"

144

* * *

Vera stood at the end of the path like a bride in a reception line. First in line was Scott Henderson, a stocky, middle-aged broker, thinning blond hair slicked back against a receding hairline. Scott was something of a placater when it came to his peers, but like all elders, he ruled lessers in the coven with an iron fist. Next to him was Andrew, Father Andrew to those who worked in the Diocese of Albany. A tight looking man, disciplined, charming, the kind of man with that "I understand how you feel" diplomacy. Beside him was a deceivingly mousey looking woman with short hair, bangs, and glasses. Lucinda Struthers worked in government—not for it, in it. With dozens of connections in Washington, she breezed in and out of the back doors of the Senate and the House, and even the White House. Next in line stood Philip Cole, about the same height as Lucinda's 5'5, and at least four times as wide. Philip was in the shipping business. He transported just about anything all over the country, including the coven's ceremonial sacrifices. Emmett Pierce flanked Vera and the position was gratifying, whether she was recognizing his position or merely keeping her enemies close. Emmett, a lawyer of some renown, was always playing a game, always hedging his bets, and playing an angle, and forever hungry for power. He watched envious as Vera received the most elite coven members from around the country.

Member after member curtsied or bowed kissing the giant onyx ring, which Emmett had relinquished and placed in the center of the pyre before the ceremony. The ring had appeared on Vera's finger at the same time the great one as a flaming god had entered her body. As the vessel, she would wear the ring until her death, a symbol of her place, and the embodiment of her power.

The last few lessers were paying their respect, a lanky brunette with silky long hair and her preppy looking male sidekick. The pretty brunette remained kneeling after kissing the ring.

"House of my lord, I beg you to consider me for a place among the elders. There must always be six, no? I have been studying all the old ways, and no one is more loyal or dedicated. I was the one who—"

145

"We are quite aware of your work, Aldea," Vera cut in. "However, for someone who claims to be versed in the old ways, you my dear seem completely unaware of the arrogance of your request."

"I . . . I," the young woman stuttered, and a look of pure fear crept over her face.

"Oh," Vera's voice sang, "I see you do know the old ways."

"Please, don't…no…forgive me mistress. I wasn't thinking, I—I"

"Think before you speak," Vera cupped her hands and between them appeared a golf ball of fire. "Consider this a gift; we'll see to it that your thoughtlessness will not be a problem." Vera pushed the ball forward, and it burst on the young face. The girl screamed in pain, her open mouth full of the fire. In seconds, the tongue was blackened and shriveled. Vera addressed the preppy sidekick while the girl, still on her knees, writhed in pain clutching her mouth.

"Take your girlfriend home. Be sure she understands we expect her work to continue in the Chicago coven, and tell her to be grateful that her big fat tongue and impertinence will no longer trouble her—or us."

The young couple scurried to their car as Vera followed by the elders walked to Cooper's black and white patrol car. Vera leaned on the hood in much the same manner Cooper had leaned on the trunk only hours before.

"Shame about Putrino," she said holding her hand out for Worm to outfit with a cigarette. A doting Worm slid a Slim 100 between the two waiting fingers. "He was useful. It will be inconvenient replacing him." Vera took her first drag smiling up into Worm's ugly mug. "Lucinda, you will see that Officer Putrino's car is disposed of properly, and the right people will discover it. Scott, you and Andrew will remove the roadblocks on your way out of town." The full moon cast a cool glow, and a breeze crept across the empty field. Vera's eyes still burned like red beads as she puffed on her cigarette, her new ring looking heavy on such a delicate hand. "Now, she said, a puff wafting from her lips, "about Sergio Valenti, a minor but irritating loose end that keeps snowballing just out of our reach."

Vera shared a portion only of what she now saw as the new mistress then stood away from the car. "Emmett, you will accompany me. Phillip will drive your, uh roadster."

The last five cars drove across the empty field towards the road as the smoldering bonfire licked its chops on the remains of Officer Cooper Putrino. His charred bones like dozens before him lay like poison on the land, choking life from the once green forest. For miles around, dead trees pointed their lifeless limbs in judgment of the many unjust deaths caused by the century old coven.

17

Once In Never Out

NOVEMBER 6, 2006

Dust billowed behind the BMW as it turned sharply up the dirt drive. Sergio recognized the small blue farmhouse on the top of the hill. It still wore the plywood he had nailed on the downstairs windows. The master made him put that up before they left last year, even though the small farm lay at least five miles from the nearest property. At the time, he remembered thinking how vandals hardly seemed a possibility out here. Yet now, Sergio found himself driving past the front of the house and barn and pulling in around the back, so any cars going by wouldn't spot his vehicle and ask questions.

Well, he made it. He had driven this cursed car twenty hours without incident—no weird music or creepy hand haunting. He should have dumped the beamer and flown or rented a car, but he was playing it safe incase the cops had connected his name to the Ranch or the Miller kidnapping. No telling what Mark may have said either. Besides, this haunting stuff was crap, anyway.

The door was locked as expected. Standing on the tiny landing, Sergio looked for something to smash the window. His hand wriggled the loose railing, nothing more than a painted two-by-four. He ripped it off from the penny nails holding it and gave the windowpane a whack. The open door let in warm sun illuminating a sparse kitchen right out of the 50's with a blue Formica table and red counters. The air was stale yet dark house felt cool. Sergio went straight to the tap on the huge porcelain sink and turned the fat white handle. Nothing. In the dark living room, he made out a couch and chair covered with sheets. He strode toward the slivers of light on the wall and with small effort tore off a few pieces of plywood. Dang, he was thirsty! Man, for November it was pretty hot here. He wished he'd brought water— better yet beer.

Anxious to get the box and get on with his life, Serge bounded the narrow stairs. At the end of the hall, he pulled the attic door down from the ceiling, and a wooden ladder unfolded to the floor. The hole was black, and Sergio checked the wall looking for a switch then remembered there wouldn't be any electricity anyway. The thin wooden steps creaked under his sneaks as he climbed. He paused on the last few rungs, his arms resting on either side of the frame opening, and letting his eyes adjust to the new darkness. He remembered exactly where he'd laid that box and covered it with insulation. Gingerly, he crossed the beams, a tiny octagon window at the end of the eaves shedding just enough light to aid him. The attic smelled of sweet, dry wood. It was empty except for a couple odd pieces of broken furniture, a rack of hanging garment bags, and a few boxes of what looked like old toys. Sergio knelt in the far corner, tore off the strips of pink fluff, and lifted a fat box up to rest across two beams. His hands rifled, lifted a few folders, hoping to see something, but it was just too dark to read. Hoisting the box and balancing on the beams, he carefully made his way to the attic door when he froze, hearing a familiar laugh.

Vera called up into the attic opening, "Mis-ter Valenti, come down i-mme-diately and bring that box."

Sergio knew that voice, coarse, distinctive, chopping syllables like a short order cook. She was an elder...the one called Ms. Wheaton. They never travel alone. Who was with her? Was there any chance he could escape? He looked longingly across the attic toward the miniscule window in the eaves. No hope there. The only way out was down. And how the hell did she know about the box? He should have known they'd know. But he heard no car drive up. Were they already here when he got here? Parked in the barn, maybe? His mind raced with unimportant questions.

"We're wai-ting, Sergiooo." Her gruff sultry voice held the final syllable of his name hostage. *Think, think. Keep your head and think.*

150

Sergio began the descent holding the heavy box of files in front of him like a shield and climbed down the ladder stairs frontwards. At the bottom, he faced Vera dressed in one of her signature suits, a black number with broad white lapels and cuffs. He was aware there were at least two solid guys behind him, that seven-foot sidekick of hers and some other dude. Wheaton stood, one hand across her thin hip, and the other bent at the elbow, waving two long red nails at him like the antenna of a praying mantis.

"I saw you,"—the fingers wagged—"two minutes after I was chosen. The great one and the Legion showed me you, crawling around up here like a rat in a city dump." There was the pot calling the kettle black, he thought.

"Really Mr. Valenti, how droll." Shit, did she just hear his thoughts? Oh man, is she the new master?

"Sergio, Sergio," she sang his name. "We have not giv-en up on you, despite your treach-ery. Did you real-ly think you could leave us?" Those obscenely big eyes with glued on lashes stared up at him, holding his gaze. The red-tipped antenna fingers flicked in a signaling motion, and just as the purpose of the signal came clear, Sergio met with a heavy thud on his skull. His body flung forward, the box fell sliding towards Vera's pointy patent leather pumps as she stepped back. Sergio's head hit the wall, and his face landed on the gold shag carpet, the musty smell of which was the last thing he remembered.

Sergio awoke tied to a chair with his chin on his chest and his head pounding with pain. He listened. A few voices buzzed in the next room. Careful not to move, his eyes scanned what little he could see, recognizing the living room in Menger's house in Indiana. The voices were coming from the kitchen. By the angle of the sun through the one plywood free window, he guessed he'd been out maybe half an hour. Shit, the elders had him. This was it. It had to be over for him. They could have killed him, instead of just knocking him out. They probably planned on sacrificing him, the sick bastards. He could be seen from the kitchen, but apparently, since he hadn't moved, they had no idea he was awake. Yellow nylon rope cut into his wrists behind the chair and wrapped tightly across his chest. Sergio flexed his calf muscles, verifying his legs were firmly secured as well.

Whoever tied him made damn sure he wasn't going anywhere. He followed the rope's path as best he could in his mind, contracting this and that muscle, searching for weaknesses and possibilities.

As he did this, Sergio listened, intent to hear any plans they had for him. Emmett Pierce was speaking. He was here, that prick. He used to come to the Ranch, order everyone around. He reminded Sergio of those prison guard types. The sort that get off yapping commands and controlling people. The kind that find it especially sweet to lord it over those who are powerless to resist them.

"Of course Mistress, you will do what is best. May I ask what you know of this third protector? I only ask that I may serve you more completely." Emmett's fake sentiment slid out, a forced respect floating there like oil on water. Serge remembered the rivalry between Wheaton and Pierce. From the sound of it, she must be the new leader. Only that would force such groveling from Emmett.

"Yes, Emmett, as you suspect I have been shown many things by the Legion I now house. We will tell you as much as you need to know in order to serve our needs." There was silence. Sergio imagined her pause was a calculated and torturous reminder to Emmett of his new place beneath her. Her throaty voice in that inimitable staccato speech continued, as one of the ropes slackened against his barely flexing right bicep.

"The third protector is completely unaware of her part. The light of the archangel has definitely chosen her, although spiritually she remains unconverted. Her light, therefore, is only potential. That is to our advantage, of course."

"Unconverted," Emmett said, as if mulling it over. "Where is she? What does she know?"

"At this moment, she is nothing more than a two-bit crack whore in Vegas. But I have seen the light she will become if she is allowed to heal. If she transforms, opens to the light, she will be reborn as the third protector." The voices were silent again. Sergio wondered if they were checking on him and paused his flexing. After a minute, she continued.

"Do you not see the importance of the girl then, Emmett? The child will exit the forest sanctuary after his time of preparation. Once he reenters the world, he will be as vulnerable as any other soul, unless we fail to turn his protector. If this whore is cleansed and born into the light destined for her, she will then have the power to defend him. That must not happen, Emmett."

Sergio heard steps circling him, Godzilla steps.

"Worm?" Vera called, "what is it?"

Worm grunted in response, and Sergio wondered again if he was mute.

"He's awake," the other Neanderthal answered. Sergio opened his eyes unable to figure out what gave him away, unless it was his breathing.

"Well, well Mr. Valenti," Vera said approaching him, "I'm glad you came to before I left." Vera leaned in close, to Sergio's right ear. Expensive perfume mingled strangely with the scent of rotting flesh. "I know how your former master has had some fun with you since he parted this life. Tell me, were you scared? Did you want your mommy?" She pulled back and laughed, "Oh, I for-got you don't have a mum-my. She couldn't stand you, couldn't wait to leave you. Your prec-ious Mrs. Lass-ko left you, too, and every fos-ter par-ent thereafter despised you. Even your own gang of Italiano Wops want you dead. Your whole mis-rable life was one long re-ject-ion, that is till the coven saved you, adopted you, made you a child of the Leg-ion. Sergio Valenti, right hand to the master, a position you should not have taken so lightly. Tsk, tsk." She wagged a bony digit in his face then circled him stopping somewhere behind him.

The two goons each stood to his right and left grinning. Worm cracked his knuckles, and the other one was sipped diet coke. Sergio recognized him. It was Juice, fat and mean, he always reminded Sergio of Bluto, Popeye's nemesis. Juice worked at the Ranch a while back, even shared the rack below his in the bunkhouse. For convenience sake, Sergio had always worked to stay on Juice's good side. But occasionally he had found himself between a rock and hard place, juggling Mark and Juice, two egos whose combined IQ's couldn't challenge a moron. Sergio tried to read the expression under Juice's pad of black Brillo hair, wondering if he'd remember any of the good times they'd shared, and praying he'd forget any incidents where they'd squared off.

Emmett Pierce came in from the kitchen, suave in his grey suit accenting the grey at his temples. He carried the plastic bag of the contents from the safe deposit box that Sergio had left on the seat of the BMW. "It's all here, less whatever cash he spent." Emmett stepped forward addressing Sergio. "How much did you spend, Valenti?"

"I...uh." Before he could even formulate a number, which he was pretty sure the creature behind him knew anyway, a fist came out of nowhere and slammed his jaw. The force tilted the chair, his head snapped back, and his lip released a trail of blood down his chin. So it's begun.

"Well? Answer the man," Juice's rumbly smoker's voice croaked.

"Less than a grand," Sergio glared at Juice, aware now where he stood. But hitting was good. He'd already decided that was the only way he'd have the distraction he needed and a chance to get away. When the blow came as the chair leaned back, he'd managed to push against the nylon tethers, loosening them more. As much as his instincts rebelled against the idea, he knew he needed to provoke Juice. His main concern was the new leader behind him. If she could read minds like Menger...any plan of his would be thwarted. Quickly, he made his thoughts turn. *Let's see, all-time best hitter was Ty Cobb, lifetime batting average of .366. Ok, ok...next top five...Roger Hornsby—.358, Shoeless Joe Jackson with .356, Ed Delahanty had .346, and Ted Williams uh...uh, Ted had .344...*

Sergio continued the trick he'd learned when he served the master, playing stats in the front of his mind while Vera came from behind and gave him a queer look then laughed. He hoped she was assuming his odd thoughts were some kind of avoidance mechanism to prepare for the expected torture. Apparently unconcerned with his thoughts, she moved over to Pierce and crooked her red nails in a gimme motion. He handed the bag over to her, and she sat in a chair by the desk in the corner of the room. She went about examining the papers from the safe-deposit box. The move distracted Emmett, who spoke only half looking at Sergio.

"Were you out of your mind, Valenti, leaving us buried alive in the cave while you came back and helped yourself to our holdings?" Emmett refocused, turning his head fully to Sergio. "And what did you think burning those papers would do for you?"

Sergio remained silent, playing stats in his head against a loose plan for escape.

"Emmett, look." Vera, who sat crossed legged, a pointy shoe turning circles in the air, held up the license he doctored to impersonate Menger. "I told you he was a clever boy. He will be of use when he's learned his lesson."

"Fricking should be killed." Juice's voice hacked out the words, sounding like a toilet flushing in his mouth. "He offed Hui and Jimbo, and he left us to suffocate in the cave." That was it, thought Sergio; Juice had been friends with Hui. That was all he needed.

"Hui was a useless chink," Sergio licked blood from his lip and stared defiantly at Juice, as his hands grasped the slat between the posts of the ladder-back chair. "Hui couldn't catch a three-legged dog in a fenced lot."

That did it. Juice gave one glance to the elder for permission, received a nod from Pierce, who then turned back to read papers over Vera's shoulder. When Juice hauled off with pleasure, Sergio was ready. As the punch came, square on the jaw as expected, Sergio yanked his shoulders forward pulling on the slat with all his might. It loosened and slid out of its hole. His forward motion calculated to look as if he were merely bracing himself for the blow worked and holding the now free slat his mind quickly returned to baseball. *Yankees, Yankees batting average…Babe Ruth-349, Gehrig-340, Combs and DiMaggio-325, Boggs and Jeter-313,Dickey…Dickey, uh…Mattingly 307, Mantle 298, who else—who else? Home Runs, think. All time best, Babe Ruth-659 then comes Mantle-534…no, 536, Lou Gehrig-493, Joe DiMaggio…."*

One eye on Vera and Emmett still unconcerned hanging over the desk of papers. The rope slid down the slat. He needed more. Sergio licked blood from the corner of his mouth and lifted it in a wicked grin. "Juice you're losing your touch. J'ou put on more weight? That it? Them chips 'ill do it. Gotta lay off the chips."

"F- you, Serge."

Not enough… Vera looked up and over his way. His mind returned quickly to stats. Emmett pointed to a sheet, and her head returned to the desktop. Worm remained near the chair but watched the elders.

"Aw Juice, you don't gotta be so sore—Hui never liked you. I did you a favor."

"Shut up, Valenti. Hui was—"

"A human shield," Sergio said, and spit blood to the side, "that's all Hui was good for. Your Jimbo, that's who offed Hui. All I did was put Hui in the way; piece of cake really—"

The blow came fast and hard, and Sergio was ready again. His hands braced two more slats, and he pushed his feet into the floor and his shoulders backward as the punch was delivered. As planned, he and the chair turned over, and the diametrical force of his straightening legs and his shoulders busted the cheap chair in half. The yellow line hung slack about his wrists and legs. Sergio wasted no time, grabbing a fat post from the busted chair even as his legs kicked to free themselves of the rope.

It took longer for the move to register on Juice, who stood stupidly enjoying what he thought was the result of his awesome wallop. Worm, on the other hand, stepped in rather quickly. Sergio saw the looming figure and struck at once kicking his legs like a donkey into Worm's gut. The move would barely have fazed the solid tower, had it not been so well placed. Steel parts he had not, and the giant doubled over in pain. Juice was just gaining his wits as Sergio righted himself, swinging the ripped chair post at his Brillo head.

Both Vera and Emmett, who had been engrossed in reading the letter from Mrs. Menger to her son, looked up after the chair-blasting blow, their view mostly blocked by Juice and Worm.

"Idiots!" she yelled. "I should have known those ridiculous thoughts were a ruse."

Juice clawed blindly for the array of yellow nylon still tangling Sergio. The move turned out fortuitous for Sergio, for as he pulled away with a few turns and quick twists, the rope unraveled from his legs. He sprang for the door still freeing his wrists from the trailing tether.

Sergio burst down the front steps and turned left behind the house, sprinting across the weedy yard for the beamer. Juice lumbered somewhere behind him, cursing his head off. Outrunning him or Worm, who was no doubt recovering from the kick, would not be a problem. Sergio reached the BMW, fumbling for the keys in his pocket, which thank Lady Luck were still there. He yanked the front door. The handle slipped from his hand, and the door slammed shut in front of him. He pulled and tugged, but the door seemed to have glued itself shut. Hairs on the back of his neck stood on end, and he jerked around, looking to the tiny porch with the broken rail where Vera stood smiling, her hands tucked neatly in her elbows, long red nails tapping.

Sergio tried another door with the same unbudging result then sped off yelling expletives in triplicate as he ran towards the barn. He slipped in between the two giant barn doors, and blinked. Inside was jet black after the blazing sun in the yard. He stumbled forward knocking against a white car as his eyes adjusted. He heard Lurch and Bluto yelling in the yard. He had no seconds. The Lamborghini was open but devoid of keys. No time for hotwiring. Banging on the dash, he let loose a string of curses.

A fat stream of light cut across the center of the barn as the two doors separated. In seconds, Worm was at the car door. Sergio scrambled out the other side, ran across the barn, and climbed a ladder to the loft. He saw a second car behind the Lamb, a red Ferrari, but had no idea if it had keys. Reaching the top, Sergio turned around to look down. Worm started the ladder; Vera and Emmett peered up at him, but Juice was nowhere in sight. Serge bounded over bales of hay, amazed the loft was still piled high with the stuff after all these years of the house being abandoned. Sergio was glad of it, pretty sure he could out maneuver Juice and Worm. He ducked between and around bales when he could, keeping low so he'd be harder to spot. He looked this way then that as he clambered forward towards a window, really more of a wide opening at one end. He came to a space against the wall where the bales had been cleared away. The floor had a trap door in it. Sergio quietly pulled the black ring handle, lifting the heavy wood, revealing a giant square hole probably for shoving bales down to feed the cows. There was a ladder of odd boards messily nailed to the wall for climbing up. If he could get down without them knowing, he might be able to sneak out of the barn, try the car doors again. Serge heard Worm grunting, plowing through bales, overturning them, and heaving them out of his way. Quickly he pulled a few bales in closer so the space wasn't quite so empty and noticeable. He might have missed the trap door himself if it hadn't of been so cleared of hay. Satisfied he lifted the handle, holding the door part way open. Then he lowered himself two rungs down while his arm dropped the trap door over his head as quietly as possible.

"Where the hell is he, Worm?" Juice gurgled from below. Worm grunted somewhere in the distance.

"You lazy ox, get your arse up that ladder and help Worm find him."

"Yes sir."

Sergio heard Vera and Pierce's voices moving away from him. He tried to judge in what part of the barn the ladder would plant him – the middle of the barn or closer to the door? He took one step at a time, inching his way down, looking for clues to his location. To his right and left, hanging from chains in a long row, like giant wooden necklaces, were a dozen stanchions where they used to hold the cows while they were milked. Sergio eased himself off the last board and crouched down. He heard nothing for huge seconds that dragged out to a full minute. Seemed like he should be able to hear them thunking gorillas in the loft. He couldn't even hear the elder's voices. He tried to make out the red of the Ferrari or the white Lamborghini, both parked in the center of the barn. Maybe they were in the car, or had gone outside to look for him.

Strips of daylight from between boards, as well as the open door somewhere in front of him gave him an idea of his position. The opening had landed him in the middle of one side of the barn. The voices he'd last heard would put the elders more to the other end of the barn away from the open door; Juice and Worm had to be skulking in the loft. Finally convinced it was safe, Sergio stood slowly, turned towards the door, and stepped into the long cement trough. The trough looked clear and would be the quietest way to go.

Chink.

He heard a chain sound when out of nowhere a wooden contraption came flying at him. It whammed him in the head and knocked him off balance. He landed on his side, across the hard trough, hearing Juice's phlegmy laugh. "Shoot, buddy, where do you think you're going?" Sergio righted himself and could barely react before Juice's boot met the side of his chin. "Thought, you was so smart. Thought I was in the loft with Worm, huh, Sergio?"

Despite the pain, Sergio was ready for the next kick. Juice was nothing if not predictable, he thought as he captured the incoming foot. Shoving up and tossing the offending limb out like throwing a shot put, Serge gave it all he had, and Juice flew back with a satisfying thud in the trough. Sergio leapt up, his head reeled from both recent bangs, and the one that had knocked him unconscious earlier. Juice was rolling like a turtle trying to get up as Sergio ran towards the middle of the barn.

Wham.

Between the dim light, and his disoriented head, he thought for a second he'd run into a barn post, when he realized it was the seven foot pole called Worm.

"*Arrrrg,*" Lurch grunted in true mute manner placing his giant paws on Sergio's neck. Sergio threw his fists up hard and fast to break Worm's hold, but all he met was an iron grip. Worm lifted him off the ground; Sergio's legs flailed, making the giant hands tighten for control, killing his neck. Sergio tensed his stomach muscles and thighs and managed to hoist both of his long legs around Worm's trunk. He squeezed his legs as hard as he could and jerked himself hard to the side, throwing Worm off balance. The tree of a man fell backward into a beam, loosening the neck hold just enough that Sergio was able to scramble free.

Behind Worm, Sergio saw Juice wielding a two by four full of nails. Thinking quick, as Juice raised the board, engaging Worm's eye with a challenging glare, Sergio made a fake move to the right, guessing Worm would meet his move. The board meant for Sergio's head, instead slammed into Worm's left arm as Serge darted out of the way.

An insanely weird sound accompanied Worm's shock of pain, and he turned instinctively grabbing the board and hurling its wielder backward. For the second time in an hour, Sergio delivered a well-placed kick to Worm's groin. He turned on Juice, pounding him with two jabs to his thick skull. With both his adversaries dazed, Sergio shot towards the open barn door. He was just coming to the cracked opening when the two huge doors slammed shut.

"ENOUGH!"

Vera Wheaton's voice seemed to bounce off every beam and rafter in the old barn.

Sergio gave the huge door a tug, but his heart fell, immediately aware of the diabolical force holding it shut. He turned to face Vera and Emmett, when his left and right shoulders were pinned against the wall by Juice and Worm. Worm laid a fist into Sergio's gut doubling him over.

"There, there my pet, let that be enough for now. You too," Vera looked at Juice. "Mr. Valenti, tis a pity you don't see the error of your ways." His back was to the wall, each man pinning a shoulder and placing their leg on his knee. Sergio lifted his head to see her. A spear of white light stabbed between a gap in the boards and cut across her aging features. Those huge doe eyes and tarantula lashes, the old movie upsweep and ruby red lips, she could have been a star of silent pictures a hundred years ago. It was surreal as she approached. Her high heels ticking on the cement sounded like a tiny death knell to Sergio's ears. Something in her voice told him the worst was yet to come. *Tick-tick, tick-tick…*

Sergio glanced behind her at Emmett, picking a piece of hay from his Prada suit. He returned Sergio's look with an odd grin that forebode as much as the ticking shoes. Wheaton stood over him.

"Mis-ter Valenti appears to have a problem see-ing our position," she said chopping her syllables in singular fashion. "He has trouble see-ing where his loyalties must lie, see-ing who his only real friends are, see-ing where he be-longs. You know love," she looked down towards Worm, who with Juice was now crouched restraining him on the floor of the barn, "so many need to lose some *thing* to appreciate something, and sometimes the loss, it's just for their own good." She patted Worm's face and traced a long red nail lightly over his scar. Sergio had wondered for years if Vera had something to do with that scar. Now he was sure. Not only that, but maybe he was mute because of her too. Yet, he was so loyal. He adored her. Sergio's head was killing him—his chin, his jaw, his crown, every inch of it. All he could think was whatever happened next, it better not happen to his head.

Vera slowly dropped, folding her thin old knees until she was crouched on her bony haunches like the rest of them. She was in

Sergio's face. "You know a lot of people don't understand hu-man nature, Sergio. But you, I'm bet-ting, you will understand . . . a little theology lesson shall we? You see Sergiooooo, hu-mans have two natures really, their bo-dies and their spir-its. Oh, they seem so united; it's nearly im-poss-ible to tell that they are really and truly separate." Her hand reached for his face and she tipped his chin higher to look at her. Looking in her eyes, big black saucers, was like looking in a pit, a sort of abyss, the kind of hole you walk up to and look down wondering how deep it is.

"For most, and most of their pa-thetic lives, the bo-dy rules the spir-it. Tsk, tsk, but that's not how it was de-signed. No, no, the biggest secret of all, the truth that makes you powerful, is the spir-it must rule the bo-dy. Without that, no man has power. But there's only one way for the spir-it to rule su-preme. Hmm? Did you know that dear? My Worm, he knows."

Tension mounted, the longer she talked, the more Sergio dreaded whatever was coming. Every punched word was like a drum roll—tad dum, tad um.

"Of course, Missssster Valenteee, the fast-est way to sub-jugate the body and allow the spir-it to conquer is to pun-ish the offending member. Let us see now, what were we saying before. Oh yes, your problem was see-ing wasn't it? You were see-ing all the wrong things, making all the wrong decisions. Oh I know," her raspy voice raised a notch and a thin finger tapped her lips. "Did you ever have trouble focusing? —and you just needed to see things a little differently, and you put your finger over one eye, like this." She demonstrated, and in that moment he caught a terrifying notion of what she might be leading up to.

"No!" Sergio yelled and began struggling anew, but the two men held him tight.

"Yes!" she said. Her index finger shot to his left eye, the long red curving nail jamming fast into a corner—excruciating pain as the instrument dug behind the eye ball and then yanked outward, scooping his eyeball until it lay on his cheek dangling by loose threads of veins. Reeling in pain, he heard her gruff voice.

"He's yours Emmett, a gift from me to you. Now he will be as loyal as my Worm."

He heard Emmett's voice in his ear, talking sweetly and realized with incredible shock the man was holding his eyeball, still linked to him by stringy blue veins.

"You belong to me now. I know all about what you've been through, Sergio. The Legion and Vera have shown me, and given me the power to make it all stop. I will make it stop—the haunting, the fear, the torture, the police—all of it. And only I can. This will be a fresh start, Sergio Valenti, a chance for you to redeem yourself." Emmett's free arm slid to the back of Sergio's neck, supporting his head. "Your indiscretions will be as lost as your eyeball."

Emmett Pierce yanked his hand up, tearing the eyeball completely from his head, and Sergio Valenti passed out on the floor of his former master's barn in the arms of his new master.

18

Shelter and Sister Eva

In a pink hospital gown, Angela sat on the end of the stripped bed, embarrassed and shaking. With arms were crossed and hugging her middle, she rocked imperceptibly back and forth. A dozen identical beds lined the long room—six on one side, six on the other. Hers was near the window at the end. Everything was clean and crisp, and empty too. It was dinnertime, and the other residents had gone downstairs to eat. All of the beds were made, belongings stowed underneath or in the lockers. Rules were strict here. It was supposed to help restore order to lives torn apart by violence. Anyway, there was nothing for her to stow. Like so many others, she'd fled with nothing but the clothes on her back. This was her third day in the shelter; she would have to go tomorrow. The rules were strict, and the neat and clean beds weren't meant for her kind.

Even the streets in this part of town looked clean, she thought looking out the second story window. No people streaming back and forth, no casinos or endless construction, no porn leaflets littering the sidewalk with naked women staring back up at the very passers-by who dropped the shocking filth as soon as it was forced into their unsuspecting hands. Filth that was a good word for it, a word that summed up the last ten years of her life—filthy johns, filthy apartments, filthy addicts, filthy Eddy…filthy her.

In the midst of this new heartache, her physical pain barely mattered, but it was there all the same. The left side of her face was so swollen it looked like a balloon with a face painted on it. Her gut hurt worse than anything. She was checked at the ER, and the ribs were bruised but none cracked. Looking down at her thin purple-splotched legs sticking out of the ugly hospital gown they'd given her, she was one giant bruise. All this for refusing to get high with Eddy. He'd come home with two jumbos of crack, and at first he didn't seem to care when she turned it down, but the higher he got, the madder he got that she wouldn't join him. Of course, all she could think of was the baby. The tiny life tucked away inside her, her second chance, a chance to do a good thing.

"Stinking whore! You think I ain't seen what-chu doing. Been going on for months." Eddy had shoved her against the dresser, and she knew he was working himself up. "You think you can get clean—clean up and leave me?"

"No Eddy, it's nothing like that; I swear." She'd edged towards the bed thinking if he slammed her, the cushioning would help. She was determined to stay clean now for the baby's health, but Eddy was right she'd been backing away from the drugs ever since those dreams with the boy began back in August. No idea why really, but the dreams made her feel different about herself—see the world different, too.

"You owe me bitch. There's no out while you owe me." He threw the first punch smack into her left eye. She fell back on the bed with a pathetic yelp.

"I know it, Eddy. I know what I owe. I'm working ain't I?" She rolled to dodge a second blow, falling off the bed in the process. "I take care of you Eddy. I love you, baby."

She was in the same situation as most of the whores here; they were "debt slaves." Every stinking thing went into their debt, even rolling paper for a stinking joint—you name it. And she barely got any of the money from high-end tricks, between the cabbies, the bellhops, and Eddy's take. And working direct for cheap tricks on Freemont and eighth was risky. Last month she was one of 184 rounded up by operation P.I.M.P, Prostitutes Incarcerated by Metro Police. The pigs really thought they were sending a message to pimps, making them pay to bail the girls out. It was the girls, who always paid in this business no matter how you looked at it. P.I.M.P. just put them further into slave debt. And there wasn't much help out there from charities if you wanted out. Safe houses were for women with kids, who were beat up by their boyfriends or husbands. As soon as they found out you were a hooker, the helping hand was yanked back at lightning speed like you had leprosy. Guess they figure these girls chose this life. She'd heard it time and again, but what girl really chooses this? And the longer you're in, the more impossible it is to get out. But she wanted out now. She was determined to find a way.

On the floor, like a whimpering animal, she had cried, "Don't, please Eddy. I'll be good," when Eddy's foot found her before she could dodge it. He got her in the ribs then reached down for her hair pulling her head so far back she thought her neck would break. He was yelling all kinds of shit about how grateful she should be, about how she thought she was too good for crack now. "A crack whore, too good for crack," he had said. He spit in her face then rammed another fist in her left cheek.

This time he nearly killed her, he hadn't stopped till he was too tired to continue. Mostly kicking her back and sides and legs as she curled into a ball and covered her face. He was literally out of breath when he stopped. She must have passed out awhile for when she came to he was gone. She should have left two weeks before that when she'd called her brother John in a panic. Eddy had hit her pretty hard then; all cause the crappy AC unit broke—like it was her fault.

Never would she have gone to that extreme of calling John. She was so ashamed of all she had done—what she'd become. Turning to John had been a desperate attempt to save her baby. She'd romanticized about seeing her brother again; that was the only reason she even had his number. She kept tabs on him over the years. She kept a newspaper clipping of his wedding announcement for years. His wife looked pretty and petite. They looked so happy. Johnny deserved happiness. She kept the clipping under her clothes in her dresser drawer. She would take it out when Eddy wasn't around. Then one day, he found it, made fun of her, and then set it on fire with his cigarette. Angela rubbed the tough patch of rumpled skin on her right index and thumb, burnt trying to save it. It felt like her tie to Johnny was really gone then.

165

Oh God! Oh God! She rocked back and forth on the bed staring down at the blue striped ticking of the bare mattress. It was all over—no baby, no second life. She should have known it was too good to be true. She heard footsteps and saw it was Sister Eva returning with clean sheets.

"I'm so sorry, so sorry," Angela looked up into the round face and bright eyes of the woman who called herself Sister Eva, in a simple jean dress and a blue scarf on her head, half covering wiry black hair. She was cheerful with her thick Brooklyn accent. She was heavy, too but in that capable pleasing way, the sort of woman who bears her problems and yours with a hearty laugh or good-natured joke to lighten the load. She had explained that she wasn't a real nun, but a lay sister, someone who dedicated her life to God and works of charity, but who still lived and worked in the world. Angela had no idea what the woman was talking about the night she came here from the ER. That was on the tenth, she thought.

Four nights before that, she had hurried as best she could from the apartment, swiping Eddy's cell phone off the kitchen table on her way out. Her head reeled, every bone screamed, and her vision was blurry, but she managed to call 911. They kept connecting her to different hotlines as she ducked down side streets and avoided running into Eddy or anyone else. She limped and dragged herself like Quasimodo. Once or twice, she fell and found herself crawling to the next doorway where she could hide. She was in bad shape. Eventually, they had her rendezvous with a volunteer who took her to North Vista's ER. It was there she'd learned her due date, August 9 same day Reef's baby had been taken. After four days in the hospital, the same volunteer picked her up and brought her here. What'd they call it . . . , Haven something or other?

The woman held the clean sheets out to Angela and studied the tortured face.

"Angela, don't worry about the stains. Lots 'a women have surprise periods."

"No. . .no it—it wasn't my period," she said, her voice sounded high and whispery. "I was pregnant."

Sister Eva nudged beside Angela, and Angela scooched a little to make room. The woman placed the neat stack of sheets on the

166

mattress behind them trying to digest the miscarriage and probably trying to figure out what this loss meant to a common hooker. "I'm sorry. Do ya want to talk about it?"

Angela was quiet. Eva lightly touched Angela's bruised thigh and took a breath like she was ready to speak, crack a joke, or something then swallowed it as if thinking better of it. They sat there silently looking out the window to the side of them. "Your clothes may be dry by now. I could go check an' maybe bring ya back a little chow from the dining room. It's only hotdogs tonight, but we make a pretty mean chili ta go with it."

The kindness in her voice, the offer to fetch food, the way she reminded Angela of a chubbier version of Lisa from back in high school—Angela looked at the blue kerchief draped over this woman's head as a self-proclaimed sign of her devotion to God, a God Angela was sure she could never understand or please.

"Why...why does God do it?" She broke down crying.

"I don't know honey"—the usual cheery voice sounded somber—"I don't want ta say he's mysterious, that sounds so...trite, I guess." Sister Eva smoothed Angela's hair. "His plans are beyond our imagining, but I do know they always have a purpose." Her hand moved down the hair and ended in the gentlest patting on her back. Eva had seen enough of Angela's purple body to be wary of causing any more pain. "Even if it's true, it's not what ya want to hear. I know it doesn't help ya understand."

"I deserved...I didn't protect my first baby. I didn't—didn't—" She could barely get the words out for the heaving. "I didn't protect this one. I let—let Eddy do that."

"Oh sweetie, ya didn't cause this," Sister Eva said.

Angela swung her head back and forth. "But I did, I did, and this...all of this is my pun—punishment. Who was I... kidding? God could nev—never give someone like me a second chance."

Ever so lightly, Sister Eva brought a plump hand to Angela's chin turning the swollen face, battered eye and ripped lip towards her. "Angela I may not know much about your life, but I do know one thing about God. He is the King 'a second chances. God is all merciful. The only thing He ever really asks is that we turn to Him."

167

Angela's good eye stared at the woman in the blue scarf, who continued to give her full attention and looked totally undistracted by the three women and one screaming child who had just returned from dinner. Eva's words rang true, and she wanted to believe in the King of second chances, but as Angela listened to the baby crying in the woman's arms just four beds away, all she could think was somehow she had blown her second chance and the sooner she faced it the better.

One of the women who came in, a young, lanky redhead approached Angela's bed looking at Eva, and the room erupted as several more women returned, chatting, and laughing.

"Eva, er Sister Eva, I need to make a phone call and the day room is locked."

Eva stood and gave the barest rub to Angela's back. "I'll get your clothes while I'm gone. You shower an' change, and we'll go down ta the kitchen an' talk again after things settle down." The redhead stood waiting in the aisle by Angela's bed. Eva leaned into Angela, head to head and spoke low, "We're not done, ya hear Miss Angela Miller? God has great plans for you." Eva stood and joined the other woman.

By the time she returned with Angela's clothes, a purple skirt, a sage V-neck hoodie, which had been sown at the shoulder where Eddie had ripped it, and a black leather jacket, the room was abuzz with other residents, rescued women and children of all ages, several as bruised and beaten as she was. Sister Eva left again to attend to one of a hundred chores she fulfilled at the shelter, and Angela changed into her street clothes as quick as she dared since so many moves brought pain. Last, she slipped on her black ballet flats, relieved they weren't heels. All she thought of while she dressed was that this place, which she'd have to leave tomorrow anyway, wasn't meant for her. She reached the street, glad she hadn't run into Eva in the halls, having to see her jovial features ruined with disappointment.

On the sidewalk, feeling chilly, Angela zipped her leather jacket and headed west on Owens. Temperatures in Vegas went between sixty and seventy during the day this time of year and dropped to the forties at night. It was dark already, and she was glad of dusk hiding her bulging face and battered limbs. Despite the pain, she picked up the pace a bit to keep warm, taking a short cut down side streets, instead of going directly down Main. She headed back to the familiar territory of Freemont Street maybe two miles away, with no plan and no clear idea what she was going there to do. Couldn't head back to her place yet, even if she wanted to, and she wasn't sure she wanted to, but also not sure she wouldn't have to, eventually. She'd taken Eddy's phone, run out, been gone for five days, although, it wasn't unusual for her to disappear for a little while after a beating. Sometimes she'd stay with other girls, or just hang out in a casino bar. If you kept a low profile, ordered a few drinks, you could hide out there, but she'd never been beaten in the face like this. Hell, she couldn't even score on Freemont and eighth with a face like this. What was she going to do for money?

With a cool breeze on her hot cheek, Angela walked forty minutes or so. With racing thoughts, painful memories, pained ribs, and now painful feet, she found herself under the giant canopy on Freemont street. The "Freemont Experience" they called it. The huge greenhouse looking canopy, which stretched 1500 feet (the length of five football fields), was really the largest projection screen in the world with something like twelve million synchronized LED lamps, including one hundred eighty strobes and eight robotic mirrors per block. Ok, she knew way to much about it but everyone who worked these streets did. You learn stuff in between tricks. The light show blasted overhead playing "We Will Rock You". Freddie Mercury's face curled massively around the screen and screamed at her—directly at her.

> *You got mud on yo' face. You big disgrace*
> *Kickin' your can all over the place*
> *We Will, We Will, Rock You, Rock You*
> *We Will, We Will, Rock You, Rock You*
> *Buddy you're a young man, hard man, shoutin' in the*
> *street, gonna take on the world some day*
> *You got blood on yo' face. You big disgrace*
> *Wavin' your banner all over the place*

All Angela heard over and over was "You big disgrace." She walked a numb, un-crying kind of walk, turning on Casino Center between Golden Nugget and Four Queens. Her head was down, barely aware of the stares of curious tourists and a few fellow whores, whose looks were always less curious, less sympathetic and more matter of fact, like they were looking in a mirror at a face they sometimes knew but never wanted to recognize. All of it flew past her—the lights, the music spilling out on the sidewalk, the curious as well as the unsympathetic faces. She walked further and further, no money, no friends, no ideas, but somehow that base survival instinct bubbled to the surface as it often does in even the most down trodden. Tired, hungry, and shaking with cold, she paused on the sidewalk in front of a pair of big wooden doors, which stood wide open like welcoming arms. Holding prayer books and rosaries, half a dozen Latino women flowed out. With no forethought, just the hope of warmth in a public building, she turned hugging the edge of the wide steps as if her very presence could taint the tiny stream of church-going, short, dark haired ladies. She slipped into Saint Joan of Arc Church keeping to the side as a short couple and a laughing young man came out of the inner church doors. Immediately she felt like an intruder, and in a mini blast of inexplicable panic, she looked for escape. Behind her, a door was cracked, and she slid inside what turned out to be a closet storeroom with a few dusty bookracks and a small window. She closed the door then sank down on the cold wood floor, pulling her chilled legs up and tucking them to her sore middle. She laid her head against the wall, exhausted and mentally drained. The uncomfortable position, the cold wall, and pungent odor of mothballs notwithstanding, feeling safe and hidden, Angela Miller fell fast asleep.

Which explained why she was completely unaware when Father Lawrence made his rounds. The priest locked the large front doors. Then, kissing two fingers and tapping the foot of the statue of Saint Pius X, he climbed the narrow turning stairs to the choir loft. It was empty, and he climbed back down intending to lock the storeroom, which now served as a lending library for parishioners. Seeing it closed, he assumed Maria had already locked it. He flicked off the foyer lights, satisfied the "Charis-maniacs" as he playfully termed the Monday night prayer group had all gone home. The priest left for the rectory by the side door, assuming his church was empty and safe from the nightlife of Freemont Experience and the poor souls he served, who he knew might, if given the chance, rob the church blind.

It was pitch dark when Angela awoke, scarcely remembering where she was or how she got there. The church was dead quiet, but outside the noise of Freemont's lightshow drummed in the distance. After a minute, she unfolded herself, stiff as a board. She felt her way to the closet door and quietly turned the knob. Making her way along the wall, her fingers landed in a bowl of cool water, a holy water fount. She patted the water to her face letting it run over the sore cheek. Damn that Eddy. From what she could feel as her hand explored her face, it seemed the swelling had gone down some more. They said it would take a while, and it was.

She pulled out Eddy's cell. The phone had no charge and quickly gave out, but not before she found the big door handles. She jiggled them. Locked. *Oh jeeze.* Leaning her back on the doors, she looked ahead to the two interior glass doors, which led to the main body of the church. There, a single votive on the wall of the sanctuary cast the palest red glow. It was a smallish church, one wide aisle flanked by blond pews, walls of pink marble, simple statues on either side, and a huge mural behind the altar. It was a Catholic church. She hadn't been in a church since she left Endicott.

Back home, you couldn't chuck an apple core without hitting a Catholic Church. Seems a century ago, every nationality of immigrant had to have their own church, whether Italian, Irish, Slovak or Pole. They built their churches right next door to each other, in spite of the fact that they worshipped in the same Latin tongue and with the exact same Mass. The last half of the century, ethnic lines had been mixed and crossed so much, only the oldest church members still considered their church Italian or Slovak or whatever. The Millers had gone every Sunday since it was a sin not to do at least that much. Angela, like her brothers, knew little of the Faith. She gleaned what she could from sermons that caught her attention. Sometimes, she read the words to songs or the bible passages in the missalette during Mass. Like her brothers before her, she was made to take a handful of religious education classes in order to receive the sacraments of Communion and Confirmation, which were another of the things considered the "least" a good Catholic must do.

Leaving the vestibule, Angela pushed open the swinging doors, and crept into the thick stillness of the church. High on the walls

171

stained glass let in some light from the street, and she worked her eyes to make out the huge mural behind the altar. After some minutes of curious study, she decided it was Joan of Arc—had to be—flames leapt below the figure of a young woman clad in armor, clutching a sword the top of which was a cross. Above the saint, an angel held a crown to place on her head. Angela dropped into the first pew and thought back to the old-time movie with Ingrid Bergman she'd watched with her mom when she was a kid. What a story! A peasant girl who claimed to hear voices telling her to fight for the crown then trying to get the King to give her an audience and listen. Her request to fight was all the more ridiculous from a poor insignificant girl. She was laughed out of court, but persisted until eventually she was believed and led the French in battle after battle reclaiming French territory. The Maid of Orleans! She kept her faith through all kinds of trials and troubles; she never gave up. Even when she was being burned alive at the stake, the nineteen year old saint asked someone in the crowd to hand her a cross. Angela loved that movie, loved that story.

In a sudden self-conscious pang, she tugged her lavender miniskirt as if she could lengthen it. Directly below the colorful mural lay a bright gold box with the words *Sanctus, Sanctus, Sanctus* engraved in the top or Holy, Holy, Holy. This was the Catholic treasure chest, Jesus himself. It would be hard for Angela to say that she believed that in that box holding what looked like the little white wafers was really holding the son of God. But she could say she always felt closer to God in church. Yep, that she could say. On all those Sundays, sitting between her big brothers, Angela used to talk to God and to the statues in church representing different saints, and every time she did, she left a little more comforted, a little more loved than before, and a little more determined to do something good and right. Her eyes drifted around the muted church, and her hands unconsciously rubbed the smooth pew. The quiet space spoke to her as though the church itself had wrapped a warm motherly arm about her and whispered, "There, there."

"Oh God," she cried aloud rocking back and forth, oblivious her cry could alert someone to her presence. "I—I don't want to go back to Eddy. I don't want to make money the way I do. I don't want to use anymore. I want out, out of Vegas, out of this life. Please, please give me another chance. I can be good; I can be more if you help me. Please, please." She slumped to her good side crying on the bench, the thick mess of blond curls falling across the pew. She wept hard, her nose running, her face wet with tears. A paper stuck to her face, and she peeled it off looking at it.

It was a faded blue holy card of Saint Michael. The Archangel stared back at her, his great wings outstretched in his soldier's armor, his roman boot square on the enemy's back, a mighty sword pointed at the devil's head. She flipped the thin card in one hand and pulled her sweatshirt up with the other to dab her running nose. Angela read the washed out words slowly.

"Saint Michael the archangel defend us in battle. Be our defense against the wickedness and the snares of the devil. May God rebuke him we humbly pray, and do thou O Prince of the Heavenly Host, by the power of God, thrust into hell Satan and all other evil spirits who prowl about the earth seeking the ruin of souls."

There are some truths every human soul is meant to discover—not every day facts or philosophies, nor teachings or lessons in life, nor even aha's or eye-openers, but the kind of truth which lies hidden like gold in an untapped vein, the kind of truth which changes everything. And just as surely it seems, this kind of truth lies hidden until the perfect moment in the soul's journey back to its Creator until the God of Time says its time because He knows that timing is everything. Call it an epiphany, a revelation, a defining moment, but as Angela Miller sat alone in the cool church, wiping her nose on her sleeve, she struck that vein and found a golden nugget of truth...

Good and evil, light and dark—it was all a battle, a giant battle for souls. Whether it is for the saving of some or the ruin of others, life is a battle. She looked up at the wall searching the face of Saint Joan in the flickering red light. Joan of Arc ran into battle, not away from it. The Maid of Orleans had fought for even the right to fight. Only a fifteen-year-old girl and she had stood her ground and made her stand. Whereas Angela had run away, and run, and run. In that sacred space of God's own house, shut like a lion's mouth against the world, Angela felt safe and sheltered, free for a time from the hustle and greed, the struggle and schemes of man, the mindless pursuit of endless pleasure for some, and a fierce struggle of base survival for others. Outside the battle raged as real as the neon lights and cacophony of the Freemont Canopy, which muted sounds thumped against the walls of the church like a drunk demanding entrance. But inside, here in this womb of solitude, a soul was free to reflect as it ought now and then on its Creator, on its purpose, and its end.

Angela did just that when she noticed a beam of bright blue light cutting across the sanctuary floor. Her eyes followed the line of light back to a side entrance where the priest gets ready for Mass. Moonlight? She noted two small windows high above the were dark. She looked once around as if for permission to investigate then rose and shyly crossed the altar area. As she stepped into the sacristy, the light intensified illuminating three stained glass windows. The center panel, wider and off the floor, depicted the angel Gabriel appearing to Mary. Two more narrower panels, one on each side were of angels as well. The words *Saint Michael* were under the right and *Saint Raphael* under the left. All three angels, depicted in armor, looked powerful. The blue light grew to such intensity that Angela was blinded. She stumbled back, shivering with fright and shielding her eyes.

* * *

Father Lawrence Mulumba, his overcoat slung over one arm, juggled a grandé coffee and a dozen doughnuts while his left hand struggled to unlock the heavy side door of Saint Joan of Arc Church. It was an hour before Mass, and at least twenty minutes before Robert, his trusty sacristan, would come. Father had bought the doughnuts, six cinnamon, three sugars, and three jellies for November 14, the feast day of St. Lawrence O'Toole. A feast day should begin with a feast, the Ugandan priest reasoned, feeling only a twinge of guilt. Let's see, he counted mentally, himself, Bob, and the golden girls, Mrs. Ramirez, Rosalie, and Maria, (the ladies from the altar rosary society who clean the church. He knew exactly how many each would eat after Mass, and he knew he'd eat the leftovers. It wasn't the calories; it was the self-indulgent gratification of his sweet tooth he would regret.

In the first pew, Angela looked as surprised as Father Lawrence when her head popped up from a sound sleep. Neither quite knew what to say to the other. As he approached, Father saw a poor

174

wretched girl with a lopsided face and bruised legs matching her purple skirt. He guessed the beating was at least a week old, probably a pimp but could have been a john. She pulled her skimpy leather coat closed over the low cut sweatshirt then made a pathetic attempt to smooth the wildest mane he'd seen since Phyllis Diller played at Caesar's.

Angela saw a tall, sturdy looking, dark-skinned priest balancing doughnuts and coffee, keys and coat like a waiter with a big order. Father Lawrence broke the surprised silence.

"Well, hullo there," he smiled warmly.

"I'm so sorry…I'm—I didn't do it on purpose. I mean I was—I was in the …the little bookroom, and when I came out all the lights were off. The door was locked and I was worried about an alarm…," Her words trickled off as he continued to smile, white teeth flashing in the dark face.

"My girl, it is quite all right." His deep, sonorous voice was careful and enunciated. "I am Father Lawrence, and you are…?"

"Angela," she said, starting to stand, when the priest waved her down jiggling keys. He hurriedly sat in the pew beside her. First, he dropped his keys to the pew, then he awkwardly worked the box of doughnuts between them still balancing his grandé. Finally, he flung his long black coat over the front pew.

"There you go,"—he pointed with his coffee baffling Angela— "you have the perfect name for someone who spent the night sleeping with the angels."

"Huh, what?"

A deep laugh rolled from Father Lawrence. "I am sorry. I forget that not everyone who visits us is Catholic." Angela thought of correcting him since she was baptized Catholic, but who would she be kidding? "Many angels keep Jesus company in the Church." He nodded towards the gold box. "Let me tell you, Angela, as a young boy, I always wanted to be locked in a church all night. I think maybe it was because of Idi Amin's soldiers and their machine guns. But," — he point outside and giving her a wink, "it is not so good out there either."

She didn't know what to say. He had trapped her in the pew more or less. "I, uh, I didn't mean to do it,"—he smiled so big, it was impossible to believe he minded her trespass—"but I know what you mean. I guess when I was a kid I wanted to be locked up in K-Mart, but I mean…it was really peaceful last night, I mean really." Her mouth turned up in a painful smile, stretching her cheek and reminding her of how she must look. Her hand went up. He sat on her right, and Eddy had bashed in her left cheek so at least the good side of her face was toward him. She avoided turning her head as she spoke. "I, uh…I figured out some stuff."

"Jesus is like that," Father said, and nodded to the box again. "Anything you want to share? I am told I am a good listener."

This was odd. Her head down, she absentmindedly stared at the red letters on the doughnut box between them. She kind of wanted to open up, talk with him, eat a doughnut—could she be any hungrier?—It would be nice to talk about God with a religious person. Last night it seemed like she'd really had a breakthrough. Hope had dawned like the rarest rainbow in a gloomy sky for the first time in so long. Apparently, it left her as hungry physically as spiritually.

"An-gel-a,"—he paused at every syllable. She liked the way he said her name with gravity and lightness all at once—"I would be indebted to you if you would do me a very large favor." She sat stone still. "Let me just tell you, it is this coffee and these," he tapped the box. "I am not supposed to drink too much caffeine, and I bought far too many doughnuts, many more than we need. I will be the only one to gorge on the leftovers. I have not touched this yet, aaaand… you look like you could use a strong cup." He held the cup out to her.

"Um, that's ok," she said, her head tilted shyly. As she spoke, the smell of the coffee was so strong. She hadn't eaten since breakfast yesterday at the shelter. Part of her wished she'd just accept the cup and be done with it, but she was never like that. Her version of polite didn't work that way. Suddenly, she remembered yesterday and how she thought the mild cramps were from something she ate. Instead, it had been a miscarriage when her insides and unborn baby had spilled all over the sheets. She struggled to stop her face from wincing at the memory.

"Please An-gel-a, it is the least you can do for me after a free night in casa de Hesus." He made her laugh. "Will you please eat and drink, and after, maybe we could talk—if you like."

Her lips bit together and she cocked her head, before accepting the cup. The priest pushed the box toward her and flipped open the lid. "Eat at least two, An-gel-a. Promise?" Father Lawrence said, gathering his coat and keys. He disappeared somewhere behind the giant mural to the room behind. Angela nibbled a jelly doughnut and mulled over staying to talk with the priest.

19

Denver

715 miles away in Denver, Colorado, Vera Wheaton paced the posh living room of the penthouse suite. Her suit was a steel grey, double-breasted number with delicious glass buttons, paired with a flowy silk blouse and black patent leather pumps. Though since housing the legion, she found no pleasure in her ensembles as she once had. Her wardrobe was a means to an end—whether intimidation, control, or making the expected impression. Worm and her affection for him, such as it was, had altered as well, she realized. He, too, was a means to an end. Formerly when she served their master, even though everything she did and every decision she made was done for him, something of her own will remained. Now, it was as if she and the master were one; she was, after all, his vicar on earth.

"The government will control the Ranch in Cobleskill for years." Vera spoke out loud, though hardly for Worm's benefit. Her seeming monologue was a way to wade through the voices in her head. These were literal voices, not running thoughts—voices which argued and bit at each other and at her. She slowly crossed the hotel suite airing her thoughts. "Deed or no deed, there will be no way to claim the Ranch as yet. Still, we will regain the land one day for the coven, and the Master will be worshiped there again." She reached the end of a bank of windows, turned back and harrumphed looking at Worm who stood attentive as always. Worm never sat unless she did—or she ordered him to, which was rare since she rather enjoyed the lengths his adoration of her took. Yet at times, the 6'7 tree trunk towering near her 5'1 person annoyed her. Vera snicked her red lips and waved a bony hand. "Sit, sit, sit, how is a per-son to think with you loom-ing over them."

Worm gave a mute grunt and hastened to sit on the white couch opposite the wall of windows. His huge knees jutted out and high, as if he were sitting on kid's furniture in a playhouse. The three-bedroom penthouse suite was chic, filled with white leather, black lacquer, and polished granite. Sweeping views of the jagged Rockies formed a scenic backdrop for the sitting and dining area. Worm looked awkward anywhere he landed, she decided, but more so here, wearing his enormous black suit in this creamy modern suite.

"By the time we get the Ranch back, our master will be worshipped openly," Vera said, as her eyes searched the stone coffee table for her cigarettes. "Then we will welcome newcomers daily."

She spied her gold cigarette case on the credenza behind a second couch, just as Worm, whose eyes had eagerly followed her wandering gaze, launched himself from his seat (no small task) to outfit her with a lit cigarette. She allowed him to perform the service then brushed him back to the couch. "Ah yes," she puffed, "the world will be clearly polarized—sheep and goats, indeed! The sheep will be scattered and destroyed not gathered as that sorry excuse for a book claims."

She turned her back to him, fingering the silk drapes, thinking of the many things she'd been shown…how it will be in the near future—how it must be. They would all have to do their part to secure the world for their wondrous master and themselves. Her eyes pierced the distance to the east of the Westrio Hotel, built and owned by the *Triune Ordinatio Orbis* or The Order of Three Circles. One day, the hotel would house members as they prepared for end times, but for today only the thirteenth floor was used by the cult, while the rest was rented as any hotel. It was three miles to the airport; so in point of fact, she wasn't trying to see the airport but to envisage it. The airport would play a key role in the end times, and so far, each and every plan for it had fallen into place as neatly as a row of fallen dominoes.

Denver International Airport or DIA, which opened in 1995, stretches over some 53 square miles making it not only the largest in the United States, but the second largest airport in the world. As expensive as it was expansive, the total construction cost of 4.8 billion dollars blew past the original budget by 2 billion dollars. The airport's control tower is the tallest in North America; its runways happen to appear in a swastika-like formation with the sixth runway being the longest in the world and able to land any plane known to fly.

For the average traveler, the airport appears clean, well run, and modern, but for conspiracists, the DIA was filled with hidden symbolism, new world order secrets, and Hollywood illuminati riddles. The internet daily gave birth to new and wildly elaborate conspiracy theories involving the design and ultimate purpose of the new airport. So many now it was difficult to keep track of them, but keep track of them she did. Vera could hardly help grinning at this morning's DIA entertainment involving those outlandish murals. What was that site called. . . World Watch something or other. They focused in detail on one part of the 28-foot mural titled, *The Children of the World Dream of Peace.*

She pictured the four colorful murals, painted by Chicano artist Leo Tanguma. They covered the walls of the baggage claim area and stumped travelers daily with their confusing array of images. The four murals were divided into two sets of two. Dominating the first diptych, or set, a massive skeleton in Nazi uniform holds a giant machine gun in one hand and an equally oversized scimitar in the other. The point of the scimitar threatens to obliterate a white dove. The second half of that diptych shows happy children dressed in costumes from around the world, holding their country's flag and handing their weapons to a German child in the center. The next diptych, titled *In Peace and harmony with Nature*, depicts environmental destruction of the earth with dead animals and children in coffins, burning forests, and smoke. In the second half of that set, happy children frolic, surrounded by live animals and colorful landscapes.

It was impossible for her to imagine any murals with more disturbing imagery, controversial metaphors, or confusing symbolism. The artist had unwittingly outdone himself, as far as the secret objectives of *Triune Ordinatio Orbis.* His murals were so jamb packed and open to interpretation they quickly became the target of every wacko group out there, and for *Triune Orbis*, the more and wilder the theories, the better. While the average person might find the images baffling and disturbing, they could, at the same time, be expected to distance themselves from crazy conspiracy talk. Eventually educated minds will be closed to all talk or even news of anything odd at the airport. News media will scoff at stories of mysterious plans of the new world order or secret underground buildings. Their plan of hiding in plain sight was ingenious.

When the elders were given this plan, Vera had to admit it seemed far-reaching. The idea of concealing something as large as an underground headquarters capable of holding friend and enemy alike, large enough for extermination chambers, and tunnels wide enough to drive a Mac truck through, even for his greatness, seemed beyond attainable. But they were in the midst of it now, and the plan was working beautifully. In phase one, Tri-O had orchestrated the planning, funding, and design of the airport using every political and social connection they had. Elders formed the New World Airport Commission using Coloradan business leaders and philanthropists to further infiltrate design elements and manage events surrounding the airport's opening. The phony commission was dismantled after its work was done with very little paper trail left behind. Through the commission, Tri-O had been able to implant myriad symbols throughout the airport: the ominous rearing steed with laser eyes; messages of black suns; sacred Navajo mountains; riddles in the ridiculously expensive granite floors; and the capstone with Masonic symbols. All of this and more was slipped in during the planning stages with no fanfare, no explanations, and—thanks to well-placed cult members—no opposition. What fun it was too! It took a little time, of course, but daily, the conspiracy theories flourished just as they had planned.

Meanwhile, behind the scenes, a massive coordinating effort reaching to the highest levels played out in the construction of the airport. No less than five construction companies and dozens more in minor roles oversaw different legs of the project. It proved even more difficult than expected to assure that no one company or group could ascertain the scope of the work. However, the constant changing of the guard as it were along with the colossal size of the project, allowed the entire network of underground tunnels and buildings to be secretly built. Only the most trusted Tri-O members were a constant workforce—and there were hundreds of them—working day and night for nearly a decade.

Vera's mind returned to the entertainment of the latest theory concerning the murals. It began when a crazy website had surmised that the mural was nothing less than a blueprint of the New World Order's plan for whole scale genocide using Australia Antigen. Most of the speculation sprang from the depiction of a miner's cart with the letters Au Ag in it. These are chemistry symbols from the Periodic Table of Elements for gold and silver, both mined in the Colorado Mountains. The artist Tanguma, who had simply wanted to paint gold and silver bars, was asked to use the letters instead. The theory was downright silly. After all, it was not as if someone could wreak havoc on society using Australia Antigen, which indeed is sometimes abbreviated Au Ag, the Antigen for Hepatitis B. Exposing populations to an antigen is not the same as exposing them to the virus itself, Vera laughed. It would be more like inoculating the world against Hepatitis B. Yet, planting the letters instead of a clearer image of gold and silver had served its purpose and spun yet another wild theory. Vera coughed a smoker's laugh to herself. Worm cocked his giant head, looking for the reason for her laugh.

The airport and all the other bunkers lay in wait until all was ready for his purpose. Those days ahead would be triumphant...

Naturally, much depended upon the fate of Angela Miller. She saw the girl, an insignificant waif cowering in a shelter for women off the Las Vegas strip—or had seen her until somehow last night when she'd lost her. Vera had already been able to incite that pimp to beat her hard enough that she lost the newly created life in her womb. The partial possession, Vera's first of another soul, had been mildly amusing. Monkeys like Eddie, weak and evil, were as susceptible to impression as silly putty to a comic strip.

Miller could be turned, alright. A little tramp, feeling unloved, surrounded by users of drugs and sex. To all she met, she was nothing but a piece of meat, an object to be used and discarded. She retained no ties to family or friends. In short, she had no one; she was no one. Angela Miller could be turned before she ever knew the reason for her existence and her mission as protector. Should they not be able to turn her . . . she would have to be destroyed at all costs. Vera saw

183

clearly what the girl was, and more importantly, what she would become. At the moment, she was safe in that shelter. She couldn't stay there much longer; the shelter had rules, thank Satan.

"Love,"—Vera turned from the window and used the familiar pet name—"I want you to reach Scott Henderson." She moved to a black lacquered desk and chair covered in zebra fabric in the corner. She sat and fished in the drawer for a scrap of paper. Worm had noisily relaunched at the word love and was now hovering over the desk with a pleased-to be-of-service look on his huge square mug. She scrunched her nose looking up the tower of him and wondering at her sudden disdain for his slave-like devotion. "Henderson is to fly to Vegas and coordinate this." With a flourish, she wrote and handed it up to him. "Give him this address. The girl is there. See that he has someone there to follow her when she leaves the shelter. At the first opportunity, he is to have her taken. She's a dead flame at present, but even if she flickers, she must not be allowed to ignite to a flame.

20

One, Two, Three — Shoot

From the baggage carousel, Scott carried his brown leather bag twenty feet and dropped it, surveying the half dozen drivers holding signs. He stood uncomfortable in his wrinkled beige suit, tight snakeskin shoes, and dampish black tee shirt. Seeing "HENDERSON" off in the distance, he gave an obnoxious whistle, blowing air past two ring-festooned fingers until every eye turned to him. He waved to the uniformed man holding the sign and pointed to his bag, then watched the young man hustle his way through the crowd. Following the driver and scratching his blond goatee, Scott reminded himself to have a trim while he was in Vegas. He kept his hair long and slicked back, but at this length, it almost needed a ponytail. Things had been moving fast since the master's death. The pace was irritating him.

Outside, the pair snaked their way around the long queues of passengers waiting for a cab, and the driver led the way to a white Lincoln across from a line of yellow taxis. The kid headed straight for the trunk with the heavy bag, when Scott gave an *ahem*. The young driver dropped the bag and hurried to open Scott's door.

"Sir, I suggest you leave the door open until I start the car and air conditioning.

"You may profit from a bit a advice 'ere," Scott said, ducking into the vehicle his heavy gold chains clinking in rhythm to his British accent, "the limo should be left running and the air on while you fetch your client."

"Sorry sir, but your plane was delayed, and I had to move the limo twice and the gas —"

"What are you on about?" He cut the youth off and flicked a finger. "Stop fannying around and get on with it."

The driver placed the luggage in the trunk, went around turning on the engine and AC, and then exited again to shut Scott's door, which hung open waiting for attention. He climbed back in and looked in the rear view relaying a message. "Mr. Henderson, Mr. Lafferty is waiting for you. He said to tell you he was at your disposal."

Bloody well better be, thought Henderson. Guy Lafferty was a lesser, a powerfully rich one. He owned controlling interest in several casinos, including the newest one just off the strip. Lafferty poured tons of money into the coven and offered myriad services to the elders who frequented Vegas.

"Shall I take you to the Dream Catcher Casino or is there somewhere else, sir?" the driver asked as the limo pulled onto the highway.

"Dream Catcher, and call ahead; I won't be kept waiting. Are we clear?" The driver nodded, and Scott rolled up the dark dividing glass.

Only 45, Scott Henderson, had been an elder of *Triune Ordinatio Orbis* for less than five years, but in his estimation, he'd earned the position by every inch of his long clawing, climb to the top. His stamina came in no small part from his growing up in Hackney, the poorest borough of London in a cramped one room flat he lived with his alcoholic mother and her passel of smelly cats. He lied to gain his first position as a bank clerk and continued to hone his craft (of lying) throughout his career. It wasn't long before he fully understood wealth was meaningless without power, and he spent every drop of his blood and every waking hour scheming to gain both. When it all hits the fan, as they say, Scott would be in the best position to rule with the Master's elite.

The limousine turned off the strip onto Tropicana Ave. and soon pulled up the circular drive of the Dream Catcher Casino. Wind carried a light spray from the imposing water feature over Scott, and he scanned the two story high boulders and the cascading water. The Native American theme was echoed on the Casino building with

186

stacked stonewalls and rich colors of Nevada's red rock mountains. The driver passed Scott's bag to the doorman and stood waiting for a tip as if Brits tip. Scott breezed past him commenting over his shoulder.

"Next time keep the limo cool, consider that your tip."

Indian themed casinos are all about expressing the tribal culture through the décor, and *Dream Catcher* did it in a most upscale manner. Guy Lafferty had a knack for hiring the right people Scott thought, looking beyond the main lobby to the casino floor. Beneath the clanging slot machines and busy tables, the carpet looked like a traditional Navaho blanket. The tables and chairs were covered in warm earth tones of beige, browns, and rust and the chandeliers had pops of turquoise the color of Native American jewelry. Equally impressive the lobby's ceiling mimicked the waves and swells of desert sand, as did the sweeping curves of the teak front desk. Scott walked toward it when Guy Lafferty hustled forward his hand extended for a shake.

"All right?" Scott said, ignoring the gesture. "We'll just have a *dekko* and get settled. You come round 'bout 'alf an 'our then, right?" Scott turned to the elevator.

Lafferty snapped his fingers and signaled the bellhop, handing him the key saying, "Show Mr. Henderson up and get him anything he desires immediately.

Half an hour later, Henderson was more than settled with a martini in one hand and the hotel manicurist bent over the other. Lafferty was let in by the personal butler who came with the 5,000 square foot $10,000 a night penthouse suite. Their talk was brief. Lafferty made several phone calls, and two of his best men were sent to collect one Angela Miller, who'd been *seen* outside Golden Nugget on Freemont.

* * *

Late afternoon sun streamed under the canopy. This morning's coffee and two doughnuts helped take the edge off, but Angela's stomach still snarled. Either her ribs were less sore, or hunger was masking the pain. Pacing back and forth between Golden Gate and Golden Nugget on Freemont, Angela decided whether to wander inside by the bar where she might score a handful of nuts before being shown out. Better yet, maybe she could score a pity dollar or two and buy some ninety-nine cent shrimp. *Oh, that would be so good.* Her head popped up looking with sudden hopefulness at passers-by. A couple of men made quick eye contact then looked away uncomfortable. Her purple face, no doubt. A woman, her arm linked in her mates, held Angela's eye with sympathy. Moved by hunger, Angela approached her.

"Just a dollar," she said, "for shrimp, I swear."

The woman hesitated, and the man she was with looked disgusted and gave a tug.

"I haven't eaten, please," Angela begged. Dead air hung above her in a humiliating heap. Angela dropped her head, her hair swinging over her eyes. Embarrassed, she turned and walked away. Without warning, something shoved into her hand. The woman tossed a, "God love you, honey," over her shoulder as she hurried to catch up to the man. *Huh?* Angela uncrumpled the three dollars—two more than what she asked. She headed through Golden Gate. Not twenty feet in, a suit placed a rough hand on her bruised forearm.

"Hey, you know better 'n that, sweetheart." Despite the message, the grandfatherly man delivered it gently. "Move right back on out now, 'kay?"

"But, I only want shrimp." Angela quickly produced the three bills. "I haven't eaten, please."

"Awright, honey, g'wan in," he said his eyes giving a quick look around. "Get your shrimp, and then off with you, right"

She thanked him and hurried to the back of the casino getting in line with the other shrimp eaters. She thought of begging off of the tax so she could have three cocktails, but she'd had enough of begging for now. She sat as far back in the room as was available and peeked up from her shrimp now and then looking around at the people. Several ate alone like herself. Two big men in jeans and Hawaiian shirts were talking beyond the roped area and looked over at her once or twice. They might be interested in a trick, even as banged up as she was. Lotta men wouldn't care probably.

She dipped her last shrimp in sauce when the old guard appeared and gave her a nod. *Yeah, yeah I know.* She stood and popped the last shrimp in her sore mouth. It hurt to chew a whole one, but she didn't want to make him wait. She needed to use the ladies room, too to wash her sticky fingers but dared not.

A blast of cool air whipped her hair as she stepped back outside, feeling better having something in her stomach. Turning east on Freemont with exactly 83 cents in her pocket, she stopped at a newsstand and bought gum. Chewing two pieces, she turned into Binion's and made a beeline to the bathroom. Afterward while taking a long drink at the fountain, she caught a glimpse of the same two men she'd seen at Golden Gate. One was bigger than the other, both looked like lineman and neither looked like your typical tourist. Oh brother, last thing she wanted was to turn a trick. She had to get off Freemont, especially as it got later, or someone might tell Eddy they saw her.

She breezed out of Binion's and continued past Freemont Casino and Four Queens. Fitzgerald's was coming up, and she debated what to do at the intersection. *Unbelievable, there they are. Those two don't give up. Jeesh!* She quickly decided to turn north down Third with no plan except to stay away from Eddy and lose these two johns.

Expecting them to leave her alone now that she was leaving Freemont, she half turned to see if they were gone. *Nope!* They seemed to step it up as she looked at them. Her chest took a dive; her eyes whipped left and right hoping to see another soul. What could they want? It should be obvious she had no money— that left rape. She swallowed her fear telling herself to think as she crossed Ogden Ave. Where was everybody? *I am not going down.* She broke into an unabashed run towards the closed down Lady Luck ahead, following a chain link fence covered in green canvas. At the end of Third Street, she was coming fast to a barrier of cement blocking traffic for construction. Hearing their heavy footfall behind her, she turned the corner of Lady Luck. Panicked, she pushed on a steel door then another door just beyond that. The abandoned casino was locked tight. She came to a cement wall. Sticking out of it, about two feet up was a meter of some sort. Without much thought, Angela stepped on it, hoisted herself over the wall, and pinned her back to the cement. She held her breath hearing the two men clomp past. From where she stood, she could see their heads, but the wall ended in more chain link fence, and if they turned, they would see her through the fence.

189

Angela ducked behind an air conditioner unit and prayed they would just give up. As soon as they were out of sight, she cut across an open dirt area and headed up a delivery ramp ducking in behind giant hanging flaps. In the dark, her eyes worked to adjust while her heart slowed down a notch. She stepped tentatively into a warehouse like space, surprised to find the bay wide open. Late sun slanted through a high window revealing pallets of building materials piled high and wrapped in thick plastic Straight ahead was a door. She heard the two men yell something outside and then heard the fence rattle.

Oh God, they know I'm in here! Please be open; please be open, she begged tearing across the space. The heavy door was open, and it swung back hard banging loudly. She ran blindly along a narrow hall in dense black. Construction smells of sawdust and plaster were strong. Her ballet flats tapped softly on a cement floor, and her hand ran along the wall covered in drywall dust.

The Lady Luck Casino had been closed since February of that year. After a thorough gutting, it lay like an empty carcass awaiting renovation. The cavernous space was a skeleton maze of cinderblock walls, steel beams, dangling wire, and exposed pipes. Little light slipped by the boarded up windows helping Angela dodge stray tools of sledge hammers, bolt cutters, shovels and five gallon buckets. Heavy footfalls echoed in the space as she plastered herself to a cinder wall where it was particularly dark. She continued moving but slow and quiet.

"Friggin' dark in here," a deep voice peeled.

"Who you yellin' at, I'm like two feet behind you?"

"I ain't talkin' to you." The deeper voice boomed, "I'm talking to Angela."

What? Did they just say my name?

"Come on, sweetheart. You know we got you now," the voice continued but headed away from her. "Maybe if you come out now, we'll go easy on you!"

She froze. How did they know her name? Eddy? He wouldn't pay for goons . . . would he? She continued moving trying not to make a sound until the wall opened to what in the dark light looked like a giant room. Sheets of plastic hung in some crazy pattern. She ventured forward to a stack of drywall. Feeling her way around it, the

190

second man called, "Yoo-hoo, Angela." Her panic intensified, and she sped forward knocking into a bucket and shovel.

A loud clank resounded in the yawning space as the metal shovel bounced to the floor. Simultaneous with this the sound of running feet drew closer. Her eyes scanned the ground for something to defend herself. She picked up the shovel, but quickly pictured them catching the end as she swung. She tossed it down making a second clang. Through some plastic, she made out a crate with something big on top of it. She tried to lift the plastic then to tear it down, but it was stapled firmly between two by fours above and below. Like mouse in a plastic maze, she moved along till she finally reached the crate and found the something was a huge nail gun. She picked it up, just as a thin glow flashed through the layers of plastic. The men were using cell phones to light their way. She tried to control her terror and function with logic. Weighing about eight pounds, the nail gun had no wire and no air hose. It was combustion driven. Angela remembered learning about them in a shop class. The teacher had a table of different examples, and they wasted a whole class on the safety issues involved as if the kids were all slated for construction jobs. Every gun is different; some fire sequentially, some you just hold the safety and the trigger at the same time. Most would only release a nail though if the end is in contact with something solid. She had to figure out the gun.

"Angelaaaaa." The voice was high and whispery.

She yelled "No" in her head, squatted, and held the gun to the floor pulling the trigger. Nothing.

"Hal, I see her."

"Where?"

"Through there."

Angela heard a familiar sound of a switchblade opening. She jumped up and began following the maze of plastic again. She heard the knife slashing through the thick plastic. These two had no intention of working the maze. A yelp escaped her when right behind her a knife flew down parting the plastic.

"Gotcha darling."

A hand shot between the plastic and laid hold of her arm. Angela screamed, at the same time swinging the heavy gun up towards the man's head. There was a pop and hiss, followed by a piercing scream. Angela was thrown backward landing on the floor. It took a second to process the scene lit in the blue haze of his dropped cell phone. His body fell back into the plastic, his right eyebrow pierced with a three-inch nail, blood streaming down his face. He rolled in the sheet of plastic, his body jerking uncontrollably. The nail must have punctured something in his brain.

She scrambled up, snatching the switchblade by her feet just as a second pair of shoes stepped over the plastic.

"Hal, Hal! You dumb whore!" He shouted hunched beside the still twitching body. "I don't care what they say; you're dead. You hear me? Dead!"

She shot around a sheet of plastic out to an open area. The sun had gone down, and only the smallest slivers of streetlights seeped through spaces between the plywood widows, cutting here and there across the floor like laser beams. Her eyes strained to make out a few huge pillars, and she dashed behind one peeking back to the plastic area and breathing hard. His cell phone light came first and she ducked back behind the cement. What now? What do I do? She squeezed the switchblade in her hand and wondered if she would have the guts to defend herself with it.

"He was a good guy, Angel-er; you gotta pay for that," the man wailed. "Who'm I supposed to shoot craps with tonight, huh?"

She waited till she thought his steps had passed her, and then she inched her way around the three-foot wide post till she faced the plastic area. She couldn't just stand here. If she could make it back through the maze, she might find her way to the narrow hall, back to the bay and then outside. His steps faded across the floor, and he threw a board or two—conceivably to flush her out—against the wall opposite her. If she crossed the open area, he might see her. Even in the dark, you could still make out shapes. She had to decide whether to move fast or slow and quiet. Could she just outrun him? Did he have a gun or anything? It was so dark! Her hands balled in sweaty fists. The space had such an echo, and the goon was anything but quiet, thank God.

He hurled another board, and in that instant with her nerves shot, she made the decision to run. She sprang from the pillar and ran across the floor. He was fast on her heels, the light of his cell closing in on her. Her hands ran blindly along the plastic retracing her steps, turning a couple times when she tripped and fell onto the other man's still chest.

"Oh, God!" she screamed clambering to get off him as her hand landed in a pool of his blood on the way back up. The guy was dead for sure. No time to freak, later, freak later, she told herself diving through the gaping plastic he'd torn down. Out of nowhere, a board flew at her head clipping her right temple and knocking her off balance. She clutched the plastic, at first for support then in an effort to get something between her assailant and herself. His cell fell to the floor, the light disappearing on impact. She yanked and tugged the heavy plastic, till some came down in a bunch, and she backed out of the way. "Leave me alone!" she screamed, ripping wildly at the plastic wall behind her with the switchblade. She jumped through the new opening and found her way to the narrow hall tearing down it as fast as she could.

Pitch black here, she ran smack into the closed door. With her right hand still clutching the blade, her left fumbled to work the handle while hearing his footsteps coming full speed behind her. She had the heavy door less than half open and was turning sideways to slip through it, when, running as fast and blind as she had moments before in the solid darkness, he ran smack into her. If the blade had been lower, if she hadn't just raised her hand to maneuver herself to fit through the opening, if he had been shorter or taller—his literal run-in with Angela Miller might not have been fatal. As it was, the highly illegal Italian Stiletto with a full five-inch blade sank deep and easy between the fifth and sixth ribs of Ernest T. Almand, ultimately causing his death.

Angela screamed, releasing her hold of the blade. The man slid to the floor at her feet blocking the door from opening any further. She squeezed through and burst across the loading dock heading back the way she'd come completely unaware of her own screams. Reaching the chain link fence, she flopped like a rag doll and threw up the remnants of her shrimp cocktail. Her body shook as she yanked and climbed the chain link fence. She threw herself over the other side and broke into a dead run on the sidewalk.

21

Drop a Spoon, Company Soon

John was out front raking the last of the leaves when Clarice heard a car drive up. She took a quick appreciative look at the piece in front of her, wiped her brush, and stabbed it in a jar of turpentine. Still wiping her fingers, she stepped to the French door and out on the porch. The maroon LaCrosse pulling up was unfamiliar, but the smiling face of Father Tom was as familiar as it was welcome. She waved and the priest waved back as John carrying his rake went around to meet him. The two men embraced, and Clarice ducked inside to scrounge up something to offer the priest. They could visit on the wide front porch and enjoy the fine Indian summer.

She carried a tray with three glasses, a pitcher of Iced Tea, and a bowl of animal crackers outside. The animal crackers were sad, but it was all she had, and they had way too many. She had stockpiled them for Jax and couldn't bear to waste them.

"One good turn deserves another," the slim priest cried, standing on their porch, She could hardly believe what they were seeing—not only his release from prison, but how much weight he had lost. He looked even younger than before. The three sat in the Adirondack rockers with the tray on a little table in front of them. The tension between she and John seemed to melt in his presence. It felt good sipping tea, each of them with a handful of crackers popping them in their mouths like peanuts at happy hour.

The conversation went from the details of Father's upcoming trial, to prison life and finally to St. Elizabeth's. John shared the news about his missing sister, Angela and her recent resurrection as the priest listened interjecting a few leading questions and hearing about John's wild goose chase on the Tracfone number that could not be traced. The conversation turned to John's parents.

"But as you say John," Tom said putting his empty glass on the wicker table, "your dad never expressed himself emotionally. It may be that he felt her loss very deeply."

"Deeply would be a stretch, I think."

"But surely they have right to know?" The priest sounded slightly incredulous. Clarice refilled his glass, silently grateful for his words, which echoed her own thoughts.

"I don't know if you can say he has any rights concerning her," John said.

"Everyone is redeemable. Everyone makes mistakes," The priest reached across and briefly placed his fingertips on John's knee. "My advice as your pastor and your friend, give your dad a chance—your mom too."

John was quiet and no one spoke. She knew he would not take anything this priest said lightly. Two seconds more and the awkward silence was broken by the buzzing ring of John's cell phone.

"Yeah?" John said, picking it up, "Bear." Turning to them, he said, "It's my partner. I better take this." John was up and heading across the porch slipping through her studio doors heading towards his office. Clarice lifted the glass pitcher and emptied it into hers and John's glasses. "I'm not letting anything go to sh-- . . . " John's deep voice carried back out to the porch and Clarice smiled apologetically. His voice continued yelling something about the business being his and he would always care about it, and what did Bear know about pressure.

"Clarice, do you mind my asking how he's been? How he's adjusting."

"He's… well, he doesn't share a whole lot with me… I mean we're…"

"It's alright. I kind of know how he's been to you. He confided a lot in me on his visits. He is a strong man, a just man, Clarice. He'll forgive you. He just has to find his way a little bit." The priest crossed his legs and rocked with one foot, listening to the echoes of Johns' raised voice. "Is he having trouble with the business?"

"He doesn't work the way he used to. Around here," Clarice said, her hand flourishing the air, "he can't do enough—endless chores, fixing things that are barely a problem, building stuff we don't need. He rarely goes into the office, and not even to the job sites. He's kind of been running most jobs by phone. Probably what Bear is complaining about. I think in some way he feels like he's even farther away from Ja—" She pursed her lips, swallowing the last syllable of her son's name, and put her mouth to her glass.

"There's probably something to that. I'll see if I can get him to open up more. He needs to talk, and if not to me then to a counselor. How about you? I saw an article about you in the *Journal.*"

"Oh, that. I guess it proves people will buy anything, huh?" she said, with more than a twinge of guilt. Here John's business was beginning to suffer, while her own career was taking off. Art dealers seemed to replace the Paparazzi press like new leeches, and in no time, her paintings were being noticed. "Just someone feeling sorry for us probably."

"$10,000 is hardly a philanthropic gesture by a well-meaning socialite. No, you're paintings have real value, Clarice. What did the paper say? Let me see," Father Tom said, ceasing his rocking and putting a couple fingers to his chin, "Oh yes, vivid surrealism, whatever that means."

"I'm sure I don't know." She laughed with him.

It was the dog painting that sold for the dizzying amount. An easy painting to let go, what with all the bad memories of that day. Those fiends from hell had chased her clear to the Glen then disappeared when she entered its borders. That was the first time she'd discovered the Glen's healing powers. But none of that mattered to the art crowd, who decided the darkness portrayed represented her fear for her son and the dangers he faced before dying. There was no proof of his death, of course, but the unspoken consensus was that he was dead. It seemed generally accepted that not only had too much time gone by but that too many deaths were connected to the cult.

They rocked pleasantly. The wind blew gently sending a few leaves dancing across the lawn. John returned just as another car made its entrance crunching around the long winding drive of white stone.

"Wow when it rains, it really *does* pour," Clarice said, watching Gretchen something or other exit a Mercedes Benz. She realized with dismay that she still did not know the last name of the art dealer with a slight German accent. She excused herself and walked down the wide center steps to the car.

To Clarice, the woman seemed tallish, not as tall as Roxy, certainly, maybe only five eight. The combination of the brown pageboy, very square jaw, and deep-set eyes gave her a masculine quality. It lent her almost instant respect of a sort, the kind where total strangers might listen and act upon what she says. The cigarette that had been dangling from her mouth as she exited the car was now being extinguished on the tire, and to Gretchen's credit, the butt was neatly placed in the door's ashtray. Her simple brown pants suit was topped with a handsome antique brooch on the lapel. Her strut was business-like.

It was only after introductions were made and while walking to the studio space that Clarice read her full name on her card: Gretchen Opdenweyer. No wonder, Clarice mentally shrugged. She paused for a moment before Clarice's latest work looking thoughtful then sailed into John's space uninvited and sat down in one of the two leather high-backs in front of his desk. Clarice sat in the other, hoping John would not come in thinking she'd initiated this office hijack. Gretchen flashed a toothy smile. Her smile, thankfully rare, was notable for her teeth were large, and when too much of them showed, she looked almost frightening. As distasteful as it was to behold, the awkward smile seemed equally unpleasant to the bearer as if she were remembering to smile and then forcing her lips apart to comply with a social convention of which her nature could not see the point nor understand the need. One quickly preferred her natural demeanor, a blank hardness that was nevertheless comforting in its professional sincerity. Clarice pictured her cutting a tough deal with a gallery owner, or pushing ahead of a crowd to raise her bid marker at an auction, or giving orders to uniformed soldiers and cracking a riding whip.

"Vell den, let us come to the point," she said, and Clarice had to stifle the urge to giggle over the fact that there had been absolutely no conversation whatsoever with which to come to any point. "You are a very talented and desirable artist." Clarice looked down shyly at the woman's sturdy Mary Jane heels, the kind in which a ballroom dancer would practice. "You are, as dey say, hot...you are hot right now."

"But...no one even knows me—

"Know you? My dear, dey are ready to eat you alive. I have received already an offer for your next painting, and dis, I must tell you is from a client of my own. Unt, I have advised him dis is foolish, but now I have seen your latest composition...there, no?" Clarice nodded, and they both twisted, glancing to the back of the room. "Ja, I think it is most valuable; perhaps his five thousand dollar may not be the highest bid.

As Clarice's head spun with talk of art galleries and shows in NYC, Montreal and Berklee, John walked with Father Tom in the woods.

"I wanted to stretch my legs anyhow. I have never felt so energized John, so alive so purpose-filled," Tom said.

"Oh yeah, you must be relieved being free and everything."

"Er yes, and no...I mean my freedom is so insignificant. I tell you I get it, really get it now. I'm on fire." The young priest's step was matching his excitement and peppy even for Johns' long legs. "I have so much to do, so many to reach... and prayer, whew! I can't tell you the heights—it all seems so different, so much more full than before."

"That's great, Father Tom," John said, breaking a snag off a tree as they walked.

"Oh wow," the priest said, his fingers tapping his forehead, "I'm dense. My enthusiasm sounds out of place here...now, with you and Clarice."

"It's ok," John said, snapping the branch in half.

"No, I... I just hope you see a bigger picture; I pray you do, John." The priest stopped walking and regarded John. "Your son is at the very heart of my joy. It's spilling out because it can't be contained.

199

God's mercy is so endless so unfathomable. He will use you and Jax; you'll see. He'll give a broken world one more chance to turn to Him, one more merciful chance before . . . the end.

The end, John questioned in his head with no desire to actually verbalize it. They continued silently, leaves crunching under their feet. John wanted to talk. There were so many things he wanted to discuss with Tom, he hardly knew where to begin.

As if reading his mind, his pastor spoke. "John, about your marital problems... The longer it stays this way, the harder it will be to get back what you had.

"What did we have?" John said, throwing the stick with a sudden violence against a tree. "What was it?"

"John, John, your heart is so hard; It's not like you. Could this be more about the loss of Jackson?"

John showered before bed that night thinking of all Father had said. They had talked about his failing business, his failing marriage, his missing sister, his family. His body ached with fatigue, not born of work. There was only so much a man could take. How much more could he? The young priest seemed to have solid, reasonable advice, but he just wasn't ready for some of it.

John dried off and headed to the spare bedroom where he'd been sleeping for months. He lay on the futon, pulling a sheet over him and his mind turned again to his family. Next week was Thanksgiving . . . . He could call his brothers. They hadn't descended as a big family on mom and dad for years... He'd have to call his brothers, get them all to agree to come. Would they? Maybe he could sort of hold the news over their heads without giving anything away. They'll come. He found sleep with the smallest glimmer of good conscience that he was doing the right thing.

In the next room, in her sleep Clarice tossed and kicked the sheet away. She was running, hearing pounding feet behind her. Her fear was palpable. She heard a fence rattle as she ran into the dark. She groaned and stretched her palms, patting the mattress as if she were feeling her way out of a maze. Psychedelic images flickered before her, flashes of skin, blood, eyes, a glowing blue light, a huge yellow bucket, a shovel—none of it made sense, and all of it felt real. A blade of wavy steel sliced through a translucent wall behind her. In her mind, she screamed and ran; in her bed, she yelled and kicked. The flash of steel plunged again, and she was conscious now of holding tight to the cold handle, aware of it pushing deep into soft flesh, aware of warm blood oozing down her fist. Not mine, not me—her mind insisted. She pulled away from the one holding the blade. A pair of incredible sunken eyes pleaded with hers for just a moment, and Clarice awoke hearing her own scream. She flipped over breathless looking up into John's soft brown eyes.

"You alright?" he said, leaning over her. Her mind refused to process the question, instead drinking in the look of love and concern on her husband's face. "Reece?"

"Yeah . . . I, uh, I guess it was just a nightmare."

"That's all? You sure?"

Boom. There it was; the look of concern completely obliterated by distrust. She hesitated. Was he asking for details, a rundown of a crazy dream? No, he was making sure she was not hiding something supernatural. And she wasn't. She reached for the sheet, self-consciously shoved her bare legs under it.

"I dreamt I was being chased—no, not me. It wasn't me, it...I..." she trailed off, turning away from his eyes.

"You alright then?"

"Yeah, thanks," she said, and began to say more when he turned and headed out. The door shut behind him and Clarice lay awake trying to recapture not the eyes of the dream, but those of her husband filled with loving concern.

22

Run, Angela! Run!

The day before Thanksgiving, Angela shivered and rubbed dry, chapped hands over the fire in the rusty barrel. Of all the lows she ever pictured, this was not even on the radar—being on the run, eating out of dumpsters, ducking in and out of abandoned hovels, and living with the other homeless of North Las Vegas. In the near distance, lights and noise from Jerry's Nugget Casino played over the makeshift shelters of dirty tarps, ripped plastic, and cardboard. The shantytown on the twenty-acre lot at the corner of Owens Ave and Las Vegas Blvd. sprang up practically overnight. Cash-strapped, the city of Vegas lacked the funds to keep areas like this clean. They would clear it out, but the homeless would just filter back until the next roust a month later.

Her feet continued marching in place, warding off the numbness. Nights had been dropping below fifty. In desperation, she'd stolen a hat and scarf set, socks, and leggings from a kiosk on Freemont Street. She was a sight—purple mini skirt over black leggings, red fuzzy socks shoved in black flats, multicolored scarf wrapped around her sweatshirt and black leather jacket, her thick, tangled hair shoved under the knit hat. For the pièce de résistance, she had a rough wool blanket tied around her waist to keep the wind off her legs. She'd found the blanket in the stairwell of a condemned building this morning. It looked like the ones from New Haven shelter where Sister Eva worked. She thought of Sister Eva, of getting her help—should she go back there? Would Sister Eva turn her in? Angela's picture was on the news already, some mug shot from her last roundup with vice. It was hard to believe. Maybe a security camera caught her going in or out of Lady Luck. Anyway, she doubted Eva would even listen to a story told by a whoring, crack head.

Angela stared into the licking flames, telling herself to stop thinking. It was all surreal. And why she didn't want a snort of coke or even a buzz was puzzling too. With the baby gone, and all this stress, and her life crashing around her, it made no sense *not* to get high..., but the church, that talk with God.... Yet, if she was changing, why did He ...? Her mind refused to go there, to blame Him. She turned instead to her satisfied stomach—the dumpster dive behind Main Street Station was another new low. Probably eat a lot worse in prison once they catch her. *Oh, man!* What was happening to her? Why were those men out to get her? How did that guy know her name?

Her head hurt; she was exhausted. Angela pulled her hood up over her head and started back to the stairwell a couple streets away. It was her third night in the small, condemned building. It was safe and quiet, just a few old people still there waiting for the day they would finally be evicted. Turning in the alleyway, she looked around making sure she wasn't followed and then ducked inside. Under the row of metal mailboxes, she curled in a ball and pulled the blanket around herself trying to think of anything pleasant. She fell asleep thinking of the boy, her little boy in the forest glen.

"I've been waiting to meet you," he spoke without words, "but you are not ready."

He gazed at her his lips not moving, yet she heard his voice as clear and sonorous as a choirboy. The setting was as fantastic to behold as it ever was, and she wanted to collapse on the moss and take it all in. But she wasn't there. He was alone. She knew that.

"What do you mean?" her mind asked him.

"We can truly meet once you change,"—he smiled wordless—"Open your heart; repent not of those sins you think you own, but the one you continue to hold on to. Believe in Him and His mercy."

He moved to the water, waded in, his back turned from her. Mesmerized she watched him scoop handfuls and let them fall like crystals dropping to the stream. "What sin?" she asked him. "Which one?"

"There is only one," he said, looking at her briefly then turning back to the water. After a minute of silence, he spoke again. "How can you believe that your sins are greater than His mercy?"

Angela was jarred awake. Someone was dragging her out the door. *Eddy?*

Numb all over, she tried to move but found somehow she couldn't. Were her limbs asleep? They tingled. She made noises that sounded only half right and tried like mad to move her body, which continued to be dragged. She was on her stomach, and the person had her legs, although she did not feel his grip. A flattened cardboard cup popped up from under her, and she continued to be tugged across the alley over garbage and stones. She watched the pavement slide beneath her as she concentrated on moving her arms and then her legs. They moved an inch, causing the hands dragging her a bare hiccup in their progress. Her chin hit the ground hard with only the knit scarf between her and the rough pavement. She turned her head with huge effort and tried to yell and then just talk, hearing her own slurred words come out nonsense.

"Whoa, yer a live one, you are." It wasn't Eddy. "Can't wait till you wake back up. Papa's gonna have some fun with you."

"Hederelp!" She heard the garbled sounds. "Sstepplef Leveth mae lons!"

"Shh, shh, hot stuff. Sorry about the Special K, but it really is the best way—for me that is. I don't have money for someone like you, and you girls ain't giving it away are ya?"

Ketamine, the date rape drug, the junkie had stolen from a local Veterinarian's office took full effect somewhere around the third step. Angela entered the K-hole smelling urine her cheek thumping down cold cement stairs. Like a near death experience, she floated somewhere just outside her body, aware of what was happening to her, but unable to move. He flipped her body over and heaved her into an armchair. A phone buzzed from somewhere above, or was it below her?

"Damn," he swore, "Yer so fine, but I gotta take this load to Darrell, or he'll slice me up." A face hovered in front of her. She saw grey hair, grey beard, maybe a grey monkey. "You sit tight Alice, enjoy the rabbit hole for a bit, I'll be back before your buzz is off, promise. Hoo-ee, yer gonna fly sweetheart."

For a long while, she floated there in a kind of paralyzed limbo, till her body suddenly jerked. She tried to lift herself but fell back. She had only an impression of the room being a filthy basement. Two windows, high up and narrow, stared down at her as if they were eyes. A lamp behind a ratty red couch completed the nose and mouth of what now looked like a giant Jack O Lantern. For some time, she watched fascinated then her head flopped sideways, her view landing on a…lumpy turtle? The pile of clothes disguised as a sea turtle, the stack of books in the corner she just knew were the stairway to heaven, and the carpet of floating flowers masquerading as the garden of Eden were all very lovely and entertaining. But eventually as her head rolled from side to side, and more in-animates posed as animates, she choked with paranoia.

Forty-five minutes later, her fright was at an absolute peak when the grey monkey face reappeared inches from hers. "Happy Thanksgiving, beautiful. Uncle Zack's back" A guttural scream escaped her, and Angela thrust forward pushing the monkey away and lunging from the chair. Her body woke from its numbing slumber and flailed violently. "Damn girlie, set still now."

The monkey man attempted to trap her arms, but his touch made her spastic. The two wrestled and landed on the floor. Every move he made was met with savage ferocity. It was the other side of the K-hole, and Angela was fighting her way out like a cornered animal. They hit a table toppling the lamp, which smashed to the floor. The TV stand received a kick that sent the flat screen flying. Finally, the thrashing of her long legs and arms fueled by the maddened frenzy of her emergent delirium were too much for him. He quit wrestling her, wanting only to be rid of her now before she caused more damage.

Angela crawled away crying. She pulled herself up by the red-lipped couch, her hands blindly sliding along the wall till she came to the door. Her limbs were unsteady but useable as she climbed the three steps back to the alleyway. Her confused mind divined one thing and one thing only: Run, Angela, run! Her central nervous system, however, lacked the ability to run. Instead, with frequent falls in an erratic zigzag pattern, she made her way to the street. She felt stoned. Cars whizzing by sounded like chainsaws with a sluggish hum; buildings bulged out and then in as if they were breathing. Her muddied thoughts waved in and out as well, clinging to the feeling of danger and echoing...

"Run, Angela, run!"

And she did run, from street to street, miraculously avoiding being hit by a car, looking like a crazy person with her Lion's mane blowing in the wind, her legs slowly gaining control where her mind could not. She ran on blindly, crying with no direction except to...

"Run, Angela, run!"

And she did, down North Main Street, towards East Freemont, and smack into—

Eddy.

23

Thanksgiving Day

It went Ted, Marty, Rob, John, and Angela, the order they were born, the order they lined up in every family photo. John crossed the jet bridge into Orlando Airport wondering if they should snap a photo at his parents. It was the first time they'd all be together for a holiday since his parents moved to Florida ten years ago, not counting Ted's wedding and his own. As kids every Thanksgiving, his dad would set up the tripod and snap a photo with all of them sitting around the good table, the turkey in the middle surrounded by loads of fixings in silver dishes. Things changed after Angela disappeared. Of all his brothers, he probably took it the hardest and had the most resentment towards his dad. John knew there was no question in any of their minds whose fault it was. How could there be?

There are some evils in the world, insidious and quiet, hard to pinpoint, impossible to explain. In some they fester unseen, growing like a cancerous tumor, fed by an unfortunate disregard of one's spirit. For Theodore James Miller, Sr., such an evil seethed just beneath the surface most of his adult life. At its core lay anger, plain and simple. Anger infected and influenced everything in his life. If he forgot about it during his happiest moments, it soon resurfaced like an old debt demanding payment. His father paid the debt with bouts of depression, sullen moods, and surly comments, which rather than shrink the debt, grew it all the more. If a psychologist could peel away the layers of his father's past, they might discover some childhood injury or neglect. They might surmise that it was this unacknowledged pain, which had sowed the cancerous kernel. But John's dad would never seek professional help. He would never acknowledge his misery or hatred. And the worst part of it all, thought John, was how the evil touched the whole family.

John continued to baggage claim where hopefully Ted waited to pick him up. Ted, his oldest brother, lived near Toledo with his wife and two kids, about an hour from Orlando. Ted was easy to spot, tall like his brothers and himself, but with a build more like an aged John Wayne. They embraced in a quick, shoulder slapping way and walked toward the exit. John asked about his niece and nephew, but found that Ted's family was going to his in-laws for Thanksgiving.

"Aw, that's too bad," John said. "I was looking forward to seeing them. You know, you should let them spend a week in the summer with us. We have plenty of room. They could hike and see the waterfalls. We could take them around Ithaca."

"Yeah," Ted said as they reached his minivan, "we should do that." He tossed John's bag in the back, and both men climbed in front. "Listen, I know what you said on the phone, and I respect that. I just...I wanted to say again how sorry—"

"I know." John cut him off. "Can we just not talk about it?" John looked away, watching palm trees whiz past. He had made it clear to all his family that he did not want to discuss Jax or the murders or the news. He just hoped they'd understand and not press him.

"Hey, I hope you're hungry," Ted said, punching John's shoulder. "I think Mom's been cooking since you called last week."

"I'm always hungry for Mom's cooking. Are Rob and Marty there yet?"

"Lightweight's driving from Atlanta; he wasn't there yet when I left. So I don't know. Rob flew in last night. He's staying at a Red Roof, saving you the couch...and the old man.

"Gee, thanks," John said, deadpan. "How's dad, anyway? I haven't been down twice since Reece and I married."

"He's alright." Ted had his stern face on.

"He treating mom ok?"

"Oh, yeah, Johnnie, yeah. He's mellowed out."

"How so?" John asked, taking out his phone. He held it there, deciding whether to text Clarice that he'd arrived, still angry at her—perpetually angry towards her.

"Hard to describe," his brother said, "but I've spent more time with them than you, and—" They approached a toll, and Ted fished for change without finishing his thought. John stared ahead remembering their father's attitude when Angela left, his refusal to look for her, his silence on the whole thing. As usual, it made him boil. Even when they had discussed the possibility that Angela might be dead, his dad had nothing to say. That had been the last straw for John. In his mind, he'd written his father off.

At the booth, Ted tossed the coins in the catcher saying, "Believe it or not, I think it was the last time you called. You know, when you told him what happened to—you know." Ted's voice got quiet, "It sounds stupid, but…I've been praying for him."

Surprised, John surveyed his oldest brother. "It doesn't sound stupid to me, Ted. I pray too. I didn't know you did." John paused, unsure if he should admit something. He'd always admired his big brother, who was honest and straightforward. "One of the reasons I'm here is because of something my priest said to me about no one being beyond redemption and forgiveness. I'd like to think dad could change."

"You mean the priest who stabbed— Oh, sorry. I, uh…, well anyway, believe it; Dad's changing. He needs our forgiveness."

They were silent; Ted turned the radio on and both seemed lost in thought. His dad's sullenness, his anger, and depression were a cancer, but one that had spread to the whole family. Every member of the family was negatively impacted, and every member carried scars of his abuse. John erupted. "I could forgive dad a thousand times if just once, just once, he'd acknowledge how it was his fault, how he drove her away—how unfair he was, how mean and rotten" his voice rose till it squeaked, "how he treats mom!"

"He treats her well now." His brother slowed the car coming up on a line of traffic. "He's not the same man, John—not physically either. The Diabetes really crippled his leg. Of course, losing half the foot . . . ," Ted said, grimacing, "I think it humbled him. He relies on her."

They entered the condo quietly using Ted's key, greeted by smells of turkey and stuffing. His mom in a bright yellow apron stood at the stove stirring gravy and laughing at Marty's story. On the counter were several of his mom's signature dishes. She looked younger than he remembered. John placed a finger to his lips for Marty, who stood in the corner, and he crept behind his mom. He wrapped her in a bear hug and lifted her off the ground, planting a fat kiss on her cheek.

"Oh, Johnnie," she cried, turning to embrace him still holding the gravy spoon. He relieved her of the spoon, gave a lick, and said, "Needs more pepper." She smacked his arm and reclaimed the spoon. "Johnnie, I am so glad you made this happen!"

"Hey, Hammer!" Marty cried slapping John's back. The two hugged. John hadn't heard that nickname in years. He earned it after a bar brawl, when his brothers said his fighting style resembled a kid playing Whack-a-Mole at the arcade, his fist coming down on one guy after another. *Man, those were the days.*

"So how's the world of engineering."

"Still there. How's construction?"

"Same," John said, and looked down at his mom, who was rubbing his arm and smiling like a mental case. "Rob here yet?'

"Calling him right now." Ted said from the hall. "Red Roofs about five minutes away."

"C'mon"—his mom pulled his arm—"say hello to your dad."

John followed his mom. He loved her, and he respected her more as the years went on as he realized their dad's emotional abuse was aimed first and foremost at her. She dealt with his vile moods and sullen nature in the best way she knew how—silence. Other tactics, cheerfulness, helpfulness, servitude, all backfired and often made his abuse escalate. When he said something negative, she had learned to ignore it, ignore him. It may not have been the best way to deal with it, but she stuck with him for better and for worse and that alone won John's respect. He thought of Clarice with a guilty pang.

His dad sat on a chair in the corner, reading a newspaper with the TV playing a game across the room. His leg was propped on a short stool and pillow. He looked old and kind of small, kind of deflated like an old dollar store balloon. "Johnny's here," she said and turned to leave throwing, "We eat in half an hour," over her shoulder. His

212

dad looked up from the paper, but he didn't put it down. "Hey," he said squinting.

"Hey," John said back, and stood, waiting through an awkward pause.

"Cowboys are gonna take it easy tonight. Course they'd be nowhere without Romo. Mark my words that boy can play."

"Yeah, I guess you're right." John sat on the couch, his eyes on the set. NCAA college ball was on. After another full minute, his dad spoke again.

"This is a tight game. Tied 14-14. Miami's looking good though."

John quickly noted the Miami Hurricanes playing Boston. His dad and he had always communicated around sports. John heard Ted's words: *he's changed* and wondered.

A half hour to the minute, the Millers were seated in the tiny dining space off the condo's living room. His mom had put both leaves in the table, dressed in the Irish Linen she'd used at every Holiday dinner since they were kids. John thought Robert was looking great. A smaller package than Ted—and at six foot, the shortest of the three —yet he was always the most muscular. Rob sat next to Mom across from Marty and himself. The table was set so reminiscent of Thanksgivings of the past it was easy to forget they were twenty-seven floors up in a condo in Florida. Mom's silver was gleaming piled with mashed potatoes, sweet potatoes, corn, and stuffing. Miniature glasses were filled with Manischewitz, and the good silver clinked against the good china like chimes in a windstorm. The boys fell to catching up, and John stole many a glance at his dad and mom. He had to admit something felt different. His dad was watching them and grinning. His mom continued to wear the same delirious beam as if she could hardly believe they were all together. Neither face seemed familiar, nor did the occasional looks they gave each other or the almost shocking handholding.

The conversation had mercifully stayed away from Jackson, Clarice, and the mess back home. Stuffed participants quit filling and emptying their plates. John knew it was only a matter of time before he would be asked why he'd called this family meeting. He was thinking how to bring it up when Marty returned from the kitchen with a new bottle of wine and a few glasses. While sipping sweet

213

Manischewitz on holidays was a tradition his parents had never outgrown, his brothers eagerly reached for the glasses.

"So Hammer, whassup?" Marty asked, topping his glass off.

Everyone stopped. John was aware of all eyes on him. He pushed his chair back deciding to stand then cleared his throat. "I, uh, have some news. It's about Angie. I got a call…she, Angela called my house. She's alive." He paused to let it soak in. "She called my house October 23rd,… er, last month."

"What? A month!" Rob thundered.

"John, really?" His mom was frozen, a look of incredible fear and hope at once on her face. "Really?" she repeated turning white before his eyes.

John cursed himself for this dumb idea. What was he thinking? This is no way to resurrect the dead. The room erupted. Everyone began asking questions at once, even some that had already been answered. Where is she? Is she alright? When did she call? Is she coming home? What exactly did she say?

Hard to believe but within ten minutes, even amid the excitement and accusations, all the Millers were on the same page. Angela was alive. No one knew where. She was most likely working as a prostitute. She had called for help, and it could only be hoped that she had found shelter and that she would make contact again. His mom, visibly shaken, said she needed to lie down. John's father hobbling on his cane led his wife to their bedroom. The four boys quietly picked up dishes and put away leftovers. Ted washed, Rob dried, and John and Marty wiped and cleaned. Though somber at first, after awhile, they talked excitedly about their sister. Their voices, deep and rumbly, filled the small condo. All four agreed she would probably call again. Each of them wanted to help pay to fly her home and each surprisingly mentioned prayer.

It was an hour later, when the four boys were watching the game that their mom came to them. She talked in the kind of low tones one uses when someone has died, even though joy and hope were the order of the day. Looking frail, she sat on the couch between Marty and Ted, fiddling with a Kleenex that looked pretty well used up. Their mom, usually a pillar void of strong sentiment, overflowed with tears. That alone seemed earthshaking to John. Then she begged their forgiveness, and she begged them to understand.

"I know you understand, Teddy. You've seen us. You know how things are, how *we* are now," she said, her Kleenex-ed hand pointing towards the bedroom and then at herself. Ted's arm wrapped around her small shoulders, Marty reached a hand to hers. She heaved a breath and smiled bravely. "We, I, have a lot to make up for, your father and I. I really did the best I could for Angela, for all of you. I—I tried, I might not…" Her words were lost as the remnants of the tissue went to her nose, blowing and wiping. She curled the tissue in a fist and held it in front of her chin. "It was n–never that I—I didn't care. Not like I was made of stone or…"—her fist trembled—"I felt I needed to make you all immune, make you tough, show you how to not feel it," Her blubbering confession went on, and John thought they all understood their mother's reasoning.

"Mom, it wasn't your fault. He made us all crazy. He hurt every one of us and especially you and Angie. He—"

"No, John, stop."

"I won't stop! I'm sick of you protecting him. It's wrong. He was as bad as a father could be to her. He might as well have disowned her for all the love he ever showed. He was the meanest, son of a—"

"Yes," Theodore Miller Sr. barked from across the room. He stood leaning on his crutch, his face red and tear stained. At that moment, he looked if possible smaller than their mom. "Yes. Let them say it! It's all true. I was the worst father to all you children, and especially," his voice cracked, "to little Angela." The shock of his admission mirrored the shock on their faces. "I can't explain what ate away inside of me, what drove me to hate and anger towards anything happy, anything real. I will go to my grave regretting, regret…regret—" His voice broke off. He could not continue, could not even hold himself up, and he slumped to the floor.

"Oh, my Ted!" Their mom rushed from the arms of her boys to her husband. Robert closest to him, lifted their dad and placed him on the chair. He was whimpering like a child. It was unnerving to watch this man, who had always been a heartless crank, cold and perpetually mean, completely break down in humble shame.

215

As uncomfortable and embarrassing as it was to witness, their father's breakdown and his confession that followed had a restorative quality on everyone in the room. It was only a beginning, the smallest down payment on a lifetime of overdue charges. Nevertheless, each member of the family, whose deeply scarred past yearned for wholeness, saw hope. Hope glowed for Angela's return, hope sprang for their mother's happiness, hope burned for a new beginning for each of them with their father.

* * *

Las Vegas

"It's just like ol' times, eh Angie?" Eddy rolled off of her and sat on the edge of the bed with his back to her. He hadn't abused her as far as she could tell, although her mind was blank as to how she got back to the apartment. Chunks of fuzzy memories lay before her like puzzle pieces refusing to fit—wavy buildings, being dragged by her hair, a smelly armchair, musty basement, running and then…Eddy.

"Lucky for you I found you." Eddy sniffed loudly and stretched his arms up, scrawny muscles flexing through his beater tee shirt. "You so messed up, girlie. What you been popping, anyway?" He turned his head backward waving a ringed finger. "Daddy's very upset wit-chu. You know dat?"

Angela didn't dare move. She tried to wrap her mind around the fact that she was back with Eddy as he stood up and faced her. In some twisted way, the familiarity after so much had passed while on the run, felt weirdly safe. The notion disappeared quickly as Eddy leaned back over her and poked the same, ringed finger under her chin. "Give me one good reason why I shouldn't beat you to a pulp, Ange?" She debated answering but had no words anyway. His thumb and finger moved down slowly pressing the soft flesh on either side of her larynx. "You're good for one thing—whoring, that's all. You gotta heal up, or you're no good for dat neither. Ain't nobody want a piece of this black and blue leopard suit you're wearin'." He pushed her chin up hard before backing off the bed. "Say thank you, Daddy. Say thank you for letting me live to whore again." He grinned at her and waited, then snapped, "Say it!"

She swallowed hard and found her voice. "Thank you, Eddy."

216

He reached for her mass of hair. "Say it all."

A lone tear rolled from her eye, and she held his eye, willing him to see her fear—something he wanted from her more than any amount of cash she earned. "Thank you for letting me li-ve," she choked on the word and continued in a mousy whisper, "to whore again." Eddy used her hair to shove her head against the wall before letting go. He went to the couch and clicked on the TV flipping channels and Angela released a slow breath, wishing he had killed her instead.

* * *

Henderson was in one of the two penthouse suites in the Dream Catcher Casino Hotel. With sweeping views of Las Vegas and its mountains beyond, the 4000 square feet penthouses comprised the entire top floor of the Hotel. Both rented for no less than $30,000 a week and included four bedroom suites, two sunken living rooms and a grand dining/conference room, several wet bars, terraces, a lap pool, and Jacuzzi. On call twenty-four hours a day were a live-in butler and a personal chef, who stayed in a two-bedroom apartment behind the gourmet kitchen. When unrented (which was often) casino owner, Guy Lafferty set up house there sans the butler and chef. When an elder came into town, it was expected he or she would stay in one of these penthouses at the Dream Catcher.

Bearing his own small duffle bag and a heavy garment bag over one shoulder, and pulling a stack of Louis Vitton suitcases on wheels, Sergio stepped off the elevator following Emmett Pierce. Coming down the hallway, two guys in hotel uniforms were pushing a luggage cart of trunks vacating Mr. Lafferty. "Hold up, would ja" one of them called.

Sergio held the elevator door for them and one of them openly stared at his eye patch with a snicker. Sergio let go of the door and lowered his eye patch. "Take a good look, why don't you?" he said.

"Jeeze," one said as the elevator closed.

"Quit showing off, Valenti and get the bags in here," Pierce called to him already at the penthouse door.

They entered the foyer where Sergio caught a glimpse of himself in the ornate oval mirror. He was a sight— wrinkled shirt, a three-day beard, black circle under his good eye, jet-black hair sticking up in

217

unrestrained curls as his once-shaved head tried to reclaim its former glory. Yup, his eye patch was probably the least shocking thing about him right now. No wonder, those guys stared. The foyer space opened to a sunken living area more posh than any Sergio had ever seen. High ceilings, dark wood pillars, black leather, mirrored surfaces, and rich fabrics dominated the penthouse, more than competing with the impressive stretch of skyline. Still holding the baggage, Sergio was jarred from his gawking by a shrill command, "Valenti, in here, sweet cakes."

Sergio followed the voice across the living space to one of the bedroom suites. He disciplined his mind, turning an indifferent ear to Emmett's endearments. The consequences of even a moment picturing himself squeezing the life out of Emmett's chicken neck were not worth it. He entered the room singing "How You Remind Me" in his head.

> *Never made it as a wise man*
> *I couldn't cut it as a poor man stealing*
> *Tired of living like a blind man*
> *I'm sick of sight without a sense of feeling*
>
> *And this is how you remind me*
> *This is how you remind me*
> *Of what I really am*
> *This is how you remind me*
> *Of what I really am*

Emmett Pierce smirked at him or was it a leer?

"You," Emmett said and reached out to pat Serge's hairy chin, "are so predictable." He swept his arm about the room. "Put my things away then find the kitchen and chef. He will show you where you are to stay with Fegan. You will not leave these apartments for any reason. This," he pointed to an intercom button, "will be used to call you from your room or the kitchen. Otherwise, I will reach you on your new Blackberry. Keep it charged and read the manual. No funny business. And for all that's wholly evil, shave that unsightly beard?"

"Yes, Master Emmett," Sergio intoned, letting the bags fall from his shoulder. Emmett watched him as he began the work of unpacking. After an uncomfortable minute, Pierce finally turned and left. Sergio hurried the chore, but was careful to organize everything from socks in a row, ties and shirts hung by color, to bottles of cologne and shampoo facing certain ways in the bathroom.

Carrying his green duffle bag, Sergio navigated the palatial maze finding Fegan and the cook in the penthouse kitchen. They were talking quietly, sitting at a small island, and each holding a beer. Fadge, as most called him, had been a bodyguard for the elders longer than any could say. Every inch of his five foot ten solid muscle breathed to please the elders. He looked at Sergio without an ounce of sympathy or brotherhood. Serge knew, despite his unique position as Emmett's new lackey, he was seen as a traitor. He had abandoned them all to suffocate in the cave at the Ranch, and the price of one eye had not even come close to paying for his crimes. Among the lessers, Sergio was hated. He recognized the chef, a rotund bearded man, from one or two coven events, but could not recall the guy's name.

Fadge addressed him with a look of open hostility. "You're back there, the top bunk. Keep out of my way, ya hear?"

Wordless, Sergio brushed past him to the room, dumped his gear, and left again to shower and shave. Later holding a towel to his waist, he was accosted by the strong smells of seafood and by Fadge, who instructed him to dress in a "damn hurry" and meet him in them in the kitchen. He stood in the kitchen five minutes later.

"Bring these in," Fadge said, shoving a silver tray of something warm in his hands. "Offer one to Mistress Vera first then to the others. Put the tray on the table and get your arse back in here. Simple, got it?"

"Got it," Sergio said, taking the tray and a pile of napkins. Walking across the penthouse, he was amazed again at the breath and décor of the place. From the kitchen and servant's quarters at one end of the penthouse, he could almost get lost making his way to the other end. Landing in the familiar foyer, he stepped down into one of two, semicircular living rooms each flanked by two bedroom suites. Emmett's room was one of these. He looked about unsure which door led to what, when two wide pocket doors slid back, revealing the conference room.

Sergio was surprised to see so many top elders in one room. There was Phillip Cole straining a chair to within an inch of its life. Next to him, was Scott Henderson with his cockney accent, and then Emmett and some redhead he only knew was from Washington, Lyn…Linda maybe? Finally, the Neanderthal figure of Worm stood behind Vera herself, whose presence shot a gagging chill down his core as if he'd swallowed a giant icy tentacle.

Vera waved off the tray but followed Sergio with her eyes as he offered the hors d'oeuvres around the table.

"Emmett, dear is this," Vera said, wafting her hand towards Sergio, "to your liking?"

"Uh, not my type, Mistress, but he's easy on the eyes, and he's loyal."

"Humph, see to it he stays that way."

Sergio was anxious to leave, but remained bowing to Phillip Cole, who slowly loaded one puffy treat after another filling his plate as if it were his last meal.

"Henderson," Vera said, "she has a record. She's a two-bit whore, a crack addict for Satan's sake. How hard could this have been? You better start performing as an elder."

"She got away. She killed both my men—"

"Do you see nothing as an elder?" Vera yelled, her voice unnaturally deep for a woman. "Your men are dead purely by their own ineptitude. She is incapable of "killing" your men. You disgust me."

"Mistress, we—"

"No matter; I know where she is. And you can count yourself lucky she is in the perfect place." All the elders looked surprised and stared at their leader, whose eyes were closed. Sergio placed the tray carefully making no sound and was about to exit when Emmett motioned him to refresh his drink. Sergio retrieved the glass, headed to the bar in the corner of the room and commenced mixing him a vodka martini.

"Our little Angela Miller is right where I want her back in the arms of her beloved pimp, Eddie. But we must see that she remains there. The heat must be turned up with the police."

"There is an APB out," Phillip said, crumbs falling from his mouth like snow.

"Who do we have among the police here?" Vera said.

Sergio listened as the elders made plans to plaster this girl's face all over Vegas and even on national news, curious as to why this girl was so important. He handed Emmett the drink and backed out of the room.

"See to it then," Vera said. "She has to feel cornered and desperate."

"But why do we not simply collect her," Scott said, leaning back in his chair, "if you know where she is."

"Becaus-ss-e, Ssscott," Vera dragged her *S*'s with the same sound of steam escaping a hot water pipe, "Little Missss Angela will only be grateful if she is pulled from the gutter, plucked from the clutches of Edward, and saved from the brink of jail." Sergio watched a moment more before closing the heavy pocket doors. Vera pushed back from the table, and signaled Worm, who had been standing a few feet behind her. He dutifully stooped, and she reached her bony fingers to his massive square jaw. She dragged a long red nail across his ugly earthworm scar. "That is when ss-s-ubjects are most apprec-iative of all that the Mass-ster brings them."

Sergio closed the doors, unconsciously touching his eye patch.

* * *

Ithaca

It was late. The cavernous house echoed even the soft tap of her fork across the lonely space. Clarice almost drank Thanksgiving dinner, but stopped herself after two glasses of wine. The small turkey she bought remained frozen, and instead she had fixed herself a deli sandwich, fake potatoes, canned gravy and cranberries, all of which remained untouched on her plate. She pushed the plate away, wondering for what torturous reason she had set herself a place in the dining room using the good china and crystal. She pictured the handsome dining room filled with friends and family as she and John had imagined holidays would be when they built the place—she and John, Jax, and Nicey, Mike Barrie and his girlfriend, and Roxy with one of her colorful dates. The dining room had never been used. They moved in shortly before Easter and had still been knee-deep in finish work. Then Nicey passed away in May, and everything, absolutely everything changed after that. Nary a soul had eaten at the table, and Clarice had decided to stick her chin in the air and christen it herself.

Climbing the stairs, she felt utterly and completely alone. Her beloved son was gone, her best friend ripped from her, her parents long gone, Nicey too, and now her own husband was rejecting her. No one, she thought, I literally have no one. A tear slipped from her eye and ran down her cheek surprising her. Grief gripped her chest, sinking in as if it were the heaviest weight on the softest flesh. To her right, the door to Jackson's room was open a crack. The Glen! There everything made sense. She entered his room intending to view the mural she'd painted of the magical sanctuary, but the first thing she laid on eyes on was Jackson's bed, and she flung herself onto it, hugging his pillow to her wet face.

"Oh my, God," she whined, "I can still smell you! My baby…" Clarice cried and cried allowing herself the full release only such privacy as an empty house could afford. Bittersweet memories flooded her of lying with Jackson in this bed reading to him. She saw him running across the yard yelling, "Mom, mom, look what I found," whenever he discovered some new bug. There was Jax sitting at the kitchen table, his head of adorable curls bent over his favorite Ramen Noodles, or his following John with his eyes and imitating to a tee every mannerism of his dad, his glasses so big for his little face…. Her tormented memories floated over Nicey and Roxy too, and finally, with gargantuan self-pity, landed on her John — his rejection of her, his abandonment. Her cries, so audible and foreign to her filled the room. It was beyond her to know how long it went on. Spent, she flipped his pillow now drenched with her tears, and as her head resettled, her wet gaze rested on the wall-size painting of the glen.

And it brought…peace. As if she were there, it surrounded her.

Even the mural, a poor imitation of the *Silva Templum* as the priest called it, spoke volumes of peace. It was curious because she expected to feel a longing to return there and to be embraced by its maternal borders, but the truth was, as she lay in Jackson's bed, she felt only… peace. The Glen held her, rocking and soothing her as if she were a child in its mother's arms. After a time, staring at the wall, the enormous gray boulders, the lush carpet of moss and flora, the crystal waters—all of it seemed physically to surround her as if she had stepped into the painting on the wall. Her chin lifted to the chirrup of birds overhead, searching the sun-laced canopy for the feathered warblers. Their lone calls and chatty twitters joined gurgling waters making a sonorous din, and the heavenly choir serenaded her. She sank to the warm moss, absently stroking it with her hand. She drew a deep breath, pulling in the unmistakable woodsy bouquet, drinking the scent to her very core. She did not question how it could be, nor did she wonder at the reality of what her senses were experiencing, she merely enjoyed.

After what may or may not have been the longest time since here time itself was meaningless, she received a start, when all at once the rushing waters she'd been watching gathered and rose in a form before her. The liquid took on a human shape that appeared to be running. Very soon, the transformation was complete—the figure was Angela, John's baby sister. The scene of the Glen faded away, and in front of Clarice, as clearly as though she were watching a movie at the cinema, Angela Miller was running for her life. John's sister with a crazy mess of tangled blond hair, in a leather jacket and mini skirt, seemed disoriented as she stumbled in the middle of a city street with parked cars and tall buildings on each side. She was in terrible danger; from what, Clarice did not know. The girl's confusion and fear were apparent, and Clarice heard herself yelling, "Run Angela, run!" Something was closing in; someone was close—the wrong someone. There was no way to help her. It was horrible, and all Clarice could do was yell, "Run Angela run!"

Clarice was jarred by the phone ringing in her bedroom. She was still in Jackson's bed clutching his pillow. The dreams were still vivid —one of the Glen (was it a dream?) one of John's sister. Clarice's arms and legs and toes cried of the cold, after lying without covers. Light in the room told her it was morning, although still early. She swung slippered feet to the floor grateful she had kept her slippers on. She fluffed the pillow and remade the bed. She should probably wash the pillowcase…, but no force on earth could make her as long as it smelled even faintly of her precious boy. On her way out, she stopped in the doorway and looked again at the giant mural. She thought about the dreams: one filled with peace, the other with fear, and both as real as life itself. She wondered about telling John. What would he say? How would he react? Not well, she suspected. And why should she tell him? The dreams weren't supernatural, just dreams, right? And it wasn't as if she had any clue as to where Angela might be. Or…

"Are you telling me something? She whispered to her son. "Are you?"

24

Ghost of Christmas Past

Holding his bag at the foot of the stairs, John debated whether to bring it straight up or go look for Clarice. Things felt different. He felt different. He had stayed in Florida all weekend with his parents and brothers. They talked and talked, they ate, and drank, and even spent time playing cards as they had when they were young. It was quite the catharsis for all of them, leaving John feeling lighter, brighter, and more hopeful. He wasn't sure what he would say to Clarice or how he felt about everything, her deceit and lack of trust in him. Not clear what may have changed, but he longed to see her.

Clarice heard the door but remained seated in the family room where she was decidedly *not* reading the novel in her hands. She stiffened with resolve. She would not go to him; she would not open her heart to more hurt. She had had her fill this week. She was tired of seeing his hurt, of apologizing with her eyes, of searching for the tiniest spark of John's former devotion. It all hurt too much. He left her, and she spent Thanksgiving alone. He didn't even call to say he had gotten there. Nothing. He didn't want anything to do with her.

As she listened to John's steps in the entry, for the first time since Jackson left and John had expressed his anger and hurt, she wondered if they would make it.

John came around the corner. She sensed his presence but refused to look up. Why should she torture herself? How much can anyone take of rejection? She almost held her breath waiting. Why was he standing there? Did he have something to say? If he did, he wasn't saying it. She forced herself to turn a page of the unread book.

John studied her, looking so small, curled up in the armchair by the massive stones of the fireplace. He debated, but what was there to say? She obviously knew he was there, but she hadn't even looked at him. An immediate stubbornness rose up in his heart, almost comfortable in its familiarity. He went to the sink, filled a glass of water, and carried it and his bag upstairs. John walked past the master bedroom to the guest room. He closed the door to it and perhaps, he realized, to his own heart… and Clarice.

December began as it would end in an unbroken string of Bing Crosby Christmas carols. The month inched by, painful and slow, sad and so unlike Christmas past. Everywhere were smiling faces, laughing families, and happy children, or so it seemed to her. She used to love Christmas, the anticipation, the universal goodwill from shop owners to waitresses, Salvation Army Santas ringing their bells, grateful for shoppers' loose change, streams of thick holly and twinkle lights, office parties with endless fudge and pretty little sugar cookies, finding the perfect gift for your secret Santa— how could all of that, in the course of one year, one event really, turn into this mind-numbing melancholy?

Without warning and without a word, the week before Christmas, John had brought home a tree and placed it in the family room in front of the French doors. They had always decorated the tree together as a family, she and John, Nicey and Jax. The next day, she dragged out the box of lights and the box of ornaments. John and she were barely talking; she could not bring herself to ask him if he would decorate with her. She left the boxes there by the tree, harboring a tiny ray of hope that he might say something or initiate something. Two days later, he had put the lights on the tree without her. She sighed looking at it. It was after four; the automatic timer turned the lights on the otherwise bare tree. It was getting dark out earlier. Flakes were falling, and John was out—probably walking in the woods as he did so often no matter what the weather. She saw he had placed their small nativity set on a side table in the same room. She looked at the set, the tiny Mary and Joseph kneeling by the empty manger. John always placed the little plastic infant in the crib on Christmas Eve. Mary and

Joseph looked happy. Mary's hands were folded in prayer. Joseph's outstretched as if to say, "Look, look what we have."

Her heart jerked. Is this how she would thank God for her son's safety, for His love, which He had so clearly communicated to her in the Glen? Would she not celebrate the birth of Jesus, His only begotten son? She stepped to the tree and opened the box of ornaments. She began with a few strings of pearls then added the rolls of wired ribbon and gold and silver bows. It looked pretty, and gave her if not joy, at least a droplet of peace. Reaching in the box, she rifled papers *for* an ornament, pulling out a flat, gold mailbox—the first ornament she ever bought for John. It was when they were still dating. Nicey was watching baby Jax. John and she had come back to John's apartment after a picnic in the park. John stopped in front of the mailboxes and placed his key in the lock. Before he twisted the key, he turned to her with the cutest look of kiddish anticipation and said, "I love getting the mail. It's like Christmas." So, even though it was the middle of July, she found an ornament of a mailbox at a kiosk in the mall, had it engraved, and mailed it to her new boyfriend with a card that said, "It's like Christmas."

Clarice rubbed the ornament. *Oh God, I love him; I still love him!* She placed it on the tree and rummaged for another trinket. Ten balls, a choo-choo, and three or four crystals later, her hand landed on a bumpy odd-shaped something. Out of a homemade frame of painted noodles, smiled Jax sitting on Mrs. Nicestrum's lap. She held his gaze as if by remaining ever so still and concentrating she could make him real.

She was standing this way when John tromped in the kitchen door, stomping snow from his boots and beating it off his giant coat. A red-hot flame rose to her cheeks. It was too much. It may always be too much. She threw the ornament back in the box, closed the lid, and silently pronounced the tree done by hauling the box of memories back up to the attic. How could the most joyous season of the year turn into the most painful?

25

Christmas

Fat, wet, magical, flakes sank and drifted across the backyard. They touched to the ground and disappeared, some sticking, and laying gently on blades of grass poking through their mini lace canopies. Watching for only minutes, the lawn went from a green and white patchwork to a quilt of heavy snow. Clarice glanced at the clock over the mantle. Four pm, the tree lights would be on soon. She heard John coming down the stairs and was determined to say something about Christmas Eve and having dinner. They were civil to each other. It wasn't as if they argued or anything. They just ignored each other and lived as strangers.

"The snowstorm is not supposed to let up." John said, somewhere behind her. "I hope you weren't planning on going anywhere."

She was doubly shocked, both that he had initiated conversation of a sort, and that he evidently cared if she went out in the storm. She scrambled for words, shyly turning from the sink. "It is Christmas Eve…"—her voice grew smaller—"I was thinking we could have our traditional dinner."

He stood behind the island and peered at her for half a second then reached for a cup and poured himself a coffee. "I guess."

"Good, I uh…it will be nice."

"Yeah, okay," he said, sipping his coffee and walking away.

She took a deep breath. That was awkward, but at least they would eat a meal together—not just any meal, Christmas Eve dinner. She took mental stock of her stores. They had frozen shrimp and half a loaf of bread. She checked the fridge for celery. The stalk was a little limp, but she could revive it, and she always had onions. Plenty of mayo, so the shrimp sandwiches were a go. She went to the breezeway to look for canned oysters. Fresh would have been preferable, but any port in a storm. The menu was not a tradition for her family but for John's. The first time he asked her to make it, she gave him such a squirrelly look that he was sure she must hate oysters. Truth was she'd never had them. Turned out she loved oyster stew. The warm broth, mostly cream and butter was perfect with the cold shrimp salad. She scored two cans of oysters. No oyster crackers, but a pack of saltines would do. She set to work with a light heart.

With the meal prepped, she debated and debated about setting the dining room table versus the kitchen. Baby steps, she decided. Having dinner together, well, it's just dinner. Her feelings remained guarded, but Clarice could no more stop the glimmer of hope that sprang from her heart than she could a knee popping up at the doctor's tap. She set the kitchen table using the good black tablecloth. Candles? Too romantic. She placed the advent wreath candles in the center instead then left to change into something nicer.

In his office, John had been listening to Clarice bustle about in the kitchen for well over an hour. He had no idea what to make of this step they were taking. Is it a step? He buried his head in his hands praying. "God, oh God, why can't we get beyond this? Why can't I? Can you help me? Help us? This is torture." Every day, his heart grew colder and stonier. He hated it; it wasn't him. Stubborn, they were both stubborn. That has to have something to do with this. But if they can't get beyond this, this torture has to end…. John pulled his head up. It's just dinner. It's Christmas. Even total strangers would eat together if they were in the same house.

He left the room and strode into the family room spying the black tablecloth and good china. It looked nice. The stew was on the stove on low and when he reached for a beer, he saw the shrimp sandwiches cut in tiny triangles and piled just so on a small platter. He was hungry. He put the beer back and went to the wine cooler choosing a Pinot Grigio. He snagged a couple of their favorite glasses, set them on the table, and uncorked the wine. He decided a quick shower was in order since she had gone to so much trouble.

As she exited the bedroom, Clarice heard John in the hall bathroom taking a shower. She questioned her sweater choice, a soft pink angora blend she paired with black leggings. It needed something. She returned to the bedroom, fished in her top drawer, and retrieved a red jeweler's box. Clarice owned little jewelry. Consequently, each piece had special meaning. This teardrop opal on a silver chain was last year's Christmas gift from John. It hung in a perfect V on the round neckline. She hesitated. Was it too forward given all that they were going through? Could she bear another hurt look? *This is silly*, she decided turning from the dresser. *It's a pretty necklace, and I'm wearing it.*

John smelled shower fresh as he came into the kitchen. Clarice placed the filled soup tureen on the table and ladled some into each bowl.

"Wine?" John said, sliding into his seat.

"I'd love some," she said, controlling her smile. They began eating and sipping their wine. John got up to turn on the Bose. Every station was playing Christmas music.

"It's good," John said of the food, over Judy Garland singing *Have Yourself a Merry Little Christmas*. "Thanks for making this."

"It, ah, really wouldn't be Christmas Eve without it." They both listened to the song...

> *Next year all our trouble will be miles away*
> *Once again as in olden days, happy golden days of yore*
> *Faithful friends who are dear to us, will be near to us*
> *once more.*
> *Someday soon we all will be together if the fates allow*
> *Until then we'll have to muddle through somehow*
> *So have yourself a merry little Christmas now.*

Clarice choked at the words and found her misty eyes meeting John's. In a gush of emotion, she stretched her hand slowly across the table to his.

Bbrringg.

The phone in the kitchen rang, cracking the moment. John stood, leaving her hand where it lay, and answered the phone.

231

"Hello," John said. Clarice took a gulp of wine listening. "Oh my God! Angela! It's you. Where are you? Are you alright?" Clarice shoved her chair back and hurried to John's side. She could barely hear the voice on the other end.

"Uh huh. Yeah, yeah, but are you okay? Tell me where you are. I'll come get you." John turned around, looking for Clarice and meeting her eyes. "You can tell me, Angela . . . uh huh… It's okay. I love you too. You have no idea what this means to me—to all of us. It's the best Christmas present ever. I told Mom and Dad—um yeah…, Rob and Ted and Marty —it was on Thanksgiving. Everyone is worried about you. You know, we thought you were dead." The voice on the other sounded small and childlike as Clarice held herself as close as she could without fully invading John's space. "Dad, er, he's uh, he's sorry, he's changed, Ange. He—" His sister's voice rose some, and John listened with a furrowed brow. "Angie, never mind, we can talk about anything… Okay I promise. I understand. I just want to get you— I love you too, Squirt." John's voice became hurried and desperate. "Just tell me where you are. Ange, Angela!" Click.

He put the phone down. "She's gone."

"But why—" Clarice started to say.

"She said she just wanted to hear my voice again, to wish us Merry Christmas. She says she doesn't want to be any trouble. That all she would bring is trouble—she said something about her doing something really bad and how it's not safe to be around her. She made me swear not to call the number. It's not her phone. I think it's her pimp's. He might hurt her." John looked scared. Clarice reached up to hug him, and for a moment, he let her then pushed her back. "I need the computer. I have that reverse number thing to try and locate her."

"What's that?"

He yanked open the junk drawer for pen and paper. "Read me the number off the phone." Clarice picked up the phone and read the number to him as he wrote it down. "There's these advertising sites online with reverse lookup directories. You sign up with them, give them the number, and they can find out an address or name for the number. Same thing emergency and law enforcement have been using for years."

"I hope it works, John," she said, following behind him to the back of the West Wing of the house where his office and her studio lie. John typed furiously and finally looked back up at her. It's searching. It may take a while. If she called from another Tracfone, we'll be out of luck. If she used a cell phone with a plan, we may even get an address."

"I'm calling Sgt. Blaine and see what he can do to help." She snapped up the phone from John's desk and paced as she talked quietly with Blaine. He promised to help again and said he would call back if he found anything. She asked him to keep it kind of low key in his office, dancing around the fact that Angela may be in trouble with the law and emphasizing instead, the crazy media always hungry for another angle on the Miller family. Blaine agreed with that; he hated the media. Before hanging up, he wished them a Merry Christmas and said he knows how hard it must be. *You have no idea*, she thought walking over to John and placing the phone back in the receiver.

"Vegas! Clarice," John nearly bumped into Clarice in the passageway between the living room and West Wing. "It's Vegas; she's in Vegas" John cried. "Thank God," he said, suddenly pulling Clarice in and hugging her. "I have to get there."

John spent the next few hours on the telephone and online. He worked and reworked the number, paying numerous website companies to find him the same information. All of them promised an address, and John waited for symbols of spinning circles and flipping hourglasses to stop. He was on the phone with each of his brothers, his parents, even Mike Barrie strategizing. None of his brothers were free to get to Vegas. Ted in Florida was splitting his time between his family and job in Toledo and helping his mom care for their dad, who was home from another hospitalization. Rob, an event coordinator was running a weeklong symposium at the Mayo Clinic and Marty, an engineer, was actually in Beijing. John was determined to head to Vegas and find Angela even if he had to comb every inch of the city. In between phone calls, John and she worked on finding him a flight to Vegas. Across from each other at John's desk, their dual laptops were clicking away, but no amount of searching could change the weather. Roads were closed, snow continued to fall with high winds and ice, everything was grounded solid. It was a game of hurry up and wait. John's idea of driving south for a flight from a different airport was nixed. Even if he could make it down their unplowed mountain road, the sheriff's had closed Route 13, which was the only way to the airport. Cornell University had closed the first time since 1993. The "snow-i-cain", as media dubbed it, stretched across the Northeast in all directions. As difficult as it was, John just had to wait it out. Christmas Day came and went. The snow continued to fall, slow and steady. The house as quiet as a tomb was buried in the stuff.

The day after Christmas, John was outside shoveling when Sgt. Blaine called with the address. John was ecstatic, desperate to leave. But nothing was going anywhere. Conditions were treacherous; a state of emergency had been declared. John spent his time searching for a hotel in Vegas. New Years was coming and most hotels were booked solid and had been for some months. Ironically, the snowstorm itself helped him. A number of last minute cancellations of people from up north opened a room at a motel just off the strip. Getting there was the next challenge.

It was Dec 29, before John could leave. He headed down the mountain in the Blazer only to find out that his flight from Ithaca was overbooked, and he would have to wait for another. He reasoned, he yelled, he begged, and finally the airline sent him in a taxi two hours away to Scranton where he could board a flight to Vegas with two stops—Chicago and LA. The schedule was tight and many of the roads still bad, but the snow had stopped. By the time he reached Scranton airport, he had barely twenty minutes till takeoff. John ran through the airport sure he would break any gate that tried to bar his way. Had he known what lay ahead, he would have gladly missed the flight. He was the last to board, and everything seemed on schedule for this leg of the trip to Chicago. But the plane had other plans. Mechanical problems landed them in Cleveland, Ohio.

John stood in yet another line punching numbers in his phone as fast as he could in a race with two hundred other misplaced fliers. What a nightmare! Every flight was a mess as airlines scrambled to get to their destinations and numerous passengers were stranded in airports all across the Northeast. John secured the best possible flight, which meant a five-hour layover in Cleveland and a flight to Charlotte NC. He was exhausted by the time he reached Charlotte. Only after arrival did he learn the flight to Vegas, they were supposed to put him on was actually booked solid, and it was booked long before they even put him on this leg of the trip. John was boiling, but at the airline's mercy. They put him up in a nearby hotel and had him scheduled on an early morning flight to San Diego, and from there a quick flight to Vegas— he hoped. It was almost midnight by the time he checked in. Fully clothed, he flopped on the hotel bed.

Next morning, bleary eyed, John took the shuttle to the airport, practically sleeping through security. He made the flight to San Diego with no other problems and the next flight too. In the Vegas airport, waiting in the queue for a taxi, he peeled off his winter coat, too tired even to marvel at the balmy temperature. He noted the time, doing a quick calculation. He had been traveling for fifty-seven hours, but he was finally here.

"I'm coming Ange," he whispered to himself, "hang in there."

26

Liberator

NEW YEAR'S EVE

Of our own will we are not free,
When freedom lies within our power.
We wait for some decisive hour,
To rise and take our liberty.

Still we delay, content to be
Imprisoned in our own high tower.
What is it but a strong-built bower?
Ours are the warders, ours the key.

But we through indolence grow weak.
Our warders, fed with power so long,
Become at last our lords indeed.
We vainly threaten, vainly seek
To move their truth. The bars are strong.
We dash against them till we bleed.

                    Robert Fuller Murray

"It's time, Love," Vera said turning from the window and patting Worm's giant cheek. It was nearly eight. They stood in the second penthouse suite on the top floor of the Dream Catcher Casino. Although the panoptic view of the Vegas skyline was not the focus of

Vera's contemplation, she noted its cosmopolitan appeal. It was likely the girl had never experienced the city from this height. The green lights of MGM, the towers of New York New York, and the ocean of lights beyond as far as the eye could see looked magical and would be as welcome to her as the Emerald City. Safe above the city that once enslaved her, living like a princess in a tower, Angela Miller would revere Vera as her deliverer.

"Should I take the casino limo or one of the vans?"

"We," she corrected him. "I will be the girl's liberator," Vera's lips curled at the edge in the slightest grin, "her ... savior. We will collect the girl in the limousine. She will be no trouble, Worm; this is not an abduction." Vera's eyes scanned the sky and squinted. "We will leave now before the girl receives... other company."

"Yes, Mistress," Worm said, his lumbering figure heading across the posh living room to retrieve the limo. Before he reached the foyer door, Vera shot another instruction.

"Bring another lesser, that, uh, Sergio character. Wait . . . No, bring Fegan; he is more stable."

* * *

In the airport, waiting in the taxi queue, John debated what to do first. He pulled the two crumpled addresses from his pocket, although he had all but memorized both. The first was the address Sergeant Blaine had given him of an apartment complex in Las Vegas. Blaine said it was as close as they could come. The owner of the cell had not given his or her real name or address when he bought it. Blaine had used the departments clout, getting the phone's server to use the GPS signal to locate the phone. He gave it to John saying there was "no guarantee" that his sister is still with the phone, or that the phone was still in the same place.

The second address was for the Motel 6 on Tropicana Ave. Any other time of year, the rates were low and hotel deals were plentiful. But for New Year's, pricing was high. His business was suffering, and the flights to Florida, and now Vegas, were straining his dwindling bank account. It was a little emasculating, too, that his wife recently made more from two paintings than John had made in two months.

The driver of the cab took his duffle, and John held onto his laptop. He climbed in intending to give the first address, but reconsidered. If he found Angela, and she was in bad shape, he didn't want to be lugging his bags. It wouldn't do to make her wait in the lobby while he checked into the room either.

"Motel 6 on Tropicana, please," John said, checking his phone.

"Ho, lucky for you, your motel's close and off the strip."

"Why's that?" John asked, noting it was now after eight.

"It's New Year's, dude. Strip's closed at six o'clock from Mandalay all the way to Stratosphere. Yup, four miles and three million revelers. Uh-huh." The man looked in his rearview. "Oh uh, you better know if you go out tonight, all the hotels close their doors at eleven and don't open back up till 12:30. It's crazy out there. Whew." He whistled. John gave a polite grunt in no mood to talk. He sank back in the seat and closed his eyes. Hard to believe he left Ithaca two and half days ago. But he was here and she was here, that was all that mattered.

"It is after nine, Missster Lafferty. What ex-actly is the problem?" Vera said, twirling her lit cigarette between her thumb and forefingers.

To the staff and clientele of Dream Catcher, the owner Guy Lafferty was the smoothest of men, always in command, personable, yet powerful. In the presence of Vera Wheaton, Lafferty was reduced to a sniveling, stuttering nincompoop. "It's just that... um, you see, we had no idea you needed a vehicle. Our guests, several groups that is, have leased them for the night."

"Is this," she said, approaching him pointing the lit end of her cigarette an inch from his nose, "how you treat your most important guest? Is this" —he felt the warmth of the cigarette but wouldn't dare to back away—"how you show your loyalty to *Ordinatio Triune* and to your mistress?"

"No, no. Please don't look at it that way. It's New Years Eve, and we rented both of the limos, and all but one of the vans . . . "

Vera turned from him crossing to the wet bar, hearing him stumble over some explanation of how the hotel offers transportation for any guest on New Year's Eve who find themselves too intoxicated to drive. Although she had no interest in a drink, she reached for a large crystal tumbler. His fumbling fear of her was intoxicating, and she was determined not to disappoint him. She smashed the glass on the marble bar top, the crystal shattering in a loud crash. Vera's hand made a twirling motion in the air, and the shower of broken glass lifted and hung suspended like a crystal curtain. Her hand held still as did the gravity defying glass. She glared at Lafferty, his face frozen in delicious fear. With a flourish, she flung her hand forward sending the sharp glass through the air. It stopped bare inches from his face and again hung as a curtain in the air. She approached him, each step drawn out.

"Misss-ter Laff-fferty, I have no interest in the van. You will immediately call back one of the limousines. Substitute the van or solve your little guest problems anyway you like. Transport the drunken sots in the janitor's jalopy for all I care." She flicked her wrist and the hundreds of shards tinkled to the floor in a melodic crash.

Greeted by orange walls, blond woods, and, he supposed, a minimalist décor, it was after nine by the time John reached the room. He sat on the bed for a moment collecting his thoughts. To lie down and sleep would be great... but if he lay down even for a minute, he might crash all the way. Besides Angie was close, and he might need the cover of night and the element of surprise. He had no idea what to expect. Sleep had been ruled out, but a shower was in order. He unpacked a change of clothes and jumped in the tub.

Refreshed and excited, John headed to the lobby to hail a cab. Revelers were everywhere; the small lobby seemed to have exploded with a number of them. The front desk had a line of people. John headed outside. Groups and couples walked in a steady flow towards the strip. The air was alive with party sounds, music, whoops, and hollers. Taxis lined the drive in front of the motel, but people were obviously queued up to take them.

"Excuse me," John said, to a sober looking middle-aged couple in line, "can you tell me how I get a taxi?"

"You have to ask at the front desk." The hefty woman said, unlacing her arm from her husband's and pulling her coat closed. It was cold out. John would guess no more than forty degrees.

"Yeah," The man said, "They're keeping a list, and the cabbies know who's next. It's not as much fun as stealing one in NYC, but it gets the job done on a crazy night like this."

"Thanks," John said, leaving them, unprepared for yet another blow. It seemed at every turn something was delaying him. His frustration had been steadily mounting at every twist and turn of this trip: the snow, the road closing, the search for a room, the cancelled flight, the rerouted plane, the overnight stay in Charlotte, the outrageously long hours in airports and lines…and now no taxi?? Another line, another wait.

"God," he cried out, almost unaware and certainly uncaring of the looks he received from the guests standing outside the motel. He squeezed his eyes shut and pounded the nearest object—a stone garbage receptacle. John struggled for control. *God help me. Please take care of Angela until we can free her from this hell.* He headed back inside to stand behind the dozen guests at the front desk and wait his turn again in line. 2006 was slipping away. It was ten after ten.

Ten minutes past ten, Vera glanced from her watch to the hotel maintenance worker cleaning up the glass shards from the marble floor. The loud hum of his vacuum stopped. "Fine," she said, "leave us." He looked about as he left, slightly confused as he and she had been alone in the room. Vera, in continuous communication with the legion, had been discussing ways to stir Edward Platzmann into further mistreating Angela this evening. Not that his regular abuse, both mental and physical, would not be enough to make her desperate to escape, but a fresh assault would make her even more grateful to Vera. It would be simple enough to incite Platzman. There was only the question of perfect timing.

The door to the penthouse clicked, and a second later, Fegan stood before her.

"Mistress, the limousine is on its way."

"According to whom?"

"Mr. Lafferty himself. He begged me to ask you to be patient." She harrumphed. "He got a hold of the driver and explained the situation. They were at the other end of the strip near Fremont Street.

The ramps off I-15 North are closed, and traffic is backed up for a couple miles. It, uh, will take some time."

"It will have to do then. Er, Fegan, you have been with us a very long time."

"Yes, Mistress." Fegan nodded vigorously.

"You understand the importance of discretion?" His head nodded solemnly. "She cannot be recognized. We will have to enter by the back. Clear our way of all hotel personnel. She will be shown perfect courtesy, her every wish served, but she will not under any circumstance, leave these quarters. Have Cook prepare a variety of fresh fruit and cheeses, and perhaps croissants for our arrival. Let me know the minute the limousine returns."

Eddy burst through the door surprising Angela, who sat on the couch watching the celebration on TV. When he had gone out to ring in the New Year under the net on Fremont, she had been relieved as she was anytime he left. Stuck in the cramped studio, unable to show her face for fear of arrest, she saw no one but Eddy and a few of his regular addicts, his steerers, and supplier. They pretty much left her alone. Eddy was another story. She knew his hatred mingled with a strange love and attachment for her. Their relationship, if it could be termed that, was sick and she knew it. It was classic abuser victim behavior. Verbal assaults, character assassination, subjugation, control, escalating to physical attacks, shoving, pushing, slapping punching and finally out and out beatings. She used to ask herself why she didn't leave, but now she was really stuck with him. She was wanted for murder. Her face was on the news, even on fliers stapled to telephone poles if she believed Eddy.

"Fricking crazy out there, Ange. Like people are outta their minds. Steerers are worthless with these crowds. Everyone is drunk and already high. Sold one ball, and a few doubs, that's it." He headed to the fridge. "What is wrong with the world, you know?"

"Yeah Eddy, I know."

He popped his beer, took a swig, the foam dribbling down his chin, and he pointed with the beer. "Your fault you know. If you weren't so f--ing stupid, get yourself in trouble . . . If I wasn't out there worrying 'bout you back here alone, I'd a sold more." He came around and sat by her, wiping the swill off with the back of his hand.

"What is this?" His voice rose, and he gawked at the garbage-strewn coffee table. "Why is the remote over here? Huh?"

She hadn't touched it. She was never supposed to touch it. He claimed she messed up the programming whenever she used it, which was never. He kept it on top of the TV; that was the rule when he wasn't using it. Tonight it lay exactly where he had left it. Why hadn't she noticed it and put it away? She knew how this would end, no matter how she played it. She stared at the clock on the DVD player and braced for the first blow. 11:45 PM. For her, the year 2006 would end the way it began—big surprise.

"Here ya go big guy," the cabbie said, stopping in front of a sprawling apartment complex. "Sunny View" he pshawed, "we just call it crack alley."

The meter read $15.20. John handed the man two tens with the words, "Would you—" but got no farther.

"Oh, I ain't waitin'." John merely looked at him. "Do you not understand? There ain't a cabbie in Vegas id wait for you here." His head shook like he were the referee at a tennis match, and he mumbled. "Ho's looking for johns, partiers looking for molly, dealers lookin' for business. I ain't got no business wit dat... Dudes getting all shot up in here...." As the man rattled on, John gave up and exited the cab. He walked away when the passenger window rolled down and the guy leaned over the seat calling, "Five. I give you five minutes."

The front of the complex was gated and locked. The buildings, however, had exterior doors facing the sidewalk. The first one he came to had a busted lock. Great security, John thought, breezing in. He strode down a dimly lit hall, (not dim enough to hide the graffiti.) He landed in a courtyard on the inside of the complex. Three long rows of mailboxes sat atop each other, half of them open or busted open. Not far ahead, he found the office closed and dark and gave a half-hearted pound on the door. He stood in the bushes to peek inside the lobby window.

"Hey chippy, what up?" a voice said, followed by a sniff. "You looking to hook up?" John stepped off the Rosemary bush. "You, uh, got some biz-nesss? Yo dude, you need something?" He jiggled a hand with pinky and thumb extended. "Cause I got you—"

John caught on and waved off his hand. "No, no, I'm looking for my sister," he said, reaching in his back pocket for the old photo he had of Angela. The photo was taken in their driveway. She was holding her schoolbooks, waiting for John to drive her to school. He remembered sneaking the shot and how she had thrown a pen at him. John looked up holding the photo out, but the guy had disappeared.

The long black limousine approached Sunny View apartments. Worm pulled the limo in front of a waiting cab and clumped out getting Vera's door. They met Fegan already, on the sidewalk. The two men followed Vera to the third building. Worm rushed forward to get the door, which, at any rate, was locked.

"Move," Vera intoned, and Worm stepped back unsure whether the order was for him or the metal door as it swung open on its own with a heavy bang.

Outside an engine roared, and the cab that had been waiting whizzed past. Vera paused in the barely lit hall, which smelled of urine and Indian curry. She turned, and her entourage followed her up a set of stairs to the second floor. The door to apartment 23 burst open and banged against the wall. Eddy Platzman's fist froze two inches from Angela's back. Her cheek was pressed against the wall, her eyes squeezed tight. Her captor continued to hold her neck, yelling at Vera. "What the hell is this?"

"Unhand her, you brute," Vera commanded.

"What do you think you're doing, you dried up piece of crow bait?" Eddy said, "You better back on out old lady and mind your own skanky business. Do you even know who I am?"

"Oh, not only do I know who you are, Misss-ter Platzman," Vera's smoky voice returned, "I know what you are."

Eddy gave a snorting puff and mimicked the old lady. "I know what you are." His grip tightened on the girl's neck. "Yeah, you do? What about this?" He took a fistful of hair and rammed her head into the wall. "Do you know 'bout that?" He repeated the slamming action. "And that?"

Twice more and the room went black for Angela, who slumped to the floor.

Minutes or moments, Angela could not have guessed as time stood still for her. When it resumed, it did so first in sound then in wavy flashes of strange faces, sliding scenery, and sensory motion. She heard the old woman's voice issuing regal orders like Bette Davis in All About Eve. She heard Eddy, indignant, bawling something akin to "you'll be sorry." She heard another man too, yelling, "Shut up." The apartment rolled like a ship on waves as she felt herself hoisted in giant arms against a brick wall chest. The sensation of descent followed, and her head lolled to one side watching the familiar graffiti and metal rails of the apartment stairwell skate by. That's when she heard the shots; there were two, the sound all at once foreign, nonetheless unmistakable. She felt herself handed into a car and enclosed in thin arms. Her forehead pounded, her back thrummed. The smell of stale smoke and perfume mingled with some faint odor of decay. The osseous fingers stroked her hair, and the raspy voice repeated, "Hush, Vera's here. Your free. I freed you."

John heard two shots reverberate across the complex, the sickening distinctive crack-bang of a gun. With a bad feeling, he hurried towards the sound. He had been walking toward building 1016 intending to look for number 23 and for someone named Eddy after a pair of very bombed and affectionate teenage girls in giant 2006 sunglasses and feather boas tipped him off. They hung one on each side of him, alternately using him to hold themselves up and at the same time kissing his cheeks, when one of them pointed to the picture saying, "That's Eddy's ho." He ran now, tearing up the stairwell and oblivious of the mad exodus on the opposite side of the 24-unit building.

The door to apartment 23 lay half open. John called out, "Hello?" and pushed the door with the back of his hand. His eyes swept the ransacked studio. A lamp flickered on the floor where it had been knocked over. A card table lay on its side in front of the door. He walked around it looking left into the room at a black velvet couch and square coffee table. The first thing that caught his eye, like a red lagoon on the blue carpet was the pooling blood. One step closer brought John into full view of the victim, a dark haired man lying face up in his own blood. He had a good-sized hole in his forehead and one in his chest. Looking about helplessly, like a kid who'd lost his parents in the mall, John's panic mounted. As his panicked eye scanned the room, it landed on the fridge. He could hardly trust his eyes, seeing a mug shot of his own sister on a wanted poster. The phone call came charging back to him—Angela saying she was in trouble, her insisting she was bad news and would only bring trouble to he and Clarice....

Oh my God. Sirens wailed in the near distance. There was no question whether the guy was dead; the scene was plain. The sirens drew closer. John made a quick decision. Stepping around the table, he snatched the wanted flyer from the fridge and shoved it in his pocket. John walked out as fast as he dared.

27

John's Bender

JANUARY 8, 2007

The flight back was nothing but clear skies for John and nothing like the fated flight down to Vegas. Thus far, it was uneventful, except for the number of drinks he had imbibed. He had two in the sports bar watching the game on a layover in Pittsburg. He was downing his second one of the flight, staring out the tiny window over the plane's wing and going over the past week.

He'd walked back his hotel New Year's Eve, using his phone's GPS to guide him. He was out of his mind with fear for his sister. What the hell had she gotten herself involved in? He spent the next ten days searching everywhere, showing her picture to everyone. Most people wouldn't talk to him, thought he was a cop or worse. Those who did give him the time of day looked at the mug shot with blank expressions or pity. One bartender called the cops on him, but he left before they came. With everything that went on with Jax and the media, the last thing he wanted was to alert the cops. He worried too that he might be causing Angela more trouble. *Jeesh Squirt, wanted for murder, really?*

This was a nightmare and damn frustrating. He knew he was hitting some kind of limit a few days ago when beating a path on the strip. He'd been systematically hitting the casinos, talking to bartenders, pit bosses, and dealers. His days had begun running into his nights as he tried to cover as many shifts as possible hoping someone would know Angela. He'd been walking with a stream of people between Harrah's and The Venetian. His head was down, making his way and minding his business, when a flapping sound made him look up. Someone shoved a postcard in his hand.

The scenario happens thousands of times a day if not hourly in Vegas. A card passer slaps a card catching the pedestrian's attention. The unsuspecting pedestrian takes the card or has it shoved in his hand. He looks at the card some ten feet later, recoils, and drops the filth in the street. John, playing the innocent pedestrian, had stopped to look at the card. Staring back at him was a grossly endowed half-naked girl — someone's sister was all John could think. John grabbed the guy by his tee shirt, pulled him up, and went berserk. He ranted about invading people's rights, foisting filth on the unsuspecting public, selling girls as if they were pieces of meat, degrading women, and well, he could not really say what else was included in his maniacal speech, which at any rate was lost on the heavy set Hispanic, whose neck strained left and right for rescue and who looked about ready to wet himself.

On Saturday night, John found a church near Golden Nugget where he'd been canvassing. He was early for the vigil Mass and sat up front holding his head in his hands. He hadn't slept, hadn't eaten, he was out of control with a compulsion for answers. Even in the barest self-analysis, he could see he was replacing his grief over Jackson, maybe Clarice too, with an obsessive drive to find his sister, to have her safe and sound in his possession. "Give me this one thing," he'd cried to God, "one lousy thing to replace so much you've taken." His anger had surprised him. So when he saw a line forming for confessions, John jumped to join it. He chose to sit behind the curtain, allowing him more easily to spill his guts.

Since he was a young boy, and especially after his born-again conversion, John had enjoyed a special grace in the Sacrament of Confession. This particular kind of grace would not have been noticed by many, but for John it was sure proof of his Lord's presence. It was usually a small sign, although a few times over the years it verged on the miraculous. Almost without exception, at some point in every confession, John heard the words of the priest as if spoken by Jesus directly to him — a private and personal audience with his King, who issued tailor-made advice, encouragement, gentle reprimands or instruction. The miraculous variety was so classified by John because the priest would specifically address something John had not divulged or even mentioned— something between him and God alone. So at some point in each confession, John knew it was the Lord and not the priest guiding him. This confession, although not of the miraculous sort, was no exception. When the priest with the Nigerian accent told John simply, "You can do no more," John heard God's voice and understood that coming to ruin would not help his sister, himself, or his wife. "Go home; take care of yourself and your business. Pray for your sister and wait for God's answer." John booked the next available flight home.

John thought of all these things as the pretty flight attendant collected his empty cup. He held a finger up for her to wait, fished in his wallet for another ten, and ordered a double.

"Tough day?" she asked, leaning over, her hand on the back of his seat.

"Tough week, tough year," he said.

"Well, I hope you get a break soon," she smiled. "Hang in there. Things always get better." She returned with his drink. Something about her attitude and her smile reminded him of Clarice. God he missed her; he missed them. He sipped his double going over the past, and fell asleep dreaming of his wife.

Clarice woke to the sound of John's Blazer pulling into the garage. She rolled over to see what time it was: Eleven-thirty. She lay on her back listening. Wind rustled the bare limbs outside. A slice of slush slid down the skylight leaving a beady wet trail. Roads had been bad. It was good he made it home. The house was thickly quiet; every noise resonated as if it were announced on a loudspeaker. The door slammed, the bags dropped, the cupboard opened, a glass chinked, and the ice machine churned. Things grew quiet again, and she pictured him in his favorite spot in front of the fireplace sipping a drink. She rolled back over and allowed herself to fall back to sleep.

If she hadn't already known he was home, she would have known two hours later when his booming roar could have roused a corpse.

"Where's my wife?" he boomed, "Where are you my ever-lovin' wife?"

She heard him clomping up the stairs, and she hardly knew what to expect. It was as rare as a literal blue moon that John was ever fully intoxicated.

"It's not fair, woman!" John blustered, throwing the door open with such force it bounced against the wall and back again. The swinging motion caught his eye. He turned towards it and studied it with an angry squint as if it were trying to pull a fast one on him. He was three sheets to the wind alright; probably four if that were possible. "There...there you are, my little Ca-reese. I am sleeping in here tonight. Now what do you think about that?" She was already up, sliding into her slippers and snagging her robe to go sleep on the couch when he came up to her. "Hey, where do you think you're going?" He slipped a strong arm around her waist.

"John," she said, pushing his arm without success, "you're drunk. You don't know what you're doing."

"I know what I want," he said a little too clearly, looking into her eyes.

Oh God, she wanted it, too. She wanted him; she needed him. But not like this. "John, let go. You just need to sleep it off." His gorgeous hazel eyes stared into hers. With his free hand—for his other remained locked around her waist not letting her go, despite her wriggling, which grew fainter by the moment—he took her chin and pulled her face to his. He kissed her, and she kissed him back. Despite his lack of sobriety, the kiss was familiar and full of love. Her resolve melted as quickly as a snowflake on a palm. She kissed him again and again saying, "John, oh John."

He scooped her up, but as tanked as he was the effort was toppling, and they both landed on the bed. He laughed, and she joined him naturally. She was inches from his face, which in itself felt like heaven. "Reeth, my God, you don't know, you don't even knowwww...what I've been through, what I've seen. Angie, she'th in trouble. She'th wanted for murder. Can you believe dat?"

His words, even half spluttered as they were, had an immediate sobering effect on her, for she had begun to feel tipsy herself with the elation of being in his arms. "John, what are you talking about?" He garbled something, and she tapped his chin and spoke louder as if addressing a child. "John, tell me about your sister. What about Angela?"

"Oh, I tracked her down, Reeth," he said, his arm swinging in the air, "tracked her right to a dead man. Oh, baby it was bad, so bad. Ho, you don't wanna know…Look." John began to roll, freeing a hand and shoving it in his back jean pocket. He produced a crumpled sheet of paper, which fell to the floor, but Clarice remained focused on John.

"John, who says she's a murderer. Who did she kill?"

"Nobothee," he whined. "Everybothee, I don't know. I just don't know…" His voice rose and fell away. She rubbed his back and kissed his chin. "I axsed everyone, Reece, all day, all night, I axsked and axsed and walked…Oh man,— His voice became high and whiny— I walked so much. I never stopped, I never wouldn't stop . . . I . . . Fadder Lawrence, he said to . . . but Reeth, she couldn't kill anyone… Oh squirt…"

"*Shh, shh,*" she soothed him as she eased out of the bed. By the time Clarice removed her husband's boots, socks, and belt, he had passed out. She pulled the sheet over him, and her foot landed on the crinkled paper. She could hardly believe her eyes. With her picture on it, the paper called Angela Miller a "person of interest" in the murder of two men. She thought of the dream of John's sister running for her life. Running from what, from who? Were those the two men chasing her? What did John know…what had he seen? She climbed back in bed and nestled herself into their usual position. It felt so good. She realized she had not slept comfortably since John moved to the guest room. She pulled his arm closer around her, lacing her fingers in his. Her lips brushed back and forth on the soft hair of his forearm, ending with a kiss. Tomorrow would be a new day, a new beginning. Together they could face anything. Her eyes closed, and her blissful relief soon turned to sleep.

She awoke alone, greeted by both the sun and the smell of coffee brewing downstairs. Sitting up in bed, stretching her arms out, she felt the day. Her fingers decided it was chilly, but a clean, bright chilly. It felt new. She should make a Sunday breakfast like the old days— a big, fat feast with all their favorites. But not looking like this. She hopped from bed and scampered into the bathroom for a quick shower. In record time, even blow drying her hair and adding a touch of blush and mascara, she was dressed in a pullover and jeans she knew were his favorite. She bounded down the stairs, and if she had tried, she might have found it impossible to wipe the grin from her face. She went straight for the coffee pot, one eye searching for him. She was balancing the coffee and reaching for the waffle iron, when he approached her. Something held her back from leaping into his arms. The stern look on his face perhaps.

"I, uh…" he said, looking down as if he were in trouble with the principal, "I'm sorry about last night—"

"Oh, that—" she began to interrupt him, thinking she understood his embarrassment over the drinking.

"I want you to know I would never have…, I wasn't myself…" his voice became firm as he went on. "It won't happen again. I promise."

Her heart sank. Her grin melted as completely as that last strip of red in twilight. She turned quickly from him and busied herself replacing the waffle iron and closing the cupboard door. It was amazing how fast her previous euphoria fell changing into red-hot humiliation and shame. Did he think she took advantage of him? Did he think she was just waiting for him to show up drunk one night so she could trick him into letting bygones be bygones? Every warm and wonderful thought of this morning was swept away in a freezing blast. It surrounded her heart in a hard shell, a protective coating. She would not be hurt! She would make as little of this as he had. She forced a fake smile to replace the genuine beam of moments ago and turned around to meet his eyes.

"It was nothing, nothing at all, she said, as evenly as she knew how. "You were totaled. I let you crash where you landed. That's all." She brushed by him, taking her coffee and heading upstairs, hopefully dismissing the entire affair. Except she knew by the third step, she would cry, and she intended to do it behind closed doors.

28

Life with Grandma Vera

February 2007

Angela came in the suite laughing, her hands swinging the dozen shopping bags at her sides. Laden down though she was, she felt lighter than dandelion fluff. Her packages ranged as much in size as they did in color, from the diminutive baby blue Sophia bag holding new makeup, to the oversized shiny black Neiman Marcus cradling a white leather coat. She was a storybook character, and Vera was her fairy godmother making all her dreams come true. Her giggling continued as she landed on one of the long—so long it verged on the ridiculous—leather couches. The bags flopped on either side, flanking her in designer labels.

Her amusement was owed to the elevator ride with a bellboy, named José, who was headed to the other penthouse with a cart of desserts. In a moment of girlish playfulness, she had dared him to eat one. If he was thrown by the suggestion, he was more thrown by the suggestee, decked out in designer clothes, Ray-Ban sunglasses, and an exotic peacock scarf on her head. A modern day Jackie O, she looked far and above the teenage prank she was suggesting. Angela was aware of the impact she made and took impish delight in doing or saying things 180 degrees south of what was expected.

They both ate one with the Hispanic servant giggling like a schoolboy, his hand over his mouth, looking at her and chewing with delight while his finger wagged naughty-naughty. José hurried to rebuild the toppled tower of treats when her hand dove in for another. He made an uh-uh sound then thought better of it and stole one more for himself.

Angela's laugh wound down ending in a satisfied sigh. She looked dreamily across the room out the vast window. How different she felt. Is this what money and security feel like to everyone? The question of just how she got so lucky waved somewhere in front of her as a warning flag one chooses to ignore. Grandma Vera had adopted her or something to that effect. The why was still a question, though not a question she entertained. She had been given an explanation of sorts by the old woman that first day together. She had remembered nothing but sketchy details of New Year's Eve, the last being in a car in Vera Wheaton's arms. The next day, she awoke in the spacious apartments she has been calling home ever since and was told she had been given a sedative.

"Drugs?" Angela had asked.

"Oh nothing of the kind," the old lady said, "merely one of my sedatives, sweetie. You were so upset. Don't you recall?"

"Eddy!" she had cried, bolting upright in the bed. "Is he alright?"

"Edward Platzmann has been taken care of. Your concern for the man who tried to kill you is admirable, I'm sure, but unnecessary don't you think? We must focus on you, my dear." The aged petite figure sat on the edge of the king size bed, stroked Angela's hair, and kissed her forehead. She introduced herself as Miss Vera Wheaton, "an old and fading socialite." When Angela asked why she was brought there and what the woman wanted, the old lady said she wanted nothing but Angela's happiness and well-being. "It is a quirk of mine in the winter of my life, to expend my efforts on the needy and the…" she paused, "downtrodden, if you will. Think of me as something of a philanthropist to those society has rejected and scorned."

Angela eyed her suspiciously while the ancient arms placed a handsome silver tray over her lap loaded with hot coffee, juice, and breakfast accoutrements. It was then as she sipped the best tasting coffee, sandwiched between the softest sheets, covered in the most luxurious down comforter, and looking about the palatial bedroom that Angela ceased caring about the why. Naturally, she questioned staff and those who worked for Vera privately and found many of them had been similarly rescued, some from drugs or the police, and even one from a warlord in Venezuela. All were beholden and all were fiercely loyal, especially the giant called Worm. Angela was satisfied that Vera was an eccentric with a giant heart, whose greatest pleasure was a new project, and she decided quickly she had no problem being that project.

This was her fifth shopping trip with Vera, and the second one in Las Vegas. On the other trips, two to NYC and one to Paris, she had flown on Vera's private jet. "With me, you can go anywhere my dear, without me, you are dead." Vera had laughed and laughed. Something in the sound of it reminded Angela of a child tickled to have complete possession of a sought after toy. Like a doll rescued from the island of misfit toys, Angela was content to be pampered and saw nothing harmful in being owned.

Across the hall from Angela, with a giant grin as if he were enjoying a private laugh, José wheeled the dessert cart past Sergio and into the conference dining room and began unloading the desserts and fruit on the wet bar's granite countertop. Just beyond lay the sitting room where Vera was speaking with the elders about a girl named Angela Miller, who had been staying with Vera in the other penthouse for over a month. Sergio only knew this through Fegan. Emmett and he had been travelling up North between Emmett's law offices in NYC, one near Atlantic City, and his suite at Four Kings in New York. They were expected to stay in Las Vegas for at least a week.

He'd caught a glimpse of the girl they were talking about from behind one day in the hotel lobby—a lithe figure in skinny jeans and heels with a thick fox tail of blond hair swinging below her silk scarf. Around her waist, Vera's arm looped in an iron lock. They were close as they walked, with the girl leaning down to listen to Vera, who seemed almost grandmotherly.

Sergio let José out and returned to stand just inside the sitting room's entry and wait for a break in the conversation to announce dessert.

"I expect she's eating out of your hand after the trip to Paris," Lucinda Struthers said, "However did you manage the passport?"

Scott Henderson was most helpful in that regard," Vera answered. "You recall his connections and early experience with forgery." Vera's words stretched out in a stream of blue smoke. "As to her loyalties, how does Grandma Vera sound? I suggested she call me that today and between the Chanel counter and Christian Dior, she confided to me her fondest wish of having a family again, and then she told me how much I mean to her." Vera took another drag and grinned. "The little vixen will never see it coming. She is so easily enamored with the simplest luxuries and privileges. Her lust for the things of this world clouds her vision and stretches thin her already thin ties to the Creator and his design. She will soon be my pet, and she will give herself with all her heart to our master."

Sergio caught himself feeling sorry for this Angela girl and just as suddenly as he thought it, Vera's head cocked up. She flashed two dagger-like lasers at Sergio across the room. Just as the master before her and Emmett, she could read his thoughts, although he could swear (or was it hope?) that she could only read the surface, same as a wrestler sizes you up on the first single-leg takedown, never guessing what strength lies inside. He was convinced these minions and satan himself could not penetrate the very core of his intellect and will. In any case, his pity for this perfect stranger was enough to show his weakness. He cursed himself for the slip. She was no concern of his, and she probably made the bed she was crawling into, same as him, same as everyone in this God-forsaken business. Sergio cleared his mind, reverting to his favorite baseball stats. On the couch, a drink resting on his knee, Emmett let out an abrupt laugh at him. It was obvious he knew what Sergio was doing.

"The dessert is ready, Mistress." Sergio said, quickly regaining a stony countenance inside and out, devoid of emotion.

* * *

The months had flown by since she came here in a whirlwind of extravagant living filled with sensate pleasures. For the palette, there were gourmet delicacies and irresistible sweets. For the body, the expert pampering of Swedish massage and exotic spas. For the senses of sight and sound, the enjoyment of plays and concerts, and private sightseeing. Angela Miller was a new woman. She owned the love and respect of Grandma Vera, and the adulation of all who served her.

In a Turkish bathrobe, Angela stepped onto the patio balcony outside her room, drying her hair with a towel. She lifted her head enjoying the amazing view, looking down as she often did on the world that used to own her. From this height, it was she who owned the world. In a gush of delight, she spun in a childish circle as if to celebrate her new freedom. She settled into a walk again, whisking her hair with the towel as she wandered over to the main porch off the second living room for the balconies were all connected by short walkways.

A cool breeze ruffled her hair. Angela laid the towel over a chair and stood by the wide cement railing, ingesting a healthy gulp of air and shrugging her shoulders in satisfaction. This life was unbelievable, nothing any of the Millers could ever have dreamed. Angela suddenly thought of John, wishing he could see it, wishing he could see her now, clean, free of drugs and Eddy, new clothes, new everything. She could still hear John's voice. Maybe she could contact him now that she was safe and had a bit of dignity. She was being treated well, and she had changed. Why shouldn't she share that with John? Vera is wonderful, like a grandmother to her; John would love her the way she did. Vera is powerful, too. There's no reason to think she couldn't protect John from this mess she was in, so they could reconnect. Maybe, she could even meet Clarice, John's—

Crack—Bang!

The sliding glass door from the sitting room burst open with such force it actually bounced. Vera in a soft grey silk blouse seemed to sail forward with the same intensity as the door until she was a second from Angela. "My dear, just what are you thinking?" Grandma Vera's question seemed to bear the same passion as her sailing entrance, leaving Angela confused and wordless. Vera burst into laugh. "Don't look so innocent—out here in nothing but a robe, wet from the shower, you'll catch your death of cold. Come in at once with me."

Obediently Angela followed, but something about the first question bothered her, and something about the rest did not add up. It was as if she had been somehow disloyal, as if she had done—or was it thought?—something wrong. She settled her qualms, quietly walking behind Vera through the suite back to her own bedroom, telling herself she had given the woman a scare, although why she was unsure. Once in her room, Grandma Vera said, "Sit, sit," patting the bed. After fetching her silver brush from the vanity, the venerable old lady climbed behind her and began brushing her hair, the silk blouse sliding backward over her chicken arms.

"I'm sorry if I—"

"Oh posh." The brush waved away the apology in a magic wand sweep. "So tell Grandma Vera, just what were you daydreaming that would make you take leave of your good sense?"

"Oh, nothing really…" Angela said, her head tilted back, enjoying the stroke of the brush.

"Come, come. We are good friends, more than friends are we not?" Cold thin lips grazed Angela's forehead. "You can tell me anything; ask me anything, my sweet child."

Angela's earlier angst returned, skidding through her as if she had swallowed a chip of ice. She closed her robe tighter and considered the question, remembering her earlier ruminations on the terrace. "I was thinking of my brother and his wife—"

"Oh no, no, no," Vera said, and stopped the brush, bringing her frail figure around to face Angela. "You mustn't torture yourself with such thoughts. I won't have it!"

"But it's not torture, I know my brother, and I was thinking you could maybe arrange—"

"Say no more, dearie," Vera cut in, firmly. "You must understand me when I say this. You cannot go back; you can only go forward. Your brother is happy in his own life, and he has been these many, many years. The last thing he needs is scandal. Now wouldn't that be selfish of you?"

"I suppose, but couldn't—"

Several more times Vera interrupted Angela as she tried to express her desire to see her brother. Vera made a number of arguments to dissuade her until exasperated with the back and forth, she clasped both of Angela's forearms arms and gave a punitive squeeze. "You simply do not understand. I am so sorry to be the one to tell you this; I had hoped to spare you…," The old doe eyes and thick lashes gazed pointedly at Angela and her head tilted left and then right as if she were weighing a point with some unseen debater.

"Hmm, I can see now, you must be told. You will dress and meet me in the office beside my room."

One hour later, Angela left Vera's office in complete shock after having been shown news clippings and information about the kidnapping and murders in Ithaca. Vera said she had had her family the Millers investigated soon after "adopting" Angela. Tears etched lines through Angela's makeup, as Vera led her away from the crime scene photos strewn over Vera's desk. She was brought back to her room, tucked in bed, and given a sedative.

Vera leaned over her, patting her wet cheeks with a tissue and hissing sweetly. "So you see, my child, why we must never speak of this again. Your own troubles would multiply theirs. No, you must start new and you have already begun." She arranged Angela's hair on the pillow. "You will have no contact with your family," she said, leaning into Angela's ear, her gruff voice a bare whisper. "Anything else is impossible."

Feeling chilled, Angela watched Vera on her way out, already feeling the effects of the valium, of which effects she attributed to the next few seconds of unexplainable phenomena. For as Vera exited, something akin to scales fell from Angela's eyes, and she beheld for the briefest moment, not Grandma Vera, but a beastly creature, a cross between a hyena and boar with tusks and horrid teeth and stood on cloven feet. She squeezed her eyes against the sight of the vile creature, overcome with a sudden dread of it being an evil she now served. Not one second later, on opening her eyes, she saw only a glimpse of Vera once again as the door closed.

Even though the unholy vision did not last, and Angela chalked it up to a bad reaction to Valium, something of its raw truth would remain gnawing at her soul.

For Angela, the next few weeks passed in much the same manner as the weeks before. Yet, there had been something pivotal in the news about John and his family. While Angela's days were still a whirlwind of worldly delights and jet-setting pleasures, she found herself losing interest. The clothes, the gourmet dinners, the shows, and pampering and catering of every whim had begun to feel self-indulgent and wasteful. In the midst of these salacious and hedonistic activities, her mind returned to the homeless she'd met, their unshaved faces in

259

ripped coats diving for food in the casino dumpster. More and more whenever she was alone, she longed to see John and dreamed of hugging him and his pretty wife and being able to console them for the loss of their son—a boy… like the boy in her dreams…. The very thought, which came from nowhere, returned by the same path.

Angela ambled into her room her head buried, playing a game on the new tablet Vera had sent. She landed on the bed, her eyes never leaving the screen, and her thumbs furiously tapping the keypad. Boom. Her character blew up, and she shook the pad once and tossed it on the bed. She rose, locking her arms overhead in a long stretch, looking about the room. She threw open the armoire doors and pulled out a drawer, debating on a swim. It was rather late, and she hated to keep the poor butler awake. Although no one told her, she was aware that the servants kept a close eye on her. Most days, they were her unspoken bodyguards, but of late, it felt more as if they were her captors.

She found herself looking in her drawer underneath the swimsuits and feeling for the card. It was the Saint Michael card from Joan of Arc Church. She'd kept it hidden and safe all this time. It had been in the pocket of her jeans on New Year's Eve. Since New Year's Day, it had stayed in the drawer where she laid it when changing into the silk pajamas Vera had given her. She never pulled it out, never looked at it. Tonight she looked longingly at the angel's magnificent form. Finally, she whispered the prayer. "Saint Michael, the archangel, defend us in battle. Be our protection against the wickedness and snares of the dev—"

Abruptly, the floor beneath her rumbled. Alarmed, Angela's hand reached for the armoire, except it too was shaking, and as it bounced in a tremulous little walk threatening her toes, she screamed and lunged for the drapery. In all the years she'd lived in Las Vegas, she had never experienced an earthquake. Clinging to the drape like a rope climber, she wished grandma were here, but her benefactress was off on business somewhere in Denver. The rumble stopped after only a moment. Angela released the drape as well as an unconscious breath and walked to the doorway. "Fegan, you there? Rosita? Anyone? A few minutes later, questioning Rosita in the kitchen, who stood unconcerned, washing glasses, Angela learned that Rosita had felt nothing. Amused Rosita shook her head pointing to the delicate stemware saying, "Debe ser un loco, estos no se mueve." Didn't take much Spanish to know she'd just been called crazy.

Angela dreamt that night that Saint Joan of Arc came to her. Like school friends, they talked as they walked across a field of farmland outlined in grey woods. The maiden was magnificent yet simple. Her dress was of a rough, white linen, and Angela imagined this was how she dressed as a working peasant. Joan herself was glorious, covered in a happy glow and exuding love and charity. The dream was so real; Angela felt blades of hay brush her hands as they ambled through the field. They spoke quite naturally of Angela's past and her family. Saint Joan related many things in Angela's life to her own life before she was called to her great mission. They came to the edge of the field where the young trees stood at attention. The saint beckoned Angela to a rock formation of deep grey. She sat with her back upright and regal, and yet relaxed and carefree. Angela chose a rock opposite the glowing, young countenance.

"I must address you directly before we part," the noble woman said. "Angela, you must choose rightly and then you will have to defend that choice." Her words, had such weight and impact compared to the dream, she knew they were to last. "Do you remember," the saint continued, "how you once looked at my painting and admired me for not running?" Angela nodded. "If the good God had given me the path, I would not have hesitated to run from the evil they planned for me. But," she said firmly tilting her head, "never in defiance of His will. You understand? That is the difference between acceptance or resignation and just quitting. Take what God gives you, dear sister. Whether it is to run or to turn and fight. He will let you know."

Angela awoke, the card with the angel curled in her hand. She flipped on the bedside lamp and looked at the image. Then quickly she kissed the picture, and for some reason, unexamined by herself, with her finger she traced a cross on her pillow. She kissed it, laid her head on the invisible cross, and slept like a baby.

261

29

The Remnant

On the steps of Saint Elizabeth Church in Ithaca NY, Gerard walked on the narrow path that had been shoveled for daily Mass goers. All around him lay piles of the white stuff from yesterday's two-foot dump on the city. Gerard came in from the blinding whiteness and adjusted his eyes to the dark interior of the church. He lightly thumped clumps of snow from his boots as he took in the wood beams of the flying buttress ceiling and the colors of the two-story high stained glass windows. The church smelled faintly of incense and wet stone as his Evangelical eye roamed the half dozen statues, gold boxes, and haunting chandeliers over a sea of dark pews. He wondered how a body could pray without distraction in such a place. In the last pew, sat a tanned old lady in an unexpected hat that could have been his own fishing hat, with medals instead of the hooks and lures. Eyes closed in a tight crinkle, lips pursed and murmuring in the deeply lined face, brown-spotted hands pressed tight—she was hard at prayer. What, he thought, could such a lived-in soul have to pray so hard about? From under the khaki hat peeked soft wisps of yellow white hair, which brushed the corduroy neck of the tan barn coat, too big for her thin frame. Gerard gave her one last look and decided someone so absorbed with the business of talking to her Creator should not be disturbed for his question.

Up front a couple of cackling elderly women stood by the front pew in animated conversation. Approaching the pair slowly and waiting for them to acknowledge him, an involuntary twinge rippled down his middle, the kind a black man experiences now and then when meeting new white folk, a kind of preemptive reaction to anticipated prejudice or fear. It wasn't just that he was African American; Gerard was also a big man at 5'11 and 250 pounds. It wasn't fat either, he thought proudly of the 325 he had benched last night. The taller hawk-nosed woman looked at him with polite indifference, erasing his initial expectation. "Are you looking for Mass, cause it just ended."

"Really Dot, it didn't just end. It's been over for half an hour."

"Oh, go on; it's not even..." Dorothy checked her watch and tapped its face tittering, "I'll be, it's 9:00. Joyce we do go on, don't we?" Both of them nodded vigorously at each other and seemed to have forgotten him. Gerard fake coughed and both heads turned to him again.

"I'm looking for a Father Tom O'Donnell." The two stopped smiling and gaped at him like he had asked for Lucifer in God's house.

"Well, I don't know what this is about, but he didn't say Mass this morning—"

"His privileges have been revoked." Dot butted in.

"That's right, till the trial. Murdering a man with a crucifix! Do you know about that? Is that why you're here?"

What a cold change came over the pair! Gerard wondered if they had ever thought to pray for the priest. "Does he reside here? I was told—"

"Yes, he's outside shoveling the sidewalk by the chapel."

The taller woman pointed to the side entrance, and Gerard left them with a quick God bless you as he silently prayed for their gossipy tongues. He stopped outside the double glass doors observing the priest, who was working his way to the street with a shovel. By the look of the heavy snow, there was at least an hour's work ahead of him, maybe more at the rate the priest was going. He was giving it his all, there just wasn't much all in him. Gerard pushed the doors and called cheerily.

"You want some help there, Padre?"

The priest stopped, leaning against his shovel seeming grateful for a break. "Oh, hello. Are you new? I mean you must be. Some would consider this my purgatory."

"What?"

"Never mind," the priest laughed shyly, "it's nothing. I'm Father Tom O'Donnell, and if the name doesn't mean anything, well…"

"Oh, I know who you are. I wanted to meet you and talk. My name is Gerard Healy. I have a long story. Mind if I grab a shovel and help you finish this off."

"Oh, you don't have to; I can finish it later. We can talk in the chapel. I—"

Gerard ignored him and walked to the open storage unit by the wall to retrieve a shovel. He loved a workout, and it showed as he lifted the heavy snow, hoisted it, and heaved it backward to the yard with vigor. He lifted a couple more before he spoke, sending sheets of the stuff behind him as effortlessly as tossing back a beer. "It was May last year," Gerard spoke his shovel not stopping, "a friend of mine died, from my Bible study group. Oh, I should tell you, I'm a born-again Christian. My church is kind of, uh … all over. We bring it to the streets, lay hands, pray, have revivals. Anyway, there was this beautiful old soul, Mrs. Nicestrum, she would come every Thursday. It was her church we were in; they were letting us use their basement." Father Tom's shovel stopped, perhaps out of confusion, but perhaps in admiration, watching Gerard cut a swath in a few minutes that had promised to take him an hour. "Ah … "Gerard laughed, without stopping, "I'm getting off track. Anyway, I think you may know what I witnessed in that cemetery May thirteenth in a little graveyard in Newark Valley."

Tom's shovel dropped. "You, uh, you were there?" he said, and Gerard nodded. "I don't know exactly what happened, but I've heard the story from my friend John. Mrs. Nicestrum, she was his child's nanny, actually, more than a nanny…,"—the priest stumbled for words as he bent to retrieve his shovel— "I'm uh, involved …. I, uh, should tell you—"

"It's okay. I followed your case," Gerard said, his shovel rhythmically digging in, lifting and flipping. "You're out on bail, awaiting trial. You're claiming self-defense, right?" A pained look crossed the priest's brow, and he nodded leaning on his shovel and watching Gerard. "The thing is a group of us have been praying in that graveyard ever since the miracle we witnessed. I mean that light we saw rising from the casket, it spun and spun, and then it smashed into Mrs. Miller...well, you don't get over something like that. Then after reading about the kidnapping and all the murders—"

"Self-defense, actually. The man, Christian Menger, he was choking my friend. I had no choice . . . ." Tom's voice drifted.

"Thing is, Padre, I believe you. I also believe it was evil you were fighting. I mean that man, Menger was a satanist, wasn't he? It was sick what went on at that farm. I don't see how any jury could . . . " he paused, scraping a line of ice. "It couldn't possibly go against you!" Gerard felt the awkwardness and decided the best way to overcome it for the young priest was to throw his strong back into another shovel-full of snow. For a minute, all that could be heard was Gerard' shovel scraping the sidewalk. Then a second scrape joined his and the two continued silently working their way to the street.

"Thing is," Gerard began again, "I was hoping you would join our prayer group when you, you know, get cleared."

"Wow, I'm, uh, not exactly getting many invites like that these days." Tom paused again leaning on his shovel and catching his breath. He took his scarf off and shoved it into his coat pocket. "I'd have to hear more about it, but I would be honored to pray with you, Gerard." The priest seemed animated and hope-filled. "Actually, you might think I'm worried. I'm not really. I feel alive and full of joy. You just threw me, that's all." Tom smiled and thrust his tool into an ambitious pile that required an actual grunt to lift.

"Hey Padre, save some for me."

Tom laughed. "I think we're going to get along Mr. Healy, and I can't wait to meet your friends. You give me hope. See, I feel something happening in the world, a separation forming, good versus evil. I've had a lot of time to think lately. My social calendar is not exactly full," he said, sounding amused, his shoulders shrugging. "Anyway, the way I see it, there's a lot of people caught between the two sides of good and evil right now. But when the end comes, it won't be like that. No fence sitters, see? The sheep and the goats, you know? Meanwhile, we have to prepare the world, and there are very few souls to help do that. You know?"

"A remnant will be gathered." Gerard's voice was deep with conviction.

Tom dropped his shovel a second time, arresting Gerard's arm. "You do understand. You feel it too!"

Gerard's eyes fixed on the priest. "God is calling his remnant, and no religious lines will separate them. He wants them to pray side by side, Catholics, Methodists, Lutherans, Jews, it absolutely won't matter to the Remnant."

The two looked at each other as surprised as two boys discovering they knew a secret handshake. Tom spoke first. "I will explain about the boy but not here, in the church, it's mostly empty by now." One more shovel full finished the walkway, now cleared to the road. They put the shovels back in an outdoor shed and entered the side door of the church. Tom pulled his skull cap off as they walked. The cackling hens were gone, but Gerard saw the fish hat lady in the back her head bent and hands still folded in prayer. He slipped in the first pew beside the priest, noticing how young Father appeared with his brown hat hair sticking up in untrained tufts and his tapered Irish eyes grinning at him.

"The child is safe." Tom said, wiping his red nose with a tissue. Gerard regarded him blankly. "The Miller boy . . . the one they said was kidnapped."

"What!"

"Shh, I'm absolutely trusting your discretion. The boy really was kidnapped, but then we got him back, or at least Rabbi Gabriel Katz did, for which he paid dearly." Tom's brow furrowed. "Gabriel Katz was the child's second protector. His nanny, your friend Mrs. Michelle Nicestrum was the first."

"Protector?" Gerard leaned in. "Were the cultists always after the boy, then? Are you hiding him from them?" Gerard thought of the little Miller boy at the funeral that day, an intelligent looking child, blond curls, and big green eyes, quoting the Good Book like he had it memorized. It was such a relief to think he was alive.

"God is hiding Jackson in a way and in a place that no one else could." Father's finger rose making his point. "Your friend Mrs. Nicestrum was more than she appeared as was Rabbi Katz. You admitted that you believe in evil, Gerard. That's good because it is real, and never more than a threat than when it is not believed."

Hot from shoveling, Gerard shifted his bulk inside his leather coat. "Why are these cultists, er . . . Satan worshippers... after the boy?"

"Good question." Father gazed at the altar ahead. "I'm kind of in the dark on a lot of this. I can say this much; Jackson is key to a merciful plan our Lord has for a world lost in sin. Simeon . . . Father Simeon, my friend who was killed by Menger, he called Jackson Miller,"—his voice dropped to a bare whisper—"The Preparer. Like a hungry lion, Gerard, evil still seeks the child and all who are destined to help him."

"Help him what? I'm a little lost, padre."

"Oh, of course, forgive me. Let's see, you believe in the Remnant to be gathered?" Gerard nodded, unzipping his coat. "We . . . you and I and your band of graveyard pray-*ers*, we'll begin with prayer. I believe the Lord will reveal what He wants of each of us over time. What is needed is prayer and a good dose of blind faith. I would be grateful to join you, that is, if you really think the others in your group will want me."

Gerard regarded the young and inexperienced looking priest with something in him so profoundly not young. He must have been through a lot, and it was obvious that he had already shared far more than he intended to divulge. Especially, the fact that he knew the child was safe and secreted away somewhere. Gerard judged that was probably enough to start their new fellowship.

"We accept all who accept Him, Padre," Gerard said. He was really getting used to calling the priest that. He had trouble calling the man father as Catholics do. It rubbed him all wrong. After all, Our Lord said call no man Father. He never got why Catholics did that. Someday he would ask his new friend. For now, Padre seemed a good compromise.

After exchanging a little more about the graveyard prayer sessions in the cemetery in Newark Valley, Gerard stood to leave and glanced to the back of the church. He saw the fish hat lady still at work and leaned back down to ask about her.

"Oh Anna?" Tom turned with his arm over the back of the pew. "Yes, she's something all right. Have you seen her around . . . I mean at any of your church events or services?"

"It's funny, I feel like,"—Gerard screwed his mouth thinking— "yeah, like I have."

"You probably have." Tom's head bobbed with a laugh. "Anna spends day and night in prayer all over town, churches, temples, rallies, novenas, revivals, anywhere really. Anyplace she thinks good souls are gathering for prayer. Years ago, she and her husband could be seen together, one church service after another, from church to church to church. Pastors wondered when they even ate. Her spouse passed on, but Anna still prays and prays. I'm not sure if she's Catholic, but she lands here a lot for morning mass. Course that might be because we're the only show in town at 8 am."

"She live somewhere?"

"Yes, yes, she's not homeless. Nothing like that."

Gerard left the way he came in watching Anna as he passed. She lifted her hawk nose under the funny hat, examining him for a moment with sparkling blue eyes. Then the worn face smiled, a warm, approving kind of smile, same kind his grandmother would give him when he brought her a handful of wilting dandelions. She went straight back to the hard work of prayer; for whom, Gerard no longer wondered, deciding Anna was the first of the Remnant called to prayer for a world in sin. Back on the narrow swath cut into the snowy world of Saint Elizabeth's Churchyard, Gerard joined his praise and petition for the world to hers.

30

Anna's Day

In the very last pew, Anna Stoltz got up to leave. She gathered a large quilted bag of faded blue paisley. It was hand-stitched and patched, and had served her long. It would continue to do so, she imagined, until her death. From it, she pulled a red knit scarf and wrapped it twice round her chicken neck. She held off on her thick wool gloves incase she needed to make a note at the bulletin board. Her head was already covered, as it always was in her favorite khaki fishing hat. The hat, decorated in a menagerie of medals and crosses, was neither practical nor warm. It was sentimental.

At the exit, her old eyes squinted down to twenty-twenty scanning fliers, odd scraps of paper and index cards plugging everything from Pre-Cana to used bicycles. She held a garish notebook covered in butterflies. It was nearly full, and Anna made a mental note to buy a new one from the dollar store. Arthritic fingers ran down the pages, double checking dates. There was nothing new to include for this church—Rosary Forum next Saturday, Miraculous Medal novena every Monday, and a Forty Hours devotion end of the month. Her fingers continued to flip pages filled with her scrawl. Nothing going on anywhere today.

She would head to the café and eat her sandwich with some tea, maybe get some nice young person to look up stuff online for her. Some said the internet was evil but evil is in the hand of the user. The internet and those whatchamacallit engines were a marvelous gift for sharing information. Just about all of the youngsters had a laptop computer or thingamajig in their hand. They often found prayer services or events for her, which she dutifully recorded and made her best efforts to attend.

Downtown, Anna parked the old Ford pickup across the street from Bookworm Joe's. The owner with the gray ponytail never minded when she brought her own sandwich and only bought a fifty-cent cup of tea. Tea was a dollar and had been as long as she could remember. But Ken and she worked it out long ago that a dollar was highway robbery for a five-cent tea bag and boiled water. So for Anna and Anna alone, the price was fifty cents. The cafe was cozy with couches and tables set up like a living room in someone's house, a fancy house, she thought, full of young college students and Ken, the age-old hippie running the place.

A hand of harassing wind at her back chased her through the door and dissolved in the thick warmth of the café. Smells of cinnamon toast and burnt coffee swirled around thick shelves of earthy mahogany and worn leather. From somewhere above, diaphanous strains of classical music tiptoed on the air. Just two students sat at the red velvet couch, their heads buried in their laptops and two giant white-capped mugs of rising steam on the table before them. Time enough to ask for their help after she ate. Ken came over as soon as she settled herself at a bistro table in the corner, removing her gloves and unwinding the fuzzy red scarf.

"Anna, how are you?" he fairly yelled. "You been out visiting this morning? Ken was a nice fella, but he always talked to her as if she was special or touched in the head or something.

"Fine, fine, I'm fine. Yes, yes, I've been to Saint Elizabeth's to Mass. Yes, Mass this morning. Not too many worshippers…still, good folks, good prayer. Yes."

She heard herself sometimes talking fast like this and wondered why she spoke this way. Perhaps it was the Irish in her, or maybe as one preacher had told her, she spoke as if there were no spaces between the words because it left more time for prayer. That was a good one, she chuckled.

"You want a mug of hot tea, Anna?" Ken asked, still a smidge too loud.

"That would be fine, fine. Yes, yes, tea is what I need. Just the ticket."

Anna carefully unwrapped the wax paper from her cheese sandwich and spread it on the coffee table for a makeshift placemat.

Ken brought a giant mug of black tea, a sugar shaker, and milk, at the same time, dutifully sliding the two quarters she left on the table into his hand. She was stirring the caramel brew, when the tinkling shop bells clanged and in bounced a group of delightfully young faces. Several held bibles and one a blue plastic milk crate high in the air above their heads. A rush of cold whooshed in changing the air as jarringly as the animated, gay procession changed the dull and hushed library-quiet of the cafe.

"Anna! What's going on Sister?" A heavy girl led the way, taking off her puffy black coat and displaying a yellow T-shirt with the words, "Jesus is my main Man". Her greeting was followed by a chorus of, "Hello Anna's."

"Oh, yes, yes, Latisha, Rocco, Dion... yes, yes. Hello. Have you been busy? Have you been working?" She just loved this bunch of proselytizing, Bible thumping, youngsters. Always up to some good, somewhere. "What is it? What were you doing just now?"

"Street revival, Anna," the tall thin one called Rocco answered, shaking a worn zippered bible case. "We took it to the street this morning."

"Yes, yes, the street. Oh my, yes. Good, good, sounds good."

"Alleluia, sister!" Rocco said, "The Holy Spirit was everywhere. We laid hands on the brothers and sisters in the street and called on the name of Jesus." Rocco continued to describe this morning's evangelization effort with his usual animated passion, throwing his hands out and up like an Indian chief doing a rain dance, and all to a continual disbursement of "Amens" and "Praise God's" from his peanut gallery of disciples.

Rocco, who was all of a half decade older than his followers, was a kind of pied piper for youth. From what Anna knew, for he was open with his personal testimony, he had come from a troubled youth, been involved with gangs, and had his share of scrapes with the law. He was in juvenile detention, as he tells it, when one day, he picked up a bible. He was last in line that afternoon, and so, beside a worn set of the Hardy Boy novels, a Highlights magazine, and two comic books, the holy book was the only thing left on the cart. Rocco said reading the Psalms was like being struck with lightning rods of pure truth, convicting him to his very core and filling him with the love of

273

God. Even beyond his Brooklyn accent, black leather coat, silver chain earrings, and worn jeans, it was easy to see Rocco's appeal and why God called him to lead these youth. Rocco had a fire in his belly and a generous heart anxious to share the joy within him.

"Woo, praise God! Praise his holy name," Rocco finished praising, and the pack threw up one further series of "amens". Hands lowered, and the little troupe sat down and around Anna. A pretty, blond thing wearing a small silver cross spoke shyly, holding her hands between her legs as if she were putting a golf club.

"We went down to the Commons, and Rocco stood on a book crate and preached the Word. We prayed and we sang, and I think we got through to some people today." Heads nodded in agreement.

"That one guy, like he definitely accepted Jesus." Rocco said. "He gave it up, you know? God is sooooo good." This elicited a series of "amens", making Anna's dry lips crack in a smile over crooked, buttery teeth. These were good kids, Anna thought, doing God's work in a whole different way from her own. Called as each and every soul is called, called to share, called to work for each other, called to be your brother's keeper and care as much about his soul as you care for your own, and all for the love of God.

Soon the merry band headed back outside, and Anna watched as they set up shop right in front of Bookworm Joe's. Rocco planted the crate, flipping it as neatly as a magician's top hat, stood on it and held open his Bible. The others stood behind him holding hands out in salute as if channeling their unified prayer and sending it upward. What a good bunch, Anna thought finishing her tea and the last bite of sandwich. She wadded wax paper into the tea cup and got up, crossing to a nearby table where she asked the nice looking Chinese boy to google for any religious events in Ithaca. They found one to add to her notebook. Rebundled and repacked, Anna headed out with a final wave to Ken.

In front of the store, a few people clogged the sidewalk in a pile, either watching the spectacle or, just as likely, hesitant to cross the Christian gauntlet. Three thumpers were singing a song of praise, Rocco was calling out scripture as Latisha and another boy cheerfully approached sidewalk passers. The curious watchers huddled underneath the Miller Construction sign: three middle-aged shoppers

274

wearing skeptical frowns, a blank-faced crumpled man, two college boys pointing and snickering, and one young blond girl biting her nail and thinking, but Anna knew (for she could feel prayers going up the same way a high-power line hums with current) no one was praying. Nope, not a one was praying. That was sad, she thought, as a strapping man with brown hair in a heavy work coat stepped out from the office next door. He stood behind the half-dozen gawkers. Now, he had a pleasing aura about him! Anna waved to the kids as she crossed the street to her rusty red truck. When she cranked the old engine, it made a horrible grinding sound but wouldn't start. She tried again with the same result. Maybe it needed a jump. Careful not to flood the engine, she gave it one more crank. Nada. Plenty of noise, but no giddy-up.

Wistfully, she scanned the glut of people across the way, when the burly man with the fine aura caught her eye. Anna waved at him vigorously as if she were pulling a giant sheet off the clothesline. She churned the cold metal knob round and round, rolling down the window. As the man passed between the trapped onlookers, they parted and moved on as if he had broken some spell.

"Having a little trouble?"

"Yes, yes, a little trouble, that's right. Can you help? A jump maybe. Hmm?" Anna spoke a might slower for the handsome young man. This one prays, Anna thought.

"Pop the hood; I'll have a look." There was no popping, more like propping, on the antique Ford. She sat patiently as he figured it out. From under the hood, he hollered, "Start her up." The car made the same funny sound. After two more tries, the propping bar was released and the hood slammed back into place. The man came around to her driver's side window. "She's turning over but not cycling properly. I'd say it's your timing belt. Nothing can be done here. Do you need a ride?"

"Oh my, yes, yes a ride. Oh, that's fine of you. Oh yes, thank you." She opened the door and slid out clutching her blue quilt bag. "But what about my truck?"

"I'll call a mechanic if you want. It has to be towed."

Anna showed the man her Triple-A card, and in a few minutes, it was settled that the towing company would tow the truck to an auto shop on First Street. The keys were left in the truck, after Anna's arthritic fingers removed her house key. Introductions were made, and Anna climbed into the Chevy Blazer of one John Miller.

"So where to?" he asked her.

Anna adjusted her floppy hat thinking. "Well, ha ha...I don't think I....the thing is it used to be called something else, my street, that is. Now it's just a number or letters or some such foolishness. Oh boy, I'm the fool, yes a fool. Now I seem as crazy as I look. Oh, don't think I don't know how I look, what folks think."

At this, John shook his head good-naturedly. "Listen, I'm in the construction business. I've seen some squirrely games played on road names. Probably happened when they instituted 911, right?"

"Oh you're charitable, yes, yes, your kind. But no, it's been changed a good while now," she said, scratching her cheek. "I just never, hee hee...never had to know the new name. My son, he comes calling. My bills they just come. Yes, yes, try to stop a bill. Ha-ha. I can direct you there. If that's all the same to you."

Anna gave John a few directions, and they were on their way.

"What—uh, what did your road used to be called?" the man asked, as her wrinkled hand explored the buttons on her door, and then caressed the uncracked leather on the seat.

"Prey Hill Road. Yes sirree, Prey Hill is what it's always been."

Taking his eyes from the road for a second, the man gave her a curious look. "I'm thinking I know the road," he said, "but I don't know of any houses except the blue one at the bottom. Is that yours?"

"Blue, no, no, not blue," she said, pursing her lips. "Oh, I see, yes, you're thinking of the East Side of the mountain. I'm all the way over to the other side, all the way around. Prey Hill Road used to connect, up one side of the mountain and down the other. But that was when I was a kid."

"Wow, we'd be neighbors if the road still connected. I had no idea. I live on the top of the hill."

"Oh it connects alright, but not for cars. No, no, not for cars, just for hunters and dogs, and deer and such. You can have a good hike someday if you find it, yep. And if you find yourself at my cabin, you'll find yourself welcome, yes, yes you will." The mini truck (for that's what John Miller's vehicle seemed to her) stopped, allowing a group of college kids to cross. Anna frowned at the sausage pants on one girl—pants so tight they looked like sausage wrap. She also noted the lost and bored looks. "John Miller, can I ask you something?" She waited, and when he shrugged, she continued in a careful voice much slower than her usual cadence. "John Miller, do you pray"

"Sure," he said, without much hesitation.

"Do you pray hard, John?" she asked, barely pausing then plunging forward with all the speed of a roadrunner in her familiar style. "We need you, John, oh yes, my yes. We need all the good prayers. Yes, yes, we need you. The world, John, yes, yes the whole world needs you." Anna looked first at his strong light, and next at his face, which seemed a little unsure but politely listening. The Blazer rumbled over the narrow dirt road that led to her lone cabin, tucked in the foot of a mountain and embraced by scraggly pines like a coveted possession. The car stopped, and from the woods bounded a brown collie. John Miller unlocked the door and smiled at her.

In that moment, nothing could have prevented the words that poured from Anna's good mouth. Although she could not see it, her eyes glazed over in a whitish haze covered in the thickest cataracts. The eyes were unseeing, and yet, saw more than this world could show. She turned them on John Miller and spoke plainly in a voice as clear and unblemished as her eyes were not.

"Three archangels are destined to aid your boy. Two of these lights have been shared and their purpose fulfilled. Michael and Gabriel have imparted theirs, and the carriers have accomplished and met their fate. It remains for Raphael to communicate his light. Your sister," Anna said, her sinewy arm reaching for John Miller's hand and taking it in a strong, bony grip, "she was born to share Raphael's light. She has been blocked. You must pray for her." The milky green film slid from Anna's eyes, her body relaxed, and she repeated the final admonition in her customary tones as if she had never morphed into a zombie-eyed psychic. "We need you to pray. Yes, yes, we all need to pray."

Anna got out of the car, leaving the young man dumbfounded. She walked around to his side, ignoring the brown ball of wet fur, pushing his muzzle into her hands beside her. "You want to come in?

277

Have a cup of coffee? Always have some at the ready on the stove. Yes, always, always have some. Like to say thank you for the ride."

"S'all right, no thanks needed. Uh, it was nice meeting you."

"Maybe you'll, find that path sometime, yes, yes; I can thank you then."

Standing in her doorway, a cat rubbing against her leg begging to be fed, Anna waved at John Miller as he drove off. "I hope he finds that path soon, Lord," she muttered, reaching for the cat, "Soon as you need him to."

31

Fight or Flight

Angela launched from the bed and tripped across the room in a mad rush to reach the toilet. Grabbing her hair in a ponytail and convulsing, she flung to her knees and buried her face in the bowl. Smelling chlorine and gripping the cold porcelain, she waited for each wave. The spasms produced nothing more than a modicum of phlegm. Panting, she sat back and banged her head against the wall, rubbing her clammy chest and damning the dream—the fourth one in a month.

Dreams? They hardly seemed like dreams or even nightmares, for that matter. They felt allegorical or emblematic of something—life, maybe, choices like picking sides in a dodge ball game. Whatever they were, it was no wonder they made her sick. Even now, sitting on the cold bathroom tile, her spirit continued to slosh inside her as if she were strapped into a seat on the giant pirate ship at the amusement park, waiting for the pendulum to stop swinging. She tried to recapture any particulars, to lay hold of the dream and examine it in the light of day. It melted as a snowflake in a warm hand, refusing to be studied. Feelings of confusion, terror, longing, and excitement, Eve reaching for the forbidden fruit, dissolved and fell away. On waking, only gauzy traces lingered. Bare powder–puff images of heart-racing moments, passionate sensations, and frightening choices, these are all that remained to meet the light of day.

Buried in the night were any details of the dream, but impressions of it lingered just above her subconscious. It was the pirate ship ride after all. Angela gripped the rail before her, bracing against the gargantuan swing of the ship, drawing her towards pleasure, powers, and possessions. As the ship dropped again, slicing like a guillotine through the air, it rushed her backwards and away. From this distance, she saw with eye-opening clarity how base and vile were these false treasures. Then just as she was about to reject his ugliness, to loathe his trickery and his power over her, the heavy pendulum dropped again, slicing through the air, hurtling her through space back to him and that place of burning desire and carnal yearning for everything *he* offered.

Angela swung back and forth, back and forth, strapped into the seat, helpless…at least, she told herself she was helpless. But was she? She bought the ticket, didn't she? Or had someone else purchased it for her? Either way, she took the ticket. She stepped onto the pirate ride, didn't she? Or had she been pushed? Who strapped her in? Who twisted her arm? Was she free to get off? The ride slows down; all rides slow down eventually, and they stop, too. People get on and a few get off.

For some people truth dawns slowly, coming together one puzzle piece at a time until the puzzle's image becomes unmistakably the sky, or the trees, or the little brown cabin. Sometimes truth sits plain as day right smack in front of a stubborn soul who refuses to look at it lest he should be responsible for it. And for some folks, truth is both apparent and acknowledged but put off. Such a soul decides there will be time to settle down later, to straighten out later, to be saved later, later—just one more ride. Was that her? Angela questioned as she stood a little shaky and straightened her cotton cami. Leaning on the bathroom sink, she stared into the mirror as if she were meeting a forgotten face on the street. She felt dirty, alive, and dead all at once. She snapped the cold-water handle, pumped the soap dispenser, and scrubbed her face hard. Dripping wet, her face lifted to the glass again, and her shoulders convulsed in an involuntary shiver. She was being prepared for something, something big . . . and soon she would have to make a choice.

Later that night, Angela stood in her walk-in closet overwhelmed with choices, racks of designer dresses, jeans and tops, drawers of silky intimates and jewelry, and a rotating collection of shoes that would rival those of Imelda Marcos. Finally, she donned the floral chiffon by Donatello Versace and paired it with yellow Jimmy Choo lace-up heels. With her hair straightened and silky, her makeup flawless (complements of the hotel hairdresser, who seemed on call day or night), she could have posed as a model. The very thought of it thrilled her. Angela had never looked more stunning in her life, and she knew it.

She fairly floated over the terrace, the wind catching the layers of her dress; sheer chiffon fluttered freely about her in a cloud of yellow and green. Standing to the side of a pillar, she caught a waiter's approving eye. She felt pretty and powerful at the same time. Vera waited at a table where hotel staff had prepared an intimate setting for an early gourmet dinner. The air was a comfortable seventy degrees, but ahead, hungry-looking flames danced behind the screen of the looming, outdoor fireplace.

"My my, don't you look scrumptious. Spin, spin" Vera's painted finger pointed down making a circle. Angela timidly complied, to which timidity Vera tsked. "My dear, you could be on the cover of Vogue. Surely you realize this."

A cool, but welcome breeze accompanied their repast as Vera listened amiably to Angela's exploits as a flower child. Vera made all the appropriate comments as they clinked and scraped their way through a Waldorf salad. She smiled and nodded as their forks poked at the second course of roasted artichokes, and she frowned and looked grave in all the right places as their knives slid through veal medallions of the entrée. And throughout the meal, from the first sip of lemon water and bite of buttered roll, Angela got the idea that Vera was here tonight to conduct business with her. The absurd thought took hold, and even with no basis in fact, it clung to the meal, overhanging every savory morsel in the same way the lone server waited unseen (but seeing), ready to collect their plates as promptly as the last utensil would be laid to rest after the last bite. By the time their long spoons were cleansing the parfait glasses of tiramisu, the absurd presentiment was verbalized.

281

"My dear," said Vera, her napkin dabbing the wrinkled corners of her red lips, "this has been lovely, has it not? But now we must attend to serious business."

"Really, Grandma Vera?" Angela said, unexpectedly choking on the adopted moniker. "What business is that?"

"We won't play coy now, hmm. We shall put our cards on the table as they say. You, child have a choice," Vera said, leaning back in her chair and rocking as Angela watched her red wine slosh gently back and forth. "These many months we have been... preparing, hmm? Showing you much of what we have to offer."

We, we she kept saying *we*, and it seemed there was a *we*—a *we* unseen, a *we* unannounced, unacknowledged, but not unknown and not exactly hidden. The warmth drained from Angela's body as sands through an hourglass, leaving a bloom of goose flesh in its wake. She carefully pushed her chair back and rose. Rubbing her hands over her upper arms, she approached the fireplace, keeping her back to Vera and her thoughts to herself.

"You have always been free to choose, Angela...."

Vera's voice was directly behind her now, and it droned on explaining a concept Angela had learned in religion class once upon a time. Vera was talking about free will. She never spelled it out in those words, but took a more circuitous route. As a serpent winds itself around the jungle vine until serpent and vine are indistinguishable, Vera wove ambiguous ideas and nebulous half-truths around a topic both understood, that indeed everyone understood on some naked level of the soul. Free will—that one untouchable element that makes one human—that sacrosanct gift of our creation. The only thing we are born with and die with—our free will.

Staring into the leaping blue flames of the gas fire, Angela held her questions. The words would sound ugly. Her queries, she knew, would leave no place to retreat, no place to hide in that part of one's self to which everyone lies.

"You will be one of us, Angela, a proud member of Triune Ordinatio Orbis, the Order of the Three Circles. You are almost prepared..."

Vera's voice soft and low continued, but Angela staring into the fire no longer focused on the words. In the reflection of the glass

282

fireplace insert, Vera's wine sloshed in her glass up one side and down. The lapping blue flames flared to cherry red. It was him. She saw herself stepping into the fire to meet him. She could not have known, but somehow knew, so many before her had done this too. A fiendish tickle burst inside her with the same intensity of her dreams, a pendulum swinging up, up, up, swooping her up, up, up to her wildest fantasies. She heard voices hissing a litany of her importance to him, her being a prize like no other, a glorious triumph. She felt pretty. She felt powerful.

Bzzz. Bzzz. Bzzz.

The familiar sound of Vera's cell phone cracked across the dizzying spell, and Angela, a little wobbly in her heels, was surprised to find she was not, after all, engulfed in red hot flames, but standing as she had been, the sun a little lower in the sky and Vegas before her as always. "Oh, how terribly inconvenient," Vera snicked, her tone back to normal and snatching her cell from the table. She excused herself and spoke into the phone at some distance from Angela, who, feeling hot and a little woozy returned to her seat. The dishes had been cleared and her wine glass refilled by the invisible help. She played with the glass and a napkin between sips. Soon Vera returned.

"Angela, I must leave for Denver on an urgent matter."

"Again? How long will you be gone?"

"Three days at the most. I trust you will follow all the rules. You know it is not safe without me."

"I know; I will."

"We will go somewhere special when I return, hmm?" Vera's paper-thin fingers lightly stroked her cheek. She delivered a bare kiss on the top of her head. "Order anything your heart desires; the time will fly by, dearie," she called as she left to pack.

Vera was gone within the hour, and Angela searched for something to do. She was free to roam the hotel at will, but usually cautious that no one outside regular Tri-O or hotel staff saw her. Angela loved the roof and often hung out there to think, but as she headed there now, it was with a certain compulsion and that same inkling of unfinished business.

* * *

283

"*¿Como 'ta la cosa?*" a bullish figure of a woman said, straightening up from where she had been wiping the underside of a sink. As she rose, it half looked as if the weight of her ponderous chest would send her sailing downward again, and she held the edge of the sink like an anchor, seeming to prevent the same. She smiled at Belia coming forward shaking her head and holding her stomach.

"Not so good, Paquita," Belia said, "*Yo tengo* nauseas."

"*¡Ay, mi madre!*" Paquita put her bottle of Windex in the sink and tossed her paper towel. "Come, come, sit down." She flipped a toilet seat down and when Belia hesitated, she ordered her, "*¡Siéntese!*"

"It's the baby."

"Si, I know it is the baby. You know it is the baby," Paquita said, and pulled a handkerchief from her pocket and proceeded to mop a bit of sweat from atop her ample bosom. She pointed outside shaking her fist, "But Belia, they must not know it is a baby."

How well Belia knew that. Three girls had been let go in the last year. Management made excuses giving them poor reviews, but everyone knew it was because they were pregnant. Belia needed this job for as long as she could keep it. Her husband had been out of work for six months last year, and their bills were high. She intended to work until and if she was discovered. By some miracle, if she could stay small as her cousin Inez did with her first baby, she might be able to hide the whole thing. Inez barely showed at eight months when she wore the right blouses. Paquita and she were both from the Dominican Republic; she could trust her to help.

"I just need air, you know?" Belia said, fingering, as she often did, the medal of the Madonna around her neck.

"*No hay problema.*" Paquita put her handkerchief in one pocket and reached in the other pulling a thick set of keys. "You go up to the roof. I will cover for you."

* * *

The sun's rays tapered to a fierce streak, smearing periwinkle and pink across the horizon. Angela stretched her arms over the low wall, overlooking the entire city to the mountains beyond tinged in a flush of rose. She'd taken in this view a dozen times, but today, in this moment, it seemed almost as if it were for her alone as if he were showing it to her. The world was here for the taking, as much of it as she dared to hold, hers—all hers, or it would be if she said yes…

To him…

How long she stood this way could not be told for time had ceased. As it slipped away, it left her off-balance and light headed. She reeled in the stuff of her dreams—scorching lust, saturated senses, hot and fawning admirers, power over weakness, things and more things, the gratification of every sense. It swept over her, frightening and pleasurable all at once. Deep inside, she ached for sweet release. This seemed to go on and on. And just when it seemed there could be no more, he showed her the ultimate powers he could bestow and how she would govern even the physical world. She saw herself move objects with just a thought. Then soaring in spirit, leaving her weighted body, she entered another body at will . . . .

Even as these terrifying *joies de vivre* swam before her, they were accompanied by a gnawing, empty loneliness. The ugliness of her selfish indulgence was as transparent as glass. Empty of life, barren of love, as full and fascinating as it seemed, it was so much nothing. For self-love is just that, dry as parched lips downing copious quantities of alcohol that feigns to quench but leaves the mouth dry as the desert sands. Love of self can never fill, never satisfy; it can only leave you thirsting for more.

A choice was being laid out for Angela, who was afraid there was no choice. She owed a loyalty to Vera, who gave her a measure of security she had not experienced in years. She felt respected and valued, from the staff that fawned over her to store clerks and passers-by on the streets, who openly admired her looks and classy style. For the first time in her life, she mattered when she entered a room; her presence was felt. Yet, for all that attention, for all that show of grandmotherly doting Vera poured over her, Angela sometimes thought she'd gotten more real affection from the likes of Eddy. Vera had power, she had style, even for someone so ancient she had looks, but inside she was dead. Outwardly, she wore a sarcophagus covered in gold and jewels, while inside lay nothing but filthy wrappings, dust, and bones. Angela knew it as surely as she knew how empty she felt and how shallow she had become. Did she want to be like Vera? Is that what awaited her final yes? Just what was her choice? Her spirit

285

screamed, twisting her in knots of indecision. Lines of wet tears, pricked by the wind, tickled her cheeks. She wiped them with the back of her hands and spurted from the wall frantic to get away.

She sped unseeing around the corner of the building, running smack into another woman. Despite Angela's arms thrusting to arrest her fall, the pretty, little maid went down. The sun, too, had ideas of going down. It shot forward that piercing last shaft of light as it sometimes does, blinding the poor fallen creature and concentrating all its last, glorious silver-white beam like a laser on the woman's medal. The effect was so outstanding, it was impossible for Angela to ignore. So as much as she wanted to help the woman to her feet and send her on her way, and as much as her own red and teary face begged her to continue her flight and hide, and as much as she practically observed a present darkness insisting she return to her room—Angela did none of those things.

Mesmerized, she leaned down to the silver medal and with no qualm of social convention, brashly lifted it from the woman's chest, held it like a precious stone, and stared at it. All manner of childhood memories rushed back at her – going to church, Johnny, her mom, even Father Lawrence and the windows at Saint Joan of Arc Church. Etched in silver, the image of a lady in a long robe with her arms outstretched and her head tilted modestly downward looked humble and delicate, and yet the tiny figure stood upon a large snake, crushing the snake which lay on top of the world. Angela knew that snake, his evil…she had seen *him* without seeing *him*.

The woman was struggling to her feet. Ironically, she was apologizing profusely for using the roof. Coming to her senses, Angela relinquished the necklace and helped the housekeeper up, whose nametag read Belia.

"Please, it's alright, Belia," Angela said, holding her hands up to her own mouth and shaking her head, "Stop apologizing. You didn't do anything wrong."

It took several more tries to convince Belia that A, she was not in trouble, and B, Angela would not tell anyone. By the time it was settled and thanks to Angela's self-deprecating jokes, Belia was at ease enough to ask Angela why she had been crying.

"I…guess I have a decision to make and I—I'm not sure I have a choice."

"Oh, bella dama, we always, always have a choice. You know whenever I am cloudy in the head, I think it is the evil one. He is nothing but pain and confusion." Belia held the medal. "You see this? Madre de Dios is all humility. God uses her to crush the evil. And see, do you see, Santa Maria is over the world, too. She can help you talk to God.

"I wouldn't know what to say."

"Ask her anything; she will give you courage."

Belia was gone in a flash, as was the sun, replaced by the glow of the lights of Vegas, which sparked to life in a thousand yellow eyes.

He is the evil she crushes. He is the evil…

All at once, it seemed as simple and clear as the stars coming to life in the night sky. He is evil, Vera is evil, these people who took her in are evil. God is Good. "I reject him, I reject Satan." Her renunciation of him, all his show and his works was quick and complete. *I love God. I want to love God.* Her mind was made up. Angela tore down the single flight of stairs trying to control her thoughts. She flew to her room and went straight to her walk-in closet, desperate that she not be discovered. Her hands fingered along the top shelf till they came to the pile of her old clothes. She wanted nothing from this life, and she would take nothing. The scales had fallen from her eyes. Joyfully, she stripped off her Jimmy Choo heels and the designer dress that cost more than a year's rent and ecstatically donned her torn jeans and sweater.

KNOCK. KNOCK.

Angela froze at the sound then quickly threw on a robe. "What is it?" she called out.

"It's me, Fadge. Mistress Vera called and wanted me to check on you. You need anything?"

"Oh no, no, I'm fine. I'm just tired. I'm taking a shower and going to bed. Er, uh, tell grandma, I'll talk to her in the morning."

"Okay. Night Miss."

"Night Fegan."

Heavy footfalls echoed away, and Angela dropped the robe. She turned the shower on incase he returned, retrieved the St. Michael

287

card from her armoire, and locked the door on her way out. The EXIT sign by the stairwell blinked like a beacon. She took the stairs two and three at a time, fearless and full of a freeing elation. She felt lighter than Styrofoam as she landed, pushing the bar across the outside door and bursting to the sidewalk. Angela Miller ran into the night, hitting the streets again.

* * *

Scott Henderson looked up from his game of Blackjack, his spidey senses tingling. Keen eyes scanned the casino in search of a light of some sort. It was gone almost as fast as it came. An enemy of the Order? A harmless passer-by? Vera was in Denver as is Emmett where they are handling a situation with a group of nosy wackos demanding access to underground airport tunnels. Scott was the only elder in Dream Catcher tonight—the only one who could sense a light.

"Twenty-one, sir," the dealer said, and the drunk man in suspenders and a cap that said "I ate Las Vegas" slapped the table and gave Scott a go-man grin, as if they had just outwitted a tightwad uncle. All the players at the table were of the same mind—a win for one was a win for all. The trouble was Henderson was on a streak. Chips were multiplying as fast as paramecium in a Petri dish. No self-respecting Blackjack lover would leave a table this hot. Scott motioned the dealer then stepped back from the table a few feet, keeping his eyes on the cards and pulling out his cell.

"Uh, yes, this is Mr. Henderson. This Antonio?" The butler confirmed, and was probably in the kitchen as Scott heard a utensil clink. "Kindly check on Miss Angeler and see if she needs anything. Call me immediately at this number if anything is, uh, amiss?" He returned to his seat sliding two black chips to the bet. "Right then, hope I didn't put the kibosh on our luck." He cocked his chin sideways, stretched his neck, and rubbed his hands as if he were warming them over the chips. The Dealer showed a six to Scott's ten, and the count had been high when he left the table only one before. The whole table stayed. The Dealer took his hit…

"Busted!" the table shouted with him, everyone "chuffed as nuts" as they say back home in England and giddy with their good fortune.

The butler Antonio had a problem too. He was in the middle of a delicious meal, when Mr. Henderson called. He had heard the girl come in from the roof as usual. He also knew Fegan had checked on her not twenty minutes ago. She had eaten earlier this evening, and she never seemed to need anything. Besides, she just asked when she did. Obviously, his employers wanted him to check on her. He wasn't stupid. He knew she was a prisoner of sorts; even knew she was wanted for murder. She was a willing inmate at the penthouse; where would she go? Henderson was not the usual one giving orders. He was probably being overprotective or paranoid.

No, Anthony would finish his fish sandwich and glass of vino, thank you very much. Then he would call the number back and assure Mr. Worrywart Henderson that Little Miss Murderer was tucked in for the night—cause she was. Yep, the problem was this sandwich; it was too good and he was too bushed to traipse down the hall and wake sleeping beauty just to ask if there was anything she wanted other than a good night's sleep. Antonio took a satisfying bite followed by a sip of wine and thought no further.

* * *

"Sister Eva is not working tonight," a wiry older woman said, not unkindly.

"Can I spend the night? I—," Angela stopped mid-thought. How do you explain being held captive (sort of) by an evil group, being wanted for two murders that were really self-defense, and being afraid your ex-boyfriend slash pimp who beats you up? How do you explain wanting a second chance, wanting to start over, wanting to be a different person, a good person? "It's my boyfriend; he beats—"

"Sorry hinney," the fibrous voice answered in that turned up decibel nursing home aides use on the elderly, "even if we weren't full, and we are, you'd have-ta be admitted by a doctor or a social worker. Sumpin' like that, 'kay? Haven's not zactly that kinda shelter. You could try the Y or Oak Tree over on Main Street. It's not so bad as they say, hinney." The sinewy arms holding the door let go, and Angela boldly stuck a hand out to arrest it.

"Could you just give me Eva's number or tell me where she lives "

"Oh, my heart, hinney, you are a funny thing. I can't give out information like that about any of our workers."

"But she said I could talk to her any time. She said—"

"Well, he-he, I'm sure she meant here when she is working hiney, not at her 'partment in the middle of the night." She sniggered again, when at once a loud argument broke out somewhere in the distance. Women's voices shrieked like maniac cats behind her followed by a booming thunk. "Oh boy, I gotta go, beautiful. You move on now and try the Y, kay?"

She turned screaming as she went, "Hey, you girls are going to your beds, you keep that up. I'll lock it down. I swear to . . . "

The heavy, self-closing door was barely an inch from shutting the warmth and light of the shelter on Angela's face when she shot her fingers in the cracked opening. She bit back a scream as the hefty door crushed the life out of her fingers, and putting her shoulder to it, she pushed it open slowly. She saw the woman's short rangy form recede, arms pumping like a locomotive's wheels as she hustled toward the Day Room to intervene in the escalating altercation and crashing furniture. Angela massaged her squashed fingertips and headed toward the office. "Be open. Be open. Be open," she chanted under her breath, turning the handle and letting herself in. She rifled through papers on the desk, ransacked drawers, combed two file cabinets, and scanned a bulletin board beside the door, all yielding nothing. She questioned the feasibility of her cockamamie plan— searching for the first name Eva with no clue as to a last name, pinning her hopes on a woman she barely knew and who for all she could guess, would turn her in, or at the very least, want nothing to do with her and her troubles. For the briefest moment, *he* flitted across her mind followed by an immediate sense of despair and hopelessness. "Jesus, no," she whispered and fingered the Saint Michael card in her jean coat pocket.

It was on her second pass through the file cabinet, that she spied a W2 form. Angela, who hadn't had three real jobs lasting more than a handful of months in her whole life, nonetheless knew W2's meant information. She searched for the name Eva, when suddenly the quiet hit her. It was over; the fight had ended. Shoot! She shoved the whole folder in her coat and eased the file drawer closed. Thirty seconds later, the heavy maroon door banged behind her, and Angela leapt down the steps walking as fast as her long legs would carry her.

Eva stood in her kitchen making tea, wearing the same blue kerchief and blue dress as before. Peering in the door's curtained window, Angela rapped twice, jarring Eva, whose overfull teacup sloshed a wet plop to the floor. For what seemed like minutes, but in reality was shorter than half a thirty second commercial, Angela feared the shocked face would call 911, scream, slam the door, or yell, "Help murderer!" or all of the above. Instead, Eva opened the door, grabbed Angela's forearm, yanked her inside, slammed the door, and bolted it shut.

"Heavens ta Betsy!" she gasped, still holding the forearm, "I been worried sick over you!"

An hour later, the two sat together on a tattered plaid loveseat. The only other seat in the room was a dilapidated rocker with purple cushions that looked as if it had been resurrected from a neighbor's curb. Most of the furniture in the four hundred square foot duplex apartment, no doubt, fit the same bill. After wearing only the finest designer silks and satins, now in a worn blue chenille robe that might possibly be older than herself, Angela Miller was more comfortable than she had been in two and half months of "living the dream". Sitting with her thin legs tucked under her, cradling a cup of herbal tea in a chipped mug, and reaching for an Oreo cookie, she felt truly safe and loved.

Eva was a most patient listener, and after Angela recounted everything that had happened since her stay at New Haven, Eva said she never believed that Angela had killed anyone and that she thought something was fishy in the police report and news casts. Eva heard every detail from the date-rape drugging to the kidnapping by Eddy to the so-called rescue by the woman known as Vera. Her breath caught at the honest admission of the evil in Angela's dreams and the humble divulgence of how close to giving in Angela had come. When Angela broke down and cried, Eva's plump hand rubbed circles on her back. After a time, perhaps a seasoned counselor's best guess of enough crying time having passed, Sister Eva, relieved Angela of her empty cup and placed it on the scratched coffee table. She took both Angela's hands in hers and said, "Hey," waiting for Angela to look at her. "Hey" she repeated, ducking her smiling red cheeks to catch

Angela's red eyes. "Ya were brave. Ya been through more in your life than ten 'a anybody I know, and I know a lot." Eva's voice low and lilting, the stuff of bedtime nursery rhymes, ended in a jolly grunt. "Ya guarded your heart. Ya suffered, ya waited, and when it mattered most, ya answered God's call."

Angela slept curled on the tatty loveseat, and regardless of its smelling of disinfectant and threads that itched her skin, she slept more soundly than she had slept in months. Even in sleep it was as if her life were her own again. Eva had gone to the store for a few groceries, and Angela had explored the unassuming quarters. Eva lived simply, sparsely, and free of possessions. She owned one set of sheets, which she washed once a week with the handful of garments that constituted her wardrobe. The tiny bathroom had one bar of Ivory soap, one cheap shampoo, one toothbrush, one toothpaste, one towel, and one washcloth. The shelves of the boxy eight by eight kitchen, held four cups, four saucers, four plates and four bowls, two glasses, a few cans of soup and one cereal box. Rattling in the drawers was a Spartan supply of utensils. The nickel tour ended at the tiny table where Angela sat in one of two ladder-back chairs when a pleasingly plump Eva came in the kitchen door holding a grocery bag and the newspaper.

She plopped the bag on the minute space of counter and placed the paper in front of Angela. Staring her in the face were two photos, one her own mug shot and the other Eddy's. It took a moment to sink in . . .

"Eddy's . . . dead?" She said. "I can't . . . I don't understand. I didn't know."

"Hmm, it sounds like this cult or coven or what have ya, has managed to pin this Eddy Platzman's death on you too." Eva's voice, which had been almost conversational as she unpacked milk, eggs, and cereal snapped to attention. "You're really surprised he's dead? I mean when ya told me the whole story just now I, uh," Eva grunted and rubbed chubby fingers across her chin, "I just assumed they kilt him. Never crossed your mind, huh?" She sat down opposite Angela with a look of sympathy.

"He was alive as far as I knew. I really never thought...I loved him in a way. I—I know that's crazy. I can't explain. It's . . ."

292

Eva took the paper, which hadn't moved from Angela's hands since she'd first picked it up. "You don't have ta explain. I may not get it, but I've seen enough women in your situation to know ya cared. Caring never needs an explanation. It's just the sign of a good heart," Eva said, patting her hand. "Ooo, the ice cream," she said, jumping up. She put away the remainder of the items and folded the bag methodically saying, "We need a plan."

Four cups of coffee, two sandwiches, a pint of rocky road, and two hours later, the plan was in place. Eva was coolheaded and Angela quick thinking. The coven had obvious power over police and media, which were all on the lookout for anyone matching Angela's description. The first order of business then was a haircut and dye job. Eva's talents lay in other directions, but the hacked results, which left Angela looking like a redheaded Anne Hathaway, transformed her looks. The second order of business, daunting as it seemed and executed in two days no less, obtained for Angela a fake driver's license. Eva was apologetic as they completed the shady business conducted in a surprisingly upscale office off the strip. "They, uh, feel indebted ta me. I kinda, at least they say…I saved their sister's life one night . . . " Angela had hugged Eva and examined the flawless fake license, which would allow her to travel, hopefully undetected, to the third order of business—a new job and location.

293

32

Four Kings

MONDAY, MARCH 26, 2007

For Angela, Four Kings Casino in Upstate New York rose out of a farmy landscape like the Emerald City in a field of poppies. As she stepped off the Greyhound bus, an icy North wind whipped her cheeks and menaced the oversized grey sweatshirt. She waited on the side of the bus with others as the driver opened the baggage door in the underbelly of the beast and extracted one swallowed bag after another. Angela claimed the dated blue vinyl number Eva had found at the Salvation Army. With her head tilted against the biting wind, she focused on the pair of heels in front of her and followed fellow passengers inside.

It was exactly one week after scaring the beegeesus out of Sister Eva in her little flat. Angela had flown into Syracuse airport then taken the two hour, twenty dollar bus ride right to the casino's front door. Eva had insisted she bring at least one warm coat, and after some disagreement—mostly because Angela did not want Eva to spend another goodhearted dime on her—they settled on the BUM Equipment sweatshirt from Goodwill. Eva had no concept of sizes, least of all Angela's size. Angela tried on everything in the pile and came up with only a couple leggings, skinny jeans that were too short and had to be rolled into capris, several tee shirts, and the big grey sweatshirt she now clung to in gratitude. How could she have forgotten what winters were like up North? And it was still March — Gadzooks!

She rummaged in her slouch purse for her fake ID and stared at the name Rachel Hart. The guy who made the ID suggested she use her middle name Raphaella. Ridiculous, of course. Absolutely no one is named Raphaella. Her mother had chosen it, and after three days of heated debate with her father, who said it sounded like a "gol-darn cat," a compromise was reached. On her Birth Certificate, it read Angela Raphaella. She was baptized Raphael, so her Baptismal Certificate said simply, "Raphael Miller." Angela figured her mother had a thing for angels.

The gray skies and scruffy March landscape outside were drab compared to the sweeping ceiling and sunny yellows of the casino lobby. Angela took in the two-story, blue-lit waterfalls. Far from natural looking, it was nevertheless impressive in its sheer magnitude as tub-full sheets of shimmering water cascaded down sheer rock. The aquatic monster left her feeling small and out of place as she approached the long front desk. It too lay yawning before her, dwarfing the lone attendant. Upon hearing her request, he called Garry Oleson, the Four Kings' manager. Pointing up with a bored expression, he told Angela to wait in the bar just off the stairs on the second floor until Mr. Oleson was available. Letters screaming Uptown Tavern in a giant circular curve loomed over the lobby leaving no question as to where he meant.

The tavern had a cutting edge appeal. It was rustic with brick walls, an orangey tin ceiling, and rough-hewn wood, all playing against clean modern lines of industrial windows, black tables, and boxy lights as if a saloon had stepped into a city loft. It was still quite early, and the space was empty save one striking figure sitting at the long, curving bar. She stood in the doorway a moment debating where to sit. Thinking it might look standoffish if she sat at a table, she sat on a stool at the bar two down from the lone drinker. She was lightly jarred by his eye patch as she shuffled onto her seat, not only the patch, but with his dark look and wavy stream of hair, her first impression was that of a pirate.

A rumply woman of maybe forty, her figure trapped in a pinstriped uniform blouse and pressing through the spaces between buttons, plopped a napkin in front of Angela and said, "Name it, sweetie."

"Oh, uh, I was told to wait here for Mr. Oleson. I don't need—"

"You interviewing for something?"

"Housekeeping, I think."

"You think?", she snickered, looking at the man then back at Angela. "Now, that's a fine start. Coffee, soda, or water? And relax, Red, it's on the house."

"Oh, that's cool. Actually, I would *love* a cup of coffee. Thanks."

The entire time she exchanged words with the woman, she was aware of the Italian stallion next to her, head down, big hands framing his beer glass, head tilted, glancing her way. He had a slight grin and spoke just after the bartender left. "You travel light," he said, nodding to the marbled blue suitcase with fat silver clasps, sitting by her stool, looking lonely without its matching siblings lost somewhere in the 1970's.

"Yeah, I, uh, don't need a lot," Angela said, acutely aware of being underdressed next to his black slacks and crisp cotton dress shirt. Unsmiling, she dug her hands a little deeper into the center pocket of her sweatshirt and hunched down, engaging an invisible force field.

"Sorry, you, a, probably don't want some strange guy talking to you the second you get here," he said, turning back to his beer.

He caught on quickly, Angela thought. Here, she had hoped that guys hitting on her would become a thing of her past. His apology hung in the air. Maybe it was the eye patch, making her feel sorry for him, or maybe she was just a tad lonely herself, either way she intended just to say something innocuously social, but the next words out of her mouth made her want to kick herself. "S'ok, I guess. Depends how strange you are." She had positively not intended it to sound flirtatious. Inside she writhed, thinking she had no idea after all these years as a hooker of how to respond to a man without any snippy innuendo, sassy sarcasm, or ulterior motive.

"Ha, I'm not the one rocking Marsha Brady's suitcase," he said.

She caught herself laughing and responded, "Whoa, low blow, Mister. It's all I could find."

"Oh, now I'm really sorry. I thought maybe you were into Vintage or something."

"Yeah, right," she quipped, "my BUM sweatshirt is all the rage with trendsetters, I suppose."

"Truce," he said, revealing adorable dimples and extending his hand waiting for her to unleash hers from inside her sweatshirt force field. "I'm Sergio."

Her hand slipped into his just as her coffee arrived. For a split second, she felt a thrilling charge at his touch, and she found herself wishing it could linger. Flustered, she said, "I'm An—Rachel." Her tongue twisted over the fake name.

"Well, Ann Rachel—"

"No,"—her head shook once—"just Rachel."

"Funny you don't look like a Rachel."

With a twinge of guilt, she swirled a creamer in her coffee then pursed her lips into pout. "Really, what do I look like?"

Ignoring her question, the guy asked from where she had come. She evaded his question as well, choosing to talk about her hometown in New York. Over the next half hour, as the two of them talked casually and freely, her defenses melted away. His slight accent, the shy way he cast his look down when their eyes met, a self-effacing kind of humor and an unassuming strength—he had a humble frankness, all of which placed this Sergio on a working man's level, a level on which she could relate. She studied his curling black hair, sharp cheekbones, and ripped body, and when she came to his eyes, somewhere in this Italian Adonis, she sensed hurt, beaten down and deeply buried—much like her own, she imagined. For just a moment, they were two wounded birds peering at one another in perfect sympathy.

Angela was mid-sentence when his cell phone hummed, and Sergio jumped up like the white rabbit in Wonderland. He slapped a five on the bar, excused himself, and wished her luck.

"Hey Sergio," she called, "You never answered my question."

He paused only a second thinking then turned back with a grin. "An angel," he said, "you look like an angel."

Not much later Eva's cousin, Mr. Oleson, the manager of Four Kings, met her and led her to his office back on the first floor, asking her on the way if she had any experience as a maid. He was a short man of delicate stature, with greying temples and a lightly furrowed face. His manner was matter-of-fact, but held a certain warmth, like an uncle who slips you a five when he firmly shakes your hand.

298

"That's okay," he assured her, stepping into his office "you'll pick it up pretty quick. If Eva is any judge of character, you're no shirker." He took a seat behind his desk and indicated a chair with his palm. She sat tucking the blue case behind the chair and clutching her slouch purse on her lap. "Sally will be in charge of training you. She's good—just don't ask too many questions or she'll write you off as an idiot." He leaned back in his chair and twiddled a pen between his fingers. "Now, uh… I know you have nowhere to stay…" There was an uncomfortable pause, but Angela had nothing to add to the statement of fact, so she waited for him to continue.

"This is entirely unheard of, you understand," he said, clearing his throat. "It will just be temporary. You'll have to work something else out later. You, uh… have to keep this under the radar, and for pity's sake, be discreet…I'm—cough, cough—going to give you a room. It's one of the ones we rarely rent unless we're chock full. It's actually smaller than a single—not exactly sure how those came to be rooms." He tapped the pen lightly on a stack of papers in front of him. "It will be on the books as a comp. But I expect you to be saving up. Don't blow your paychecks on booze or fancy clothes or anything like that." His tone was more and more the stern uncle. He pointed the pen at her. "You'll have to save enough money for a security deposit, *and* first and last month's rent on an apartment in Merna. Oh, I'll be comping your meals, too, for a little while, anyway, till you get on your feet."

Angela uncrossed and re-crossed her thin legs nodding.

"Lemme see that ID." She passed it to him as he continued to speak. "Your pay will have to be under the table, obviously. Can't issue you an employee number or do any of the usual paperwork. Okay, er…Rachel, it's not bad," he said, sliding it back across the desk. "Your ID will be good for most other stuff." He said the last at the same time picking up the desk phone pressing a button, and turning his back to Angela, who sat in the chair looking about the boxy office, devoid of any color, save a few photos, presumably of his family. "Yeah ok, who then? Whose around? Yeah alright. Have him meet me at the elevator outside the first cage." He hung up. "That your only bag?"

She looked down embarrassed at the outmoded case, for which Eva paid all of three bucks. As small as it was, it was still not full, with only a pair of jeans, three tee shirts, a package of Hanes size five, cotton, bikini underwear, two tanks, one pair of socks, and a pair of used sneaks. All but the undies and socks, which were purchased new at Walmart, had been found at Goodwill.

"Yeah, I don't need much," she said for the second time today.

"Welp, you need a uniform for starters," he said, getting up. "Walk with me."

She followed Mr. Oleson out of his office, past the gilded cashier cages, over predictably kitschy red and gold rugs, past dozens of garish slots towards the elevator. What is it with casinos and the reds and gold, she wondered? Had some researcher revealed that it made people gamble more, be looser with their money, or be so engrossed in the illusion of money that they wouldn't notice losing their own? They arrived at the elevator, just as the doors opened. There stood a diminutive figure in classic-blue, handyman attire. His brown hair was combed back like a young man from the fifties and his open, smiling face made her immediately think of someone special.

"Clyde, this is Rachel, Rachel Hart, joining our housekeeping staff. She'll be staying in the lower level, room B13. I need you to show her around."

"Sure thing, Mr. Oleson. Whatever you want."

"Oh, and go down to the laundry and outfit her with a housekeeping uniform. Include the shoes, too." Oleson caught hold of Clyde's forearm, causing Clyde to jump back and stiffen. The manager immediately held his palms up in a universal take-it-easy sign, as if he were calming a skittish horse. "Tell them I said no paperwork on this one. Tell them I'm taking care of it, 'kay, Clyde?"

Angela stepped onto the elevator with Clyde, and the two traveled in silence. He seemed to be sizing her up, almost literally. His eyes traveled slowly all the way up to the top of her head, like a kid watching the red ball ascend the meter stick at the fair. Then down, down, down, his look traveled to her feet, returning to her face with an unabashed smile. Angela thought if any other man had traveled the length of her so boldly with his eyes, she'd have tried to charge him. But this guy! Just look at him, his open, honest face, curious eyes peering into hers same way a kid does the first time they meet you. He made no comment, and seemed content with her silence. Normally, she might have expected some attempt at small talk given the situation. Just as she would have expected to feel at least somewhat discomfited with this complete stranger's odd behavior. Instead, this man exuded a comfortable kind of non-demanding, unselfconscious quiet.

After visiting the laundress, who sized Angela up, this time with a tape measure, they returned to the casino floor. Pit bosses and dealers acknowledged Clyde as he passed with big grins and smiles. He told her the rules about not crossing the casino floor and about being invisible to customers. Then he cupped his hand like a grade school girl and whispered, "If you really havta, you can. Just stay over here by these slots and cut this way. It's only a couple a managers that'll give you the business. Clydey'll help you learn the ropes." And he did. As he warmed up to her or she to him, she wasn't sure, she found Clyde Stoltz had something to say in every department. With so much inside information, Angela thought, someone would think he was the owner and not just a janitor, except for his unmistakable, artless candor and—she shook head and inwardly laughed at the thought for nothing about this simple soul would make anyone think he owned anything.

A few weeks later, Angela was happier scrubbing toilets than she had been for more than a decade. She lived so purely now compared to before—her heart was light and young again. Sometimes she caught herself daydreaming that she had just graduated high school and gotten this job here, as if the last fifteen years never happened, as if she never ran off, never was a hippie, never had an abortion, never sold herself to eat or live.... Still when the dark cloud of her past would descend, plunging her in fear or despair, there would be Clyde, showing up in the hall or appearing just over her shoulder, cheering her with his unfeigned interest, his uncomplicated, guileless trust that absolutely everything was as it should be. In Clyde's view, not a hair in the universe was out of place. Clyde really did seem to sit in God's hand, fitting as comfortably as an old man in an easy chair. And from this comfortable position trusting in Divine Providence, Clyde

301

accepted every person as this beautiful creation of God's. He held empathy for absolutely everyone, good and bad alike. He kept a childlike faith in every soul, believing each person was as well-meaning and charitable as himself, assigning his own good traits to all he met, and assuming the best of everyone. Angela came to believe Clyde was more than special, much, much more; Clyde Stoltz was a peek at what mankind was meant to be.

With these thoughts, Angela wheeled a cart of glassware collected from room service into the Uptown Tavern. She delivered the load and was turning to leave when she heard a voice calling from a booth in the far corner. It was Sergio, the man she'd met the day she arrived. He was motioning her over. She approached, intending just to say hi, but he caught her hand and pulled her into the rounded seat with him. He ignored her pleas that she was in uniform and not allowed to sit in the restaurant.

"They can't see you over here," he said. "Besides, I'm in good with Zelda. She won't give you away. C'mon, stay. I'm lonely."

"You're gonna get me in trouble." She could not help but grin. He seemed a friend, and she had none of those here besides Clyde Stoltz. "She really called Zelda?"

"Yes," he said, and squinted then admitted, "No," laughing, "I just call her that cause she's German and"—he waved his hand as if he was erasing a sentence on a chalkboard—"It's a long story, a thing between us. Sides it bugs her. Rachel, right?" She nodded. "How's the maid thing going?"

"It's alright, actually,"—she gave an apologetic shrug—"I like the work. It feels good," she said, stealing a French fry off his plate. "This will sound weird, but taking something dirty, making it clean…it's gratifying, like I'm, you know, making a difference somehow. Crazy, right?" She heard her own laugh, a tad nervous but natural. The fact was she did feel—as if for the first time—what she was doing made a difference. When she entered a room it was a mess; when she left, it was clean. That little factoid was more than she could say for a good part of her life, and it felt damn good. It was work, good, honest, hold-your-head-up-high work. Why she wanted to tell Sergio all that was beyond her, and she told him so.

"No, no, Rachel. It sounds good. I get it. I wish I could feel that way too," he said, sipping his drink and looking beyond her out the long window, which had no view except the sunlight that filtered through more windows towering over the lobby. He was far off for a moment then returned. "What I do—what I have to do, er, it's… almost the opposite. I feel…dirty in my line of work." Looking down, he twisted his drink on his napkin. He glanced back up at her with an incredibly soulful look. "I'm glad for you. I'd give anything for that in my life."

He seemed remorseful and distant. The natural question would be to ask him what he does for a living, but she sensed it was a question he neither wanted to hear nor answer. "So, why don't you quit," she asked, filching another fat fry. "Do something else."

His head thrust back gazing over the copper ceiling tiles. "It's more complicated than I could ever explain. My life, it's not my own. I don't know when it ever was."

Her heart did an empathetic lurch. His sadness, that feeling of being trapped. Though she barely knew him, and though he never said what it was he couldn't walk away from, or who, and even though he had revealed nothing of his problems in these scraps of shared regrets, it was as if she knew him because he was just like…her. Sergio was caught in a trap, perhaps one he stepped into as she had with eyes wide open but seeing no other way, perhaps he lay in a bed of his own making, yet completely unable to set himself free. But why? She couldn't say why she herself had been set free. How is it that she was here and not turning tricks in Vegas or worse, in league with the devil incarnate Vera. It was beyond her, yet Angela, of all people, was uniquely qualified to understand this man's sadness.

She let him change the subject, and relaxing more and more, they talked of everything from the weather to baseball. He pushed the plate of fries in front of her and offered her his untouched water. It was genial. She might have been twelve and kicking her legs over the garden wall, sitting comfortably close to a best friend, discussing the world or nothing at all. She hadn't hung out with someone in forever.

"You like my eyewear?"

"Oh, I'm sorry. Was I…I didn't mean to stare," Angela grimaced.

"Naw, you're fine. It, uh, I had a run-in with a nail, of sorts."

303

A nail gun flashed in her head. She heard the pop and hiss, saw the uncontrollable jerking and crimson stream running down his face in the blue light. "I'm so sorry," she whimpered. His expression became quizzical, and she wiped the memory clean and spoke as naturally as possible. "Will, uh, you need the patch long? Is it bad?"

"Not bad—gone," Sergio said, lifting the patch, revealing the puckered skin hugging soft pink flesh, a little like the inside of a red grape. The empty socket was macabre, but she swallowed her instinctive recoil and maintained an even look as he spoke. "I could get an acrylic eyeball, Doc says in a month. Not sure I will though."

"Why not?" she said, watching him pull the patch back in place.

"It's a reminder of my own stupidity,—the price I paid for—besides," he said, straightening up with a Rhett Butler grin, his fingers drumming the table. "It's debonair. Makes me mysterious."

She snickered. "Oh it does, does it?"

"Yup, the ladies can't resist it. Look at you."

"Hey-o, woe Tiger. I'm not..." She gave him a slap, and he made a show of rubbing his chiseled arm. It was easy with him, easy to talk, easy to sympathize, and scarily easy to flirt. She was a teen again in his presence. He was kind of debonair. She wondered if he sensed it too, that they were both scarred, both simpatico, that perhaps both of them saw the world through the same pair of scratched lenses. Perhaps he too suspected that they had as much in common, and neither of them were ready to burden the other with stories of the past, let alone worries of the future. Perhaps too, both of them knew the other was holding back, and perhaps both knew that was for the best. Either way, it seemed fine for both of them, for now.

33

Clyde's Day Off

Clyde Stoltz was a good son. His widowed mother could count on his visits every Thursday as surely as she could a priest for Sunday Mass. Clyde's hours at Four Kings had been the same since the day he was hired, second shift Monday through Wednesday and first shift, Friday through Sunday. Thursdays were for his mom. The rest of the week belonged to Four Kings. Excepting Thursdays, anyone could find Clyde Stoltz at Four Kings either long after a first shift or long before second. And if he was there, he was working. That was just Clyde. On duty or off, he gave a hand, ran errands, grabbed a mop or a screwdriver, whatever was needed. Managers, fellow custodians, bar tenders, hotel clerks or maids, there was no one who didn't call on Clyde, and no one who questioned if he was on shift or not. When Mr. Oleson was hired to manage the casino and hotels, he noted Clyde's strange hours and continual presence, and it became quickly apparent to him how much everyone took advantage of this open, generous man. Oleson sat Clyde down in his office one day and sounding like a father to a son, he proceeded to expound on the replenishing benefits of time away from work.

"For what?" Clyde had asked Oleson with all sincerity.

Phrases such as, "take it easy", "relax and watch TV", "take in a movie", or "enjoy time for yourself" fell on a blank face as if Oleson were explaining physics to a first grader. After several attempts, Oleson sighed and patiently explained that even if Clyde should want to hang out around the casino after work, he should at least tell his coworkers he was off duty. Clyde listened to this fatherly advice with a mix of curiosity and wonder. Though this last counsel, left him thinking that maybe the new manager thought he was in the way. Truth was Clyde saw the whole casino as his home and the workers as his family. Who wouldn't want to be near their family and to be helpful? He got plenty of rest, and what was there to do in his place in town, anyway?

Clyde lived in a one room flat in the tiny town of Merna, New York. His apartment had a hotplate, a six-inch black and white, pop-up TV his dad gave him in the 70's, and the tiny Frigidaire a college student left behind. Just to make tea or instant coffee, Clyde had to exit his room, walk a long, narrow hall to the back of the Victorian house, ascend a narrow flight of stairs, and fill his pot in the bathroom sink. The same route was traversed to relieve himself. All that way too, to hit a toilet so many seemed to miss, he often chuckled to himself. In order to shower, yet one more even narrower flight of stairs was necessary. Nine of the thirteen renters in the hundred-year-old house had their own lavatory or kitchenette. Clyde, however, rented only the one fifteen by fifteen foot room above the stairs for fifty dollars a week. He had rented the first place he saw. It had a bed, a folding table, a couple chairs, and solid chest of drawers, and that was all he really needed. He had tossed the classifieds with half a dozen red circled one-line ads in the trash can and shook the landlord's hand saying, "Yup, this is good," and that was that.

The low rent allowed Clyde to take good care of his 1965 AMC Rambler Ambassador 440 he had inherited from his dad. It was the last year they made the Rambler. She was robin's egg blue with a white top and black interior, four doors, a split bench front seat, and a 327 V8, four barrel, "easy muscle" engine with the power of a Mack truck. What more could a guy want, Clyde wondered, rolling the window down by hand and inhaling some of that fresh fifty-degree day. Funny he thought, how fifty degrees on a day in July would feel downright cold, but here in April, it was sweet with the promise of spring.

He was enjoying the hour and a half drive to his mom's in Ithaca. She lived in the tiny two-bedroom cabin his great grandfather Uriah Prey built over a hundred and fifty years ago. Crafted to last generations, it was simple, plain, and practical, much like his mom, Anna Stoltz. Originally, the cabin was not outfitted with toilets or running water. Then both were added in the late fifties. It was long after most folks had gained such conveniences, but convenience was not a word that registered even a blip on the Prey radar. No, Preys were known for and most comfortable when, "making do."

For Preys, life was good; it was every moment of every day taken exactly as the good Lord handed it to you. What could be better, a Prey was taught, than what the all-knowing, all-powerful, and all-loving God had planned for you? If God handed you a loaf of bread one day and a stone the next, a barrel of good crops or a passel of crop-ruining bugs, what difference should it make to you? God feeds the birds, he'll feed you. In short, Preys learned to accept all from the hand of their Creator. Where others suffered anxiety, Preys were trained to accept. Where others wore themselves out questioning their maker to tears, Preys enjoyed an inner calm and happiness. This is how his mother Anna was raised and how she raised him. Truly, the only pain they endured was in their empathy for others. It pained them to see sin, to hear of evil or violence, and most especially it pained his mother and himself to watch the pain folks piled on their already faith-deprived lives, when around the corner and within easy reach, the joy and tranquility he and his mother enjoyed were there for the taking.

Clyde reached his mom's dirt drive going slow around a couple of strutting chickens, who scratched and bobbed their way in front of the Rambler as completely unthreatened as they were unhurried. Swinging the car door open, a grainy, wet nose attacked his knees, and his hand reached out to rub Mable's soft brown fur. Her tail wagged furiously, and she danced excitedly in circles about him as he walked.

"Mable you old gal, you never lose any of your pep, do you girl?" Despite her great age of nearly fifteen, Mable, a collie mix, could run with the best farm dogs. Not much of a watchdog though, as the greeting Clyde received was the same Mable gave everybody. She was just happy to see you. His hand continued to pat and caress whatever jumping part he could reach. His mom stood on the porch watching her only son approach. He was aware what a blessing he was to her, and how she had not received him till her forty-second year. Long after her family and even her husband had decided she was barren,

307

she had hoped for him and prayed to be blessed. As she often reminded him, he was truly the answer to her prayers.

Clydey, my Clydey. Aw," she said from the porch, wiping her hands on a kitchen towel. "Mable's been hankerin' for attention like yours—just hankerin'."

The screen door screeched and banged behind them, and inside, Mable settled at his feet as Clyde sat at the thick-varnished table, letting the cozy kitchen and comfortable routine hold him close. On the floor, the roughhewn wide planks were smooth with years of use, scrubbing, and linseed oil. The same maple although whitewashed, lined the walls, covered in odd-sized shelves and splattered with penny nails and railroad spikes, holding roped utensils, black pans, coats, faded aprons, and a menagerie of fishing hats. Postwar steel cabinets topped with red linoleum and a chrome band stretched around the chipped porcelain sink and drain board. A fat Frigidaire and a giant Tappan stove flashed more chrome like dimples on a smile. Two short rows of shelving held a few dishes and pots, and an assortment of glass jars. These were stuffed with peaches, red beets, green beans, and pickles, stuffed much like the room was stuffed too, a comfortable mess of everyday living without any semblance of order, where nonetheless everything had its place.

His mom moved to the stove and gave the stew a stir, turned the flame low, and put the lid on. "Kettle's hot, yes hot, and there's a mess of spring smell in the air. What say I grab a coat, an' we sit outside on the rocker with some tea while the stew sets up. Yes, yes, you fill me in on all them shenanigans up there at the casino and in that crazy maze of a house you bunk in, ha ha."

"Remember Eileen?" he said, up now and helping to reach the mugs from the hook behind the stove. His mother scooped tea leaves from a giant wide mouth mason jar into a chubby brown pot. She grew the chamomile herself.

"The practical joker?"

"Uh, huh. She's gone and done what she said she'd do."

"No, you don't say. With all the flour and the bucket, an all that?" he nodded and her laugh erupted with a slap on the counter that shook the tea in the pot to an eighth inch from spilling. Following his mother to the rockers on the porch, Clyde carried the tea tray avoiding Mabel close at his heel.

Later they were back at the kitchen table finishing lunch. Anna held the basket of warm biscuits towards Clyde, who declined a fourth.

"Dogs is the best kind of people, Ma. You ever think about that?" Clyde wiped his mouth with the big napkin erasing the last of the homemade stew.

"Well, Clyde I don't really know, now. What do you mean?" She patted his arm with satisfaction as she collected his empty bowl and scooped up the basket of rolls. He always brought a good appetite to her table. Never could understand why he was so slight.

"See, they're happy just to please you, Ma" Clyde said, tilting his head back, and stretching his legs forward as she began the dishes. "Dogs just wait on you, ready to follow you, happy just to be with you, trusting you to provide for 'em and love 'em…. Dogs live for you, and they're happy about it. It's like me and God, you know?"

She thought about it. Clyde *was* something like a loyal, happy dog. He looked at his Creator the way a good dog looks at his master. Living to please God, looking for Him, waiting on his commands, and happy just following wherever he was led. "I guess I do know what you mean, Clyde. Yes, yes, I guess I do." Anna finished sloshing soapy water round the last dish, rinsed it and placed it in the plastic drainer. "Now, Clydey you g'wan an tell your ol' mama what else is going on up there at the Casino. Something more'n tricks on Sally has got your mind in a bunch. Mr. Oleson? He ok?"

"Oh, Mr. Oleson's doing a fine job, Ma." Clyde said, getting up and retrieving a striped towel from the oven door handle. He picked up a bowl and carefully dried it as Anna wiped the sink. "Everything's running smooth as anything." He got quiet as he rubbed the second bowl dry. He was working on getting something out. It was just his way. He spoke again while running the towel over the copper bottom of a Revere Ware pot older than himself. "There's a new girl. Her name's Rachel."

"You don't say?" She sprayed water, rinsing Ajax down the drain.

"She's the nicest young lady. Very sweet, real polite, but…she's not 'zactly who she says she is. I think she's running from someone."

309

"Who, Clyde?"

"I don't know, but I make out she had some trouble from where she came. The thing is, Ma, her light is powerful strong, and she has no idea."

"You can see light round this girl?" They both ceased working.

"Oh yeah, Ma, powerful. Brightest I've ever seen." His gaze went past her as if he were seeing the girl and her aura right there in the kitchen. "Only I get this feeling when I'm with her too. Them darks, they're looking for her"—holding the wet towel, he made circles in the air—"looking, looking, looking." Clyde finished and plunked back into the painted wood chair.

Anna squeezed the dishrag and hung it on a nail then sat opposite him at the table. As her son stared at the ceiling, Anna couldn't be sure. After all, there were no guarantees with this sort of thing. This Rachel…she could be… Anna reached across to Clyde's hard-working hand, whose big knuckles mirrored her own. She held it firmly. "You must stay very close to this Rachel, Clydey," Anna said. "I think she may be very special, very important. Now, I don't know for sure but…"—her voice was reassuring and careful—"She may be in danger. Oh yes, danger whenever you are not near her. If she is who I think she is, she'll be coming to the light fast now" Anna began mumbling almost to herself. "The legion will be able to see her more easily. Oh yes, her danger is very real,"—her voice rose—"Clydey, you're the key," Anna said, coming around the table and wrapping her wiry arms around his frail shoulders with an awareness of how thin he was compared to his strapping dad gone these thirty years. "You, my dear, are special too; you can mask her light, and only you. We knew the good God had a reason for placing you at the casino all these years. Didn't we know it, Clydey?" He nodded but looked wide-eyed. "Awww, you just g'wan and be yourself, Clydey. Never you mind about it. You just g'wan an do for that girl like you would anyhow. That will be fine enough for the Lord."

"Welp, I best be headin' back then." Mable commenced dancing about Clyde's knees as he stood.

"You not staying the night? No, no?"

I better not." They both knew it was because of Rachel, but neither brought it up again. "You wanna hand with anything before I go?"

"Naw," she pshawed, "I been keeping up with this old shack pretty good. I'll ask when I need it, oh yes, yes, you know I will." She walked him to the door. Reaching down for Mable's ears. "Stay girl; Clydey's got work to do." Clyde kissed his mom on the cheek. "Awww, my dearest boy, Mama loves you child. You need me, I'll be right here. You can count on that, Clydey. Oh yes, yes."

"I know mama. I'll see you next Thursday."

34

Peek-a-Boo, I See You

In the laundry room, Clarice twisted the dryer dial and hit the start button to give the sheets another toss in the heat while she sorted a tiny load for the washer. The new detergent smelled fresh. "Spring Fresh" she read on the blue container. spring was here, too. Last week, Easter had come and gone quickly, and with it the wistful hope she'd nursed in the back of her mind that John and she might have a repeat of the Christmas dinner. Instead, he'd gone to Church and not returned till evening, spending Easter with Mike Barrie and his family in Endwell.

Her arms full of the warm load, Clarice banged the dryer door closed with her foot. The door bit with such force it bounced open again. She gave it another satisfied kick, and this time it stuck. It felt good to kick something. Her spirit was more peeved than hurt as it had been more and more of late. John's bender, the imagined closeness, however fleeting and illusory, had left her damaged. Her heart in an effort to protect itself against the continual pain began to thicken its outer shell, holding itself aloof and void of emotion, lest it be hurt again. This unconscious protective shield with its cold and bitter shell so foreign to her, slowly ate at her normally warm personality. The effect of this hardening heart was to leave her angry. She was mad at the situation, mad at John, and mad at life.

Abruptly a concentrated stream of cool air blew against the back of her neck. She spun towards the open laundry room door, holding the warm clothes closer. John was outside working on something or other, but he could have come in through the studio office and left a door open. She stepped gently into the passageway, checked the studio, but the doors were shut. Continuing to the family room, she let the clothes tumble from her arms onto the couch. She began to folding them. Snapping a giant sheet in the air, another prickly breath brushed against her neck. Her hands flew to her nape, leaving the sheet to billow in a pile at her feet. Clarice's heart tripped as her fingers pressed the skin to block the air, which, at any rate, had gone. It left behind an arctic chill, whether real or imagined, for it was impossible to distinguish if she felt fear or actual cold.

"John," she called softly then a little louder, "John, you here? He wasn't. In fact, just then she heard the buzz saw in the distance and knew he was cutting down the plum tree that died. Calling out to John, though, proved to be the dose of reality she needed. This was silly. Houses have drafts, and you, Reece, have one, big, fat imagination. With that thought, she finished folding the sheets, trying not to hurry, as if, hurrying would somehow confirm her irrational fears or give some unknown entity permission to haunt her further.

Clarice carried the neat pile to the stairs aware of, yet purposely ignoring, a growing sense of being watched. She glanced left and right at murky shadows and dark corners, hearing her own steps on the wood. Exactly three steps from the top, her foot rose to step when the edge of her shirt jerked down and up as if someone were tugging it. Clarice shrieked and lost her balance. The folded clothes pitched in the air spilling en masse in a cascading trail down the stairs. Clarice, too, fell in a similar way, one hand clutching the landing, the other the stair below, and her legs sprawled beyond that. Unexpected tears pooled from the scare. She bristled, sensing the presence still near, and in a panic scrambled up the last steps headed to her room.

"M-o-m?"

She stopped short. It was faint, yet so recognizable; she turned and froze.

"Mom?" It came again from Jackson's room, his own sweet and familiar tone. From the time he was an infant, even when experts, pediatricians or nannies said to let him cry it out, Clarice never could. She would cradle her newborn son and rock him for hours on end—

as long as he needed her she would always be there. As he grew, no matter what the circumstance, Clarice would drop everything to run to her son when she heard him call. With no other thought than he needed her, and overcoming her fears, Clarice walked purposefully to his room. She turned the knob and pushed the door gently. It creaked slowly open. Nothing was unusual or out of place. She stood in the center of the room his bed on one side and the tremendous mural of the Glen on the other. The air hung thick and stuffy since the vents and door were normally closed.

She stood very still. Waiting. Nothing happened. She shifted her weight and sheepishly looked around the room. "Jackson, honey," she said, half afraid it wasn't him who had taunted her but some malevolent energy. "I'm here baby. Mommy's here." Nothing answered. In another moment, she would question her sanity. She squeezed her fists, and made the decision to leave when all of a sudden, her shirt tugged again. She stiffened as prickles sped up and down both arms. This time was different; this time, she sensed him and looking down, her breath caught. The same gold curls, the big green eyes that used to peer behind his Poindexter glasses—the same six year old she left in the care of the Glen. Tears glazed her eyes, and unconsciously, her mouth formed an O, holding the unspoken syllable in a kind of limbo as she gazed in his face. He was here. Her boy was right here… or was he? Her tremulous hand hovered above his head afraid to touch him, afraid the vision would dissolve.

"Don't mom, he said, though his lips did not move. She tried to process the disconnect of hearing him speak without seeing him speak, while at the same time unable to get over the fact she was seeing him at all. "I'm not really here in my room. I'm with you but not here." Her hand pulled back to her lips. He paused, and she wanted to say something but no words would form. "I have a message for you and dad." Her son smiled and looked up at her with such love. It was so familiar, so reminiscent of countless times he would tug her shirt and just tell her something or ask her a question. "Angela is for me, my last protector. She made a choice for God, but as her understanding grows so does her light. Evil is seeking her Mom, to destroy her before she reaches me and the Glen. She won't be safe till—"

315

A door banged in the distance. "Reese?" You all right?"

John had finished the old plum tree, cutting it into manageable branches and hauling the bundles off to the burn barrel behind the shed. He smelled of smoke and sweat, a combination that offended even himself. With only a shower on his mind, he uncharacteristically chose the front door for the quickest beeline to the stairs. Seeing the strewn laundry, he slammed the door and bounded the steps by twos following the trail and calling out to Clarice.

John found the door to Jackson's room open. His steps slowed, as his head ordered his heart not to leap to any wild imaginings such as Jackson being home from the woods. Instead, he saw Clarice, a quivering, beautiful mess. Why did she always look so attractive to him? And why did it hurt so much to look at her? No matter how he scolded his heart, the old pull remained. He stayed in the doorway, assessing the scene. Her tiny frame in leggings and slouchy shirt, stood still as if someone had pressed pause on the remote. Her arms were poised in the air, her facial expression suspended in time, even her mouth hung open. For a second, he wondered if she had left her body, but he would have expected it to go limp, not stiff. Then again, Jackson's trances used to leave him about as moveable as a light post. Before he could speak, she moved, curling her fingers and turned glistening eyes to him. Her face contorted, and it was obvious she was having trouble forming words or maybe there were none.

"What happened?" he said, stepping in the room. "What's wrong?" At this moment, there was nothing between them —no lies, no hidden past, no omissions, evasions or prevarications, and *no* distance. He saw only his wife. The wife he still loved, his wife in shock and pain. As if in a few strides he could erase the damnable distance between them, John strode with purpose to his wife, placing his hands on her arms and looking in her face. "It's all right. It'll be okay." She seemed to relax a bit under his touch. She bit her lip but looked him directly in the eye searching his face . . . for comfort or courage, he was unsure. Even with this unknown threat hanging over them, her look melted his heart. He never could stand to see her in pain. Whatever it was, it had shaken Clarice to the core. "Take your time," he said, rubbing her arm.

She stuttered, "Jack…, Jackson," as she shook her head, giving him a whiff of her perfume. "It was…Jack…son" She choked on their son's name. "I s—saw him… right here."

John seized her elbows, "When, Clarice," he yelled, "Answer me." Barely giving her a breath to answer, he shook her. "When? You saw Jackson? Is he back? Where?"

Clarice's head swung slowly in the negative, and she seemed to recover, squaring her shoulders and stepping back from his near embrace. "John, please calm down. I can't think. I saw him, but he wasn't here."

"Where? Where!" John interrupted her. Hearing his own panic, he realized he'd been squeezing her arms, and vaguely that he had shaken her. He released her.

"It was a vision or an apparition of some sort."

"Jeeze, Reese," he gave her a disgusted look and was about to say the words, "a dream?" when she answered.

"It wasn't a dream if that's what you are thinking."

She related her tale beginning in the laundry room, telling him about the breath on her neck and her strange feelings, right up to the tugging of her shirt and calling of her name. If he had any idea of not believing her, it was gone as he watched her recount the story. Trembling, she ended, holding her hands out as if she were touching his blond curls. Sympathetic, John led her to Jackson's bed and sat beside her, tracing with his eye the glistening path of a tear crawling across her cheek. He barely knew what to make of it, except the account stirred a sort of dread in his gut. Concern for his wife overcame his panic, and he asked in a calm almost reverent tone, "What message?"

"Jax said Angela was for him, that she is his last protector." She wiped her nose on the back of her hand.

"Angela? I don't … what…what does Angela have to do with Jackson?"

"I *really* don't know," she said, emphasizing the word really and making him brace himself for something he couldn't quantify. She rubbed her palms over her thighs ending at both knees and clasping. "I don't know how to tell you this, John. You have to understand though, at the time I had no idea that it wasn't just a dream." Her

317

palms returned to her jeans and rubbed the length of her thigh again. "I absolutely did not relate it to our son. I mean I didn't think there was a connection. It never dawned on me . . . I had a dream, two actually" her voice trailed.

"I'm not following."

"I know; I'm not making any sense. Believe me, I'm not claiming to have any real answers. Okay," she said, taking in and letting go of a deep breath, "a while ago, I dreamed of Angela. I dreamt she was being chased. It was intense and incredibly real. The first time, it was just a girl. I didn't know who she was. The second dream happened when you were in Florida. I fell asleep on Jackson's bed and dreamt of him in the Glen. Then it turned into your sister running for her life." He looked at her without voicing his thought that she had somehow betrayed him again by keeping something from him. As if she knew what he was thinking, she answered his allegation. "I didn't say anything cause it was just a dream, you know. I was worried after her phone call and…I didn't look at any of it as a message."

John's anger swelled. It was more of a reaction to his helpless confusion than any real animus toward Clarice, but it threatened to sound like the latter as he spoke through his teeth. "What *do* you know?"

"Nothing, really," she whined, "I…only what Jackson told me. He said evil was seeking Angela and trying to keep her away from him and the Glen. The last thing I heard him say was she wouldn't be safe until…"

"Until what?" John cried then waited all of a second before repeating. "Till what?"

"I don't know. I don't know. I heard your voice then Jackson vanished. I think my mind had found him, or . . . his mind found me and our connection—Ooo, this sounds insane. Our connection was broken. I—I think she needs our help. Angela needs the Glen."

John buried his head in his hands, tearing at his hair. "If she's his protector, then she's…she's like Nicey was or Rabbi Katz." His head popped up. "They're both dead, Reese! Katz was torn to shreds by some evil force. The Glen didn't save him!"

"Gabriel Katz was saving our son. You know that."

John knew. His chest expanded, taking a deep, exasperated breath. "It's so frustrating. I still don't get any of this. Why my sister? She was dead, and now, she's alive and someone's trying to kill her. My God!" He cried the last to heaven, his eyes squeezed shut, and his chin pointed to the ceiling. Sitting together on the edge of their son's bed, both parents fell silent. His mind went back to Mrs. Nicestrum, Jackson's nanny. Unknown to them, she had been protecting him since birth, like a… guardian angel. Her name was Michelle, which fact suddenly struck him. "I can't believe it. Nicey's name was Michelle, and the rabbi's name was Gabriel."

"So? What does that mean?"

"It's just, my sister's middle name, it's Raphaella. It's weird, but my mom said she owed Archangel Raphael for healing her dad's eyes while she was pregnant with Angela, and she wanted to honor him."

"I still don't get it."

Reese knew little Scripture. He tried to explain the connection, more to himself than to her. "There are three Archangels named in the Bible. Michael, who cast Satan from Heaven, Raphael, God's healer, and Gabriel, who announced the coming of Saint John the Baptist and of the Savior, Jesus." He shook his head. "I can't think this out right now. What am I supposed to do with all this?"

The rhetorical question was met with expected silence. Both of them sat, uncomfortably close as John now realized, having trouble concentrating. His gaze travelled from the Berber carpet to the wall mural directly across from them and the vibrant greens and blues of the Glen. Three realities solidified against the image. Jackson had needed the Glen. If Clarice is right, Jackson needs Angela, and Angela needs the Glen. One thing John knew for sure, Angela was not safe. He knew it. Every fiber in his being knew it, and had ever since the first phone call from his sister. John boosted from his seat.

"Reese, take her there! Guide her. You can leave your body. Use your spirit like you did that night when you flew to find Jackson and Gabe. You said you could see his light. Maybe you can see my sister's. You can—"

It's not like that, John. I don't just leave my body at will. I can't close my eyes and take off like a genie or something."

"You could try. She needs you. My sister needs the Glen; Jax needs her. You said so yourself."

"I see her in the visions, but her light is clouded. I'm not sure I'd sense a thing. Besides there's another problem, John. How can I lead her to the Glen when I no longer feel its pull? I have no connection to it. It's gone; I sense nothing as I once did."

"Why?" He heard his voice rise with his frustration.

"I don't know. I'm not meant to, I guess. If I could, I might be tempted to fly to Jax and never leave. We both know that's not what God wants."

"But the Glen may call to Angela. If she's meant for Jackson, Right?"

Clarice looked up at him, rocking forward her arms thrust between her knees now. "I guess if we could find her, bring her here, maybe."

They fell silent again, each ruminating in his own way, Clarice her hands tucked behind her knees and rocking slightly, and John pacing two or three steps to the wall and back. Finally Clarice spoke, "John, I know it's not much to go on, but in my dream, it did look as if she was running in Vegas."

Her words like an edict spun John around. "Vegas! I have to go back. I have to find her, bring her here. She's not safe. I know it. I've known it all along. I'm calling my brothers."

Clarice, still seated on the bed, caught his arm just before he was out of reach. Her teary face was composed. "I'll do anything, John. Just tell me what you need."

35

The Millers Take Vegas

The old-fashioned music was the first thing John noticed as he stepped on the bus sliding his metro card. Jimmy Dorsey Band if he had to guess. The cool relief from the blazing Vegas heat was the second thing he noticed. Choosing a bench in the back that faced inward, John pulled his T-shirt away from his sweaty chest, fanning some air up his shirt. He was riding back to the hotel to meet his brother Rob and compare notes. They'd both been out all day. He glanced at his phone—nearly 6:30. Man, it was coming on twelve hours now. But all of them had been hard at it all week. After Clarice's vision or whatever it really was, he was more convinced than ever that he was supposed to be looking for his sister. She was not safe; he'd known that since that first phone call. Now though, his fears took a more sinister turn. The same evil that had hunted his son was hunting for Angela. It was surreal that she, who was more or less thought to be dead, should now be resurrected only to be involved in the mystery of the Glen. Yet, he had no doubt it was true. He even believed on some subconscious level that God had been leading him to this role all his life. If Angela is one of Jackson's protectors.... It was almost too incredible tracing the finger of God in their lives: his meeting Clarice and Jackson, his falling in love, his born again conversion, Clarice meeting Nicey in the hospital, Father Tom being his pastor and Father Simeon—God bless his martyred soul—being Tom's spiritual advisor, Rabbi Katz finding them through Bookworm Joes and that picture of Clarice's painting. When he looked at it all that way, why not Angela? Angela Raphaella, he reminded himself. But what would be required of her?

An oily stench from the bus' exhaust seeped in the side door as a number of passengers hopped off. John found his foot unconsciously tapping much as Clarice's would when she had a lot on her mind. Clarice . . . why hadn't she shared the dream sooner? She said it was when he was in Florida for Thanksgiving. They weren't exactly communicating then or now, and that was more his fault than hers. He knew that much. She had been trying hard to help, and he appreciated it. He had called his brothers and convinced them to take time off so they could look for their sister. Ted had already taken a week off for Easter break with his kids, so he had flown in from Orlando for only two days. Marty, too, could only get a few days off but stayed till Thursday. Only he and Robert remained, and Rob was leaving tonight on the red-eye back to Rochester, Minnesota. It was a huge sacrifice for all of them. And so far with dismal results.

They had canvassed the neighborhoods near where their sister had lived, tried every convenience store and casino and just about anywhere girls of her type were known to work or hang out. It was so much like the old days, when they were young and meeting at Grateful Dead concerts combing the crowds, showing fans and security personnel her picture, hoping someone would recognize her. It had been heart wrenching, and their search and time together this week was reminiscent of that. They joked and enjoyed each other as they always had in the past, and the love and camaraderie of the brothers eased the pain of the reality they faced.

For his siblings, it was different for they knew nothing of Jackson and Clarice and the Glen. It would sound insane. John got them here under the pretext of him having received "more information." He hated not being up front with them, but the whole truth was too far-fetched. Perhaps when they find her, he could confide in all of them. As it was, his determination to find her bordered on crazy desperation compared to theirs, which while dedicated had a que-sera-sera flavor.

Tired and defeated, a crushing weight on his shoulders, John sagged in his seat. It was over—over again. The trail was cold. This week was ending the same way it always had in the past—without a trace of Angela. How many times would they come close and fail. Why, why, he thought, shaking a mental fist at all of heaven. The words of an Eddy Arnold's voice drifted over the bus speaker and caught John's ear.

> *Make the world go Away*
> *And get it off my shoulders*
> *Say the things you used to say*
> *And make the World go away.*

He took in the words. At home Clarice sat alone. She had been supportive over all this stuff with his sister—someone she had never even met. If the first lyrics grabbed him the next verse killed him.

> *Do you remember how you loved me*
> *Before the world took you away*
> *Well if you do then forgive me*
> *And make the world go away*

John, so absorbed in thoughts of Clarice, was unaware of the young African American mother with a baby on her lap, who had been watching him. John's fist gripped the paper flyer with the photocopy of Angela; his throat was dry and his eyes moist when she spoke from across the aisle.

"You a cop?"

"Huh?" John swallowed the dry lump and raised his brows, opening his eyes wide while his brain worked it out that someone was speaking to him, and he was not alone on the planet brooding over the pain in his life. "I'm . . . no, I'm not a cop."

"Detective?"

"No," he said, opening his wet eyes wider to the air and seeing the tired looking teenage mother in a tank top and pink bandana for the first time. The baby sat on her lap clutching a stuffed Elmo. Holding a big black purse, the handle of an umbrella stroller, and a cuppy looped through one finger, she performed something between a juggling act and a wrestling match with the little one, whose cherub wet fingers explored one no-no after another. Big walnut eyes laughed at her as she gently pulled his hand from her open purse then away from her necklace. John watched the performance with a distracted interest remembering similar times with Jackson.

"Oh alright, okay," she said, smacking gum and unhitching a wet finger from her hoop earring. "You looking for that woman?"

323

John glanced at the paper, and it dawned on him why she had asked if he was a cop. "Yes, she's my sister," he said, almost flatly. They had had several false leads this week. It seemed a number of people who lived and worked in Vegas, liked to connect, to talk, to help, and apparently, they liked to feel as if they were helping, or look as if they were helping even when clearly they knew nothing of Angela. Reluctant to ask any leading questions, he said no more and waited.

"Uh, huh. So listen,"—her gum smacked—"I seen her. I didn't wanna tell no cops or nuthin, you know? Cause like, I don't know if she hurt them guys or not, but . . . I don't trust cops, not here, not here in Vegas. Sides, I liked her."

"You know my sister?"

The baby made an all-out lunge against his captor, and while the mom managed to hold the child, the stroller clattered to the bus floor. John picked it up and she motioned for him to put it back in her fingers. "It's ok," John said, "I'll hold it for you; you have your hands full.

"You know that!" she said, as she shifted the child and repositioned things, ending by zipping her purse. She pointed to the paper, which John still held in his lap. "I was with her in the shelter a long time ago. This one was . . . not six months, I guess."

"What shelter, when?"

"Hold on, now," she said, looking down at her son, who finally decided to drink from the cup and threw himself backward in her arms to drink it. "I remember," she continued, "his daddy came home high, hit me with a bat. Took two swings, but I had dodged the second, you know? I called 911, and the cops brought me and my son, Tyreece—this is Tyreece. Say hi, Tyreece. Wave hi to the man." Tyreece eyed John while holding the cuppy in his mouth. His mom repeated the request, and the baby's little fist opened and closed, making her voice rise an octave as she said, "Gooood boy Tie. That's a good boy to say hi to the nice man." Across the aisle, John opened and closed his own hand in greeting.

"Anyways, I remember your sister all right. Came in my second night there—you only get three—she was beat up something awful."

John cringed as the woman, who seemed to have a fantastic memory for detail, described Angela's multiple injuries, her huge swollen cheek, bruised ribs and thighs. "Where was the shelter?" he asked.

"Oh it's the one over on Oak . . . is it . . . Lemme think . . . what the heck is that place called?" She strained to remember for the next three bus stops, as Tyreece fell asleep in her arms. John helped her off at her stop, unfolding the stroller for her. As he hopped back on the bus, which was headed up Las Vegas Blvd. still a good five stops from John's hotel at MGM, she called, "I'm sure of the street. It was Oak for sure."

John pulled up to New Haven on Oak street, knowing he would not find his sister, yet excited about the first real lead he had since coming to Vegas a second time. The shelter was a simple building, outside and in. It was furnished sparsely in early Salvation Army décor. Posters of smiling women hid the peeling stucco walls, and the rooms of wool-blanketed bunk beds resembled the barracks of an army camp. New Haven, though, was anything but simple as John saw in all of fifteen minutes he spent there with Maria, the acting administrator. John and she were interrupted with the regularity of hiccups by girls and women in need of attention, by phone calls from police, hospital personnel, angry boyfriends, and at least once a very loud bang that needed investigating in the cafeteria-style kitchen. John learned New Haven used to be an elementary school, slated for demolition, when three women pooled their resources, called in favors, and bought the place, founding a shelter for battered women—something of which there is no shortage in Vegas.

Sitting in Maria's tiny office, after the show-the-visitor-around-in-hopes-of-gaining-a-new-donor tour, John knew he would become a monthly contributor, although he did not tell that to Maria. He was humbled by what he had seen and grateful they had taken care of his sister.

"Yes, I remember her," Maria said, "pushing the photo back across the bare metal desk to John, "I didn't personally take care of her, you understand. It was the weekend; I mainly work during the week. Sister Eva, er Eva, was the one who brought her here from North Vista Hospital on Lake Meade.

"A nun, I don't understand."

"Oh, Eva is not exactly a nun, in the traditional sense. I see your wearing a medal, are you Catholic?"

John fingered his miraculous medal bearing the image of the Madonna."Er, yes."

"Eva is a what she calls a lay sister. As she tells it, she felt a sort of calling to dedicate her life to God, and she asked everyone to call her Sister as an outward reminder of her own personal vows." Maria leaned back in her chair, giving it a quarter spin left then right. "Don't ask me to explain Eva. The only explanation you will get from me is that Eva loves these girls; she loves helping them and dedicates every breath to them while she is here, and I might bet, even when she is not. She is the one who helped your sister. I only remember your sister in the sense that we all remember her because cops were crawling around here after those murders."

John frowned and studied the scuffed linoleum.

"I'm sorry."

"It's ok. I just . . . I know my sister; she wouldn't hurt anyone unless they were threatening her own life. I—"

"Scuze me, Miss Maria," a little round face peeked in the door, "they's fightin' over the channel again. Manda says she's goan-a watch whatever the hell she damn well wants, and we all better just," she snapped her fingers and wagged her head.

"Jaylena!" Maria said.

"Oh, I *am* sorry, Miss Maria; you got company. But… they's about to come to it."

Maria took a deep breath and shoved her chair back. "Alright, I'm finishing my conversation with Mr. Miller. Try and diffuse the Manda bomb till I get there." The head disappeared, and Maria gave John an apologetic grimace. She walked to the file cabinet, rifled a second then returned to the desk, pulled an envelope out and scrawled on the back, the pen making a loud scratch sound. "This is Eva's home address." She handed him the paper, walking him out to the front door. "I wish you luck Mr. Miller, and, um, our address is on the envelope," she said, raising her brows and clapped her hands together

326

as if she were praying, "if you should decide to donate. We can always use the money."

John had little doubt of that as he stepped to the sidewalk, and punched the address into his phone's GPS. Twenty minutes later, unknown to him, he stood in the exact spot where his sister had stood just one month before. After the third hard rap on the side door, he saw a large shadow approaching behind the curtained window on the door. A sign under a tiny floral wreath read, "Me casa et su casa."

"Who is it?" the heavy shadow asked without moving the curtain in front of door's window.

"Uh, ..my name is John. I just came from New Haven."

Silence.

"Uh . . . Maria gave me your address." The sound of a latch being slid followed.

"Why? Is something wrong?"

"I have some questions about Angela Miller." He heard the latch sound again in reverse.

"I have nothing to say about that. You're on your own."

It suddenly occurred to John, he was taking the wrong tack again. More than one person today had wanted to protect his sister. He was glad of that, glad Angela was still so sweet she could inspire loyalty from complete strangers.

"Please, you don't understand. I'm John Miller, Angela's big brother." No sooner than he said it than he realized that is how he still saw himself. In his mind, she was frozen in time, perpetually sixteen. "I can prove it, please."

Silence

"Just move the curtain. I'll put my ID against the glass."

There was a pause then the curtain moved just enough to fit his license. John followed that with one of his Miller Construction cards, which is when he heard the latch slide a third time followed by the doorknob. Pudgy fingers shot out, and he was yanked inside in much the same way as his sister was a month before.

"It may not be safe. We have to be careful. Did anyone else know you were coming?" John was quickly feeling as if he was in a spy novel. The woman, more excited than worried, brushed a curtain aside all of an inch and peered both ways before returning to him.

327

"Ange didn't tell me she had a brother. She played it cool on that one. I know she doesn't get along with her parents, but when I asked about siblings, she avoided the topic, so I left it alone. But here you are in my kitchen!"

Within the hour, John was in a cab and on the phone with Clarice, who sneezed upon answering.

"I may know where my sister is."

"Oh John, that's wonderful," she said, her voice hugely nasal and sandwiched between snuffles and tissue wiping. "Where? How?"

"You okay? You sound awful."

"I'm fine; it just sounds deadly. Where is she?"

"An Indian Casino, up North, Four Kings. The how is complicated, but my information is solid. We got her, Reece."

"Okay…, but John, you have to hurry. You need to come home now."

"Can't change my ticket. It'd be like a thousand dollars. And wait—why?"

"I had another d-d-…hachoo—dream. It was pretty bad."

"What do you mean bad?"

"It wasn't all that clear, more like a regular dream where you can't…." Clarice coughed and huffed into the phone. "I only have a kind of leftover impression. All I know is we have to get to her. We're not the only ones looking for her, and I don't mean cops. It's not just for her, John. It's Jackson's mission or whatever we're calling it; she's key to his success, John."

John listened to his wife, and accepted what he was hearing. At this point, he wasn't going to question any source of information, whether gut instinct, crystal ball or a fuzzy flu-infected dream. "My flight is not till tomorrow. I'll drive to Four Kings straight from the airport and get her. This could be it, Reece."

36

Busted

Angela finished in the bathroom, folding a neat triangle in the top of the overhanging toilet paper. Moving to the bedroom of the suite, she worked quietly but with a vigor foreign to coworkers that would have set their maid tongues wagging if they saw it. She was just tucking the sheet when she heard a "Hullooo?"

The list of things yet to be completed—pillows to dress, comforter to arrange, and a pile of towels and linen to carry out—ran quickly in her head as she continued to smooth the sheets. Two seconds later, a handsome head in a charcoal grey suit popped in the doorway, which Angela, leaning over the bed tilted her head up to see.

"You can finish up; just wanted you to know I'm here."

Her breath caught as she recognized the elder, Emmett Pierce. Swallowing hard, Angela nodded yes and quickly turned her back to him, snatching a pillow from the chair, and struggling to control the well of rolling panic. Did he recognize her? He seemed to stand there an eternity as she bounced the pillow into its case. With creeping flesh and a racing heart, she forced herself to turn and place the pillow on the bed, but he was gone. Angela finished the room and loaded her arms with laundry, holding the pile a little too high in an effort to hide her face. Peripherally, she saw him in the armchair by the window texting on his phone.

Out in the hall, she took a couple of deliberate breaths before shoving the sheets in the laundry bag hanging from her cart. Her hands ran through her cropped hair reminding herself that it was short and strawberry red now. She still had to vacuum.

Emmett Pierce looked up from his phone and watched the young woman briskly pushing the vacuum back and forth across the carpet. Not to stare, he moved his glance to the wide windows where lay a dull sky thick with grey and heavy with the promise of rain. His thoughts remained on the girl. He smelled rather than saw, her nervousness. Too, she was decidedly not looking at him. Her behavior, along with something familiar about her, captured his attention. She finished in record time and was gone. He stared into space for some moments, trying to place her. Unable to, Emmett shrugged and went back to his emails. Then, as often happens when something escapes someone, in the same way stretching a rubber band, whose true shape and size are not revealed until one stops stretching it, a half an hour later as his mind relaxed, it hit him—the *Summo Custos* (highest guardian.) It was her! Angela Miller.

The elder paced the suite as he weighed his options. But no amount of pacing could change what he had to do, and by the time Emmett admitted that to himself, he had wasted another half hour before finally breaking down and Skyping her from the laptop on the coffee table. High noon, he noted mordantly, how farcical and appropriate.

"Emmett, do get on with it," Vera snapped, irritated as she sat in her private jet, waiting to taxi on a runway in Denver. His news was likely to upset her plans. Emmett irrationally noted her steel grey suit with satin trim, distracting himself, admiring the exquisite material, which silk threads shimmered just so, catching the light in the subtlest sheen, and causing him to wonder if his tailor had such fabric. Though this imagining was swiftly checked as he took in the coifed upsweep of grey hair, the signature red lips, and landed on those Betty Davis eyes. Vera's eyes had always been large, but now the virtually black iris, so like the Master before her, was beyond unnerving. "We found her," he finally said, bracing himself. But Vera's countenance remained blank. "She's a maid here at the casino in New York."

After a painful gap, his mistress spoke. "Do you mean to say, Missss-ter Pierce, the *Custos Vocem* (Guardian of the Voice) is in your employ?"

Emmett hesitated, afraid to say how long, but knowing full well the cost of any prevarication, he answered, "Uh, about a month now—"

"And how is it"—her voice, scarily controlled, sent chills down his arms and back—"that she is just under your nose, Mr. Pierce?"

"I'm not sure, I . . . Do you remember the retard, the janitor here, the one with the strange aura? His stinking light must have been masking her light."

She snicked, disgusted. "You should have got rid of him, when you first gained interest in the casino."

"I was . . . he's very uh . . . every department counts on hi—"

"Enough!" The order was spoken in no less than ten voices. "Your excuses are pathetic"—Vera's voice returned—"If you denied yourself as you should, as an elder, instead of living as a lesser, overdosing on pleasures like an escaped convict in a whore house you would have recognized her sooner."

There was a pause. In a weak attempt at bravado Emmett swept a delicate hand at a piece of lint on the lapel of his silk suit, trying not to wonder whether corporal punishment awaited, and if so, what limb he might lose.

"Has she very much light?"

"No . . . I mean, not really. I—I can't say," Emmett stumbled because the truth was he discovered the girl more by sight and could not read her light at the casino. He couldn't even tell what floor she was on, let alone what room she was cleaning. "When that janitor is near her, he messes up my ability to—."

"Stop!"—the voices returned in a sonorous, unified, cacophony that shook Emmett's frame to the core—"Cease making excuses. Listen and mark our words; if you want to live to see anything beyond your testicles implanted in each of your ears for all eternity—you will see to it that the girl stays put."

"I'll take care of—"

"No!" the legion roared in stereo, the huge black eyes searing him and the face contorting unnaturally. "Don't even think of *taking care of it.*" The voices melded into Vera's alone. "We will take care of her. *You* will see to it that she remains at the casino. She should have been eliminated a month ago."

"So, we are no longer interested in turning her?"

"No, she has proven unspeakably dull and ungrateful. We should have known; The creator always chooses the weak things to work His plans. Now, she must be stopped, every speck of her extinguished, so she may carry no light. If we fail, she may help the boy in ways we dare not even consider."

Emmett slammed the laptop's lid. Vera would be taking the coven's jet from Denver through Detroit but would have to use a commercial flight from there to Hancock International in Syracuse, the absolute nearest airstrip. Her precious Worm would have to stay behind. Emmett was to pick her up, a prospect he dreaded. His mind unwillingly conjured the image of Scott on the rooftop. When the girl was discovered missing from the penthouse, the casino had been combed, and Scott had been sure she was still there. It made no sense to him—or Emmett for that matter. The girl had been as loyal as a puppy dog and even defensive of Vera in her absence. She was so in love with her mistress, she rivaled Worm, who himself had an instant and vehement jealous hatred of her. In an eye blink, she had gone from that idolatrous reverence to running. From that point of view, it seemed hard to lay the blame for her disappearance on Scott Henderson. Nevertheless, no one questioned the punishment. In the coven, a price is always exacted for such extreme failure, and the higher the stakes, the greater the payment.

He pictured Scott on that roof, staked out like a piece of meat. Emmett shuddered as he crossed the suite to the desk. Pigeons rarely entered his realm of thoughts, let alone crows, but he saw them now and even the sparrows that had showed up. The ravenous fowl had fought over every inch of flesh on Scott Henderson, who had been covered in layers of suet and birdseed, for more than thirty-six hours. At first, the birds only squabbled, dive-bombing each other to nab seed from the helpless body. The first blood drawn brought a scream from Henderson, whose wagging head and yelling tongue had kept the birds at bay for a good twelve hours. But birds, despite their reputation, are nothing if not savvy scavengers. They came to be

332

unafraid of the living food strapped down for their pleasure, an immobile target of delectable delight. During the last twelve hours, Scott became a slab of living road kill. As new wounds opened, old ones were being enlarged, and muscle, fat, and veins harvested. Even for the Elders, who regularly watched infants torn limb by limb in covenal sacrifice to the legion, this display was too gory. The placement of straps covering vital organs had been calculated to keep him alive as long as possible. He was given drugs to wake him when he passed out from the sight of his own evisceration by the birds. It was ingenious.

Emmett shivered and held the edges of the desk. He leaned there heavily, picking up the receiver of the old-fashioned phone and pressing the button for the Front Desk. "Send Sergio Valenti to my suite. Tell him not to delay."

Sergio entered Emmett's suite, wearing his pinstriped dress shirt and black jeans, hoping the petty dress code violation would be ignored. He found Emmett standing at the mini bar by his desk pouring a drink, which Sergio assumed was vodka. Emmett drank only the best. His present favorite was Chopin, a potato vodka straight from Poland and the best Sergio had ever tasted. So smooth it was almost a sin not to enjoy it straight. Emmett waved the glass in the air and said, "I'd ask you to join me Love, but it is only tonic. I— we have to keep our wits about us just now."

Sergio controlled his immediate cringe at the endearment. Although, he found with Emmett that his mind was far less penetrated than it had been under his former master, who like Vera could read his every thought. Emmett was powerful, no doubt, yet his ability to read thoughts was hampered somehow. He was unlike Vera and Menger, and seemed to lack a certain self-control. Perhaps that accounted in part for his weak powers. Emmett was also gay.

Sergio had been the subject of his advances on and off for months. It made him puke the first and only time Emmett tried to kiss him. Sergio was duly punished for his reaction and made to rinse his mouth with Clorox. He'd rather drink the whole gallon of Clorox than let Emmett touch him. Unable to control his distaste, Emmett eventually settled for teasing him. Sergio was just not his type. Still,

Emmett kept up the endearments and certain gestures in public and sometimes in private like this just to humiliate and subjugate him.

"Sergio, the girl, the Miller girl is here," he said, holding his drink directly under his mouth and settling his skinny arse on the desk's edge. "She's been right under our nose for some time, in fact." He slurped uncharacteristically. Sergio said nothing, as a ball began to form in his gut. "Oh, you know who I mean," Emmett swigged the remainder and banged the glass down on the desk. "Get me vodka. I need it. When Angela Miller ran in Vegas, it cost Scott . . . well, you know what it cost Scott.

Course he knew. Wasn't he right there for most of Henderson's torture? He and two others had to stake the poor guy. They used six-inch screws bolted right to roof deck. Secured him with rawhide straps. They were made to take turns monitoring him from a distance so as not to disturb the birds. Twice Sergio had to use ammonium carbonate (smelling salts) to revive him and shots of epinephrine to keep him awake. The entire affair weighed heavily on his conscience. As an elder, Henderson deserved what he was getting, but Sergio had trouble believing anyone should be tortured to this degree. He did what he could secretly for the guy, but his every movement was known if not to Emmett always to Vera.

Sergio handed Emmett the vodka and waited for more, tucking a big hand into his shirt back and then hiking his jeans. Emmett tossed one back and poured the last two fingers from the glass decanter into his tumbler. Then pushed it across the desk away from himself. "Have to stay clear, now. One to calm my nerves, that's all," he said. "She chopped her hair and dyed it red too, but it's her all right—Angela Miller."

Sergio knew right off whom Emmett meant. Short red hair, chopped—it was Rachel, his Rachel! At least she was his in his unexpectedly clean, romantic fantasies. Something made him dream of her, but not to possess her in the usual sexual way, but to protect her, to shelter her. It was weird. And now she was in imminent danger. To think all those months ago, she was the girl in the Penthouse; it was unreal that he'd never met her! Just as well too or he wouldn't be planning what he was planning right now in the deepest recess of his gallant Italian head as Emmett talked about recognizing the maid in his room. Sergio had trained his mind well under Menger, and because of that, he found he was more than a match for Emmett all these months. He knew how to put certain innocuous thoughts at the forefront and hide his true ruminations deep in his own psyche. He had graduated past baseball stats to a game of playing back or echoing the conversation. He imagined it sounded more or less as if he were thinking only of the present dialogue or trying to remember details. At present, while he was sure he planned to save Rachel, er Angela, from the hands of the Coven, he drove this thought deep as he repeated Emmett's story internally like rote.

"I have an hour drive ahead of me to pick up our Mistress Vera," he said, walking to the coat rack and slipping into his grey trench coat. "I will be in constant contact by phone. You must not fail, nor I, or sweet cakes,"—he reached out to pat Sergio's chin—"both of us will be strung out for the birds like Henderson."

"Where can I find her? Do you know where she is?"

"Not at the moment. Her light is useless. Go and question staff until you locate her. When you find her, keep an eye on her. Be her shadow and never leave her. If she attempts to leave, you will waylay her in any way possible. Our Mistress is reserving the right of kill on this one, but she is slated to die, so if it looks as if you cannot contain her or any threat that may come up, do not hesitate to the kill the bitch.'

Both men left Emmett's suite in a purpose-filled stride heading in opposite directions. Sergio rushed towards the escalator intending to save Angela Miller as his boss, with the opposite intention, hurried to the elevator and parking garage.

In room 374, Angela was emptying the small wastebasket in the bathroom. The TV buzzed in the room, although Angela never stopped to watch it. Other maids seemed to have a code about this— everyone had it on, or no one had it on. She stooped to pick up the can of soda and wrappers that spilled off the top and shoved them into the bag before tying it off. More often than not, the waste cans were overflowing. People ate; they drank; they lived, up to four in a room at a time. She shook her head wondering at the stupidity of the woefully-inadequate, minute wastebaskets,.

There was a loud rap on the door, which was wide open. Angela jumped, remembering the elder. She'd been a nervous wreck when she left his room. If he had recognized her, he hadn't shown it. She peeped around the corner of the bathroom toward the hall spying two deck shoes and jeans. It wasn't him, but he could have sent someone.

"Hello, Rachel? You in here?"

"Oh, it's you," she sighed, relieved and stepped out of the bathroom into full sight. "What are you doing up here, Serge? It's great to see you, but I'm—"

"Um, can we talk?" he said, looking up and then down the hall. "Who else is cleaning this floor?"

"Consuela," she said, tilting her head at the question. "She's doing the West End. Why?" She still held the bulging plastic bag, and she went around him to throw it in the bigger bag on the cart.

"I need to talk to you in private. Right now. I know this is going to sound wrong, but we need to use your key and go in another room."

She filled her hands with two shampoos and creams. "Umm . . . sure, I'm almost done and—

"No," he said and yanked the little bottles from her hands tossing them back in the cart. "Leave this. Leave the cart, and leave the door open too, so it'll look like you're still cleaning 374. We need to go in one of the rooms you just cleaned."

He was so insistent; she knew without knowing, it had something to do with the elder. She looked in his face and saw genuine concern mingled with panic. With no argument, she turned and began walking down and across the hall. She stopped in front of room 365 and quickly let them in with her passkey.

The door had barely closed behind them when Sergio seized her wrist and yanked her into the room. "It's not safe. I have to talk low and fast, so just listen please. I know about Vegas. I know your name is Angela, not Rachel."

Her eyes grew wide as he spoke. The size of him, broad shoulders, his block like chest pressing against the dress shirt, his way of looking about between sentences—it began to dawn on her like seeing the answers on a final you blew. She'd studied for the test, put her time in, knew what to look for, knew not to trust anyone, and still she missed the signs—he was a bodyguard; he was coven. She pulled back, shaking her wrists, but he held them fast.

"No, no," he said, as she continued to struggle, "please don't be afraid of me. I'm not one of them, not really, I mean not exactly." He released his grip. "I'm more like . . . a slave really. I . . . they have me. I was hunted, just like you. This,"—he patted his eye patch—this is their handiwork. My boss, he's Emmett Pierce, you cleaned his room. He recognized you."

"Oh my God! I have to leave. I don't have—I don't know—I can't let them catch me. I can't go back to Vera."

"Rachel—Angela, they don't plan on *catching* you, except to have you killed by Vera. Pierce is supposed to pick her up at Hancock International in Syracuse; it's about 40 to 45 minutes away, I think. Not sure when he is leaving, but playing it safe that times two is about how much time we have to get you out of here. Really, you need to be long gone before they get back."

Angela ran thin fingers through her short hair. "Sergio, oh my God, what am I—"

He seized her and hugged her to himself, his striped cotton shirt smelling fresh against her cheek. She sank into its cleanness, feeling his strength, his firm chest and strong arms, all good and solid. It wasn't just his physical strength; it was having someone care again and an overwhelming need to rely on someone else . . . . He spoke into her hair, his breath soft on her red waves. "I won't let anything happen to you; I'll die first."

"No! Don't say that," she said, pulling away. "Don't ever say that. No one is going to die for me. I can't let you get involved." He held on to her waist and back, not letting go.

"You don't have a choice."

"But—"

"Rach—listen . . . Angela,"—he said her name as if he were tasting wine.—"I like it; it suits you," he said, his grin indenting slight dimples. "I've done a lot of wrong in my life; I can never make up for it. I can never be good, but you . . . you're"—his eyes filled, and he tenderly brushed a strand from her face—"I sense something in you, something good, you know, something so opposite to all I've known, especially them."

She shook her head violently at his words, and began to cry. "You don't know me; you don't even know what I really am."

"It doesn't matter," he said, holding her chin gently between his thumb and forefinger. "Sometimes it's not the choices we've made, it's the choices we will make."

She was silent over that, his words resonating truth. Her eyes searched his. "If it's true, it's true for *both* of us. You can choose, too."

"Right now I'm thinking of you. I think we should take the train. There's an Amtrak in Rome. It's only about ten miles from here. We have to score a ride, and I don't have a car. Do you know anyone with wheels?

"Hardly anyone, I'm still pretty new, and I've kept pretty much to myself, afraid of being recognized. I guess that boat sailed, huh?"

"*Pff*", he snorted, releasing her from the embrace they had held awkwardly long. "You could say that." She turned, pacing between the two queen beds as Sergio dropped, sitting on the edge of the bed. "Wait," she said, turning back around. "There's Clydey—he might help."

"Who?"

"He's kind of special, but not exactly. He's a maintenance guy, 'bout yay big," she indicated his height. "Clyde's here all the time and lately, I mean *right here*." Her hand patted the air by her side. "Sometimes he follows me like a lost puppy from room to room while I clean, and we talk and make jokes."

"I think I know who you mean. He is around a lot, like… he never goes home. Seems to do a bit of everything."

"Clyde owns an old car. He took me to a drugstore once . . . " she trailed off.

"We have to go. We have to move now."

Five floors down, the pair headed to Angela's room intending to throw her scanty belongings in a bag before looking for Clyde. They hurried down one corridor after another, following the dizzying Navaho blanket pattern on the rugs. When they reached Angela's room, they saw Clyde pacing in front of her door, holding a brown lunch bag.

"Ra-Rachel,"—He waved the bag and eyed Sergio suspiciously.— "I bought us dinner."

"Ohhhh thanks, Clyde. Uh, this is my friend Sergio."

Clyde paused looking up at Sergio, a good foot taller than himself. His head tilted one way and then the other as if he were a bird deciding if he should peck and where. "Pleased to meet you, Sergee-o." He extended his hand and said, "Uh; I don't know if there is enough for three."

Sergio's larger hand met Clyde's rough knuckled grasp, and Sergio gave a hurried smile. Clyde held the hand a little long, and when Sergio attempted to pull back, Clyde brought his other hand around clasping Sergio's in both of his.

"Oh, ohhhh," Clyde exhaled, "what is wrong? Why are you so worried about Rachel?"

Both Angela and Sergio exchanged a curious look. Angela opened the door and swept past the two going straight to her closet, pulling down her suitcase, and flinging it on the bed. Clyde followed Sergio into the small room.

"Clyde, I need to ask you a big favor," she said, unzipping the top and flipping it open. She turned back to the closet capturing all of six hangars with various jeans and tees, and tossed them into the case, hangars and all. Turning back, she scooped up a pair of flip-flops and sneaks from the closet floor and thunked them into the case. "Clyde, I'm in trouble, and I need a ride out of here." She brushed past him to the three drawers under the TV. Sergio moved to the end of the room and out of the way of her tornadic movements as she gathered undergarments, socks and a pair of black leggings.

"Ra-Rachel," he said, "Stop, stop." he said arresting her stuffed arms.

Her determined face softened seeing his confusion. She took a deep breath, "I'm sorry, Clyde. I know I'm moving fast, but I have to leave. I need to pack quickly and I, we," she looked at Sergio and gave a weak smile, "we need a ride to the bus station. Oh, and I hate to dump this on you, but my real name is Angela, not Rachel." She pulled gently away and placed most of the items in her arms into the suitcase. His dazed face was killing her. "Oh, Sergio, can you explain?" she said and disappeared in the tiny bathroom with leggings and a sweatshirt. Mystified, Clyde stared after her.

"She's in trouble," Sergio stepped toward Clyde, who seemed frozen where Angela had left him. From the bathroom came sounds of glass and plastic items being collected. "Some bad men are trying to hurt her that's why she changed her name. She can't stay here. She's been recognized." Sergio paused and waited for Clyde to look at him. "We need a car. We have to get her to Amtrak. It's up route 365 in Rome, NY. Only about 15 minutes from here."

Angela emerged with a zippered cosmetic bag, a hairbrush, and deodorant, letting go of them over the suitcase. Her uniform lay on the floor of the bathroom. She hopped on one foot and then the other, pulling her feet into a pair of low suede boots. She zipped the case, and then came to Clyde, placing her hand on his elbow. "I don't want you to worry. I—"

"No," Clyde said, animated, "no time for talk. I will drive you. We can leave right now!"

Angela looked at Sergio, lifted her eyebrows and shrugged. She reached for the suitcase handle, but Clyde dove for it and whisked it off the bed.

"Need this?" Sergio said, lifting a brown purse from the small table by him.

"Thanks," she said as he tossed it at her. Angela and Sergio left the room and followed Clyde, who was half way down the hall.

Under a threatening, wind-whipping sky, the three figures hurried across the side parking lot. Clyde held Angela's battered suitcase and used it to point forward as his head turned back toward she and Sergio. "Us employees have to park the farthest out; it's the rules." It was a bit of a hike, but at last, they advanced upon a boxy old blue car sitting alone in the absolute farthest corner of the lot. It appeared as if Clyde was the only employee aware of the rules. Clyde stopped, set the suitcase down, and reached in his pocket. A ring with three keys dangled from an inch of chrome letters spelling DAD.

"What kind of car is this?" Sergio asked as Clyde unlocked the passenger door of the car, which had fading blue paint and rust, but was otherwise clean.

"This is a Rambler, Ambassador," Clyde said, perhaps the way a butler would announce an eminent visitor.

Angela, who never paid much attention to cars and never understood why makes and models seemed essential information to guys, listened indifferent, her hands buried in the same BUM sweatshirt she had worn on arrival, and her legs chilled in the thin jeggings. The brisk wind was reminiscent of that day, as well.

"What year is it?" Sergio ran a big hand over the white roof.

"It's a 65. Last year they made them. It was my dad's." Clyde sounded solemn. He reached a hand around the inside to the back, pulled up the door lock then opened the back door and carefully deposited Angela's bag. He left the door open and flapped his fingers for Sergio to enter.

"I think I should drive; we need to go fast."

Clyde stiffened and seemed to hold his key a little firmer. "I know how to drive." After a moment's more hesitation and one concerned glance at his watch, Sergio complied. Clyde shut the door hard. He situated Angela in the front and scurried around the car to hop in the driver's seat. "You both need to buckle in my car. Th—that's the law."

Sergio sat in the middle of the back seat, and Angela could see him in the rear view mirror, his black leather jacket open over the navy pinstriped shirt. She searched for the ends of her lap belt and shoved the metal pieces together reminding her of airplane belts. The three were silent as the car rumbled to life and soon the Four Kings sign grew smaller in the distance as they turned onto 365 heading east.

341

37

Unfriendly Skies

John waited behind a young family feeling impatient. Moments before, the plane had been emptying at a good clip. John had half-stood, reaching long arms up to the overhead compartment and retrieving his compact duffle bag, ready to fall in line and file out. First it was the mother who blocked the aisle, choosing that moment to wipe her son's nose and sticky blue fingers. Technically, the family was behind John, but their father was across the aisle from him. The dad had slipped out just after the mom, standing in the aisle and tugging at this and that bag of theirs in the overhead. So far he'd plunked down four items and was working on the fifth—and hopefully the last—wedging it left and inching it right. It had been the same routine in reverse at the start of the flight. Some folks just could not abide by the size limit, happy instead to inconvenience everyone around them. John chided himself for his lack of charity and looked benignly forward. The mother's bent and bounteous bottom swung even further in the aisle as she began the wiping ritual on the second child of about three years of age. The little boy caught his eye, stuck an intensely blue tongue out at John, and laughed. The mom smiled apologetically, thanked John for waiting, and finally proceeded to inch the boys and bags forward, following her husband out of the 757.

Exiting gate A74, John went straight to the nearest flight board. The earlier announcement of a ten minute delay had him concerned. The next flight was on time and his connection was tight. Damning his luck, he noted the gate change. He debated on catching the express tram to the center of concourse A. It probably made the most sense. Even with it, he had a long haul ahead. He hoisted his duffle to one shoulder and commenced jogging to the nearest escalator. Waiting for the tram, he checked his phone. Still twenty minutes to boarding—ample time, well, if not ample, sufficient. Passengers piled in the Tram, subway style, and two minutes later filed out,. Once free of the plodding crowd, John's big legs set to work again, passing the water fountain shooting spidery streams in time to Mozart. In the underground tunnel, he stepped on the moving sidewalk and got trapped behind two elderly men. John tried to remain patient bathed in purples and surrounded by whale sounds. He checked his phone a second time. Coming off the belt, he weaved and bobbed around meandering forms, turned right at Einstein's bagels, wishing he could grab a bite, and finally, jogged the last half mile of Concourse C. He was making good time till he saw her. Hers was a face he would not forget, emblazoned as it was in a series of unfortunate and memorable events.

Dr. Vera Wheaton stood a few feet from an exit door used by airline personnel. She seemed to be negotiating with a pilot and a couple of airline staff. John's thoughts flashed quickly to the Sunday morning he and Clarice had decided to take Jackson to the clinic. He remembered his son's resistance, the frantic search when he was missing, the trashcan fire set by his own five-year-old son before crawling through ductwork and running through fields, a stranger's house, and finally finding Jackson in the barn. He remembered the poor man that died of a heart attack, the sheriff's department, the trial, and the accusations of social services, and at the heart of it all — somehow or other was the altruistic Dr. Vera Wheaton.

He never understood her role in the whole clinic fiasco. That is if she even had one. He had no proof of her involvement; it was more of a gut feeling, and, as John thought back, he wasn't the only one who was leery of Wheaton. Mrs. Nicestrum, God rest her solid soul, would not even shake the woman's hand. In hindsight, Nicey's mistrust fed all his suspicions. Dr. Wheaton spied John, just as he had her. He paused only a second then tilted his head, continuing on his way, when her gruff voice called out. She said something quickly to the pilot with whom she was speaking then approached John with hand extended.

"Misssster Miller," she said, dragging the s like a snake ready to strike, "it is indeed a sssmall world, is it not?" John gave a polite nod and met her cold and bony grasp. She had the same big eyes and aristocratic demeanor he remembered. Her silver suit, a designer label, no doubt, had such a high sheen its luster was almost as distracting as her queer halting speech. Everything about her was as he remembered, except a certain look beyond her black eyes that seemed to mock him. "And what brings John Miller so far from home?"

"Just coming home from a long flight," John answered guarded and noncommittal. "And you, Doctor?" She regarded him, and for a hair's crazy moment, he could have sworn a hundred people were eying him at once. John shifted his duffle off his shoulder to his hand, allowing his eyes a reason to drop.

"Oh, one conference after another. I'm sure you can only imagine," she said, equally vague. "I was so sorry to hear of your son's, ahem, disappearance. I do hope you and your lovely wife are coping."

"Thank you. We're managing," John said, glancing at his phone.

"Dear, but I won't keep you. If you or Mrs. Miller are in need of grief counseling, or even marriage counseling, I can refer you to several expert colleagues." John squinted, his brows furrowed. "It's no secret these things tend to tear couples apart, young man. Don't hesitate to call."

"We're fine," John said, meeting her gaze now, full on and defiant. "Good to see you, doctor."

"It's difficult to be separated from family." Her eyes bore into his once again, and the feeling of being scoffed at by not one soul, but perhaps a hundred, while it made no sense, was eerily present. He was outmatched, or was it outnumbered, in this staring contest. John turned away, walking. "It's best to just accept these things, John Miller, you'll see," she called after him, her voice churning in his gut like a tapeworm.

Out of his peripheral vision, he saw her sashay back to the waiting pilot. John's gate lie directly across from them, and he quickly joined the back of the line already boarding for Ithaca. A glance back at Wheaton, confirmed the sensation he had that her eyes were still following him. Just as John came to the front of the line, the attendant, a snappy little brunette in a maroon uniform, closed off the entrance, pulling a stretchy fabric from one post to another.

"I'm sorry sir, but the flight is full."

"What?" John said. "I just…I have a ticket, my seat is confirmed."

"No sir,"—her chin jutted and her tight lips pursed—"you are in fact late."

"What? I'm not late. I'm right here. I'm…You just boarded. You can't be full—I have my ticket. Just look at it." He realized he was spluttering. The attendant took the ticket, and something (like a hundred eyes burning his neck) made John turn back to look at Dr. Wheaton. The pilot had gone through the door and was holding it open for her to pass. She paused, glaring at John, and then she threw her head back in a deep laugh, conceivably laughing at something the pilot said to her, yet for no good reason, it seemed to John she was laughing at him. Somehow—and he had nothing, less than nothing to base this on—somehow, Doctor Vera Wheaton was stopping him from boarding his plane. Moreover, she was stopping him from finding his sister! This realization woke in him, a tiny epiphany across a horizon of doubt like a streak of Windex across a dirty pane.

John immediately turned his mind to prayer, sending ejaculations of "Jesus, have mercy" heavenward. The flight attendant, whose name tag said simply "Janine," held his ticket scrutinizing the numbers. John refrained from further pleading as she began punching numbers into the computer. His phone rang just as she spoke, which she did without looking up from her keyboard. "…supposed to be here thirty minutes before boarding…I know, right?" She seemed to be speaking to herself, so John went ahead and answered his cell.

"Yeah," he said, his business like grunt betraying his angst.

"John, it's me, just listen. I just had another vision," Clarice said, still nasal and wheezing. "I was outside, getting the mail when a wind kicked up. It was so strong I had to fall back against the trunk of the big oak in the front lawn. The wind started to swirl. It looked like a mini tornado, John; I'm not even kid—" Clarice gagged and coughed mid-sentence. The barking turned into a fit of sorts and it seemed the more she tried to control it the worse it got. John thought it sounded so bronchial, it might be bronchitis. He told her as much but she was

346

intent on finishing her story. Through a series of hacking stutters, puffs and whistles, John gathered the rest. She had been clinging to the tree out front, her fingers gripping the bark and hair whipping across her face, when at her feet a hand clutched her ankle. It was old Father Simeon, lying there just like after he was strangled. She screamed and screamed, but she couldn't take her eyes off of him. He pointed at something beyond them where the wind spun faster and faster in some fantastic mini tornado. John waited again as Clarice had another full on fit. "I'm sorry," she said, coming back, "It's just the talking, makes me cough. John, I saw the doctor."

"You went to the doctor?"

"No, I saw the doctor in my vision."

"What doctor?" John stepped away from the tight-faced Janine, trying to process Clarice's phantasm.

"That one we took Jax to, you know, Dr. Wheaton, Vera Wheaton. I think, no, I know she has something to do with the coven. I think she is planning to kill Angela."

"Jesus," John whispered, as much in prayer as surprise, "I just, I mean just this minute, had a run-in with her." He gave a quick account of his chance meeting, ending with his present dilemma. "Now they aren't letting me on this plane, and it was bizarre, just bizarre how Wheaton looked over here, and now they're claiming the flight is full."

"John, you have to get on that plane. I feel it. You have to reach her first. I'll pray."

"Pray hard, then. You, uh, should take some Tylenol or something. I gotta go, Reece. I better get back." John tapped his Blackberry, and stepped in front of Janine, who had hung up the airline phone and now busied herself with a stack of boarding passes. "I don't understand why you are refusing me. I'm not late. You boarded early. I was in the line and"—his voice squealed as he fought for control—"and I checked the flight an hour ago and there were still seats available."

"Things change, sir."

"Yeah, when you overbook a flight, things change." John leaned forward, his head a good foot over hers. "I need to get on that plane."

"I'll ask you not to raise your voice, sir."

Hearing that made his blood boil, especially since he had actually lowered his naturally deep voice so as not to yell. Try as he might, John's next words were indeed loud. "My ticket was full price, and I purchased it a week ago. That should take priority over whoever you put on this flight last minute!"

"Sir, I *will* have you removed. I'm asking you to move back." Janine reached for the phone, when a short man in his thirties, loosely wearing the airline's uniform, that is, his tie hung like a hangman's noose about his neck, his shirt barely tucked and his suit jacket slung with the garment bag over his left arm. He had a small suitcase that looked as tired as the man wheeling it.

"Hey Janina, what's the problem?"

"No problem, Mr. Sessler, your seat is ready, 1C." She unhooked the stretchy band to let her coworker go through and flashed him a phony smile. "Go on board." John stepped politely aside noting the man wore a silver cross.

"How about the jump seat?" John queried. "Can I ride in one of the jumps?"

"I'm afraid that is impossible, Mr. Miller. It is against airline policy. Only employees may ride the jump seat."

"You don't get it; I have to get on this plane," John said, making an unconscious, nonetheless threatening, step forward. "It may be a matter of life or death."

Janine shook her stiff head as she and John went back and forth a few more times. The entire time, John was inwardly pleading with some guardian angel somewhere to pull a string for him. Just as John was sure all attempts at reasoned arguments had failed, he saw the man named Sessler half way down the jet bridge, do an about face and return to the desk.

"Listen Nina. I can take a jump if this man—"

"You don't have to do that Mr. Sessler, and really, your seat is first class. Our policy is—"

"Hey, hey" he said, cutting her off and cutting in front of her, effectively separating her from the keyboard and scanner. His smile was warm and playful, his voice soft. "Since when do we follow every policy? C'mon Nina, call it a random act of kindness. Oprah says I need thirteen every day. This can count for mine and yours. Ha ha."

Mr. Sessler then relieved John of his ticket. He crossed something out, wrote something else, did the same to his own, typed a bunch of numbers and words on the keyboard, and finally scanned the ticket. "Your all set, Mr. Miller. You've been bumped to first class. Enjoy your flight."

John hardly knew what to say. Obviously, his prayer had been answered, and after a quick thank you to God and his angel, he said, "Thanks man. I don't know what to say. It's really, really important."

"Don't mention it. This leg of the flight is so short flying jump is nothing. We better get on board now." They walked together down the Jetway to the aircraft as John pulled his phone to call Clarice.

Sitting at John's desk, Clarice hung up the phone, thanking God he was on the plane. She clicked out of MapQuest where she'd googled directions to Four Kings for John. Please, please, please, get him home, she prayed shuffling to the kitchen for a drink of water and a handful of fresh tissues. Thus armed, she ascended the stairs, her aching head pounding with each step as if it were full of wet cement. That last vision—*Oh God, don't let that be so. John has no clue.* Both calls were cut short, and she'd had no chance to tell him the rest of what the old priest had shown her. She could still see John's sister, writhing in tendrils of black smoke. It wrapped around her waist and bleeding arms, pinning her helpless to a tree, one tentacle squeezing her neck, her face bulging, purple and suffocating. Flashes of carnage, two maybe three bodies, were fresh in Clarice's mind. It was going to be a blood bath. *Oh God, no.* At the top of the steps, Clarice abruptly turned for Jackson's room. She sat on the bed, downing her water and wondering who was with Angela right now. John wouldn't even touch down for another hour and a half, and it was at least another hour and forty-five minutes to the casino.

Heavy as an anvil, her head dragged her down onto the twin bed and pillow. Miserable, she lay on her side staring at the mural, a tissue under her nose. In her mouth lay a foul taste as if someone had fed her strychnine; and her nose felt as if she'd snuffled chlorinated pool water. In no time, whether she was nodding to a flu-induced sleep or stepping as fancifully as Mary Poppins into a sidewalk painting, Clarice was lost in the Glen.

* * *

A half an hour before Confessions were due to start, Father Tom stood in the small shrine dedicated to Saint Francis outside the rectory kitchen. The howling wind whipped a few of last fall's leaves in circles as if they were errant sheep. It blew up his cassock with urgency as if he too must be herded. The air tasted thick with the promise of rain. Father's cell phone buzzed in his pocket. Before answering, he sat on the cold stone bench facing the little statue of Saint Francis and begged the little figure's intercession that he would not be resentful for the interruption in his planned prayers. As soon as he heard Gerard's upbeat voice, he was relieved, and when he heard Gerard's request, he was humbled. The saint's likeness seemed to have a knowing smirk as he talked to Gerard.

"I'm sorry about last month," Father Tom said, "I got your message, but First Fridays are tough for me. I should have gotten back to you—"

"No worries, padre. We know how busy they keep you priests. That's why we changed it to Saturday. Now I'm the one who needs to apologize because somehow I forgot to call you sooner. Ahem, it's this Saturday, tonight."

"Tonight? Oh, ah, I have the vigil Mass at four-thirty. What time?"

"We were thinking six, but if that's—"

"Hmm, that's rough; I might be a bit later than that."

Gerard assured him it was no problem. He asked if he knew the way, and Father Tom told him he'd actually driven out there after Gerard's first visit, and that it was a good half hour from him. He hung up promising to do his best. What he did not tell Gerard was on that visit to the grave site of Mrs. Michelle Nicestrum, he had consecrated the tiny cemetery and blessed all the graves. He would probably tell them, although they may misunderstand his intentions. He was looking forward to meeting this little group and joining them for prayer. Okay Saint Francis, you're invited too, you know. We need all the help we can get. Tom extracted his fat black breviary and began his evening prayer.

38

To Anna's House We Go

They had only been on route 365 for a few tenths of a mile when Clyde veered to the right merging onto 90 West toward Syracuse.

Sergio leaned forward and tapped his shoulder. "Uh, Clyde, we were supposed to stay on 365 East. You'll have to take the next exit and get back on 365."

Clyde shook his head but said nothing. Angela turned around to look at Sergio. "Clyde's lived here a long time," she said. "You probably take a different way huh, Clyde?" Again, Clyde shook his head in the negative but said nothing. Sergio shrugged and sat back in his seat. Angela squeezed her lips in a flat line and then watched the road. Within minutes, 90 had looped, and they saw another sign for 365E and Rome NY. She pointed to it expecting Clyde to take the exit. He ignored her and concentrated on the road. Again, she imagined he must know a different route. She glanced in the rearview at Serge, who was typing something into his Blackberry. "Uh, Clyde, are we—"

"Hey," Sergio said, and held up his phone, "90 West will not take us to Rome."

"Maybe Clyde knows—"

"Maybe Clyde doesn't know Jack. There are no more turns. He's driving one hundred and eighty degrees in the wrong direction." Sergio shoved the phone, which was open to MapQuest, between the seats. "See."

She took it from him. "I'm not very good at maps...but Clyde, it does look like we need to turn around. Clyde shook his head now back and forth and continued shaking it.

"Hey, you need to turn this around, chief," Sergio raised his voice, "like now."

Clyde continued to shake his head like a bobble head winding down. "No, no," he said, "not the train."

"What?" Sergio yelled.

"Clyde," Angela said softly, "Are you saying you're taking us somewhere else, to a bus or the airport?"

"No," Clyde said staring at the road. "Not a plane, not a bus. We have to go to mother's. She knows you are in trouble. Mother will know what to do."

"Are you kidding?" Sergio shrieked, sounding desperate and mad. "*Porca vacca*, we have to get her out of here now."

"Clyde,"—Angela remained patient, throwing a backward glance at Sergio, begging him to calm down—"what are you talking about?"

"Clyde, turn this thing around now!" Sergio ignored Angela and spoke with the force of a bodyguard who meant business. Clyde's head shook again and he gripped the wheel tighter, his face showing a remarkable purpose.

"Clyde," Angela said, her voice reasoned and sweet, "I need you to drive us where we say, sweetie. Sergio knows these men. If he says—"

"Listen,"—Sergio laid a heavy hand on Clyde's shoulder—"If you don't turn this heap around right now, I'll do it for you." Sergio grabbed for the wheel roaring, "Pull off! Pull off now."

Clyde yelped; Angela shrieked, and a minivan's horn blasted as the Rambler swerved into its lane at sixty-five miles per hour.

"Stop it," Angela shouted, "you'll get us kill—"

"Tell him to stop!"

With both of them yelling in tandem, Clyde yanked the wheel left and slammed the breaks. The car screeched to a stop on the thin shoulder. In a blink, he cut the engine, unexpectedly, yanked the keys, and shoved them down his pants pocket.

"Oh this is great," Sergio fumed, his hands slamming the back of Clyde's seat. *Cavolo! Hai la zucca vuota*! You think that is going to stop us?"

In this moment, Angela admitted to herself she barely knew Sergio, and this, this side of him, which certainly matched his tough hardcore build and stern looks, frightened her. She became more afraid he might actually hurt Clyde. The back door flung open, and he made a leap out the backseat. Angela followed suit and jumped in his path arresting his thick forearms. "I can deal with him, Sergio. Give me a chance to find out why he is acting this way." Sergio's face was steaming and his fists clenched. Just then, his phone buzzed. He yanked it out of his pocket, looking at it then back to her. It's Pierce.

"Five minutes," he said then repeated it yelling towards Clyde, "you got five minutes before I rip those keys off your scrawny trunk." Sergio walked a couple paces off, speaking into the phone, "Yeah, she's cleaning rooms."—Pause—"Yeah, I'm watching her cart; she's still on the third . . . "

Angela moved to Clyde in front of the car where he stood, hands in pockets, eyes down, bobble head twisting slowly as before. She crouched to get under his eyesight. "Clyde, I know you want to help me. But we need to get to Amtrak as fast as possible. Remember, we told you there were some very evil people after me?"

"Mother knows what to do."

"Clyde, I'm sure your mother is—"

"No, she knows about you. I know about you. You have to be protected. Dark is coming for you. You have light near you, not all in you but some—"

"What? What do you mean?" Even as she asked, she knew Clyde saw something more than herself standing before him. She felt the same angelic presence that she felt that night in church and again when she ran. Part of her, the logical, reasoned part, questioned what this normally transparent creature could possibly know, while another part of her, the spiritual neophyte, heard raw truth—darkness was after her and light was near her. "How does your mother know me, Clyde?"

"We talked about you," he said, hanging his head shyly and hunching his thin shoulders. "I see the lights and the darks, the ones in people and the ones outside." Clyde's frame straightened, and he looked her straight in the eye, "Your light has a name; it's Raphael."

Angela gasped. No way did she tell Clyde her middle name. Just then, Sergio stormed back and demanded, "We need to go, NOW. Pierce is coming, and I just checked, we're on the same road he has to take to Syracuse." Angela put her hand up in a stop signal and continued to study Clyde. All three were silent for a good moment, Sergio with a look of a panicked bull, staring at Angela, Angela, her hand still raised, staring at Clyde, and Clyde staring somewhere above her.

"Clyde, can your mother tell me about this light, about Raphael?"

"Yes, yes. I see the light, but mother understands. She prays, and God shows her stuff."

Clarice lowered her hand, and still looking at Clyde, she addressed Sergio. "Clyde is taking us to his mother's in . . . "

"Ithaca," Clyde answered, his chin forward and challenging Sergio.

"Stay here," Angela addressed Sergio, "hitchhike back to Four Kings or disappear; do whatever you want, but I need to speak with Clyde's mother." Her voice was make-no-bones-about-it firm. As Clyde wiggled keys from his pocket and reclaimed the driver's seat, she softened it, placing herself under Sergio's chin. "You need to let him take me there, but you don't have to come. I know they have a claim on you. I know they can hurt you. They're not interested in you. You should escape now; go find a different life. Live free, get away."

Sergio pulled her in fast, stealing her breath and planting a hard kiss on the lips. "Let's go," he whispered in her ear as he withdrew. He opened the passenger door, and held her elbow as she entered. "Wear this," he said, stretching the lap belt across her. Clyde fired the fat engine just as Sergio climbed in back. The Rambler rambled off at the law-abiding pace of fifty-five miles an hour down 90 West toward Syracuse, New York.

39

Where is She?

Emmett's white Lamborghini whizzed around the circular drive of the Casino, the engine winding down like some jet coming to a stop. The Lambo's long doors lifted, and it hunched there, hanging its metal batwing appendages in the air. They were barely raised before Vera was exiting. A yellow-jacketed valet sprinted forward to park the car. Emmett flicked his hand and the attendant quickly backed off. Vera stood in the lobby, her head slowly scanning the vast space, her serpent neck craning and tasting the air for prey. Emmett was just coming behind her when she spun on her heels and demanded, "Where is she, Emmett?"

"She's here," he said, immediately reaching for his cell, his thumb busy and punching. "I just have to—"

"Fool!" she screamed, stamping forward. Emmett quickly followed blathering something about trying to reach Sergio and them being on the third floor. Still ten feet from the elevators, Vera waved her hand and the doors flew open. Her chin tilted up, her spidey senses sniffing the air. Once on the third floor, Vera swept ahead, striding down the long halls. As she passed, door upon door burst open and banged heavily on the wall behind it. Most rooms were unoccupied, and several had their chains and bolts ripped out. Amid the screams and growing chaos of guests trying to decide if they were under terrorist attack, they came upon an abandoned housekeeping cart as a few guests popped their heads into the hall to see what had burst upon their room. The open display of power could hardly be a good sign for Emmett. He felt somewhat certain the girl was here and that the Mistress could not sense her for the same reason he had never been able to on his visits here—that janitor, the one called Clyde. His thumb flew over his phone.

"I'm looking for the janitor called Clyde." Through the phone, the girl at the front desk promised to reach him as soon as she located him, but Emmett was unable to answer being literally hung up by his mistress, whose long fingers squeezed his neck and slid him effortlessly upward against the wall, leaving his feet to dangle a foot off the floor. "You have very little time to redeem yourself," a dozen voices hissed in stereo. In minutes they were storming again, and after stopping on every floor and not sensing the girl's light, they ended in the managerial offices on the second floor. The outer doors flung open before Vera. Cabinet doors and file drawers flew open, lights flickered and cracked, and the three office personnel stood like frightened deer amidst a swirling cyclone of papers. Ignoring them, the Mistress pushed past the short one named Carol, assistant to the manager, Mr. Oleson. The door to his office popped open, and Vera sailed in.

"Video now!" she demanded of a blank-faced Mr. Oleson.

"Now, see here, Pierce," he spluttered, looking past the unfamiliar woman to Emmett. It was understandable, as Oleson sitting in his closed office had entirely missed the paranormal display of power. "I don't know what this is about," he said, squinting to the hurricained mess of his outer office and watching one by one of his staff come to life and bolt for the door, "but your interest in this casino is just that, an interest. You are a heavy and valued investor, I understand, and for that we cut you all kinds of slack, turning a blind eye to all your comings and goings, and granting you access to—"

"Enough!" Vera blared in that hellish symphony. Oleson's mouth literally hung open. She crossed a fist over her shoulder and flung it forward releasing her fingers as if she were playing Rock, Paper, Scissors, Shoot. A sheet of tacks, staples, pens and pencils came together from every corner of the room and raced through the air at Oleson's face. A mild attack, really, thought Emmett, seeing the thin face covered mostly in tacks that stuck and a few staples on both cheeks. Excellent reflexes had saved the man's left eye, which lid lay closed lanced with a red push pin.

356

Emmett approached the shivering body, flicked the push pin and shoved him into his desk chair, which then rolled a couple inches away under the weight. "I wouldn't question my mistress any further if I were you," he said, leaning over Oleson and picking a few staples from his cheek. "We require the videos taken of the parking lot today. Say everything from…" he paused, thinking when he last knew for sure the girl and Sergio were accounted for, "noon on."

Soon a cooperative and bloodied Oleson was swiping his card and punching codes to enter the Security office where two stunned armed guards sat before a wall of TV screens monitoring the casino. Oleson showing a remarkable and selfless concern for both men, calmly instructed them to cooperate fully with "this woman and Mr. Pierce." He assured them he had suffered only a minor accident; he was fine, but more than anxious to help these investors get to the bottom of something quite urgent. They brought up the parking lot videos on several screens and played them in fast forward. Within minutes, Emmett was pointing to a screen, and they watched Clyde, followed by the bodyguard, Sergio, and the redheaded housekeeper, scurry across the lot to a sky blue antique looking car sitting by itself in the farthest lot.

"Where is he going, Emmett? Where!?"

"I . . . I," Emmett stuttered then turned on Oleson. "I want Clyde's address, now!" Oleson dabbing his face with his hanky, led the way again, but seemed deep in thought as they walked. Finally on reaching the empty offices, stepping across reams of strewn paper, he stopped. "Uh, his file, it would be here," he indicated the litter.

"Surely, you have records in your computer," Emmett said, evenly.

"He's…Clyde is special. He's a good man. I'm sure whatever you think he has done, he—"

Emmett slapped Oleson hard across the cut cheek. "Clyde is NOT your concern." He pushed Oleson ahead of him to his office and towards his chair. Oleson began dutifully typing and then nervously scribbled an address on a paper, sliding it to Emmett. Vera stood behind him looking about the room and snapped.

357

"He's lying." With no more said, she waved a hand. Two electrical cords on the floor took on life, rising like deadly cobras and poised before Oleson.

"No, I … I won't let you hurt Clyde. He is a good man, a harmless soul. I don't care what—" His last words were quickly swallowed as one cord crossed the other before his neck twisted in unison to the twisting motion of Vera's red-taloned fingers. The bottom drawer of a file cabinet in the corner of the room bounced open, and a single file rose and floated through the air like a scene from the invisible man. Heading out the door, Vera said, "Take it," as it landed in Emmett's hands.

Emmett gave one last look at the murdered manager, thankful at least, that his office had no cameras. It hardly mattered though as half a dozen or more people had seen them storming the place. Still it seemed prudent to at least lock Oleson's door. On his way to the Lambo, an idea struck him. He was on the phone as he climbed in the car with Vera already seated in the passenger seat. "Yes, that's right," Emmett spoke into the phone, "it's registered to me, my own phone. I need to know the location, and direction, too, if possible, not just the end result. Ping the phone every fifteen minutes, and text me the location." Emmett continued the conversation with his carrier representative, who as Satan would have it, happened to be a lesser in the coven. All he needed was the phone ID and authorization. Upon giving the phone to Sergio, he'd kept a record of the ID for just such an occasion. The authorization was swiftly arranged by a coven member in law enforcement. With no better alternative, they were on the road towards the Amtrak station, Vera's best guess for the trio's destination. The first text from Emmett's phone carrier came back that the phone was somewhere between Syracuse and Ithaca NY, probably on Route 81. At this information, the Lamborghini did a body-spilling U-turn and tore in the opposite direction.

40

John & Clarice's Journey

By the time John landed, retrieved his car from the long-term lot, and gassed up, it was near 5:30. Leaving the gas station and heading north, he tried Clarice again. No luck. Her cold sounded pretty severe, and she may be sleeping off a fever. The route was simple enough, so he should have no problem. About a half hour in, he saw a powder blue car on the other side of the road obviously broken down, hood up, two men buried under it, and a third traveler, a redhead in a big grey sweatshirt killing time roving in the field. His curiosity piqued as he passed them and satisfied itself in the knowledge it was indeed an old Ambassador from the late 60's. John wondered if he should try to help them somehow, keeping his eye open for an easy exit or somewhere safe to make a U-turn. Ten miles later, not seeing anything he could do, he told himself they had probably already called for help. The redhead looked unconcerned, certainly not flagging anyone down as the two men worked under the hood. No, he decided, it was too important that he reach Angela. He said a prayer for them and left them to God and their angels.

* * *

In the Glen, Jackson sat opposite Clarice, legs crisscrossed, before a small fire, holding a stick and poking embers. If it looks like a dream, and quacks like a dream, it's a dream, right? But this…this … Clarice leaned across attempting to kiss her son. She seemed to scoop nothing. "You're still at the house, mom," Jackson said, looking up from the fire. "I'm still here." Clarice, or some kind of ghostly version of herself, felt disappointed. Nonetheless, she drank him in. He looked the same, and he looked strange. He seemed still her tiny precious boy, and he seemed independent and confident. "Where are your glasses?" she asked him, "Did you break them?" She felt far away as he said, "No, the Glen takes care of all my needs. After drinking the water and washing here, I found out I didn't need them to see stuff."

"Why am I here?" she asked.

"*Tri-Magnus Custos*, mom, the third protector. She is in danger. The Great Raphael is her mentor, but all three archangels will guide you to her. She must be brought here. It is the only place she will be safe while she becomes a channel of angelic light, which God wills for her. Go, mom. Get dad. Bring Raphaella Custos...go, go, go..."

Go . . . go . . .

His words floated about her; she floated somewhere between her dream and her bed. Oddly, her thoughts turned to her cannonball head, which, at the moment, felt weightless and no longer like the misshapen alien head she'd been lugging about for three days with this flu. Her nose, her muscles, in fact all of her symptoms seemed to be suspended. It took a full moment, as if she were coming back from a commercial until she realized she was watching herself sleep, hovering over her own sleeping body. It had been so long; she hadn't been like this since the night Jackson was taken. Why did it have to happen now? Now when she felt desperate to reach John, now when she needed fingers to dial a phone, when she needed feet to press gas pedals and hands to turn the wheel? What good was she like this? Panic welled. How was she supposed to help?

Bring Raphaella...go...go...go....

Clarice looked on her prone shape, thinking she could concentrate her way back to the corporeal. She noticed beads of sweat spotted across her brow. Apparently, her body was running a fever. How much good might she be if does reenter? In a sudden realization, it just made sense to search for John and his sister in spirit instead of flesh. "Father, I surrender myself to You. Use me in any way You see fit."

She made several back and forth efforts willing her spirit to move. If someone who could see such light were watching, it might have looked as if the Milky Way's twinkly tail were being whipped to and fro across the air. Her trail of sparkly light skated through the door and crossed the hall then slipped through the open skylight in her bedroom ceiling. The woods and trees had that fuzzy transparency she remembered. Myriad shades of grey and ethereal shadows, replaced the colors, giving everything that black and white movie effect. She seemed one with it all, the air moving in and through her as if she were the mist itself. Now what? She swayed this way and that above their house like a silk ribbon being waved on a stick. It wasn't as if she could find Four Kings in this spirit state; she wasn't a GPS into which an address could be plugged. She had no connection to Angela that she knew ....John! John, she might have a connection to her own husband.

Clarice's light soared over trees and hills using every ounce of will to think of John and their love. With a deep sense of déjà vu, she played the same game of hot and cold she had used the night Jax was kidnapped—leaning toward the sense of him, spinning around if she lost "the signal. Clarice continued zeroing in on John, gliding over a changing landscape of ghostly trees, hills, and fields. Soon something below sparked her interest. On what appeared to be a flat stretch of highway between low hills, she saw a flash of fantastic bright light. She practically dive-bombed the source, but as she lowered herself, the light which had been there dulled and disappeared. Clarice watched a figure of a woman joining two men, who were leaning over the engine of an old-fashioned car. The hood slammed; the tall one barked, "Let's go," and all three entered the car.

As the mystery light did not reappear, Clarice rose over them and once again committed herself to detecting her husband John. The incident filed itself, as inconsequential incidents do, in the back of her mind to gather dust. The thought of Angela and any possible light that might accompany her occurred to her only as a fleeting thing. The hair was all wrong—dark and cropped; besides, the third protector's light would not just disappear like that, would it? Gabe Katz's light was constant. Perhaps she never even saw a light; perhaps it was just a trick of her imagination. The landscape rushed by in muted hues of grey and green. Her spirit followed the tree line; John was still ahead she knew, and the inner voice urged her on: *Raphaella, bring Raphaella.*

41

Anna's Canticle

The hood slammed with a loud metal clang, a sound so unlike modern cars. The engine did not exactly hum or purr, more of a loud, ticking grumble accompanied by an occasional squeaking, which ended in a gurgling pop every minute or two. Despite the spluttering growl, it was definitely fired up again and revving as if it were willing and able to take them further. What possible choice did they have? They'd been stuck here a good while, and even now, though she could not be sure, she felt Vera Wheaton bearing down on them. Her immediate fear had no basis in reality, other than the fact that she had been discovered, and Vera was on her way, probably already to Four Kings. When the car first broke down, the engine just quit as simply as a wind-up toy winds down, Clyde went nuts about not touching his dad's car. His protestations were nothing short of a savant tantrum.

With the car started again, Sergio held her door open. Clyde on the other side of the car glanced up into the darkening sky, the wind curling about them. It looked about ready to open up and dump buckets any second. What was that light hovering above the trees and now lowering? Clyde remained standing by the car with his door open and looking up till Sergio barked, "We have all day or something?" Clarice settled in her seat and leaned forward to look for the odd light. She saw only a tail of glinting shimmer trailing off behind them, and then it was gone. Clyde got in and drove.

Sergio had his head buried in his phone. Abruptly, he cursed, wildly cranked the window handle, and launched his phone out the open window. "I should have known. I should have known."

"What? What just happened?"

"He's been pinging my phone. Emmett's got connections and technically, he bought the phone."

"I don't understand. What is pinging?"

"All he needs is a dirty cop and the phone ID. The phone carrier can trace a cell's signal by what tower it is trying to connect to." He damned Emmett shaking his head. "They know we're this far anyway. How much farther, Clyde?"

"Half hour, maybe." Clyde looked at his speedometer and then in the rearview. "If you want I can go a little faster. That would be alright, I think, this time."

Angela placed her hand briefly on Clyde's. "I'd really appreciate it, Clyde."

"Just don't blow the engine; we'll be worse off if we're walking, and they catch us."

It was twenty-three minutes later when they were rolling through a forest and up a dirt drive at the base of a low mountain outside of Ithaca, New York. A dog barked once and appeared at the driver's side, running alongside the Ambassador. Clyde addressed the brown collie as Mabel and assured she and Sergio as they climbed out that she wouldn't hurt a flea less it was biting her own neck. The wind kicked up, and Angela squinted taking in the sturdy cabin and welcoming porch with thick birch tree posts. The door banged open and an elderly character in an oversized sweater with huge pockets appeared throwing her hands in the air. She wore a calico house dress atop rubber rain boots with unstrapped metal straps flapping to and fro. The whole ensemble was thrown on in haste, no doubt. Loose strands of grey wiry hair were crowned by a khaki fishing hat complete with lures, which jingled as she ran forward. As she drew closer, the lures turned out to be various medals and crosses pinned to the hat.

"Oh my sweet savior! Look at-cha, just, look at-cha," she exclaimed, clapping her hands together, and then to her mouth, and then out again as if she were performing a rain dance. She stood directly before Angela, now. "My God, my God, praise Your name. Praise your name forever. For You have raised the lowly to house the mighty. You have brought up the weak and the broken to wield a powerful sword. You have made the sick and abandoned to heal the wounds of the proud and haughty. Thank you, Lord, for the sight of it on my tired praying eyes."

Angela, still between Sergio and Clyde, looked from one to the other for explanation. At that, the woman seemed to come out of her private reverie and reached out to Angela's elbow as the dog sniffed the heels of the newcomers. "Oh my dear, dearie. Oh my, oh my. Forgive me, yes, yes. I'm a little touched sometimes. Not crazy," she laughed in a pleasant chirrup. "Manners, manners is all I'm lacking. Welcome, welcome. Didn't know when you were coming . . . but for so long, oh yes, yes, a long time, I think I knew you would come here. I think He showed me that. You did, didn't you, Lord?" she said looking up in the grey sky.

Her racing speech was as quirky as her look, but there was no mistaking the generous heart and honest, happy way of her. It was curious to think this was Clyde's mother, him so soft, and careful, and almost delicate, her so abrupt and hearty, but both with the same openness and matter of fact personalities. "Mrs. Stoltz," Angela raised her voice over the wind, which nearly howled, now, "How did you know I would come here? How did Clyde know my middle name?"

"Hooo, I expect you have a lot of questions," Clyde's mom pushed a stray hair from her face only to have the wind plaster a new grey-blond strand in its place. "No sense talking out here. Call me Anna and come on in."

Clyde rushed ahead with Mabel at his side and held the screen door with a satisfied look of goodish pride and that delight of sharing his special place with others. The cabin smelled of warm bread and woods. Angela rubbed her hand on a thick beam, wonderfully worn and curiously polished, probably linseed oil. Her brother John jumped in her head. How much he would have loved this wood. John loved working with wood and making it come alive. His house is probably full of such beams. The floor showed the same worn care as did a few pieces of sturdy furniture. The place was rustic yet warm and inviting. Anna had removed her funky hat, hanging it on a giant spike by the door, and smacked knobby fingers against her runaway greys, unsuccessful at coaxing them into any order.

"See this," she said to Sergio as he entered. Anna pointed to the giant nail protruding from the wall. "It's just the right height for me

365

to hang my hat." She removed the hat and reenacted the hanging of it. "It's just the right length too, for any number of hats. Clyde Senior, that's my dearly departed, God rest his soul, he did that for me. He went out and dug those out of abandoned railroad ties, just for me. See they're all over. He was a good man; God bless his heart."

They sat around the table, which had but three chairs. Sergio announced he would stand and went to the window, adjusting a curtain to peer out. He paced the room peeping down a short hallway and out a back window then asked, "Is there a back way out of here?" Anna watched him without a hint of disapproval and said, "No, no, it's closed behind that hutch my grand-daddy built. I live alone, yes. I like one way in and one way out. Fire hazard, they tell me," she pshawed, "I can climb a window, I suppose. Yes, I can, I can. Go 'head, look around all you want. Glad you're here." Sergio took the offer, quickly disappearing down the hall.

"Bit of a pirate, that one, heh, heh," Anna got up and proceeded to make tea; Clyde jumped up to gather various mugs and cups, none of which matched. Without any further ceremony, and as she busied herself with the work of tea, Anna began to talk of prayer and God, of Angels and Clyde's "gift," and her "tiny visions." Sergio, now satisfied the place was secure, beat a path from the table to the front window, after asking if there was coffee to which Clyde announced, "There's always coffee." He then warned Sergio it was thick as engine oil. Sergio declined the offer of cream and sugar. Clyde's mom stopped talking, and she Clyde watched Sergio tasting the brew. He made no face, but held the cup and continued his pacing, stopping now and then to listen more closely to Anna's story.

Anna concluded her rather long account by saying she knew very little but had seen Angela's face several times and understood she has a unique service to perform for God as a vessel, a kind of channel of grace and power for his great merciful work in the end times. As much as Angela wanted to deny that these words were making any sense to her, the truth of them rang in her heart. She was only slightly distracted as Clyde's chair squawked backward, and excusing himself, he unexpectedly rose from the table. A moment later, the screen door banged, leaving Anna and Angela at the table alone. Sergio still paced but was obviously listening.

"Angel... my name is Angela. My middle—"

"You were named for Raphael. It is his healing and protective light you will reflect one day."

"Raphaella..." she said, "Mom christened me, Raphaella."

"God did that, sweetie, Yes, He did." Anna nodded and smiled, making rosy balls on the end of high cheekbones lighting her thin face. She placed a knuckled, hard-working hand on Angela's and said, "You are like a...tightly closed bud, no wait... a brown, dried up bulb.

"Gee, thanks," Angela laughed, relieving the tension she felt. Anna chuckled and Sergio, amused, repeated, "dried up, brown bulb."

"In the fall," Anna explained, "the bulb has to be planted just so, and in the right soil, and it has to sleep all winter and sorta cook as the spring comes. It opens itself up to the warm rain and reaches through the good earth for the sun. As it opens and grows, it becomes green, and voila, one day it's a colorful, splendid flower. Now you need to be planted. God wants to save you for some special work. You been closed up tight, to protect yourself from everything and everyone. You didn't wanna be hurt any more, or feel rejected. God understands that, but now you need to be open to Him. He's ready to feed you those good nutrients but you have to say yes. He won't force anybody, not ever." Anna's speech was calm and purposeful, slower than her usual.

"How?" Angela asked, tears welling in her saucer eyes.

"You'll know how. You'll know when, too. Everyone is given a choice, dearie." For some reason, she said the last looking up at Sergio, who was placing his empty cup on the table and continued to look at him as she said, "Everyone has to make his stand."

Clyde called his mom from outside, "Ma, can I talk to you." Anna pushed back from the table, calmly scraped some spilled sugar crystals into her hand and closed her palm. Angela too stood and made to follow, when Sergio moved in front of her and spoke low.

"You getting any of this?"

"Kinda...maybe," she said, "No, I'm really lost."

"None of this is getting us any further away." Sergio slid big hands down her shoulders and held her forearms, looking into her

367

eyes, "We need distance. Who knows how much Vera knows. Oh man," he exclaimed dropping her arms and clapping his ears. "Do they know about Clyde's mother where she lives? Like he's an employee."

"I don't know. Maybe we should ask him."

The two headed outside where the wind had mysteriously died, and the air was heavy and dark, like the calm before a storm. She looked up past tall pines to the rolling deep clouds, wondering at the change. Clyde and his mom were standing in the yard discussing something and looking out to the road.

* * *

Newark Valley was that quintessential sleepy little town of Christmas cards. Main Street was lined with dozens of proud old Victorians. The brick post office, the courthouse, and the Chamber of Commerce were a stone's throw from a picturesque bandstand wearing a giant American Flag. Turn off any street and in minutes you were surrounded again by gracious fields and quiet farms. Soon after enjoying the postcard-like stretch of town, Father was turning off the country road and pulling up to the Sweitzer's property and the graveyard behind. He parked in their dirt drive behind six other cars. The wind was still at it, and the sky bleak and threatening. He leaned back into the car snagging an umbrella. Voices in lively conversation emanated from a side door, and he found the little prayer group in the Sweitzer's kitchen laughing.

"I must have missed a good one," he said through the screen door.

"Padre!" Gerard called, rushing to open the door. "Come in and meet the gang."

Even before introductions were made, he was struck by all the happy, welcoming faces in the motley group. He met Al Sweitzer, the owner of the property, who never used to pray, but who hadn't been able to stop since "the day of the miracle." He met Mrs. "call me Fran" Pallegrini, an 'original' who was in Michelle Nicestrum's Bible Study, and Val, also an 'original.' Both ladies were pleasingly plump and animated. Next came Bob (or was it Rob) Walker and his wife Kate, good friends of Mrs. Nicestrum and of the Millers. "We saw the miracle," a petite Mrs. Walker told him in an equally petite and dulcet tone. "I guess that makes us originals, too." Val and Fran tittered, and everyone smiled at that. Finally, there was a very young couple, or just friends, he couldn't tell, in their twenties, David and Heather. It was a good group, that was clear.

Father Tom was given a short history of their gatherings, and soon the little troupe, outfitted with umbrellas and coats, was walking toward the graveyard behind the house, and growing a little more sober with each step. "I'm afraid I don't know much about the miracle some of you witnessed."

"Not much you could know, really," Gerard said, walking past the newly painted, yet still shabby, fencing. "Nice, "he said, giving it a pat and Al Sweitzer a nod, who returned, "I've been trying to keep up with it, should probably replace it." To which comment no one disagreed. Gerard addressed Tom again. "Yeah, when it first happened, we talked and talked about it. Now we realize, it was more a personal experience. Don't get me wrong; we saw what we saw. But the peace, the love, the power we felt, and especially the driving sense of the need to help, to witness to others, and mostly to pray," Gerard said, to heads nodding in unison, "it's an individual thing, our journey to God, but we do it with brothers and sisters, you know?"

The ground was soft but dry, and the long weedy grass, which had lain beneath heavy winter snow, was beginning to show signs of spring growth. Bringing smells of fieldy freshness, the wind continued to play with their garments and chase whatever leaves had thawed and unplastered themselves from the ground. After a few interesting headstones were pointed out, including Michael and Emily Prey, who were Michelle Nicestrum's grandparents, and the oldest stone belonging to Elisha Prey, 1761-1797, the group reached Mrs. Nicestrum's grave. Her simple but handsome new stone contrasted sharply with the dozen moss-encrusted tall and thin stones of centuries past. Father was told of how Mrs. Nicestrum had gained special permission to be buried in the cemetery, which hadn't seen a new resident since 1892.

"Reverend," Rob said, or was it, Bob, "we thought you might like to lead us in prayer, and then we can open it up."

Only a little thrown, and that mostly because he was so very Catholic, so very much a priest, and they so Protestant, he felt honored to be asked. The psalms he'd read for evening prayers jumped to mind, and he wished he'd brought his breviary, still much of it was familiar. "I, uh, have just the thing. He turned up his raincoat collar against the wind, and began with the sign of the cross surprised to see several others bless themselves in turn. It was going to be an interesting night. He cleared his throat and began Psalm 34:4-8.

> *Magnify the Lord with me;*
> *And let us exalt his name together.*
> *I sought the Lord, and He answered me,*
> *He delivered me from all my fears.*
> *Look to him and be radiant,*
> *And your faces may not blush with shame.*
> *This poor one cried out, and the Lord heard,*
> *And from all his distress He saved him.*
> *The angel of the Lord encamps around those*
> *Who fear Him, and He saves them...*

42

If Cars Could Talk

Dink dink---bzz --dink ding dzz.

John's phone rang unevenly in a weird, metallic, broken kind of sound. He picked it up, but no one was there. Strange. He checked for messages and missed calls but found none. Maybe Clarice tried to call him, and his phone messed up. He called the house again. It rang four times and went to the answering machine. "Hey," he spoke into the phone, "I don't know if you tried to call me, but try again if you want. I'm on the road. Still about an hour and ten minutes away from Four Kings. I'll try your cell." John dialed again, but Clarice's cell went straight to voicemail, so it wasn't even on. "It's me again. You're probably wiped out with the flu. I'll call you when I reach Angela." He paused then hung up swallowing his habitual *I love you*, which felt wrong and sad, though he was growing accustomed to it. Outside everything seemed darker. John hunched forward, gazing through the windshield to the threatening sky. The wind, which earlier had bullied the Blazer practically off the road, had died leaving a blackish sky overhead.

John's vision fell across the double lanes and grassy median to the south bound traffic where a sweet white sports car, still half a mile off, could not be ignored. Lamborghinis were pretty rare around here and this one looked new. Thirty seconds later, as the car passed him, and only in the briefest moment, he could have sworn he glimpsed Vera Wheaton in the passenger seat. It couldn't be! He must be imagining her because of the run-in at the airport. John's brow furrowed, and he tapped the wheel going over possibilities. What if she was in the

Lamb? What airport could she have flown into—Syracuse? Where could she be headed—Ithaca?

Dink dink dink bzzz—dink ding doooong.

Again the cell went off; again he picked it up, trying to figure out what was going on with it. Battery wasn't low, but the screen was full of song titles, one on top of the other, reminding him of a messed up computer screen. Never did that before. He decided to power it off for a while, and for the heck of it, hook it to the car charger. A light mist covered the windshield, and it seemed as if he were traveling through a wet cloud. In minutes, it turned to a light drizzle, that kind of rain that wets the road just enough for trouble, mixing with the oils and making the roads slick. For now, it hardly warranted the wipers, but he placed them on the lowest setting and leaned over the wheel concentrating on the road. Without warning, the loudest crackle from the radio ripped through the car as if it were between stations and cranked to the max volume. At one and the same moment, the crazy cell phone ding-buzzed so loud it seemed to bounce with the noise of it on the seat. The wipers, too, snapped to life, banging themselves at the highest speed back and forth across the windshield. The dashboard lights and the turn signal clicked on and off. All these sounds and movements John could hardly process, when the horn went off, blaring with the shrillest intensity.

John slammed on the brakes just as the wheels hit an oily patch on the wet road. The horn screamed and mixed with the other sounds, producing a chaotic cacophony like teenagers playing instruments in a garage. The car spun out of control in a full 360. In the split seconds of mayhem, John held the wheel and tried to regain control. Finally, he thought to release the brake, unlocking the tires, attempting to steer into the spin. When he felt an inch of give, he reapplied the brake. The car skidded straight for a traffic sign and screeched to a fantastic stop. The hood of the Blazer miraculously landed just between the posts of the road sign. The whole episode couldn't have lasted more than a few seconds, yet it felt like he'd just run a marathon. He sat there taking inventory of sorts; he was okay, the car was okay, the wipers were off, the phone lay quietly on the seat still tethered to the coil of charger cord. The horn, the dash lights and the blinker sat in stony innocence. John blessed himself and said a quick thanksgiving before thinking any further. He gazed ahead in dumb silence.

Someone, something was near, watching him. He could feel it. He lowered his window and hung his head out in the misty rain, his eyes searching the atmosphere. He thought he saw something, something right there, a shimmer breaking the air, the same way wavy lines appear above a hot grill or asphalt on a summer's day. Something was hovering above the sign in front of his car. He pinched his eyes closed and rubbed them before looking again; it was still there. Vera, Dr. Evil, she did this, somehow. His rage came quick and easy, pushing him like popped corn pushes a lid. John leapt from the car. "I see you, whoever— whatever you are. I see you already. If you're trying to stop me, bring it on," John hollered, adding an epithet. "I got on the plane, didn't I?" The waves hung in the air before him, and the phenomena in the chilly rain, which increased by the minute, was even more apparent and bizarre. But not as bizarre by far from what happened next.

It was the only song they had ever called theirs. It never made any sense to call it theirs, other than the memory it held for them on the first night they met while they watched some guy writhing on the dance floor to Rod Stewart. Both he and Clarice laughed so hard together. John even had the band play it at their wedding for the first dance. It was ridiculous, silly, and almost sacrilegious, but it was their memory, their fun, their silliness, and it was the only way he could have guessed right now it was her.

Toooot toot toot too too-toot, Toooot toot toot too too-toot . . . The horn tapped out, "If you want my body, and you think I'm sexy, tell me baby, let me know."

"Reece? Is that you?"

Toot, toot

"Oh my gosh, you, your—and I can see your light or your glow or something!" He paused, his brow furrowed, and he quizzed, "Wait, I need to know if it's really you. Okay? Give me one honk for yes and two for no."

Toot..

All was quiet except for rain beating on the Blazer's roof as he thought of something only Reece and he would know, something she

373

would not have shared with anyone but him. "You told me something on our second date—

Toot, toot.

"What!? I didn't even ask the question yet," He complained to the air. "Did you or did you not tell me on our second—"

Toot, toooot.

"What, you don't think it was our second date?

Toot.

What date do you think it was?"

Toot, toot, toot.

"Third?" Great, he was having an argument with a horn—it had to be her. They had always disagreed over the fact of whether the unexpected lunch they had shared counted as their second date because he had paid. "It's really you, huh?'

Toot.

He damned the air. "You nearly killed me back there."

Toot, toot.

He waved his hand in a "whatever" motion and said, "Reece, I don't know why, but I can sort of see you. It's neat. Why are you like this, right now?" he asked, waggling his hand back and forth. He waited. "Oh right. Yes or no questions. Do you know where my sister is?"

Silence.

Clarice had no idea how to answer John's question. Technically, the answer was no, she hadn't found Angela, and up until a little while ago, when she was still zeroing in on John, she would have just followed him to Four Kings unmolested. Then she saw Wheaton and the evil she housed pass John going the other direction. The blackness was so reminiscent of the night Jackson was taken when she'd seen that creature come out of the house on the Ranch—the blackest heart she'd ever seen. Dr. Wheaton's seemed the same. The moment that sports car and Vera Wheaton passed John on the highway, Clarice was sure she was chasing Angela. John was going the wrong way, and she had to turn him around. Her plan was to turn him in the same direction as Wheaton and then use Wheaton as a sort of black radar to locate Angela. She could only pray they would get there in time to be of some help.

John repeated the question, and Clarice decided to answer in the affirmative. Toot

John seemed to be thinking. Then he called out, "I can try to follow you. Can you show me which way to go?" Toot. He climbed back in the car, turned the engine, and as he backed away from the sign, she thought how close it had been. Thank you, God. He's okay. She hadn't meant for all the stuff to go haywire in his car. At first, she was just trying to mess with his phone the way she had used Gabe Katz's GPS to lead him to Jax. But the phone was more complicated. It was then she saw Vera Wheaton pass and panicked, figuring John was headed the wrong way. That was scarily clear through her guardian angel with whom it seemed she could more easily communicate in this state. The Blazer idled. She moved slowly to John's window, and he looked out directly at her. He was right; it was neat that he could see her. She continued to move slowly. John twisted himself backward following her movement until she was behind the car.

"You're behind me. I'm heading north. Do you want me to head south? Is that it?"

Toot.

John pulled back into traffic. The rain sliced down in full sheets, now. He let two cars pass him then moved to the left lane and slowed the car a bit. Throwing it in four-wheel drive, he yanked the wheel hard left onto the median where the Blazer blazed a muddy trail over the field grass. It ploughed down one side and rocked up the other, rumbling onto the side of the southbound traffic. Clarice's presence shimmered in front of him, and together they continued back towards Ithaca.

* * *

"You sure?"

Clyde nodded to his mother. Anna looked in the distance past the curving dirt drive and out to the road. The air was pregnant with wet fog. It held that yellow glow as if she were viewing it through cheap sunglasses. "Hide the car," she said not moving her eyes.

375

"In the shed," Clyde said, fumbling for the keys in his pocket. "Quick!"

"No, first place they'll look," Anna said, stepping to Clyde as staid as a funeral director, placing a light hand on her son's forearm. The khaki hat tilted up, and her crinkled eyes regarded him tenderly. "Ya got to sink it, Clyde."

"What?" Clyde said, running fingertips across his forehead. "Dad's car. Ma, no"

"Ya gotta, honey for these folks; their lives are at stake."

"But Daddy—"

"Clyde," her old voice said as gentle as summer rain, "your Daddy ain't that car. He ain't in that car. He left this world just as naked as he come into it. He gave you that car, and you treasured it all these years like a good son, keeping his memory, and honoring your ol' Dad. I'm real proud of you, too. You did right. But nothin," Anna said a hair firmer, as she lightly squeezed his arm, "nothin's more important than a real life person, Clyde. You know your Daddy doesn't want you too attached to anything down here. Not his car…not even me."

Misty rain was coating their faces. Remaining as still as if they were frozen in a game of statue, Angela and Sergio sensed, as could anyone with more feeling than a block of wood, that this was a big moment for Clyde. Even the dog stood watching Clyde as if every part of him were bronzed but the smallest end of his slowly twitching tail. "Sink it," his mother repeated. Clyde looked behind her towards a ravine then back at his powder blue Rambler, than at his mom, and then at all three again slowly as if processing the most complicated equation.

Tears welled in Angela eyes, knowing how much that car meant to Clyde. She could hardly believe what his mother was insisting upon. Thankfully, Sergio spoke up.

"Uh, Mrs. Stoltz, that's not necessary. We don't have to stay here; we can—"

The old woman's hand made a fist. "No, young man, you cannot! Forgive me but you have no idea what is at stake here. And Clyde," she said, now turning back to him, "he knows what's comin better'n we do. Clyde?"

Clyde looked gravely at Angela. Then at Sergio. He moved past his mom, who smiled approvingly and kissed his cheek. In the driver's seat, he cranked the engine. It gave a loud, burping bang and quit. He tried two or three more times, but she refused to turn over. Clyde sat, hands on the wheels, a sad, faraway look. He ran a hand along the length of the dash ending with a pat. "Have it your way then," he said, and climbed slowly out and caught Sergio's eye. "C'mon, you push with me, Angela can steer her."

When neither she nor Sergio moved, old Anna clapped her hands saying, "Yes, yes, now, right now."

Angela steered as directed by Anna, who walked along giving directions. Angela watched Sergio and Clyde's faces in the rearview mirror. Sergio had that firm, unfeeling look he sometimes carried—a look she'd always recognized in herself. Clyde was stricken, his face white, his eyes wide, that kind of stoic controlled widening one does to one's eyes to force bravery and keep their wetness from spilling. They proceeded at a solemn pace in almost total silence except for occasional directions from Anna. The whole business took less than five minutes. Though for Clyde, Angela feared it must have felt as long as the green mile.

They pushed the beloved Rambler perhaps a hundred feet behind the property to a ravine, which ended in a damned up pond at the neck of the woods. As the others watched the pretty, blue Ambassador sink slowly into the black water, Angela's attention was drawn to the woods, pulling at her as if she were a divining rod after water. How many minutes passed she couldn't count, staring off to the wood.

"You have to hide now," Anna called nearly to the house. "They're almost here. Inside, quick I have just the trick." Resembling an airplane marshaller, Anna's stringy arm waved to the three of them as if she could scoop them in with her hand.

"Come on," Sergio yelled to Clyde and Angela, understanding the urgency. Clyde was still staring into the pond, Angela into the woods. "Let's go" Sergio said, charging up to Clyde, who nodded somberly and stepped toward the house, his head bowed.

"This is it," Angela said as Sergio came to her side, "This is where he lives, the little boy of my dreams."

"Huh? What boy? What are you talking about?"

"He's real. I didn't know it, but he is, and he's in there." She said, pointing to the woods. A sudden awareness ran through her, and she clutched Sergio's leather coat. "I know where; I can find it, that paradise, that forest, the falls and rocks, the walls, it's all there I know it. I know where—"

By this time, unable to get the attention of the other two, Anna began yelling to Clyde, who waved to his mom some hundred feet away and hollered, "I know Ma. I can sense it too." He returned in a determined little stride back to Sergio and Angela.

"What paradise?" Sergio said, "What are you—

"We have to go inside, now. I know there's no time." Clyde tugged Angela's sweatshirt practically off her arm. He looked at Sergio pleading. "The evil—a whole pack—it's coming. We have to go inside. Make her come," he appealed to Sergio, "it's not safe."

Sergio wrenched Angela around to face them as she kept turning back to the woods. "Rachel, er, ah Angela, sorry. I know these people. You only think you know them. I've seen—" he swung his head and cursed, "You have no idea what they are capable of, how easily they kill, how they… torture. C'mon, please; they'll tear us apart—"

"Oh, I'm sorry," she looked at both men, finally thinking of their safety and all they had risked for her. With one more backward glance, Angela made for the house between Clyde and Sergio. Reaching Anna, they hurried inside with no ceremony. As the screen door banged behind them, Anna was yanking chairs away from the table. "Help, Clydey." Clyde pulled the last two chairs away and held the end of the table opposite his mother. Both of them hefted the table off the oval rag rug, which was likewise removed and pulled to the corner, exposing a large, black iron ring attached to the floor. This all four gazed upon for a full second until Anna looking at Sergio said, "Yes, yes, you now. Would ya mind lifting it? It's heavy as a wet bale of hay. That's fine, fine, okay far enough." Sergio hoisted the thick trap door, and she wedged a metal bar behind it till it stood perpendicular to the floor. The opening, covered in cobwebs, revealed a set of crude ladder-like steps to a root cellar below.

"There's only one way down there. Clyde Senior filled up the outside entrance for me years ago to keep critters out. You'll be safe down there. In you go, and don't come out now—no matter what you

hear. Keep quiet, and don't call out. No, no, not if you think all the
world is up here having a nuclear bash. You keep quiet. I want your
word on that." Anna Stoltz stood there in her house dress, long knit
sweater, and rubber boots, looking like anybody's zany grandma, and
not at all like someone who could withstand a nuclear blast. Yet for all
that, she held a certain wiry strength with her sundried lips pursed
determinate and her eyes burning with inner fire. Something told
Sergio this woman could stand against the fires of hell with her dukes
up saying, "You want a piece of me?" She waited, regarding each of
them in turn till they nodded their agreement. Last she addressed
Clyde, who had already headed down the steps but returned with a
frantic look at her words of doom. "Clydey, now you promise your
Mama, you won't give away where you are, no matter what you hear,
you'll protect her, keep her safe," Anna said, pausing then giving a
sharp nod she added" "Like the good Lord wants." Clyde mumbled,
"Yes, mama," at the last. Angela followed Clyde, who beckoned
eagerly for her to "Hurry, hurry up."

Sergio started down then stopped. "They'll know we're here; they
can sense us."

"No sir, they won't," Anna cackled, "Clyde's like an odor
neutralizer, only he sucks up light, and he sucks up dark. Never knew
why. Now, g'wan, and find a hiding spot just in case they snoop the
old-fashioned way."

"But what about you? You can't—"

"No, I can't, young man. I learned that a long time ago. Yes, yes, I
did. I can't do anything but what the good Lord wants. This He wants,
and I'm glad to do it. Now git, or I won't have time for my little ruse."

Below Angela watched Sergio help lower the door and listened
overhead as Anna chugged and pulled the rug and table and chairs
back to their former places.

Feeling slightly winded and excited at the same time, Anna went
to the coffee tin, the one with the top cut open for stuffing in cash.
Ripping the top off, she dumped the contents of bills and loose
change in the oatmeal bin by the stove. The empty can was carried to
the porch, but just before the screen banged shut, Anna doubled back.
She claimed her husband's fishing hat from the hook and plunked it

on her head with a satisfied tug. Her lips pursed, and her head bobbed once as if to say, "take that." No doubt, she was scared, but the hat would bring her blessings—blessings cause there's no such thing as luck. For good measure, she slipped the worn Bible from the three-legged stool, and soon the rocker outside was full of herself, the tin in one hand and the Good Book open on her lap.

She rocked furiously at first then forced herself to slow it down. She reminded herself it was a goodish plan. She also hoped to God it was His. "Let's do it, Lord. Yes, yes, whatever it is, I'll stand for You. I'll make my stand. I just beg You for Clyde is all, Lord. Take care of my Clydey."

Brushing a cobweb from his hair, and trying to adjust his eyes to the pitch dark, Sergio remembered seeing a penlight on Clyde's keychain. "Clyde, give me your keys," he demanded. Clyde, standing behind him handed over his keys with no comment. Sergio shined the tiny beam around the root cellar's space. In the corner farthest from the stairs, lay a water tank of some sort, or perhaps a heater. Directly in front of the stairs, a long workbench hugged the wall. A peg board above it held a number of cloudy glass baby food jars filled with nails and screws, a hammer, a short saw, a long metal square, and some rusted clamps. Covered in a thick layer of fine dust, the bench top held more tools, pieces of junk wood, and broken bits of rusty hardware, a miter box, and attached on the end was a large red vise, a duplicate of another he remembered in one of his foster homes. It was in Ma Lasky's garage. Her old man used to fix things. Ma showed Sergio how to use it one day, and he could still feel the hug she laid on him and the kiss on the cheek.

"Serge? You, okay?" Angela said. He continued shining the light to the right and left where he saw two narrow windows with paint chipped frames and hazy film covered glass that let in the barest light from outside.

Clyde, who had been standing at the base of the stairs, moved to the water tank corner and ducked behind it calling to Angela, who, at any rate, had already decided upon a hiding place of her own. She crouched under the back of the stairs, hidden on one side by a timeworn tallboy dresser and a crate piled high with junk, and on the other by an old-fashioned rain barrel and more junk. With these two secure, Sergio searched, not only for a place to lie unseen but for a weapon. From behind the water heater came Clyde's urgent hissing, "Hurry, hide, just hide." His imploring continued in a voice meant to be whispered but which hissed out at decibels sure to be heard by the deafest ears. In the corner to the left of the stairs, lay a cornucopia of the abandoned stuff that makes up most basements. Covering the length of one wall were wooden shelves holding mason jars, some empty and some full of peaches and tomatoes and beans, along with a couple of paint cans, and buckets. Stacked and leaned against this were wooden doors, odd pieces of lumber and paneling, and a rusty ironing board. Hearing a car, Sergio acquiesced and decided to dive weaponless between these layers. His big frame wedged and shouldered his way in, the layers sliding a little further out, and thankfully, the tottering jars not toppling to a messy death off the shelves. He clicked the penlight off and allowed his eyes to adjust to what little late afternoon sun seeped past the milky panes. Sergio observed in shadowed forms the edge of Clyde's profile kneeling behind the water tank and the back of Rachel's, or rather Angela's, wispy red hair. She glanced back toward him, and her hand went up in a weak wave and then returned to its position under her lips.

From his position, he could also see the outline of a hammer hanging on a pegboard over the workbench. Crouching there, debating about making a quick leap to retrieve it, his hands explored something cold and solid of crusty metal, lying on the bottom shelf. It was shaped like a pipe, about three foot long, and four or five inches in diameter, ending in a long handle. His best guess was it was an old-fashioned hand-operated, well pump and probably made of solid cast iron. His felt for the hinge, and his fingers began working a couple of rusted screws and pins out to free the two-foot long handle.

43

Vera's Arrival

She heard the car on the back road long before it showed up in her driveway. Anna had never seen a sports car like that. It was unexpected, adding to her nerves. Nevertheless, she forced herself to rock steadily back and forth, but when the machine's doors rose up in the air like a giant white vulture, she about lost it. Happily barking, Mabel, who had been circling the vehicle in her usual way, whimpered and shot up to the porch as the doors lifted. She parked herself at Anna's feet.

Anna was a strong woman, practical and wise. She was also a prayer warrior, fighting evil every day with scripture, her beads, her long visits to churches, her joining with all kinds of prayerful souls. In all her prayers, meditations, and visits, she felt she was doing her part to conquer the evil one and help the Lord rescue lost sheep. But never had Anna in all her eighty years had to physically stand before evil. She braced herself for what would confront her—what Clyde had seen coming—something so full of evil, her son had called it a pack. Yet, here it was in one of these two fancy packages exiting the hunching vulture car and walking her way. Rock, rock, rock, steady as she goes, Anna told herself eyeing them. The driver was suited up as if he was Wall Street itself. A real dandy that one, fussing with his sleeves. The passenger, a short thin woman was equally overdressed in heels, a silky blouse, and a shiny grey suit. Her hair was coifed, her lips and long nails were red, and her strut all business. Their corporate-like mien made inexplicable this horror Anna felt as they approached her on the porch. The man walked to the side of the house. Mabel followed him making a low growl and uncharacteristically keeping her distance. Apparently, even the dog could smell evil.

The compact woman climbed the porch steps slowly with a cold, uninviting smile, more of a knowing smirk. Her round, black, eyes, which seemed to have no iris, held Anna's. Anna's chest constricted as the woman spoke. "Miss-us Stoltz, I pre-sume. I am Doc-tor Wheat-on. You may call me Vera." Her stammered speech was strange, breaking syllables and pounding consonants. It reminded Anna of someone,…some movie character.

"I don't intend to call you anything," Anna said with a jerk of her chin.

"Oh, tsk, tsk, must we start out like that? I'm look-ing for your son, Clyde. I be-lieve he has some-thing of mine."

"Whatever you think he has, it isn't yours, and they're long gone anyway," Anna said, grinning up at the woman and shaking the empty can. "I gave 'em my savings, plenty of money to git where they want."

"That so?" Vera tilted her head as if sniffing the air then looked back down at the can. Mabel ran around the porch and commenced barking from a safe distance. The woman turned slowly to the dog and fixed on her a steady gaze. Anna leant forward, gripping her chair. Mabel howled then ran off whimpering into the woods. Mabel was a lover not a fighter, and whatever she'd seen, Anna thought, it was no match for her. She was glad Mabel wasn't the type to fight, glad she'd turned tail and run, glad if she was safe from this pair. The Wheaton woman returned her attention to Anna with a smug expression. "And just where ex-actly might that be."

"Heh, wouldn't you like to know," Anna said, commencing her rocking.

"Suit yourself, I guess you won't mind if we have a look a-round." Anna launched from the rocker as Vera sailed through the screen door uninvited. The coffee can clanged to the floor while she clung to the bible. Inside, the woman stood once again sniffing the air, reminding Anna of a snake.

"Git outta my house, you witch," Anna cried, raising the bible as if it were a weapon. Vera merely laughed at this and began circling the cabin, the whole time gauging Anna's reaction.

"Oh, ho, ho," Vera said, her finger wagging like a metronome. "You do know where they are, don't you." Startled by this revelation, with no idea where to go from here, Anna began to pray. Without warning, a cabinet door burst open and banged shut. Then another and the third, open, shut, open, shut. "Tell me where they are Miss-us Stoltz." Her voice accompanied the banging doors. Scared out of her wits, afraid to move, Anna prayed faster. Whether it was Anna's prayers or her apparent nonplussed demeanor, Vera Wheaton grew more agitated. Things began to fly off counters, some crashed into walls, many circled the room in a swirling tornado of household goods, plates, cups, the sugar and flour canisters, which smashed heavily into the wall behind Anna, who ducked just in time to avoid them. At this Anna screamed, "Jesus, mercy!" And at that, Vera stepped directly in front of Anna.

In her heels, they were nearly the same height. The owlish black eyes shimmered, and from her blood red lips a dozen unearthly guttural sounds mocked, "Mercy, oh, mercy, please, please, have mercy!" All the while, a maelstrom of kitchen gadgets, pots and cans flew around them. "I will spare your freak son," Vera's voice returned, "if and only if, you tell me where they are going. Consider my offer carefully, Miss-us Stoltz." In response, Anna spit in the old powdered face.

Just then, a can of beans whammed Anna's shoulder and a black skillet her back, knocking her half over. Fortified by a lifetime dedicated to relying on God the Father to take care of her, she continued to pray, "Whatever it takes Lord, I'll stand. I'm here, Lord." She straightened back up and faced Vera just as the fat oatmeal bin swung in the air and smashed on the edge of a ceiling beam over Anna's head, spilling its contents in a rain shower of coins, bills, and oatmeal flakes.

"Aha," Vera howled, "you deceitful lying old woman!"

"Mistress Vera," the man outside called, "there's a cellar. I can't find an entrance out here."

Vera's black eyes glared at Anna, whose gaze flitted unconsciously over the rug. Vera scanned the floor landing on the oval carpet and then smirking back at Anna. She flipped a chair off the rug and tugged at the table. Anna yelled, "No" and ran at the woman full force,

385

knocking her backward. Vera recovered her balance, flashed her hand out at Anna, whose body slammed backward with terrific force. Anna found herself a foot off the ground held by some mysterious force and plastered to the plywood wall like a boiled noodle. She tried to pull and twist able to move her arms and legs but not release her almost magnetized body. Her oversized rain boots slid from her bare feet and thunked, one then the other to the floor.

"Hold still you dried up prayer warrior." Vera looked toward the kitchen and flicked her hand. The silverware drawer wiggled then slid out heavily, hanging open so the contents were visible. The small number of butter knives, forks, and spoons shivered like a basket of fresh caught Kippers spilled on the dock. In a heartbeat, two knives in succession, one steak, one carving, rose from the tingling silverware and came racing through the air. Stricken, Anna urged her limbs to free her without success. The blades bit into her left ankle and right foot. In the length of time it takes for such excruciating pain to travel along the body's neurons and record its complaint to the brain, the junk drawer was open and two more sharp implements were sailing forth to pin Anna's wrists to the whitewashed wall. The knife for cleaning fish impaled her right wrist, and the sharpener Clyde gave her for Christmas three years ago, a long piece of carbide bar on a handle, skewered her left palm. And that is when Anna shrieked a blood-curdling cry of agony that ripped through the house.

44

Do You Reject Satan?

Still following Clarice's light through the heavy rain, John turned off the back road, recognizing the long dirt drive as that of Mrs. Stoltz, the woman he'd given a ride to that day in town. As he came to the clearing, he saw a white Lamborghini—*the* white Lamborghini that had passed him on the highway was parked near the house. John pulled the Blazer next to it, wondering to whom it belonged, when he spied a man in a dark suit crouched on the side of the log house, rubbing a manicured hand over a windowpane. Hearing John's approach, the sharp looking, middle-aged man stood. He drew a white handkerchief from his pocket and wiped his hands facing John.

"Hey, what do you think you're doing?" John said, striding forward. The man squinted against the rain and gave John a rather large diplomatic kind of smile. "I am Emmett Pierce," he said, coming toward John with his hand extended as if they were in a used car lot and John were a valued customer. Perhaps it was the pouring rain, which at the moment had decided to apply itself in sheets instead of drops, or perhaps it was the distance of time or place that threw them, but each of them did not recognize the other until they were within three or four feet, at which time both of their hands ready to shake the other's dropped to their sides. "You!" John said, ignoring the shower in his face, "You're that lawyer. You tried to have my son declared crazy and put away."

Emmett Pierce laughed at that, holding a palm to his forehead against the rain. "Tsk, tsk, taken away not put away, made a ward of the state and evaluated. There's a difference, Mister Miller."

"What are you doing here, snooping around Anna's house?"

"I might ask you as well, John Miller. What possible business could you have here?"

John said nothing. Pierce, who had retained his insipid smirk, placed the soiled hanky in his pocket and moved beyond John, who followed him back to the front of the house. In front of the steps to the porch, Pierce looked over John's right shoulder and snarled, "I see you brought the little woman."

John's surprise at this was quick. So the gloves are off, he thought, and some sort of hand was on the table, one John could only begin to guess. Apparently, this guy could see Clarice's sparkle too, and not only that, he knew it was his wife. It suddenly seemed sure this smarmy lawyer in the navy suit was here to look for his sister Angela. "Move," John told him, rivulets of water running into his mouth, "or I'll move you."

"Not to be puerile, but you and what army?"

It would be hard for anyone to say who threw the first punch since John's fist met Pierce's startling iron-like hand in mid-air. Pierce's hand closed on John's and thrust him thrust backward like so much baggage. The alarming force from one considerably smaller than himself left John flummoxed. Clarice's light whizzed in front of Pierce just then, and he laughed. "Ooooo, Tinkerbelle is ve-wy mad, Peter."

Just after Anna's ear-piercing scream, and following the sound of scraping furniture and a heavy thud, a rectangle of yellow light shone down from the top of the stairs. Heavy rain pelted the widows and the sound of it hitting the roof was echoed down into the cellar from the opening.

"Come out, come out wherever you are." Vera's voice sang as her heels clicked one ladder step at a time. Sergio's hand tightened on the iron handle. He felt as if he could hear everyone's breath being held. "No?" Vera said, "You can't hide behind that microwave spirit sucking half-wit forever." She skulked, gingerly poking a few things and kicking others. Thick with cobwebs and dust, the space was a catchall for cherished discards. "Let's just get on with it, shall we?" Without another entreaty, things started to rattle and move, mostly things on the workbench. Sergio had just enough light and vantage point to watch the show, part in awe and part in terror. The glass baby food jars slowly rotated, unscrewing themselves from their metal lids. In a second, the hidden trio were under fire. Whipping nuts, bolts, screws and nails, a veritable hailstorm of metal, pelted them reaching every corner of the cellar. The ammo embedded itself in wood, bounced off stone, shattered the light bulb, and sent jars of canned tomatoes and greens, smashing to the floor, splattering tomato blood and guts across the battlefield. Angela shrieked. The shellfire ceased as Vera turned towards the sound. With a calm step, she walked around to the back of the stairs. Sergio saw Clyde's shadow rise. Fearing he would lose his chance, he risked everything to wave him down. Vera stooped, peering in between boxes and piled paraphernalia to Angela.

"There you are my sweetest child; Grandma is here. All is forgiven now that I've found you."

Creeping behind Vera, Sergio could just make out Angela's doe eyes, wide open with a kind of fascinated look. So mesmerized was Angela, and so compelling was it watching her captivation that Sergio nearly forgot his own intent. It was the smallest sway of Vera's suit coat as her back stiffened that alerted him to the fact she was aware of his presence. His already raised arm delivered five pounds of solid cast iron straight to Vera Wheaton's back. She keeled forward into the cardboard boxes underneath the stairs. At the same time, Angela erupted, pushing the rain barrel out from the side. It rolled across the floor and banged the wall. Sergio seized Angela's her hand and steered her upstairs.

"Clyde, come on," he urged several times. Clyde remained in place, and although Sergio could not see him or even begin to guess what fear held him hostage. He knew they should not wait for him. Still holding the cast iron handle, he shot up the stairs after Angela. Lifting himself over the edge of the floor, something lay hold of his boot. He looked down, hardly believing his eyes, and kicked like a madman at a beastly arm digging at his ankle, a thick, twisted appendage, covered in stiff boar hair and ending in red claws—the color of Vera's nails. He punched his leg with desperate force, one arm holding the floor edge and the other beating down into the dark at the misshapen mass of flesh and fur. He glimpsed horns and between them a pair of tusks. What wasn't covered in fur, seem to be a kind of skinless flesh, raw and open like flayed meat. Slime dripped and oozed from the area of the mouth, which teeth reminded him of a possums. Hideous sounds attacked their ears. "Jesus!" Sergio shouted with as much faith as epithet. His leg was freed, and the beast tumbled back with a loud thud.

Sergio climbed out with his back to the opening, still feverishly shaking his leg, and stood before Angela, who stared into the hole transfixed. Sergio grabbed Angela's arms and tried to shake her out of the spell. Quickly judging his efforts a waste of time, he pushed past her to heave the heavy trap door in place, not even considering Clyde. As it dropped, the arm of the creature appeared, and Sergio flung his entire body on the door. As he yelled at Angela to run, who at any rate stayed put, the door humped violently upward. "If you won't run then help me. Get that table." Sergio's body thumped wildly with the tremendous building force. Finally the door flung him off completely. He landed on his back a couple feet away facing the wall.

His chest leapt. There, hanging from the wall, her arms spread wide, her sweater too, looking like a flying squirrel, pinned flat like some kind of butterfly trophy, was poor Anna Stoltz. Thick and wet crimson streams ran the length of the wall from her skewered wrists and feet. Her head hung down; her once charming hat shielded her eyes. Adorning the same wall, in jarring juxtaposition, about three feet away, a silent witness to Anna's last stand, hung a large crucifix.

The sound of Vera's laughing, brought his attention back to the cellar opening. Rising as slow as a waft of smoke, was Vera, same suit, same hair, same red nails. As frightening as she always was to him, this form was a relief from the monster of moments ago. Her focus was on Angela having that same mesmerizing quality as before.

Sergio, who had abandoned himself to his fate serving evil long ago, felt overpowered with sympathy for the fate of this girl. In his eyes, she was innocent. She represented something to him he could not explain. He wanted her to have the redemption he lacked. He wanted her to be free, free to be good, free to live for good wherever that existed. And he knew wherever that was, it was far from anything he had ever known. Sergio scrambled to his feet shouting, "Leave her alone. What are you doing to her?"

"Who me?" Vera oozed sarcasm, hovering in the air. "Nothing, nothing really, we can't possess her, not yet, but we can control her as easily as we can this table." Vera waved her hand. The table wobbled and rose, flipped on end, and before Sergio could react, the thing rammed him to the floor, pinning him as tight. He pushed his arms out, expecting to easily rid himself of the table's weight, but found himself held fast by some supernatural force.

"Really, children," she spoke as a floating specter, "I can call you that for you are indeed ours. Your choices were made long ago. All this running is futile. Do you know while you have been risking your life and precious limb to save her, she has been in doubt? We knew it, the moment we laid our eyes on her."

"So kill us and get it over with."

"Oh my dear lost boy, what kind of a spiritual mother abandons her children without giving them one…more…chance?" Her body ceased floating and came to rest on the floor in front of the cellar opening. "We are prepared to forgive you. You will be spared, Sergio, unharmed, and untortured if you accept the master now."

"No-ooo," A weak sound emitted from the wall. Anna's head lifted slightly and turned towards him on the floor. Her words were labored, but clear. "Don't listen to her. You have a choice. You have always had a choice."

Vera scoffed at this. "Look at you," she said, "hanging on the wall as helpless as a dissected frog. "Look what all your insipid mumbling and sacrificing, your pathetic bowing and groveling, just look, look what it got you." Anna's grey head bobbed slightly as if to disagree. Vera sniggered. "By all means, Sergio, gaze on this old crone and see what her choice has wrought. See where her fanatic religious loyalties have brought her. What you see is what you'll get, young man. Speaking of seeing, perhaps…, you have learned your lesson? Say the word, and we will restore your eye. A gesture, a gift to welcome you home. It will be nothing compared to the new life you will enjoy."

As Vera continued to ply him, Sergio felt conflicted. Truth was he had harbored hopes of his sight being restored. Beyond that, he even dared now and then to allow himself to daydream that he held Emmett's place, that he had redeemed himself with the coven and that he could wield the powers that now controlled him. Indeed his hatred for Emmett and Emmett's sickening advances, caused many a moment imagining his exquisite revenge. It was true that he'd spent a good many months—really since being free of Menger—in rebellion and rejection of the coven. But that rejection, was far from discovery, let alone acceptance of whatever lay in opposition to that life—the mystery of God and goodness. If Angela Miller was a neophyte on the journey to discover God, then Sergio Valenti was a mere zygote. He looked at Angela now. She remained as before, immobile and staring at Vera as though hypnotized. He became more and more confused, unsure of what was being asked of him.

As Sergio lay there silently thinking of his options, Anna roused herself to speak, the effort of which must have been pure torture. The weight of her body was supported by the knives with her own bones providing the only resistance. The slightest movement increased and renewed her agony. Her voice served the effort well and carried across the room. "Do you reject Satan?"

Suddenly the question was simple. It was not grey or murky. It was not bound with power or singed with revenge. Nor was it tainted with guilt, or confused with yearning for material possessions or creature comforts. It was a very simple and straightforward question. Even so, Sergio said, "What?"

"Do you reject Satan, all his pomps, and his works?" Anna heaved. "Do you accept Jesus Christ, your Lord and Savior?" As Anna wheezed these words out, the curtain behind the sink billowed straight out from the wall toward Vera, whose arm was raised and her fingers spread out. In one motion, her hand closed as if upon the rod, and flung backward as a fisherman preparing to cast. At this, the curtain rod sailed through the air, the curtain flowing behind it. It found its mark impaling itself in the wheezing chest of Anna Stoltz.

45

Turning Tides

What Vera did not know, what she could not have known or sensed, neither corporally, spiritually, nor even demonically, was Clyde. Clyde, that light and dark sucking black hole, whose spirit neutralized the appearance of light and dark as effectively as a Tums on stomach acid. The presence of Clyde Stoltz provides such balance and equilibrium that no such person or entity could have known Clyde was there. His gut reaction, having just taken in the ghastly crucifixion and the kitchen cutlery nailing his mother to the wall of their beloved home, and seeing the white rod bearing the sweet yellow curtains she had made with her own two hands, which now lanced his mother's chest and hung like some ridiculous cheerful flag, and hearing the legion of evil voices, and seeing them peering out through those old black eyes and laughing in a hundred voices...

Clyde rose up behind Vera, unseen and unsensed. Clyde Stoltz, as unexpected as he was unexplainable. Little Clyde Stoltz, who wouldn't smoosh a spider or swat a fly, but catch it carefully in his hand and gently release it outside. Clydey Stoltz, who would offer the other cheek all day until his tormentor grew tired of slapping it. Clyde Stoltz, who counted no man an enemy, no scorn an insult, and no insult an injury. That Clyde W. Stoltz rose up and stole up that ladder. That same Clyde stood behind Vera Wheaton and all the monsters of hell she housed, and that same Clyde Stoltz pushed for all he was worth, for all one hundred and twenty, meek and mild pounds of him. That Clyde pushed as hard as any fat kid ever pushed a skinny kid on the playground..., and that push was perfect!

Vera thrust forward like a lover, her arms out, her feet running, trying, but unable, to counteract the sudden propulsion and landed with her face against the wall. Here and there projections of giant nails jutted from the walls. These were railroad spikes that Clyde Senior, Anna's dear husband—rest his blessed soul—had pounded into the plank walls at just the right height for Anna to hang one of her beloved hats, and just the right height—God bless him—for Doctor Vera Wheaton and her Bette Davis Eyes, and just the right length,— God be forever praised—to hold any number of hats at one time, or as the case happened, to perfectly skewer and punctuate that evil infested brain. It took a moment, and Sergio was the first to enjoy it, before a stream of black blood leached from Vera's right eye. Her body slumped against the giant nail tearing upward to the skull just under her right brow. Her left eye flashed at Sergio, seemingly aware of a vengeful enjoyment he was surely owed. Sergio's words to her were simple, as simple and straightforward as the question Anna had posed to him.

"I do reject Satan," he said, "I do accept Jesus."

Outside in the yard, rain continuing its relentless downpour. Dripping wet Emmett Pierce was having fun. This lummox and his Tinkerbelle fairy wife are the boy's parents. All these months, they've been playing the poor distraught parents with the media and the cops when it was they themselves that hid him in the silva templum. Now it looked as if they intended to be involved again, messing with the great one's plans. At any rate, he could toy with them a while. It's not all that often he has the opportunity to use his powers so openly. John Miller was reeling back from the blow. Emmett had no intention of engaging him one on one in this manner. He spied a wood pile by the shed and had a delicious idea. The top log jiggled and rose then shot hard into Miller's arm. Emmett laughed. Miller held his arm and observed the pile unbelieving. His power may not be as strong or impressive as the Mistress, but it was plenty for this sport. He caused another to dislodge and rise. John Miller ran for cover, sliding in the mud and nearly falling. No use that, as the log neatly met the side of his head, completing his fall. He picked his face from the mud and tried to shield his head from another log. As he rose, his shirt and face covered in mud, the third log found its mark square on his back.

Sucking up the pain, John hurried to gain his footing. This scummy lawyer was one of them, John thought, part of that coven. He even had supernatural powers. This was going to end badly....I'm not going out this way, John decided, covered in mud, hearing this jackal laugh and knowing Clarice was somehow watching. No way. He ducked behind a second shed of sorts, a ram shackle lean-to with a tar-paper roof. It offered little to no protection, but gave him two seconds to come up with something. And as he barreled out from it, full speed ahead, he more than realized, it was no plan. Head down, a raging bull, John charged the smarmy lawyer taking him fully by surprise. Pierce fell backward into the porch steps with John practically on top of him. He scrambled up like someone dropped into a vat of spiders, and he leapt out of reach of John's blows. He ran, slid and fell, and it was hard to tell what horrified him more, the mud bath on his suit, or John's fists. Up again, he gained distance from John, who stopped to enjoy the spectacle the lawyer was making, and Emmett landed, facing the shed as if he were in a hold-up. He turned with a red-hot and muddy face to John. He smiled. John followed his gaze. The wood splitting ax, which lay in a stump before him, wriggled.

Clarice, who had been helplessly watching, saw the ax jiggling itself loose. She flipped as Emmett sent the ax, end over end, hurling towards John. She threw her light in front of Emmett with no sense of purpose, only a panicked righteous anger. She tried to get meaninglessly between John and Emmett. John saw the ax rise, saw it fly, saw Clarice's light too. It came to him as some sort of bizarre blinking light show. The strobe effect it produced for him caused the motion of the ax to stutter; it was as if he were watching someone flipping one of those booklets of cartoon drawings. John could make out the ax's movement toward him. Whether instinct or his guardian angel's hand, which he had instantly sought, John reached out, and rather than deflect the ax, he caught the handle, and in one smooth move, he hurled it back at his opponent, whose eyes were temporarily blinded by his wife's angry light. It sailed end over end and planted itself deep in Emmett Pierce's skull. Emmett stood with the blade splitting down the forehead, between the eyes, and to the upper lip. He tottered, and finally fell face first in another deposit of mud.

John watched with a mix of emotions, triumph, relief, and then regret over having taken a human life. But these deeper thoughts would have to wait. John nodded to Clarice's light. "Not sure what you did. Not even sure why I can see you. But thanks, he said, and took a deep breath, "Thank God!"

In the house, Clyde rushed past Angela to his mother on the wall. Sergio, easily throwing the table's weight from him now, jostled to his feet. Clyde pulled the awful curtain rod from her chest then the two knives from his mother's bare feet. He was unable to reach her hands, and his words buried between guttural moaning and air-sucking gasps came to Sergio, "Help…, help us." In two steps, Sergio was there assisting Clyde with his mom.

Facing the wall as they were, neither man noticed the black blood, which oozed from Vera. Rivulets and individual droplets writhed and squirmed about like a virus under a microscope, finally coming together into one great gurgling puddle. After cooking a short time on the petri-dish floor, the wet thing rose in a massive plume until the black soot of it filled the top of the cabin. The mass of oily black seethed and bubbled like boiling tar. Clyde saw it first; Sergio looked up, and even Anna's eyes opened to watch. From one end of the cloud, a protuberance bulged into a long extremity, forming a serpent shape wider than a boa constrictor. As it grew, its shape did indeed solidify so the very end of it had the form of a snake, complete with fangs, a giant flicking, forked tongue, and beady red eyes. It wound this way and that as if in search of something, coming inches from the trio of Clyde, Anna, and Sergio whose faces were stricken with a helpless horror. It wound away, snaking left and right of them, finally coming upon Angela where it pulled to the ceiling and whiplashed forward. She screamed as it poured into her every orifice, her eyes, nose, open mouth, and lower torso. The fat snake morphed into tangles of liquid eels, streaming in and out of her body. In a huge sucking sound, every speck of oily tar bored into her and disappeared therein. Sergio jumped up and rushed forward to hold her. She stood nearly as she'd been, only now two of the coldest black eyes stared back at him.

"Angela!" he cried, as he caught her. She pulled him into her embrace then wiggled against him.

"You want me. You have always wanted me."

"Angela, stop it; stop this. This isn't you."

She laughed, or rather the things inside her made that vile multiplied reverberation. "You know what you are? No fun. You have made up your puny mind, and you are useless to us. Done, done, you are done." She placed her hands on his chest, and he spoke softly inveigling, avoiding those eyes.

"It's okay, Angela. I know you can hear me. It's okay; we'll get it out of you. Just fight it. Just hang on."

Her long fingers walked playfully up his breast until they rested on either side of his neck. Without warning, they wrapped round his neck and clamped down. Even as she choked with super human strength, Sergio refused to believe what was happening and continued to attempt to speak. "No, Angela…This… not you. You don't know…stop… sto—" As the words were literally wrung out of him in the vice-like grip as strong as a dozen men, his struggle was desperate. It graduated to frantic, ripping and pulling at her thin wrists, unable to loose them from his neck. In complete panic, as color drained from his face, he kicked at her legs, punched her head and even tried to tear her hair. It was a ludicrous sight, a slender girl, emotionless and robotic, raising the six foot two hundred and twenty pound man as easily as a rag doll, holding him a foot off the ground. His head turned a bluish grey, his deep Italian eye bulged in a frightened globe, and his head slumped to one side just as John followed by Clarice's light entered the cabin.

The body stopped twitching, and she lowered it till his ear reached her lips. "The boy is next," she whispered. Then she screamed, "No," sounding very much like his sister. Angela still held the unconscious man with curly black hair by the neck. "No, no!" she yelled again as her two hands screwed one against the other, snapping his neck as easily as a twist off cap and releasing the insensate body to the floor.

John watched the maniacal redhead, quickly processing it was his own sister, thin legs apart, hands at her side, standing over the body. "Gotta run, John boy, places to go, prophets to kill, you know how it is." She laughed. "Aw, don't look at me like that Johnnie. You'll hurt my feelings."

"Ange, I don't understand?"

She picked up the grown man's body as easily as a sack of potatoes. She tossed it down the opening in the floor where it landed with a heavy sickening thud. "Oops, he might need some help, some CPR or something." She said, laying one finger aside of her cheek. "You better check that out." He hesitated, unsure what to do. Who was the good guy, who the bad. This did not sound or look like his sister. Her eyes... Wheaton!

"Chop chop, he might be dying. Don't you care?" She sounded crazy. "Tsk, tsk, you do-gooders are supposed to care more." When he still stood unsure, she moved swiftly to the corner where John saw for the first time the others in the room. The scene looked like a reverse pieta of a man holding a bleeding old woman, who John quickly saw was Anna. "Let go," Angela demanded of Clyde. She yanked the old woman's bleeding wrist as the small man named Clyde screamed and held onto his mother's body. His sister's strength was too much for him and a second later, she had dragged the woman's body and the man with it to the cellar opening and plunged them downward. John hardly knew what hit him. He may not know the two men, but the old woman was clearly Anna. John debated no further and leapt to intercept the descending bodies when he too was pushed headlong down the wooden steps. The heavy trap door slammed above them entombing all three in darkness.

Clarice watched all of this as the whole scenario played out in fifteen seconds. She flitted back and forth, powerless to help at all as the redhead waltzed over to the old Frigidaire and toppled it. White milk and yellow juice seeped out as she effortlessly heaved it twelve feet till it rested on the trap door. John's sister clapped her hands once and appeared to be talking to herself. "Now what, my loves? Oh yes, good idea." She strode to the stove, whipping every one of the four dials, which hissed to life and filled the air with the smell of gas. Realizing what was happening, Clarice flew in front of Angela, who swatted at her ethereal shape as if at an annoying gnat. "Be gone," a scarily masculine voice emitted from the girl's mouth, "you can do nothing here." Angela, for it was surely Angela as John had called her Ange, nosed about in cans and jars on shelves. The drawers lay empty and of contents strewn as if they'd been in a cutlery tornado. Angela was looking for matches, no doubt. Filled with dread and foreboding, Clarice flew outside and around to the cellar windows.

Under the floor boards, John disengaged himself from the confused muddle of arms and legs. "You okay?" he asked of the man who was thrown down with him, at the same time, trying to see the old woman's condition in the greying twilight.

The man ignored his question crying instead, "Ma, Mama?" He was laboring to turn her over and separate her from the other man's body. John clambered off them and after some effort, pulled the other man away. He leant over him trying to feel his breath. "The light, the light," the man in blue waved a shadowy arm upward. John stepped over them, straining his eyes in the dark to the ceiling and seeing a single bulb on a post. He felt for a string and tugged it. The bulb cast a weak yellow glow over the scene. The man wearing a blue work uniform knelt, holding a hanky over the wound in his mother's chest and whining softly. John crouched to the dark-haired man. His head was twisted unnaturally. He lifted the wrist, but could feel no pulse.

"His light is gone," the smaller man said. "He was a good guy."

Above their heads, something scraped loudly across the floor, and John clumsily dove over the pair and ploughed to the top of the rickety stairs. Several times, he threw his weight against the trap door, but it refused to budge. Whatever was on top of it was heavy as all get out. How did his sister get so strong, and what the hell was the matter with her? "Angela," he screamed, "Angela, it's me, John; let us out."

"*Ooah*," a hoarse sound, barely a moan came from the old woman, and John descended again to kneel on her other side.

"Anna?" John said, and the man regarded him.

"You know mama?"

"I gave her a ride home from downtown one day when her truck wouldn't start."

"You know Rachel, er, Angela?"

"The woman upstairs is my sister. It's hard to believe." He mumbled the last. "I'm John."

"I'm Clyde, Clyde Stoltz." He wiped a bloodstained hand on his shirt before offering John his hand.

"What happened up there? Did Doctor Wheaton do this? How?"

"I work at Four Kings with Ra-Angela. The old one upstairs, she did this. I think she is dead now, but the filth from inside her, it is in your sister—controlling her I think. It…I don't think it has her all the way."

"*Ooahhh,*" the old woman moaned again, and her eyes fluttered open.

"Mama! It's a miracle, mama. Your alive." One of his mother's bloody hands went up to his face, and he caught it before it fell, holding it to his cheek as he must have suspected she wanted. John left them and knelt by the other man's body. He lifted one arm and then the other, laying them over his blue striped shirt. He was making a sign of the cross when Clyde's head popped up. "She's doing something bad, something to the stove," he said to John. Both heads tilted up, listening. John thought he heard something, a light hissing sound.

"Gas? Is she… she wouldn't!" John stormed the ladder stairs again and pounded on the trap door. "Angela, Angela," he demanded, "Let us out! Angela!" Hunched over, John planted his feet on the second step, positioned his back against the door and lifted. He could squat three hundred pounds with his legs if he had to, just needed a good … the door lifted an inch then another two—*Crack!* The step tore beneath him; one foot rammed through the wood as his weight came down, tearing through his jean to his calf. He swore, loudly damning the broken step and his luck. Still cursing at the pain, John lumbered past the two at the bottom of the stairs to the narrow window. He tried to unlatch it, but it was nailed shut. Looking about, he found a hammer on the workbench pegboard and used it to smash the panes letting in fresh air. Something twinkled just outside the window.

"Clarice?"

46

Great Escape

"Clyde, whoever said my knives were dull, eh? Heh, heh, owww." Anna pinched her eyes and struggled for a breath. "Hurts… to laugh." Every word was labored, in fact. John thought perhaps a lung had been pierced. Her son nodded vigorously, tears dripping from his eyes. "Shh, shh," he whispered, "save your strength."

"No, no more saving for me….We're done…, the Lord . . . He's… calling me home." Clyde vigorously shook his head. "You—you have to acc—ept His will. Ma—ma lov—es you." Her eyes closed, but Clyde shook her despite her fragility. Her eyes remained closed, but her mouth spoke again. "Save the boy…it wants to find—"

Nothing more. Anna's body relaxed and lie perfectly still. "No, noooo," Clyde cried, held her closer, and rocked back and forth.

John had been examining the stone basement with a crowbar for a way out. The beams, mammoth and crude, were topped by inch thick wide plank floors, nailed in solid. The two windows, about twelve inches high and two feet wide, were surrounded by stone as well. Covered in sweat from his frantic efforts to loosen floorboards, John smelled gas in the room above through a knothole that popped out at his banging. John was keenly aware of the danger they were in but did not want to increase Clyde's burden.

Angela felt as if she were in a movie. She seemed to be helplessly watching the actions someone else was performing but from the vantage point of her own eyes. She tried several times to free herself, to rid herself of the heinous mind-shattering evil that surrounded her, but her fear was stronger than her will, and she retreated to some corner of her own soul, and cowered there, trying only to preserve some portion of her will.

She watched herself shuffling through a few drawers in the cabin, saw herself kicking things around on the littered floor, heard herself mutter something about making a mess of a simple crucifixion, and felt her own leg kick the well-dressed corpse on the floor. Now she was heading outside, and it seemed obeying a chorus of voices instructing her to search for keys to the Lamborghini, to turn it on, and to heat the cigarette lighter. The gasses in the cabin would have to reach five to fifteen percent to explode, a fact conveyed to her by the voices. She would have time to begin a small fire and escape, before the gas was just enough concentration to ignite, explode, and obliterate the cabin. People were down the basement . . . but who? The voices would not answer her, but instead subjected her spirit to incredible torture for even asking.

She felt her hands rifling in the pockets of a muddied body, seeing the head torn asunder by the imbedded ax. She crossed the yard with the keys, watched the strange doors of the sports car rise, felt her bottom settle in the seat, saw her arm push the ignition button, then pop open the glove box, feeling for the cigarette lighter. She pulled a phone charger plug out, popped the lighter in place and waited for it to heat.

Relieved that John could still "see" her, Clarice left the window to check on John's sister. The blackness was everywhere around Angela. Yet it seemed outside of her somehow, as if it were visiting her spirit, harassing her, but not in complete ownership of her. Clarice dared not enter the cabin. If her anxiety caused even a light switch to flicker, it may provide enough spark to send the cabin up in smoke. Angela had searched the axed corpse and now sat in the white sports car with the engine running. She soon exited the car holding a glowing cigarette lighter. Why had the rain let up now? *Oh my God, help us. Send help. John has to get out of that house!*

John's sister surrounded by the incredible inky blackness walked back into the house. A moment later, she hurried out and down the steps. She walked to the edge of the yard where the woods began. Angela stood there as if deciding which way to go. Clarice felt blindsided as the truth hit her. Angela knows where Jackson is hiding. The blackness wants her to take them there. *Oh my God, Jackson!*

Climbing down from the dresser, John wiped an already blistered hand across his beading forehead. He approached Clyde, crouching down and placing a hand lightly on his shoulder. "Hey, I know this stinks, but we need to get out of here. My sister, she's turned on the gas, and I think she's lighting a fire." Clyde continued to rock his mother's body. John sat on his haunches and quietly waited a full minute then tried again. "She's gone. I know it kills, but—"

"No," the man cried, pushing him, and causing John to lose his balance.

John silently prayed a moment, reminding God they had not a moment to spare, and he tried once more, this time seizing Anna's son and forcing him to look at him. "We have to get out. Your mother would want you to live. I have to get to my sister. Please, is there a way out. Think!"

Clyde blankly studied John's face then snapped alert. "The coal chute! I used to crawl in it as a boy. It goes outside. It's boarded up—"

"Show me."

Clyde gently unleashed his mother, and carefully arranged her on the floor, stopping to straighten her flowered dress over her legs and tuck her bloodstained sweater neatly about her shoulders. On his knees, he kissed her forehead, and made the sign of the cross then rose. "Here," he said, "it's behind the workbench. Dad built it here, and then I couldn't use it anymore."

John surveyed the area under the workbench. It was covered and solid. He tried to pull the piece out from the wall, but it was fastened tight, like everything else in this cabin. John began throwing things off the top, and they made loud crashes into the corner. He handed the hammer to Clyde and retrieved the crowbar for himself. Together the two of them ripped and tore at the heavy structure. John was attacking it like a crazed gorilla, his hands full of splinters and bleeding as he ripped pieces off. Even Clyde, who was more strategically removing nails, was sweating. Finally, the legs came loose and the two of them rocked the thick top off. The coal chute covered by an iron door was only half exposed as it sat some three and a half

403

feet from the floor. Without words, John and Clyde attacked the giant pegboard until it and everything still on it crashed to the floor. Behind the iron door lay a crude hole lined with black coal dust. It looked tight.

"You should go first," John said. "I might get stuck."

"No, you probably won't. Besides, I don't think I can break through the other side. You're stronger." There was no time to argue. John pulled himself up and inched his way forward in the tight space, holding the hammer. The chute was short, so short John's feet still hung out the bottom in the cellar. He felt a metal door much like the other. It was of course closed tight. John tried banging the hammer on it where he thought screws might be. The space was so tight though, he could not pull back for a decent wham. After a few more efforts, he backed out of the hole with an idea and found Clyde kneeling by his mother again. "Clyde," he called, in that deep, clipped and commanding tone he used with his workers, "I need you." Clyde returned and waited for instruction. "I'm going in backwards, so I can try to kick the door free." John made another attempt with Clyde supporting his head and shoulders. John worked himself as close to the door as possible, pulling his knees up and letting loose on the small door. It definitely felt more powerful than his arm, and he repeated the beating over and over feeling it loosen. "A few more," he announced, one word with each kick, "and...we... got it!" What twilight was left could be seen through the chute. John insisted Clyde go first, partly because he was afraid Clyde would want to stay with his mother, partly because he feared an explosion was imminent.

Rightly so, as the propane gas filling the room and mixing with the oxygen in the closed cabin had just reached that magical ratio. Together the gaseous cocktail danced over the bright little paper fire in the middle of the floor, finding the spark it so earnestly desired. The igniting spark that would consummate its union and allow it to burst forth in one calamitous and destructive blast, loudly sending everything in its path outward to oblivion.

Outside the hole, Clyde waited with Clarice's light bouncing wildly behind him. "Hurry," Clyde urged, "she's really worried about you." John did not bother to process that Clyde could also "see" Clarice, instead he yelled, "Run, go, just go," as he wiggled himself out of the coal chute. John was two seconds behind Clyde, about twenty feet from the house, when the house exploded in the loudest boom he'd ever heard, sounding like unbelievably close thunder. It cast John in the air as if he'd dove forward of his own accord. He sailed outward with wood beams and household furniture, which landed in the yard, the trees, and a choice board or two on his head. The house collapsed as if it was made of toothpicks and lay in a heap under the mostly intact roof. A fire immediately blazed forth, and John, his head smarting from the blow a board had dealt him, rolled over to observe it. "Clyde?"

"Here," Clyde said, rushing towards him. "You all right?" He reached to remove the lumber still on John.

"Yeah, I think so." John sat up rubbing his head, and inwardly thanking God.

"Okay good, we have to go. We have to stop her."

"Huh?" John said, not following at all.

"Angela, she is going to find him, the one, the Voice in the Wilderness. She plans to kill him."

John kicked a remaining board and scrambled to his feet. He had no intention of questioning this special man. He'd come this far on faith, why quit now. There was just one thing, besides his screaming shoulder and head… where was she?

As if in answer to his silent question, Clyde, already headed into the woods, cried, "C'mon follow the light."

47

Deo Gratias

Heavy rain pelted the handful of umbrellas. Father Tom tilted his rather small one back and shifted it even further right to ensure Mrs. Walker was covered. Mr. Walker was sharing his enormous golf umbrella, which he held high almost forming a roof over the originals, Val and Fran. The young pair, just fit under their blue number, huddled but comfortable. Gerard, flipped his hood up, and Al wore a baseball cap and had his hands rammed in his jean coat pockets. Both refused any offers of shelter, and Gerard told Al, he didn't need anything from the house. No one seemed too uncomfortable or even distracted during their intense prayers, which had gone past an hour now. Father glanced at his watch, 7:33. Sunset was about 7:50 these nights. He hoped they would not have too much trouble seeing their way back to their cars. Gerard Healy was praying.

"Father, we just thank you for the Millers, and ask your protection on them. And we know you have a great plan for us all. A great and merciful plan." Several amens erupted at this as they had been the last hour. "A great and terrible plan, Lord," Gerard continued, "for we know you are a Just God,"

Amen.

"a mighty God,"

Amen.

"a God of mercy, who loves us and wants to fill us with his Fatherly love."

Thank you, Jesus. Several hands shot up in the air and wagged back and forth like seaweed in the waves.

"Amen! And so Father, we just praise you. We praise your name and your son Jesus, and thank you for your Holy Spirit, who speaks to us and hangs out in our hearts."

"Glory to God, the Father," Father Tom called out surprised when the troupe answered him.

Glory to God, the Father.

"Glory to God, the Son," he said, and waited for the echo.

Glory to God, the Son.

"Glory to God, the Holy Spirit."

Glory to God, the Holy Spirit!

"Do you feel that?" the young girl named Heather whispered.

"I do," answered Kate in the same hushed tone. Several uh-huh's and me-too's followed then all of them were quiet and perfectly still. "Someone needs help, right now. Something, something is happening."

Father Tom felt it too. After a moment, he spoke. "We should keep praying. Keep praising." All nodded, and feeling inspired Father began, "Come, Holy Spirit, fill the hearts of your faithful, and enkindle in us the fire of your love."

Amen. Yes, Lord. Come Holy Spirit.

"Help us Lord, help us, send your heavenly help," Gerard prayed, "to whoever needs it right now."

Help us, help us, chimed the choir. All at once, a white glow shone around Michelle Nicestrum's headstone. It grew brighter and brighter as everyone gasped. The light condensed, formed a ball, and rose slowly. Father fell to his knees in wonder and exclaimed, "Glory to God the Father, and to the Son and to the Holy Spirit." He repeated the prayer and everyone joined him, also falling on their knees oblivious of the mud and wet and chanting together: Glory to *God the Father, and to the Son, and to the Holy Spirit.* Umbrellas were abandoned, and all hands raised in praise as two more heavenly lights appeared, one on each side of the first. Their faces, lined with rain and tears of wonder and joy, beheld the new miracle and the chant continued. The three orbs shot higher and flew northwest disappearing in the sky.

408

The sun had just about set. The trees, except for the interspersed pines, were still bare of spring growth and admitting that yellowish twilight. Their eyes adjusted as they climbed the steep paths leading up to what John knew was the opposite side of his mountain. He thought back to the day Anna told him all that. She was a remarkable person, the loss of which, even having known her so little a time, he could feel,. He looked ahead to Clyde whose eyes were on the sparkly light of Clarice floating ahead of them. He felt sorry for the man and wondered what would become of him. Hah, he caught himself, what was going to become of any of them?

They stepped over twigs and soggy leaves; the trunks of the trees grew thicker. He felt a little out of breath as the climb seemed to never end. John was coming around a big elm when Clyde stopped and pointed. "There she is."

His sister with that crazy red hair and a wild look in her eyes had stopped her ascent too, spinning around and flashing her eyes on them. Her head fell back, scanning trees then the forest floor. Her behavior was odd, threatening without actually being a threat. Or so it would seem . . . .

Clarice too stopped short before both Angela and the incredible army of demons she housed. She saw the threatening behavior in a much clearer light than John and Clyde. For coming forth from Angela's darkness, emitted with each glance, were flying black flames. They flew out from her like mini jets from the mother ship, one after another finding their targets. In the tree branches, they slipped into birds, again and again then into squirrels and rodents; they skimmed along the forest floor, finding their way into snakes and spiders, even ants.

For John and Clyde, the attack that ensued could not be easily explained. It began with a flock of Hitchcock dive-bombing birds. They came from every direction, swooping down, madly pecking their heads and hands. Their furious screeches and caws pierced their ears; wings flapped and flailed about their heads as both men waved them off. As these attacked from above, below came a number of rodents running up their legs, nipping at their pants and ankles. John's arms were flapping wildly between the airborne attackers and those biting at his legs. He stomped his work boots, attempting to crush anything he sloughed off. A fat yellow garter snake climbed on his boot. His yells were instinctive, almost as primal as the creatures attacking him. Leaves were rustling with new life, black armies of insects carrying out some paranormal directive, possessed and unstoppable.

In the midst of his personal blitzkrieg, John hadn't thought of Clyde. He looked to him now to see how he was managing the onslaught. Clyde knelt on the forest floor, his hands clapped over his head. In the dimming light, John made out his calves covered in snakes and spiders, a squirrel and several mice tearing at his blue trousers. Blood was on his hands where birds had ripped the skin. And John heard just now he was shouting at him. "Stop, stop, you must stop fighting. Only pray. Pray! Stop fighting. Displeasing God, you're offending Him. God wishes to defend us." John could hardly believe, what he was seeing or hearing. "Lie down. Assent to our Father's will. Demand he protect us!"

John hearing what Clyde was saying, and with only a spiritual instinct, howled one last time, before clapping his hands over his ears and face like Clyde. He dropped to his knees, resisting the urge to slap away insects crawling over him or the birds, which returned storming his now defenseless back. Withstanding the squirrel biting through his jeans, taking a chunk from his thigh, not kicking it but instead calling out, "God have mercy. Jesus, save us! Mary, be our help!"

Clarice had felt them coming. Her angel had pulled her towards them even as John and Clyde were under siege. Her spirit leapt at the sight of them. If they had been accompanied by blaring trumpets, it would not have seemed the least bit out of place. Their lights were the brightest she'd ever seen since the ball of light came to her from Michelle Nicestrum's grave. Three giant orbs glowing and pulsing with power and hope. The Archangel's lights spun down to the kneeling men, surrounding them in an effervescent glow and lighting the darkened forest as bright as day. One after another black flame shaped entities escaped from the birds and rodents, slipping through the air and returning to Angela. The birds gently lifted and fluttered to the trees. Insects beat a path from them scurrying beneath the leaves from whence they came, the squirrel let go his teeth, and the mice their tiny bites.

John uncovered himself first and helped Clyde to his feet, who hugged him and stood dazzled, smiling at the lights as if they were brightly wrapped gifts on Christmas morn.

Angela screamed, "Johnny, help me!" Angela's black eyes faded to blue, and fixed on John. She seemed to be struggling with the unseen demons inside her. He had the impression the lights were giving her strength to fight them off. She shrieked and her eyes turned to again the seething black holes as before. Violently, her spine jerked backward, arching unnaturally. Her arms hung limp as a rag doll and her legs slack and dangling as her body rose off the ground.

John rushed forward but was held back by Clyde. "No, no, let her alone. Wait," he pleaded.

"Oh, God, help her," John cried, "Angela!"

The three orbs each elongated into fantastic forms, shining, gauzy cloud-like beings, resembling men but with fantastic wings, which spanned the entire length of their fifteen foot bodies. If these were not the Archangels, Michael, Raphael and Gabriel, then John was a monkey's uncle. Michael, whose name means, "Who is like unto God," carried a flaming sword in one hand, a thick blue chain in the other. He was dressed in a soldier's breast plate and metal skirt of gold and silver. Raphael and Gabriel both wore long robes of luminous cream and also had giant belts of gold about their waist. Raphael, "God's Remedy," held a staff and a silver jar, which radiated light. Gabriel, which means, "Strength of God," held a spear high and ready in one hand and a scroll in the other.

These great figures surrounded the body of his sister, whose body now twitched and convulsed still hanging arched in the air and covered in a growing inky black cloud. Michael drew his fiery sword and plunged it into the dark and into his sister's chest. John charged forward to spare his sister, but found he was held tight/ Though it was not by Clyde, who only loosely held his arms; it was his legs that were held fast, as immoveable as if they were cemented to the ground. He made to scream "No", but his mouth was held closed. With the sword still thrust, Gabriel now pitched his gleaming spear into her head. John's own head dropped at this. He felt it gently raised, as if an invisible finger were crooked below his chin, and this just in time to see Raphael sweeping his sister's eyes with ointment from his cruet.

411

As he smeared something that looked like silver, her mouth opened emitting an excruciating scream. Light streamed down on Angela concentrating in a single beam straight to her face.

"My God, my God," Angela's voice rang, "Who is like unto God?" Her head lifted. The silver from her eyes sloughed off running down her cheeks. "Lord, open my lips, and my mouth shall proclaim your praise"

All three magnificent entities cried in one command, "Come forth!"

Out of every orifice, just as it had swarmed in, the dense black soot gushed into the air, poured itself into a snakelike form and reared forth at the winged men of light. All three withdrew their weapons from Angela and cast them into the beast. The serpent's thick trunk split into six slithering heads, twisting and twining about each other. The six heads struck out straight at Clyde and himself. For a split second, John felt the breath of it, the stink seeping somewhere beyond his olfactory sense and into something much deeper. He recoiled and immediately, instinctively, as a habit ingrained, he recited the ancient prayer. "*Saint Michael the Archangel, defend us in battle. Be our protection against the wickedness and snare of the devil...*" John heard Clyde's voice unite to his own. In a comfortable and comforting chorus, but louder, stronger and more desperate sounding than either of them knew, they continued, "*May God rebuke him, we humbly pray.*"

The Archangel Michael's arm holding the massive blue chain swung round and round whipping in the air.

"*Do you oh Prince of the Heavenly Host, by the power of God...,*" John and Clyde prayed even louder.

The chain slammed into one of the outside serpents and wrapped itself around to the sixth snake; it wrapped around and around, making a terrific whistle in the air.

"*Cast into hell Satan and all other evil spirits, who prowl about the world seeking the ruin of souls.*"

With the loudest thunder, a perfect bolt of lightning in classic zig-zag shape, electric and raw, as bright as the angels before them, struck the ground. It cracked the ground, which opened before them, tearing the earth, leaving a cavernous yawning hole alive with hopping flames. Gabriel and Raphael crossed their arms on their chest and looked up to heaven. The beast screeched and hissed and howled till it seemed their eardrums might burst. Michael yanked the chain, pulled the six-headed beast towards him, and clasping his sword thrust it into the beast. He hoisted the squirming mass with his mighty arm and cast it down into the blazing inferno.

The hole closed, leaving the ground as natural as it was before. At the same time, His sister's body lowered and banged to the ground. Finding himself free, John rushed to her, collecting her in his arms. He repeated her name twice then held his tongue in the presence of the heavenly princes. Now all three angels, stood with hands folded and their radiant faces turned to the sky. Saint Michael spoke, in a voice full of gentleness that rumbled like the softest thunder. "Give thanks to God for He is Good. His mercy endures forever." The angels sang the Gloria. Their light forms lifted into the sky and above the trees, and for a moment, still lighting the evening sky, they hung luminescent as white clouds. They dissolved into the starlit sky, lit now only by the full moon.

Clyde, breathing as heavy as John, fell to his knees, saying "Thank you, God. Thank you, God," again and again in a heartfelt mantra. He was surprised to see Angela's lips too moving to the words. Tears slipped from her eyes. They opened to the wonderful green color he remembered, despite the tears. Their prayers ended with a shaky yet unified, *"Glory Be to the Father, and to the Son, and to the Holy Spirit, as it was in the beginning, is now, will be forever. Amen."*

48

Back to the Glen

"Ange, it's me John," he said, allowing her to sit up.

"I know it's you, stupid." She twisted around.

"Well, you, uh, weren't exactly you for a while there."

She ran long fingers through his hair as John continued to hold her other hand. "I know. I mean, I kinda know. I remember some stuff, but it's like I wasn't there and still seeing my hands and legs do stuff." She took a deep breath. It fell from her in stuttered puffs. Then she fell into his arms in a spontaneous heap. "Oh, Johnnie, Johnnie. It's been so long, so much has happened. I wanted…," her words were lost in his coat. He held her head in his giant hand and patted her curls as she cried it out. They sat a long while this way. When he sensed she was coming under control, he poked her. "Hey, am I gonna have to call you Red now?" She laughed, wiping her cheeks with her palms, noticing Clyde for perhaps the first time.

"Oh, Clyde! I remember…Oh my God, Clyde, I'm sorry, your mom—"

Clyde frowned regarding her warily for a moment, as if deciding if she was really oaky. "My mama is happy. I saw her… saw her behind those angels. She went up with them. I saw her." Clyde nodded his head; Angela nodded hers back, and John searched the air for Clarice. He saw nothing but the little stars and a full moon through the tree tops. "She's there." Clyde tugged John's coat sleeve and pointed matter of fact to a space before them. John saw nothing, no twinkle, no light, nothing but the outline of woods and trees in the white moonlight.

"It's time; we have to go. I'm alright, I swear," she said, aiming the last comment at Clyde and standing, "I was going to find the boy. I knew it right after we sunk the car. The place he lives…it's paradise, magical. It was calling to me. Later, I was fighting it because the evil inside, around me, I knew it wanted to destroy the boy. I'm supposed to meet him. I'm supposed to do something for him…I don't really know." She stopped, looking past them and contemplating the woods. "I just know I have to reach him."

"That boy, he's our son, Jackson." Angela expressed surprise, though she admitted she suspected it was true. She'd seen a picture from the newspaper once and wondered if that was why she was connected to him. They talked a little more, but came to no conclusions. It was as mysterious as the reasons for everything else. Angela brushed herself off as they stood and said again it was time to go.

"I don't know about you all, but aside from a little moonlight, I can't see squat," John said.

"I think," Clyde said, standing and facing the area to which he'd earlier pointed, "we can follow this light."

"What light? Where is it, Clyde?" Angela asked, and Clyde pointed forward. "There? I can't see it, but I can sense it."

"I can't see it anymore, but I think whatever Clyde is seeing, that's my wife."

The light moved forward. Clyde led the way. He held Angela's hand, who held John's. In this way, they trudged the steep paths, Angela and John blindly relying on Clyde for whom Clarice's light acted as a lantern shedding enough light to wend his way through the forest. They necessarily walked slow, carefully stepping over branches and roots, ducking snags and pushing limbs. They talked in the dark, Angela and John, sharing their stories, their missed time together. John told Angela all about their parents, how their dad changed, how many times her brothers searched for her, how until recently they thought she may have died somewhere. He told her how intensely they loved her. He told her all about meeting Clarice, often forgetting Clarice could hear him. It was easy to forget in the dark. He had waited so long to find his sister, to talk to her again, and have her back in his life. So when he spoke of Clarice and their love, it was unaffected and genuine. He spoke of Jackson and how incredible a child he was.

"Oh, I know," Angela said, "I know him from my dreams. I've been seeing him for about a year."

"Hmm," John said, "that was the same for Rabi Katz."

Then Angela filled John in on the years and how it had been for her. It was cathartic, no doubt, and easy in the cover of night, walking, drawing closer to the peace of the Glen. She too was open and rawly honest. He learned of Eddy and realized he was the same pimp he'd found killed. He learned of Vera and his sister's months with the beneficent doting patron, who showered her with worldly possessions and luxury. He learned of her running and they compared notes as to how many times he had missed her. They spoke of Anna quietly and much subdued. Clyde's steps remained constant and he was silent as they offered condolences again. They touched on the Archangels and faith. They marveled at God's incredible timing, His grace and His mysterious plans. Finally they stopped when Clyde announced, "We're here."

John squeezed Angela's hand. He spoke towards where he judged Clarice might be and said, "We're back...Back to the Glen."

* * *

"We can't go any farther together," Clarice heard Angela say aware of the wall of mist which lay before them. She heard the magical waters of the Glen. Despite her being in this supernatural state, she saw nothing but forest and the mist.

She flitted left and right along the wall of mist, up and then down. She knew it was a little wrong, yet she still tried. So all of them were outside the borders of the Glen. Jackson was not visible. She floated there accepting and renewing her fiat. It was complete; her son belonged entirely to God. Still filled with His peace, she thought of all she had just witnessed of God's merciful power, his beautiful angels. No, she refused to question God's plan....still, she retained a mother's natural longing and hoped to catch a glimpse of her baby boy. She watched the trio below her. Clyde had sunk down against a tree, his legs out and feet gently tapping, appearing to contemplate all he'd seen. He stared straight ahead to the mist, and she tried to decide if he could see her son, this man who had seen her light the entire way up

417

here. It didn't seem he could. He was most likely thinking of his mother. Clarice's heart went out to him; she just wanted to hug and console him. He seemed special in the best sense of that word and innocent. She was determined to seek him out when this was all over.

John's hand was on his sister's neck as he talked to her. The pair looked happy and content. John's question belied his paternal worries. "Will you be staying with him?" Oh God, please let her say yes, Clarice thought. Give me something, please.

"I honestly don't know. I don't know why I'm supposed to meet him. It feels like… I'm…" Her head shook, and she looked back into her brother's big brown eyes. "I will do everything I can for him…everything I'm allowed."

Clarice was relieved to hear that, as John must have been. If Angela can enter that mist and disappear, it would mean an adult would be with their little boy—that seemed better on some level, though she knew it should not matter—her trust was complete, at least she wanted it to be. She prayed continually for that grace, the grace of true resignation and complete trust.

Angela hugged Clyde, who stood now. "Thank you for being my friend. Thank Sergio, too." Both men looked at each other exchanging the same silent surprise. So she really did not remember all that happened. It was for the best. "I hope he's all right. I remember him falling…or something. Tell him, I will pray for him. I love you both. I don't know if I'll see you again."

"You might," Clyde said, "God knows." Angela, tall and lanky, embraced Clyde, who came to her shoulder.

Angela stepped out towards the invisible border shrouded in the wall of mist, still attached like a tether to John's outstretched hand. She was just at the wall when, he gave a strong tug, almost tripping her and pulled her into a bear hug. "Sis, I love you so much. Be careful. Tell Jackson…" he choked on the words but coughed bravely to continue, "we're here. We will NEVER not be here for him… or for you. I_I"

"I know, John—me, too." She hugged him back, reached up a bit to kiss his cheek. As she held him, her chin by his right ear, she looked up and beyond him and whispered, "Reece, I know my brother loves you, so I love you too. Hang on. Jackson and I will be praying for you both." Now she removed herself firmly from John and freeing her hand, she stepped off. No sooner had she stepped than her entire figure seemed to be swallowed whole by the mystical fog.

"Angela?" John called. No answer, and only a blink later, no sign of her or even the mist wall. Clarice was soaring. Demanding her return, her body called, sucking her forward. Her job here was through. She wondered as she sailed away…, but only God knows, when she would ever be…back…Back to the Glen.

49

Epilogue: Feast of the Visitation

MAY 31, 2007

John was outside. When was he not these days? He was working hard sawing an opening in the side of the shed where he planned to install a wood door. He'd replaced the busted up garage door just months after that fate-filled night when Jax was deposited safely in the Glen. It seemed an eternity ago, when in reality, it had been just over seven months. Creating another exit, this side door, was overdue, John thought, hefting a board to the sawhorse and remembering how trapped he'd felt the night Jackson was taken and his only way out was the garage door. If he'd had a second egress then, he might not have been impaled. He looked with pleasure at the door he'd built propped against the shed. He'd used heavy cedar and stained it deep red. It was an old-fashioned door, the kind in which the top opened independently of the bottom. It had loads of character, a real Mr. Ed door. Who knows maybe he'd get a horse—remake the shed into a miniature barn and build something else for the mower and ATV.

He thought about the time again. How long ago had Angela joined Jax?—over a month at least. He attempted to figure it out, trying first to remember the date. Well, that was sad—May 29 or 30? He placed three more penny nails in his mouth and hammered a fourth straight into the fat doorjamb. Aha, Feast of the Visitation! It was May 31st already. His own saint's feast, sort of, being it was Saint John who leapt in the womb of Elizabeth at the very presence of Jesus. It was a bad sign he didn't know the date, and he knew it was a bad sign, too. Used to be writing the date ten times a day—whether in the office or on construction sites. His company, Miller Construction was hanging by a thread, and here he was daydreaming about owning Mr. Ed. His heart just wasn't in the business, he told himself. No, his heart wasn't in much at all these days.

Dammit! How much did he have to lose? How much could one man stand? He lost his son, he lost his wife—even as he thought it, he was aware of the unfairness of what he was thinking. He had given his yes to God's plan for his son many times and he would continue. Then there was Clarice…something between them had changed for the better he could sense it. He was just having trouble getting past the months of stewing, months of resentment towards her betrayal. It was pride, now, and he knew it. It wasn't as if she had cheated on him, or even as if she set out to deceive him. He was being unfair, and he hated himself for it. He swung hard driving a nail. The hammer slipped just shy of the head hitting the edge, contorting the nail. He flipped the hammer over and attempted to pry the nail out, but the head was buried and the claw couldn't grip anything. He dropped the hammer and headed to the garage to find his pliers. He laid his hands on the tool as well as his suede tool belt, and he strapped the latter on as he walked back to the shed.

Just past the empty clothesline, his eyes scanned the stone path to the woods as always not really expecting to see anything but a habit as ingrained as breathing by now. He was about to turn his attention back to the shed when he thought he saw something in the distance where the path dropped down a hill. A grey fox maybe? He stopped walking and turned to face the path, waiting for the creature to materialize. The wildlife here were a constant source of wonder. It bobbed again and his heart lurched, the color decidedly blond not grey, and in one more second, his sister's head popped into view. John flung the metal pliers so hard as he took off running, it slammed into the wood siding of the shed and embedded itself in a knothole.

"Ange!" He yelled, ducking under the clothesline rope and running towards her. Composed and graceful, she continued at an even gait, but her eyes greeted him with the biggest grin. Arm in arm, they walked back toward the house, John full of questions, Angela reserved and putting these off. They laughed at the chucked tool hanging open and dangling from the knothole. As they began the walkway to the garage, Angela stopped and held his gaze, serious.

"I have a message from your son for you, John." Her slender fingers felt chilly as they wrapped around his big hand and gave a squeeze. "You must forgive his mom from your heart. We can only survive what is to come as a family. He will need you; you will need each other's strength, and others will need all of you. He wants you to remember that God has great plans, but you cannot cooperate as two flesh because you are both one." Her words stung. John's heart swelled, his lungs filled by great bellows of regret, and his mind swam in a sea of remorse. The hardness of his heart, these many months, Clarice's many efforts, the dinner Christmas Eve, choked his chest till he felt it would burst. Amid all this compunctious grief, there was something loosening his heart. It was a kind of relief, as if his son's words were the key to unlocking and releasing all that was left of his hurt. His sister watched his face contort.

They entered the house through the garage and breezeway all smiles. So tightly was Angela in John's arms, it was a wonder she could even walk. Coming from the laundry room, holding a white wicker basket of wet clothes, heading to the clothesline, Clarice looked up hearing John's laugh, a sound she sorely missed. Her hands let go of the basket and flew to her mouth. The heavy clothes landed with a thud on her toes, and she stood holding her breath looking from the two huge grins and searching briefly behind them. John quickly spoke answering her eyes.

"Just Angela, Reece. She's back—back from the Glen."

Clarice lurched forward tripping over wet sheets and falling flat. Most of her weight, she caught on her left hand. Immediately, John was on the move crossing the room to help as Clarice struggled to right herself. She kicked at a damp sheet, which was tangled in her sneaker. He laughed at her, and as she turned from her struggle, she saw something more than sporting mirth in his eyes—something was different... towards her.

Angela was by her side now too, and all three of them enjoyed more than a playful laugh over the buffoonery. The presence of Angela, her return brought a giddy joy.

"I can't—can't believe it!" Clarice cried. "Am I really seeing you?"

"In the flesh," Angela said, everyone standing now. Clarice clasped her hand, looking at her hard and then dove in for a hug. Her five foot two head of light brown locks landed neatly under Angela's chin.

Eventually the trio sat around the thick walnut table in the kitchen. Clarice offered John's sister every beverage and food item she could bring to mind, but Angela had only one request: coffee

John jumped up to help, filling the pot with water as Clarice ground fresh coffee beans. To the three steaming mugs, Clarice had added a plate of homemade sticky buns left over from Sunday. She still tried to make something extra on Sundays, although John more often than not rejected the overtures. Angela scooped a spoonful of sugar and returned the bowl to the wood Lazy Suzan in the center of the round table. She poured a generous amount of cream from the pint container just as John did. They both took their coffee identically, Clarice noted, sipping hers black. It took all she had not to break the silence with the thousand and one questions she had racing in her skull. It must have been obvious judging from Angela's next words.

"Okay, okay, you're killing me with your self-control—what do you want to know first?"

"How is he?" and "Is he Okay?" came simultaneously from she and John respectively. Causing all three to laugh again. The laughs kept coming, so filled with joy were she and John, an eleventh Commandment could not have controlled it.

"The Glen is truly a divine sanctuary. Jackson and I ate manna from heaven. I would not have even known what to call it if the little guy hadn't told me. Do you know he has the whole Bible in his head?" Both parents nodded, and Angela looked from one nonplussed face to the other. "It lay like frost on the ground every morning, and all we had to do was sort of scoop it onto bark pieces and eat as much as we needed to feel full. It tastes kind of like bread, but after the first few times eating it, I just never thought of taste one way or the other again. It satisfied our hunger. We slept anywhere really, sometimes on the moss not far from the stream, sometimes under this overhanging rock in the hill."

"What did you do all day?" Clarice said. "What did you talk about?"

"Oh God, mostly. Talking to Jackson, sharing my love for God...it's hard to describe the joy you feel. I wish everyone could have time like that with someone who loves God. The praise and joy just spilled out of us. God is so amazing, so loving, so..." Angela shook her head, clearly unable to find words. She stared into her coffee cup and no one moved. John scraped his chair back and got up returning with the coffee pot and topping off Angela's cup. She nodded thanks, and commenced the sugar and cream ritual.

"Did you learn anything," Clarice said, "about when he might return or..." her voice drifted. She knew this territory was probably off limits, and even if she didn't already know it, Angela's sympathetic, almost pitying pursed lips confirmed it.

"Here's what I can tell you." Angela began. "No one will see him again until it is time, not even me." I was brought there for safety, and I must remain here until Jackson exits. My spirit has been fortified and somewhere within my own soul, I am privileged to carry the power and auras of my two predecessors."

"Nicey," John said, matter-of-factly, "and Rabbi Katz, too."

"That's right, Michelle, who housed the aura of the greatest of Archangels, Saint Michael, and Gabrielus, who housed the aura of Saint Gabriel and wielded the power of Tzaddik. John, do you remember my baptismal name?"

John, who had been stirring his coffee unconsciously faster and faster as Angela spoke, stopped, but not before a slosh slipped over the side of his mug to the table. "Raphaella," he said in an almost reverent whisper.

"Yes, Raphael is the Archangel, whose light I share." John stared at his sister as if she were a mirage, and his mouth literally hung open. Clarice spun the lazy Suzan, retrieved a napkin, and laid it over John's spill as Angela continued. "It's hard to put into words—I don't want to say channel because it sounds so... I don't know occult or something."

"But..." John said then pursed his lips, furrowed his brow, and made a weird sound blowing out his nose, "are the Archangels...uh, are they your Guardian, like your Guardian Angel?"

"No,—Angela's head shook slowly back and forth, her voice was soft, reverent—"no...no. We are all—each and every human being—accompanied by an angel from the choir of Guardian Angels, who guard, guide and pray for us all our life." Angela scratched her hair, and for the first time Clarice noted, what a tangled mess of blond curls it was. It looked wild and inexplicably natural and appealing. "No the light, the power of the Archangels is allowed at times to run through us—I'm sorry, I keep saying us. I realize Michelle Nicestrum and Gabriel Katz are deceased, but you see we never really die any of us, we just continue in spirit. Not that spirits stick around when they have attained heaven. But be careful,"—her deep blue eyes grew wider and serious—"any spirits hanging out down here never were human, they are only demons pretending to be spirits of loved ones." She stopped put an elegant finger to her full lips. "Um, I forgot what we were talking about...

"About how the Archangels work through you," John said.

"Oh, yeah, that's a good way to put it too."

"John, I think maybe your sister would like to shower and lay down?" Clarice looked at Angela, who had half stuffed a yawn down with her last sip of coffee.

"Oh, I—it's okay, I know you have loads of questions..."

"Wow, no, no, Reece is right; it can wait. It sounds like you're going to be with us for a while."

"Is that alright?"

Both husband and wife answered, "Yes!" nearly in unison, resulting in a shared laugh and what Clarice thought was a loving look from John directly at herself! Clarice pushed her chair back and stood.

"Well," Angela said, standing with them, "I asked you as if it's an option, but the truth is I was instructed in the Glen, that I must never leave the mountain top. The angels will cloak all of us until God's plan is set in motion. I'm afraid if you put me out, I'll have to camp in the woods." She gave a cheesy grin while stretching long graceful arms over head.

"There's not much danger of that," John said, getting up and stretching his own bulk. "Like I waited fifteen years just to finally find you only to toss you back on the street." Clarice inwardly winced and could tell John regretted his slip the second it left his well-meaning mouth. She watched a grey look pass over Angela's bright blue eyes. "Dang, squirt I'm sorry."

Angela's deep set eyes brightened. "Told you once I told you a hundred times Johnny, I'm too tall to be called squirt." Her big brother immediately made a play to deliver a noogie to the top of her head. She did little to duck it, and instead nudged him with her shoulder and said, "S'ok, John. It feels like a lifetime ago…at least today. Think you can set me up with a shower and maybe a horse brush to get through this hair?"

"I'm sure we can do better than that," Clarice said. "Follow me"

"Hey," John called as they turned for the stairs, "Why is it blond now?"

"Huh? I didn't know it was. Maybe the waters of the Glen did it. It healed every cut I had when I got in there."

John waited downstairs while Clarice led the way to the bathroom. Out of curiosity he watched as they went to the top of the stairs—if they turned right, Clarice was leading her to the hall bathroom he'd been using, if left she was taking her to the bathroom in the master bedroom he had not been sharing with his wife for some time. He tried to think what he would say to Clarice, how to begin. It had been so long. Would they even be able to talk normally?

Clarice led Angela through the master bedroom. Pushing the door to the master bath, she noticed her sister-in-law had stopped at the doorway.

"It's awesome. I love it. Did John…" she pointed waving her finger at all the elaborate molding.

"Your brother is genius with wood."

Angela stepped into the room, running a hand over the chair rail. "Not so genius in other departments," she said, regarding Clarice steadily.

The immediacy of Clarice's reaction surprised herself. Her eyes welled, and a lump of hurt in her chest leapt to life. The same one that is always there, always just below the surface of her routine, right there ready to erupt as she's checking out at the grocery store, ready to burst when she's talking to Bear about nothing, or when she's selling a painting, whenever the world is spinning, and she is meant to carry on polite conversation as if everything is just fine, just fine,

427

when clearly it's not, when clearly she has lost everyone dear to her… that lump. "It's my fault," she blurted. Her voice became small and pleading. "I'm afraid I've lost him. I don't—"

"No, no," Angela said, hurrying to Clarice. "I watched him looking at you, and believe me I know my brother. Besides I know other things too." She reached for her hand and leaned her forehead to Clarice's, "Just keep believing, and keep a prayer in your heart. God is always watching, always ready to step in where He's invited."

Clarice wiped her eyes. "I'm sorry, not your problem. Oh my gosh, please, you're tired." Clarice showed Angela everything she might need for her bath leaving her a pair of pajamas, fresh towels, and a new toothbrush. Clarice insisted Angela lie down in the Master bedroom after her bath. A polite argument ensued until Clarice convinced her it was actually easier for her since this bed had just had the sheets changed, Angela finally agreed so long as Clarice promised it was just for today. Of course, Angela had no idea she was about to conk out for nearly seventy two hours.

Clarice went downstairs, slowly talking to God on each step inviting Him to either fix it or end it between John and her. She just didn't know how much more rejection she could stand. John was on the big couch, kitty-corner to the giant stone fireplace they'd designed and built together stone by stone. The couch also faced the sliding glass doors that looked out to the thick woods beyond. They'd always thought the unadorned glass made the scene look like a painting, a living landscape. Tomorrow would be the first of June and the trees were pushing forth curled leaves of bright green ready to unfurl themselves in magnificent summer splendor.

He must have heard her cautious step, and for the first time in over seven months, he beckoned her to sit by him. His face was unreadable, and for a moment, she hesitated sure he might finally be ready to ask for a divorce or a more permanent separation. She went in choosing to sit on the opposite end of the couch, trying to feel brave and find some way to live through the words he might say.

He started slow, even for John. "Reece, I began this marriage in the deepest love and commitment to you." *Oh God no*, her mind could barely force itself to listen. "I vowed to cherish and love you all the days of our life, but…" *Oh, God, oh God, please no, no John don't say it, don't.* Her eyes teared, full of pain and pleading, and finally his eyes met hers. He shook his head still holding her gaze, and his gorgeous brown eyes were as teary as hers. "But I broke that commitment."

Clarice was numb, so numb she missed that key word *I.* "John, I know—"

"I promised to love you in sickness and health, in good times and bad, I broke that promise."

"Wait, what?"

"Reece Martin Miller, you were a secretive, untrusting, guarded little woman, who held back a huge chunk of herself, afraid of losing my love." John paused. "And you were also willing to risk everything to win back what you thought we had—what I thought we had." He slid over on the couch until his leg was touching hers. He took her small pointed chin in his big bear hand. "You never lost my love. You could never lose my love. I'm sorry, I'm so sorry for not accepting your apology—sorry for making you pay so dearly all these months."

Her relief turned to blubbering, most of which was unintelligible repetition of the same guilty apology she'd been repeating to him for months. He moved just enough to reach the box of tissues on the coffee table. He pulled three out and said, "It's enough Reece, enough. Please I don't want to hear you apologize again. If I were half the man I should be…I would have accepted it the first time you tried to explain it to me."

It was no use; she couldn't stop crying. She was able only to stop blubbering out words, but the lump in her chest had finally exploded, and her heaves and her tears were beyond her control. He pulled her awkwardly, wrestled her onto his lap, and held her there as she regained her composure. She honked and wiped and honked again. Then she drew her arms around his neck in the tightest hug, which he returned in full. She pulled back and found his lips and their passion poured forth in the neediest series of kisses, which soon calmed to one long and tender kiss.

The two were one flesh again and stronger in their commitment precisely because of the trial. Nothing would be taken for granted between them, nothing would be allowed to separate them. Their honest treatment of each other from this day forward, would strengthen them to endure not only the rigors of everyday marriage—from its grinding monotony, to financial headaches, to daily differences in temperament and personality—but it would strengthen them for mind-blowing losses and unimaginable heartache. They would bear it all together, as one, just as they had promised six years ago.

Mr. and Mrs. John Miller would share the couch that night, the tiny twin guest bed the next, and the next until Angela Raphaella would awaken starving for food. As they would fill her, she would fill them with news of their son and hopes for the future when one day he would come out… *Out of the Glen.* ✝

Meet the Author

Carla Coon has been happily married to her husband Darrell for 29 years, living in Upstate New York and raising their eight children and enjoying their four grandchildren. Books of *The Glen Series* are a synergy of two great passions: religious studies and the outdoors.

Carla Coon's professional experience included serving as Editor of *LifeWork*'s, a statewide publication, where she also contributed a monthly column. While homeschooling seven of her eight children, Carla wrote in-depth articles for *National Catholic Register, New Oxford Review, Faith & Family, The Catholic Sun, Press & Sun-Bulletin* and more. In other positions, she was Program Coordinator for non-profit groups and Director of Religious Education at her parish.

Once a ballroom dance instructor for Arthur Murray's, Carla enjoys music and dance, roaming art museums, and travel with her husband. Currently she works locally and online to help support families and those suffering relational brokenness.

(Left to right on couch.) Daughter Ellen Coon, daughter-in-law Angelica Coon holding Ivory, daughter-in-law Michelle Coon, daughter Stephanie Taylor holding Sophia, Carla "Nana" Coon holding Ruby, and daughter Catherine Coon. (Back row) Jacob Hawk, son Daniel Coon, son Carl Coon, Darrell "Papo" Coon, son Sgt. Gerard Coon, USMC, and son Sgt. Kevin Coon, USMC. (Missing are Sister Mary Philomena Coon, OP, son-in-law Jaime Taylor, and newest family member, James Thomas Taylor.)

Look for more in this series:

If you enjoyed Back to The Glen won't you please leave a review on Amazon, Goodreads, Barnes & Noble or wherever you purchased this book?

www.carlacoon.com

www.faebook.com/TheGlenSeries